THE ART OF MURDER

Also by Don West:

DREAM OF THE GREAT BLUE, a novel

THE ART OF MURDER

BY DON WEST

dancing bear   Tucson AZ

THE ART OF MURDER
by Don West

ISBN: 978-1-59778-111-4
ISBN: 1-59778-111-8

LCCN: 2006903801

First edition

Printed in the United States of America.
10 9 8 7 6 5 4 3 2 1

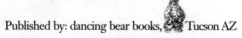

Published by: dancing bear books, Tucson AZ

www.BoomerFiction.com

Cover and interior design: Robert Aulicino
Author photo: Barbara West

To my mother, Lillian Sue, in South Lyon, and to my father, Henry Thomas, in Kentucky.

And, of course, to Barbara, who worked with me throughout, gave more than she was asked, and teaches me everyday the true meaning of the word love.

ACKNOWLEDGEMENTS

My thanks go to Trinity Parker, museum registrar, to my editor, C.E. Gatchalian, and to my friend, Bridget Roads, artist and writer, for giving of their time, generous remarks, and hard work on this book. Also thanks and love to my son, Ian West, teacher and poet, for his continual inspiration and encouragement.

Much love to my brothers Jim West, Dave West, and Jeff West, to their wives, my sisters, Janet, Lynn, and Carolynn. And to their kids, some of whom are not kids anymore: Lani and Brandon, Katie and April, Walker and Nash.

To my other brothers and sisters, Bob and Shirley Wilfong, Bill and Annette Smith, and their children, Patti, Kim, Beth, and Robbi, and Steve, Mark, and Matt.

And to my grandson, Sam Eliot. Love to you all.

Finally, my thanks to Dashiell Hammett, Robert B. Parker, Elmore Leonard, Raymond Chandler, and all the other writers who have thrilled me and millions of other readers with their hard and soft-boiled tales for years.

THE ART OF MURDER

"A creative writing teacher at San Jose State used to say about clichés: 'Avoid them like the plague.' Then he'd laugh at his own joke. The class laughed along with him, but I always thought clichés got a bum wrap. Because, often, they're dead-on."

—Khaled Hosseini, The KITE RUNNER

"Ars est celare artem"

—Ovid, Art of Love

One

I T WAS A LATE FRIDAY AFTERNOON. I SAT WITH MY FEET propped on the desk, entertaining three fingers of Early Times bourbon. The whiskey, neat and edgy, slid down my throat and melted my anxiety like a chocolate kiss. In the window, an old dilapidated AC unit stuck into the room like a short square tongue and made a noise that vaguely resembled a Bronx cheer; it fought a gallant but losing battle in this ferocious summer heat. As the sole owner and primary gumshoe of the RD Detective Agency, I was celebrating or bemoaning the end of a long, uneventful month, but who could say which? My only prospective new client that week had stood me up on Tuesday. Across the city, the horizon sliced off the bottom of the sun and left it bleeding through the blinds of my office like a big blood orange. I was reading the LA Times through the resultant voids of light and shadow that fell across my lap.

Headlines: "Carter Lee Hollenbeck III Crushed by Kouri." The body of the notoriously popular trustee, a member of the Board of Directors at the Getty Museum, was discovered just that morning under one of the famous Greek stone boys. There was no evidence of foul play, but circumstances were certainly suspicious. LAPD was conducting an investigation, and I was just about to turn the page to get the rest of the details when two over-sized, over-stuffed but well-tailored Brooks Brothers' suits sleazed through the door into my office. Muscles, sweat, some nasty vibes, and a voluminous cloud of eau-de-skunk perfume wafted into the room. Damn. I'd forgotten to lock the outer office after Felia left. I had to pay more attention. Can't have goons sneaking up on me like this; it was unprofessional.

"You Nestor Pike?" the short bald man said as he pushed into my office.

"That depends. Who's looking for him?" I said, folding the paper and putting my feet on the floor.

"You don't look like Pike."

The man's accent reminded me of that Crocodile Dundee guy. "You ever seen Pike?"

"No, but from what I've heard, mate, he's supposed to have hair, and I'm guessing he's not as ugly as a roo, like some people I could mention. You shave that?" He pointed at my cranium.

I gave him some rope and let it slide. "Lucky me. Mine grows back. How about yours?"

"I heard Pike was too dumb to have such a smart mouth. So, what are you doing at his desk?"

"I'm his personal secretary; what's it look like?"

"Nobody told me he was queer, heh, heh, heh," he smirked, more pleased with himself than any moron had a right to be.

No sense going there, I thought and left it alone. "So what do you want, Curly?"

2

"Got a message for him—and the name's not Curly."

I pulled a pen and pad out of a drawer and pushed them across the desk. "Whatever, Slick. Jot your number on that, and I'll have him give you a call," I said, testing their reflexes. Reluctantly, the two men removed their hands from inside their lapels where they'd flown when I reached for the drawer.

"What we got to give Pike won't fit a yellow pad. Who're you then?"

"Aren't you the inquisitive one? Just give me the message, and I'll make a note of it. What d'ya say, buddy?" I said, retrieving the pen and pad.

"I'm not your buddy, mate."

"I say, I em tard athees she-rod." The tall, dark, and ugly one spoke for the first time.

Was that?—"I'm tired of this charade?" His voice was so deep, it vibrated through my body like a shiver. The thought flashed through my brain that that is what it felt like when someone walked on your grave. I didn't fear much, certainly not these two rejects from Colonel Klink's goon squad. Though I have to admit, I could've used another slug of that Early Times about then. However, this was but a social call. If it were anything else, I'd already be dead. So, it wasn't exactly fear, and I wasn't exactly cold—not in this heat.

The big bruiser gave me the creeps. He was an Arab, had a musty odor, the smell of a mummy's tomb about him, and looked like he needed to be dusted. He wore greenish-looking metal braces on the biggest yellow teeth I had ever seen. I almost laughed out loud at the way he'd spoken. It wasn't the Middle Eastern accent so much as the attitude: Pharohic—in a Yul Brynner sort of style—is the only way to describe it. Before I could wipe

3

the smirk off my face, he nodded. Then Baldy kicked over a client chair and came across my desk like a loco-motive. I sidestepped the charge and Karate-chopped the back of his bulbous neck. Unfortunately, it was a pathetic, useless, and—I admit—humiliating gesture; my most formidable chop rendered no impression on the blockhead whatsoever. But for the fact that the lout's leather sole had slipped on the scruffy oak, I might've met my destiny then and there. I felt a momentary pang of regret when I realized that he'd knocked over my drink in his boyish enthusiasm to flatten my kisser.

Meanwhile, Ahab was lathering up to pummel me unconscious. Head lowered, he moved around the end of the desk toward me. Luckily, he was busy adjusting some highly polished brass knuckles and hadn't seen me break the hold. Hello! When I blasted into his mid-sec-tion with both fists, one after the other, he crumpled to the floor and flailed for air.

None too soon. Regaining his feet, Freight Train chugged around the desk and wrapped me up like a carp in newspaper. He threw me to the side, slamming me into the wall between the windows, face first into my PI license frame. It broke the glass and gashed the flesh across my cheekbone. He followed up behind with a flurry of precise and painful kidney punches. Pushing off the wall and kicking back as hard as I could, I landed my foot square in the guy's groin. He grunted, grabbed his gonads, and thumped over the edge of the desk onto the floor.

These yokels recovered quickly; they'd done this before. I had to start using my head instead of muscle; fifty was getting too old for this. The Mummy rose and walked again. I turned to meet him as he threw his fist—

with the pretty brass knucks—a glancing blow across my face, almost breaking my jaw. I stumbled back into the wall and sank to the floor. He followed up fast for a big man. On the way down, I caught his knee in my mug. My head spun, and I could feel the edges of my consciousness unraveling. No such luck; intense pain had a way of sharpening one's focus and putting an edge back on frayed ends. Not to feel left out, Pile Driver stomped me in the stomach.

Just as he was about to deliver the coup de grace and dance the Flamenco on my face, the voice of Allah sounded like a trumpet, "Just a moment there, Mr. Davie; a word for our new friend, Mr. Pike. You stay out of this, or we give you double, you understand?" When I didn't respond, he turned, looked at The Diesel then back at me. "You understand, smart-ass?" he repeated. "Keep your nose out of this business."

"What business? What're you talking about?" I spat some blood and felt to see if my nose was still on the front of my skull.

"Don't play dumb with me, asshole."

"Who said I was playing?"

"It's not possible to be as dumb as you look, Mr. Pike. Shall we, Mr. Davie?"

"I'm right behind you, Mr. Mustafa." The Hard-on kicked me in the belly one more time.

"Y'all come again soon," I gasped and doubled over.

"Just stay away from this, Mr. Pike, or it will be your last." He backed toward the door, removing the brass from his knuckles and straightening his suit. "I'm afraid the blood from your face has ruined my pants."

"Tsk, tsk, tsk. How careless of me."

The Tank tightened the knot of his tie and stared

down at me like a connoisseur craving sweetbreads. He kicked at my crotch, but I caught his pricy Italian boot with both hands and twisted the meathead off his feet.

"Hey Felia!" Donny Mack called from the outer office, catching everyone by surprise. Donny, my young colleague and general factotum, was there to pick up Ophelia Tucker, my part-time secretary, who had obviously forgotten to tell him that she was leaving early for an audition.

Mustafa hurried back, leaned down, and helped Davie to his feet. "You remember what I said, Pike," he spat like a cobra at my face and pushed The Dink toward the door. I yelled out to warn Donny, but Davie sucker-punched him as he came into the room. Donny never knew what hit him.

I rested a moment, back against the wall, stanching the blood with my T-shirt. When the worst of it subsided, I moved over to check on Donny. There was an angelic look about his boyish face. I took the pint of bourbon from my desk, tilted back, and poured some of the harsh amber elixir into the gash on my cheek. I took a deep pull from the bottle and sat down on the edge of the desk to wait for it to kick in. "Damn!" I was going to need a whole string of stitches.

"What business?" I wasn't sure that I'd spoken the words; my ears rang, and my face seemed to have melted off my head. My nose could have been buried out at Forest Lawn Cemetery in a grave of its own. It no longer drew breath. There was a time I would have gotten over on a couple of stooges like these—but an Arab and an Aussie in such an unholy alliance? I got nothing against most Arabs, or most Aussies for that matter; bad guys come in every size, shape, color, and nationality; I despised them all equally. "But what business?" I was into no business. I was virtually retired, for Pete's sake—had been since Nathaniel was killed, almost five years now. All I had was a freebie divorce case. And, God knows, I hated divorces—messy and no up side. What was left were some pictures for the bride, some fancy footwork for a homey going down on drug charges—who was probably guilty anyway—and some collection work for an older couple stiffed by a pair of sleazeball scam artists down in El Segundo. There was certainly no business that would be of interest to yahoos of this caliber. These boys did this for a living.

Obviously, they had me confused with another Sherlock—someone who worked for one of the big law firms. What would bring these toots looking for Nestor Pike? They had my name, all right, but somebody must've known something that I didn't and wanted me out of the way. Yeah, well, maybe it was time for a little vacation. Besides, I'd been promising Shirl a couple weeks in Cabo. As it was, I guess we should've left yesterday, but then hindsight's always 20/20.

I took the .357 Magnum out of the bottom drawer of the desk and loaded it. I laid it in the top drawer under some papers. Nothing like closing the door after the horses had left the barn. I went to the cooler, drew some water into a paper cone, and splashed it into Donny's face. Yeah, a little r & r in Mexico, a little sun, sea, and fresh air in Cabo would be more than welcome right now. But not before I paid a visit to the bastard who owned Messieurs Mustafa and Davie. Nobody sneaked into my office, kicked my ass, and then lived to tell about it—at least not for long, not in this life.

Two

Monday

DEXTER'S DINER AND DONUT SHOPPE SMELLED GOOD first thing in the morning. The aroma of hot fat frying the sweet batter mingling with exhaust fumes off Santa Monica Boulevard always reminded me of Shirley. Shirl had worked for Dexter Jackson almost fifteen years, making donuts and serving breakfast to the regulars. Although she always wore Shalimar, dotted with a single finger over the intimate places of her body, the smell of Dexter's Diner was her true perfume—she sizzled. But not this morning. I couldn't smell a thing with a nose like a mashed tomato. When I entered, the sound of the bell on the door announcing my arrival was music to my ears. The sight of donuts cooling on the racks along the wall behind the counter made my mouth water like Pavlov's dog—almost as much as the sight of Shirl or the sound of her voice.

"God, you look awful. Does it hurt bad?" she asked.

"Thanks, good to see you, too," I said and closed the door behind me.

"Looks like you could have used some TLC over the weekend. Why didn't you call me?"

I sat on the stool across the counter from her. "Looks worse than it is."

"You broke your nose again. What is that, about the tenth time? So, you gonna tell me how you got those shiners?"

"You don't want to know, trust me."

"Never mind, I can guess." She wiped the Formica in front of me with a wet cloth from beneath the counter. "You could have stayed at the house instead of that flop you call an apartment, you know. I would've looked after you." She tossed the rag back where she found it.

"Nothing you could do but fuss over me while I slept it off. Besides, what's wrong with my place? I like the minimalist ambiance." I grabbed a menu from the rack on the counter in front of me. "Say, Shirl, would you mind drying this off so I can put my arms down?" I pointed to the surface she'd just wiped.

"Minimalist ambiance, my ass. The place's so empty, it looks condemned."

"So what? I've got everything I need right there."

"Yeah, but what if you'd wanted something?"

"Like what? I'm a big boy now."

"I know, but . . ."

"Just leave it there, okay? Look, Shirl, if you're not going to dry this off, how about a cup of joe and one of Dexter's bearclaws?" I put the menu back in its place behind the sugar container.

"I still wish you would've called. You see why I worry so much. Someday, someone is going to kill you, and I'll have to read it in the Times to find out about it." She licked the ball of her thumb and reached across the counter to smooth down one of these wild eyebrows of mine, an exercise in futility.

"I promise, Shirl. I'll call next time."

Shirl was working on her BFA in painting, part time at UCLA. She'd quit after we got married, but went back again, off and on, when Nathaniel started school. She'd been working on it ever since I knew her, one class at a time, over twenty years now. Her love of art fascinated me, and I admired her for going to school with youngsters—not giving up, no matter how long it took.

"If that's the way you want it." She reached up and slapped the stubble on the crown of my dome. "You letting your hair grow? I'm glad. I like it better that way," she said, by way of changing the subject.

"Ow, that hurt. Yeah well, I'm glad that you're glad. I'd so hate for you to be disappointed about my hair. Besides, I might get used to this, if I keep cutting it."

Just then, the bell on the door jangled, and Bernie came in. He took off his suit coat, hung it on the wall by the door, and sat on the stool at the counter next to me. His butt cheeks hung off either side. Lieutenant Detective Maldonado liked his donuts, but he didn't like confectioner's sugar all over the front of his expensive gray suit. Bernie was fastidious and dressed well, even on a cop's salary. He and I had different tastes in clothes. When I wasn't sleuthing around in my London Fog, mine ran to these camouflage fatigues, cargo pants—I liked all the pockets—or jeans and T-shirts—a style I'd acquired in Viet Nam. That was one reason I liked carrying the Magnum. I could conceal it under an overshirt like the red Hawaiian I wore, which hung out. I used to wear suits like Bernie, only mine were affordable so it was never a problem. Bernie never wore his weapon until he arrived to work. He always left it in his locker overnight. Neither one of us had much use for guns, mostly. We worked without them when we could.

"Eh, buenos dias, muchacha, Bernie said. "This pen-
dejo coyote treating you all right? Just say the word, and
I'll have him thrown in the slammer and personally toss
the key into the Tar Pits myself."

"Would you?" she said as she descended down the
counter for the coffee. Maybe you should. He's a real
pussy this morning. I've just about had it with him,"

Bernie and I watched appreciatively as she moved
away. For my money, five-foot-nine with soft ash-
brown hair, long-legged Shirley Pulaski-Pike had the
most marvelous manner of movement—a lurid, languid
locomotion. It was that classy chassis of hers that gave a
man thought for the possibilities of what the future
might bring. With her around, every man became an
optimist.

The noise level in the restaurant dropped a notch as
people got serious about drinking their coffee, buttering
their toast, slicing their ham, slapping ketchup on their
hash browns, and munching their eggs. Though I could-
n't smell a fart in an elevator, I imagined the heavenly
smells that I knew wafted the place. Somebody dropped
a plate in the kitchen just as the bell rang, and two young
businesswomen came through the door.

"So tell me again, muchacho, why you two lovebirds
aren't still married," Bernie said.

"Look, Maldonado, you know we're still married. We
just don't live together."

"Well I don't care. It's not right. You two should get
remarried."

"I just told you. We are married. Sometimes two people, no matter how much they love each other . . . "

"Oh si, si. I know what you told me. Never mind.

Hey, nice set of stitches, zipper face," he added, pointing. "How many you got there?"

"Thirteen."

"Ay caramba, unlucky thirteen. You fight a duel for some Darla in distress, or did some puta scratch you in the heat of passion?" he asked, holding up both hands as if someone just got the drop on him. My long time compatriot liked to blow smoke up my metaphoric skirts, although he knew I was devoted to Shirley.

"Look here, Maldonado . . ."

"No, no, let me guess, ese," Maldonado continued. "You were on a stakeout and ran into some machete-wielding punks over in Beverly Hills. Had to be more than one, right? You want me to arrest the perps. That why you called me down here so early?"

"Yeah. Something like that."

"What can I get you, Bernie?" Shirley asked as she arrived and set our coffee in front of us.

"What's he having?" Bernie said, looking at me as he grabbed a menu off the counter.

"Bearclaw and coffee," she said. "But we've got your raspberry jelly, and the crullers are excellent today."

"How about one of each, esa. I got a feeling I'm gonna need some extra fortitude after I hear this cholo's sad tale." He hooked his thumb in my direction. "On second thought, esa, tell Dex I want three eggs over-easy, hash browns, chorizo, juice and toast. Hold the donuts; just box me a baker's dozen, assorted, and I'll take them back to the squad. I'll be a hero for the day." He replaced the menu without looking at it.

"Hey, Shirl, order me the same and bring the bearclaw for dessert," I said.

"Okay, but you don't deserve it," she said, going off

to place the order and wait on several other customers who had come in. The bell on the door jangled every few minutes; the place was filling up as usual.

Bernie lowered the sound of his voice. "So, ese, what's up? Who was this vato that got inside you like that?" He nodded at my face and sipped his coffee, black.

"A couple of pros I've never seen before, Mustafa and Davie—an Arab and an Aussie, new in town. Thought you might be able to help me develop some background to go with the names and faces," I confided as I creamed my coffee from the little chrome pitcher on the counter.

"And just what will you do with this background once you have it? I see by that pretty red shirt, that you're packing. You know, as an officer of the law, I cannot condone any sort of vigilante retribution. I don't remember you taking that much cream in your coffee."

"I need to go see who's running these beauticians and find out just why he, or she, had them give me this facial. Hey Shirl, could you bring me another cup of coffee?" She didn't appear to hear me.

He looked at me, intently.

I gathered he was contemplating my request.

Chops, the busboy, Dex's son was clearing a table and dropping silverware onto plates in his tray, so Bern leaned in close to be heard. "What did these cholos want?" he asked.

"I don't know. Told me to stay off a case. But I don't have a case, except that collection thing down in El Segundo and a divorce I was obligated to pursue."

"Since when do you do divorces?"

"I don't. It was a favor for a friend. I've been running a little surveillance on a wayward husband. But this has nothing to do with that. These two mugs have an agenda and someone's paying their expenses. I need to get to the bottom of this before they begin to long for my effervescent personality and decide to come back."

"Well, I guess we can't have these vatos coming in here and roughing up our upstanding taxpayers, now can we? If they are visitors to our little village, we should talk to the other states first. If that doesn't satisfy our curiosity, we'll reach out and touch Interpol."

"Figured as much."

"We'll go back to the office and run their names through the files. I know it'll be next to impossible for you, but try to keep a low profile when we arrive. Get with Artie and work up a couple composites; tell him I said so. We'll send them out and see what comes back. I doubt the mug shots would turn up anything, since you say they're not local talent. So, while we're waiting, you can tag along with me to the Getty Villa. I need to speak with some people about the recent unpleasant developments out there. You've read the newspaper?"

"I thought the Villa was closed for restoration since they opened the new place up on the 405."

"It is."

The bell on the door rang again; two construction workers came in and made their way down to a booth along the wall. I could hear the traffic on Santa Monica picking up steam as it headed in through the fog during the Monday morning rush hour. On her way back to the kitchen, Shirl set our juice on the counter in front of us, orange for Bernie and tomato, with a fresh cup of coffee, for me.

"Why, Bernardo, I'm so flattered you'd let me come along on police business. You sure that's wise?"

"Don't let it go to your head. I just want to keep an

eye on you, until we know the deal with those morons. Can't have you going off half-cocked, get yourself killed or worse—kill somebody else. McCorkle is still on the warpath over that last peckerwood you stiffed. Another one, and he and the ADA will have your license. I won't be able to do jack-squat. He'll throw your ass in lockup for good, and toss the key his own bad self. I won't have to."

Maldonado was blowing smoke again. The cops swung no weight with the license bureau. Revoking a PI's license was just a lot harder than they wanted us PIs to believe.

"Look, I know you, amigo, and I'm serious about this—you get hurt with me in charge and Shirl will have my cajones for a new pair of earrings."

Bernie was referring to an accidental death in which I was involved. An undercover DEA officer had oozed over to the other side. He was selling more horse than any dealer in town. He shipped the profits to a numbered Swiss bank account. At the time, I was the primary investigator for the defense attorney whose innocent black client was taking the fall. Luckily, I was able to flip the agent and expose the seamy underbelly on his corrupt dealings. Unluckily, he escaped the net and, one dark night, confronted me outside my office. He stepped from the shadows under the bougainvillea and leveled a .38 Special at me. Nobody sticks a gun in my face without suffering the consequences. He was killed when the weapon discharged in the ruckus.

I couldn't take all the credit. He had crossed the line when he diced himself into Chinatown business. It was just a matter of time before they peeled his onion and wokked his tofu, Szechwan style. In fact, I was about ninety-nine percent sure that the Chinese put me on to him in the first place, although I didn't find this out until later. But Deputy Chief Brian McCorkle complained to Bernie that I'd muddied the investigatory waters trolling around in police business. He then implied that I'd done the Chinese wet work. He went so far as to suggest I got paid for the hit and dragged me in for grilling. I didn't know what kind of fly McCorkle had up his butt—he was always fishing for some kind of trap to catch me in— but he was wrong. Simple truth was that I didn't have a choice. I'd had to deal with the .38.

"So what's with this Hollenbeck thing?" I said. "You sure you want me out there?"

"Si, Mon, nobody there but security, me, and maybe a couple of forensics guys. But I think forensics finished up Friday. I want to get another look at the scene and double check some facts in the preliminary report with a couple of people who were previously unavailable."

"Any suspects?"

"No. At first we thought accident; no motive for murder yet. But how does a two thousand pound statue fall on you while you're not looking?"

"Two thousand pounds?"

"It's a heavy mother is all I know. You don't just push one of those rocks over, especially one rigged on ball bearings in case of earthquakes; it takes a forklift. That was on Friday at the Villa. On Saturday, Hollenbeck, the dead man, faxes a suicide note from his office computer at the new Getty to the main desk at the station."

"Oh yeah? That's pretty weird."

"It was addressed to the Chief of Police. In it, he stated that he'd lost more dinero day-trading than Dexter's got donuts—that the death of his mother, six months previously, was when his troubles began. It seems that she'd been secretly and anonymously giving her fortune to charity for years, leaving Hollenbeck without means to cover his big losses and worse debts. Then there was the breakup with his long-time lover, Raleigh Hanson, the sculptor who had, apparently, decided to split when he heard the bad news about the fifty-eight year old Hollenbeck's fiscal picadillos."

"That's odd. Seems rather strange, not to mention a lot of trouble, to fax such personal information to the police for a suicide. Puts Raleigh Hanson in a precarious position. You got to look serious at a sculptor, for a murder by sculpture. The fax was sent from Hollenbeck's office computer at the new Getty, you say?"

Bernie nodded and drank from his cup. "Si. First computer generated suicide note we've ever gotten, I can tell you. And by fax, no less."

"Obviously, it was set on delay send. Was it actually set up the day before?"

Bernie nodded again. "That's what the computer guy tells me."

"There were no other prints on the keyboard."

"Madre de Dios, I just love to watch your brain deduce."

"Well? Be too easy if we had a bumbling idiot murderer leaving his prints all over the place, wouldn't it? So, you still don't know whether it was suicide or if someone iced him."

"You got it."

"Got what?" Shirley said, as she came over to refill our cups.

"Got milk," I said. I hadn't creamed my fresh coffee yet and reached for the little chrome pitcher.

"You want me to cream that for you—Nes Honey?"

We watched in silent admiration as she set the pot down, took the creamer from me, dolloped just the right amount into my cup, and stirred it with a flick of the spoon.

"There now. Put your tongues back in your heads, boys, and quit drooling all over my counter. Breakfast is coming right up." She smiled, set the creamer in its place, took the coffeepot, and went down the counter to catch up on her orders. She was the only waitress in the place, but she was never in a hurry.

I sipped ambrosia. "I gotta tell you, Bern—nobody ever creamed my coffee like Shirl—if you know what I mean . . ."

Bernie just sipped from his cup and smiled. "So, Nes Honey," he said. "Tell me—does she dress you in the morning, too?"

Three

BERNIE AND I SPLIT COMPANY AFTER BREAKFAST. HE headed downtown to the Parker Center Station on Los Angeles Street. I kissed Shirl, told her I'd see her later at the house in midtown, and got into my Nova Super Sport outside Dexter's. When I pulled into the Santa Monica traffic, I noticed a tan late-model Ford slip off the curb and drop in two cars behind me. I now had company all the way over to Chullsu Kim's Firearms Emporium just off Wilshire Boulevard in Koreatown. The tail was pulling into Von's Grocery parking lot across the street, when I entered Mr. Kim's place.

"Ah, Mista Nesta. How you do? You don' look too good. That got to hurt."

"Not when you take these," I said and rattled my little vial of Vicodin at him.

"Wow, that stuff make your eye bug out. How you drive with those things?"

"Very carefully."

"Ha, ha. You big card, the Joker. Wha' I do for you today?"

21

Chullsu Kim was short, thin, and seemed to never stop moving, even when he stood perfectly still. And he always spoke very fast and loud, though he never showed signs of hearing loss. I was sure the guy in the Ford across the street could hear him from over there. Chullsu may've been a tad rambunctious, but he knew his guns.

"Ah yes, Chullsu, I need shells for my Glock. Couple of cowboys drifted into town looking for trouble, and I don't want to disappoint them. All I've got is the Smith and Wesson."

"Yeh, yeh. . 357 Magnum snub-nose, only shoot five shell. I remember. Glock 19 shoot 10 shell, or 15 shell, 31 shell with big clip. You got big clip? Big clip very sexy. All the girl wan' big clip."

"Yeah, right."

"Shoot automatic. How big your clip?"

"Big enough."

"Size matter, I know. You like Glock? Hot rod, yes? How much you wan'? I get bes' shell for you. You don' wan' to shoot blank."

"You got that right. Two boxes—Glock. One box—Mag."

Chullsu put two boxes of 9mms and one box .357s on the counter.

"Free today for you. You take." He shoved them over to me.

"No, no. I'll pay like always." I took money out my wallet and laid it on the counter. We went through this every time. He always tried to give me the bullets free, but I wouldn't take them. He always insisted I take the shells. He felt obligated to keep me in cheap lead, because after two months tough digging, I had dug up the only eyewitness who could've possibly cleared his son in a triple homicide—the actual murderer. Chullsu had been generously grateful ever since, giving me the "materiel de mayhem" at cost. As I explained to him before, I was just doing my job.

"I show you something to shoot cowboy," Chullsu said, as he pulled a wooden box from below the counter and opened it. "Colt Cowboy .45, forty-two ounce, six roun', single action army, brand new. Very cheap for you. You like?"

I took the hog-leg, rolled the cylinder along my arm and listened to the satisfying sound it made clicking over. I cracked it open, inspected the chamber, then snapped it shut, clean. I held it in a shooter's grip and sighted down the store aisle. I thumbed back the hammer and pulled the trigger several times, just to feel the action.

"Very nice," I said. "But a six-shooter's just not my style, thanks." I twirled it around my finger and handed it back to him.

"You grow hair, look like John Wayne. Get three gallon hat."

"Very funny. Say, how's Jason and Mrs. Kim doing?"

"Kid, you know kid. He make his mother crazy. He got job now, pay rent. Buy car. He stay out of trouble." He put the Colt away.

"That's good. Right?"

"Missy Kim make me crazy. She take hormone for change. Now she wan' fuck all time. Come here at lunch every day. Make me close store early. She regular nympho now. I have to get Viagra keep up with her."

He made my change, as I tried to keep from laughing out loud. I told him to keep his ears to the ground and let me know if he heard anything about a couple of foreigners named Mustafa and Davie. He said he would. We shook hands, and I left.

Across the boulevard, the man in the tan Ford was trying to look inconspicuous while eyeballing me around the side of his newspaper. When I stashed the ammo in the trunk of the Nova SS, I thought about walking over and confronting him on the subject of why he was following me—so I did. He began to look uncomfortable as I crossed the street. He'd probably realized that my new destination was in his direction, and I had just left a gun shop. Initially, he might've thought I was going into Von's for some creamed herring or something, until he caught me looking directly at him. By the time he had managed to put his paper away, I was bending down, leaning on my left forearm, and looking in at his open window. Hispanic with slicked-back hair, narrow shifty eyes and a pencil-thin mustache, he appeared, up close, to be about my height—six-four, two-ten, two-twenty max. He was sitting down, so I couldn't say for sure, but it all looked pretty soft. He reached for something beneath the lapel of his camel-colored sportcoat.

"No, no, no," I said, laying the Magnum across my forearm, just below his eyes. "That wouldn't be smart."

He put his hand on the wheel. "What do you want, vato? Is this some kinda car-jacking or what?" he said.

"In this heap of guano? Are you kidding?"

"Well, what then? What's with the greaser?" He looked down at the gun.

"You're going to tell me why you're following me."

He threw his head back and laughed. "Like hell I am, muchacho. I don't know what the fuck you're talking about."

24

"You know a couple of goons named Davie and Mustafa?"

"Are they the guys who gave you the facelift? Nice work." He smiled and reached down for the ignition.

"Uh, uh, uh. Not yet, pal." I wiggled the Magnum to remind him who had the drop on whom.

"Buzz off, bonehead. You're not gonna kill me here, right in front of all these witnesses." He was referring to a couple of people crossing the lot.

"You're right. You got me there. What was I thinking?"

He smirked again.

I flicked the satin-finished, stainless steel body of the gun sideways across the bridge of his nose and broke the cartilage.

"Pinche! Sonava-fucking-bitch!" He jerked his head back, felt the blood running down his face onto his shirt and reached inside his jacket.

I stuck the end of the barrel against his temple. He froze.

"That better be a hanky you're reaching for, or you're not going to need one at all," I said.

He slowly removed a handkerchief from inside his coat, and I lowered the gun. He mopped at his face and shirt, then held his head back to stop the bleeding.

I noticed a few more people moving around, and a man on his way out of the store had started to take an interest in us. I nodded in his direction to let him know things were copacetic. He moved on.

"Like I said, you know a couple guys named Mustafa and Davie?"

"Fuck you, asshole," he spat from beneath the hanky. "I just don't believe what you've done to my nose and my good white shirt. I paid thirty bucks for this shirt. Shit. This blood'll never come out."

"I gotta tell ya, fucking around with people you don't know can be a real sartorial catastrophe." I pointed the gun straight down and rested the end of the barrel on top of his thigh. "Those beautiful Sans-a-belt polyester plaids of yours could be next."

"Toda madre. You gonna blow my leg off now? For crying out loud."

"You never know when a man's gonna to be forced to do something that he doesn't want to do." I prodded him with the barrel.

"Okay, okay, who'd you say?"

"Mustafa and Davie."

"Never heard of 'em. There, are you satisfied?—for Christ's sake!"

"I might be, when you tell me who you're working for."

He lowered the handkerchief and glared at me.

"So who sent you?"

"Oh man, I tell you that and I'm outta work. Shit, I'll hafta move clear back to Tallahassee."

"Okay, so why were you following me?"

"The guy told me to."

"You always do what you're told? Tsk, tsk, tsk! Who was it?" I applied a little more pressure to his thigh.

"All right, all right. They find out I told, I'm gonna look worse than you."

"You already look worse than me."

"You gotta promise you won't say nothin', or it's gonna go real bad for me. Those guys'll ride me like a merry-go-round. Promise?"

"Sure." I could see he was in a real fix about telling,

so while he made up his mind, I panned the parking lot to see if anyone else had been watching us. An ambulance went by with its siren wailing.

"Look. This guy named Buddy wanted to know who you talked to and where you went."

"Buddy? Is that Buddy Palmer by any chance?"

He shrugged. "You know him?"

"Yeah, if he's the same guy—security chief for Universal Paradigm, the last I heard. Does he still work for UP?"

He shrugged again. "Maybe."

"Why did he want me followed?"

"Don't ask me. I don't know shit. I just do what he tells me, and he gives me money."

"You just started dogging me this morning, outside of Dexter's, right?" I already knew the answer to that. I just wanted to see if he would lie to me.

"Yeah."

"For how long?"

"Until he said otherwise."

"Well, Zero, not that it hasn't been fun, mind you, but I've got other fish to fry." I took the magnum off his thigh and held it where he could see it. "I think you need to go back and tell Buddy that you were made, and couldn't see any sense in sticking to it. You should also tell him not to bother putting someone else on me."

"Look, man, not an option. The motherfucker'll put my ass in a sling, for sure."

"I grow another tail, or I see you again, and I'll put your ass in a sling, for sure—when I talk to Buddy personally."

"But he'll find out it was me who told you."

"More than likely. But hey, pal, you play stud, you

27

play the cards you're dealt. There's no draw." I holstered the Magnum and quickly backed away. As I crossed the boulevard, I saw the tan Ford pull out of the parking lot onto Third Street. It headed east, in the direction opposite from the Universal Paradigm building over in Westwood. Maybe he was headed home to boink the little woman, or maybe he was hungry for some Yellowtail and a hand roll down in Little Tokyo, or maybe he was actually moving back to Tallahassee. Either way, I'd seen the last of him for now. Hell, I'd probably seen the last of him forever.

Four

TWENTY MINUTES LATER, I PARKED THE NOVA SS IN the two-dollar lot at the corner of First Street and Alameda. I put my piece in the leather bag with the shells in the trunk and crossed against the light. The thought that those two snakes, Mustafa and Davie, might've had something to do with Hollenbeck's death, slithered through my mind as I walked a couple blocks to the Parker Center. Call it a hunch; I had no real reason to think so. After all, it was pretty far-fetched. And though not often, my hunches have been wrong before. Nevertheless, they were exactly the types to be involved in something that smelled like murder. It was not like Buddy Palmer to be involved in murder, at least as far as I knew. Our paths had not crossed in some years. Now that I thought about it, I really couldn't say what he might be willing to get dirty over, or just how dirty for that matter. He was no Boy Scout in any event.

At the station, I cleared the metal detectors and weapons search, then took the stairs to the third floor to find Artie. After we finished the composites, I went up to the fourth floor and caught Bernie on the phone arranging to meet someone out at the Villa. While waiting for Bern, I meandered across the squad room looking for a donut, but they were already gone. There were a lot of new faces that I hadn't seen when I worked downtown. I ran into a couple of traffic cops that I'd known before moving over to homicide. I hoped I wouldn't inadvertently happen into McCorkle. So far, my luck was holding. When I returned to Bernie's desk, he was off the phone and putting on his suit coat. I told him about my morning adventures. He confided that Buddy Palmer had been keeping a low profile, but had been questioned about the severe beating and eventual death that several of his security men had given an alleged armed burglar, over at Paradigm. LAPD had looked into it, but under the circumstances, the case was dropped for lack of evidence. It was a stonewall. Even with solid evidence, CEO G. Henry Carl's attorneys at UP could've tied it up for years and made it virtually impossible to get a conviction. Bernie wanted me to give him the name of the tail. I had to confess that I didn't get it. Since there was nothing on Mustafa or Davie yet, we put the composites out and decided to take our separate rides out to Malibu.

The twenty-five mile drive across the city gave me time to think about why Bernie had invited me to come along; it was not his usual modus operandi. Nor was it good policy for him to discuss ongoing investigations with an ex-cop, especially one that kept turning up like a bad penny, one which the brass considered tarnished copper, no matter how long we'd known each other. We didn't often sit around talking shop. For one thing, I didn't much care to be around police business anyway, except where our interests overlapped. Then, too, it simply wasn't smart for me to scull around in places I had no truck. In fact, if McCorkle found out, he would probably choke on the cream filling in his Long John.

Usually Bernie told me only what he deemed prudent. What I didn't know I couldn't divulge under oath in a courtroom. In our business, information was the thing. He and I traded only when necessary. Maldonado knew how to keep his mouth shut. I liked that about him and understood the feeling was reciprocal. Even as friends, we both knew that in our respective positions, representing different and competing interests as we often did, if push came to shove, Bernie would put me in jail. I knew that for a fact. He had done so, on one occasion several years back, when I wouldn't give up a source that he felt I had wrongly shielded from the shortsighted arm of the law. He knew that he couldn't legally give me enough jail time to make me sing. I think he did it mostly to appease higher-ups, but he wasn't telling.

Even with its kernel of truth, his smokescreen about keeping me out of harm's way as a reason for dragging me along to the Getty Villa didn't hide its lameness as an excuse. Maybe he thought my longtime interest in and knowledge of art could be of some practical value to his investigation. Maybe he wanted a second opinion, for me to get a look at the conundrum he was dealing with, quid pro quo for Mustafa and Davie. Maybe he didn't know why he'd asked me along; it could've been just a hunch he'd had about Mustafa and Davie, and that I was somehow connected. Maldonado was too good a detective to let a hunch get off scot-free. In this business, you learned to pay attention to your hunches, or you got yourself killed deader than a perch in a pond of piranhas down in Poodle Springs.

Or you got yourself killed in traffic, which in this town was murder anytime, day and night. It was even slower today, because the fog had not burned off and visibility was limited. It seemed to come and go, although it was already pushing noon. Santa Monica Freeway was bumper-to-bumper, stop and go, clear over to the Pacific Coast Highway. There was a light rain falling, just enough to need the wipers as I turned up into the Malibu Hills an hour later. When the sun came out in this humidity, we were going to swelter by early afternoon.

I parked next to Maldonado's unmarked Chevy Impala in the lot, and grabbed my trench coat from the back seat. Hot or not, I didn't want to get wet. Bernie was waiting to clear me through Villa security as I walked up to the gate.

"When you gonna get that coupe painted?" Bernie needled.

"Bout the same time you give up jelly donuts," I needled back. "Been waiting long?"

"No, just got here." He flashed his badge from beneath his trench at the guard. "This guy's with me." He arched his thumb in my direction, went through the gate, and started up through the beautifully manicured grounds of the Villa, with me in tow.

"Yes, sir," said the guard. "Dr. Eastlake and Ms. Rivero are expecting you in the marble foyer. But I still need to see some ID, sir—for the log entry, you understand."

"No problem," I said and came back to show him my driver's license.

"Could you remove it from the wallet, sir? Thank you."

I couldn't believe it. He wasn't even a cop, just a security guard, but I took it out anyway, and handed it to him.

"So that's what you look like without the Halloween make-up," he said, bobbing his head at my contusions. "Not a very good likeness is it, Mr. Pike, especially since you no longer bleach your hair like the picture?" He handed it back to me with a nasty lopsided grin.

"Well, well. Señor Gonzales," Bernie said, stepping in, brushing me to the side before I could respond. "Were you out here the night that Mr. Hollenbeck was killed?"

"Uh, no sir. That would be Pete Roberts and Rudy Laslo. But they didn't see or hear nothin', is what they told me."

"Would they be telling you the truth?" I asked, putting my wallet away.

"What else?"

"So, you didn't work that night," Bernie said. "Where were you then, say, between the hours of seven and midnight?"

"I was bowling at the Starbowl Lanes in Inglewood and then went home."

"That can be corroborated, Bro," said Maldonado. "You will, of course, give me the names of people who saw you at the lanes that night." He took a small notebook and pencil out of his trench pocket and got right into the man's face. At Bern's size that could be considered Webster's definition for the word intimidation.

"Hey, man, I already told all this to the other cops that came out here on Friday," he said, moving back a step.

"Well, ese, you may have to tell it again and again before this is all over. In fact, you could end up sitting in a cell with some other smart-ass cholos downtown, waiting to tell your story to still another detective, if you follow the drift of the river here, Señor Gonzales." Bernie tilted his head and cocked his eyebrow.

"Yes, sir. Sorry, sir. Gracias." Señor Gonzales stumbled over the words in a hurry to get them out. "Dr. Eastlake's waiting, sir. Should I phone up and let them know you're here."

"That would be appreciated. Gracias. Are you ready, Mr. Pike?" Bernie stood back up to his full height of six feet and put his notebook away.

"As ready as I'll ever be, Lieutenant Detective Maldonado." We started up the hill, and I waited until we were out of ear shot before I said, "I thought he was going to cry there for a minute."

"I didn't like that vato's attitude."

"No kidding."

"Hate to see a young Latino in a uniform, even just a security uniform, act like a prick."

"I know what you mean. It never ceases to amaze me how people's attitudes reflect their nearness to money. There's a smugness; it's a Republican idea—very democratic in its appeal—the trickle down theory of snobbism. Comes from being too close to people in power, with all that money to play with. Just adopt the nastiest mannerisms of the moneyed class. One day, you too will be rich; if not in fact, then by association."

"Is that what it takes? Madre Maria, intercede for me. And here, all this time, I thought it took just plain old hard work or a winning Powerball ticket."

"Well, Compadré, that too. And I know that I don't need to remind you, but some people will even kill you for it." For a few moments, we walked along the path in silence, listening to the fog-muffled thumping of a lone woodpecker cutting into the soft damp bark of a tree.

"Hey, I'd forgotten that you bleached your hair," Bernie said.

"Yep. Sure did—almost a year."

"Oh yeah—your Billy Idol phase. I remember. Say, could I see that license?"

Five

DR. YAEGER EASTLAKE, THE SENIOR CURATOR AT THE museum, was a tall, imposing man when seen from below, which is how I first saw him, and a young woman, under the portico as we climbed the steps to the Getty Villa. Fashionably thin, good-looking and well muscled for a man in his fifties, he had the kind of build that could only be acquired through sheer ruthlessness in the gym, a good plastic surgeon, or both. Eastlake wore his cool-gray Armani casually, with a sense of inevitability that I couldn't help but envy. Tanned, bursting with good health and glowing, he stood as if basking in the last golden rays as the sun set on the Roman Empire, although it was overcast and just past eleven a.m. He gave me the impression that he'd waited all his life to meet Maldonado and me. We were somehow more important and radiated our own fabulous glow, just by being in his presence; and now that we were, life finally had meaning for him. At the top of the steps, he was not as tall as he'd appeared from below. Some of that last-days-of-empire glow had faded. I was always amazed how things could change when seen from another point of view.

"Lieutenant Detective Maldonado," Eastlake said, as he nodded and offered his hand.

"Dr. Eastlake, my colleague Nestor Pike," Bernie said, returning the nod, showing his badge and ignoring the gesture.

I nodded in turn, hoping he wouldn't ask to see my credentials. The less said about who I was the better.

"Mr. Pike." There was no hand offered as he glanced up in my direction. "Gentlemen, this is my Associate Registrar, Ms. Veronica Rivero."

"Ms. Rivero." Bernie and I spoke and nodded in unison.

"Please call me Ronnie, Lieutenant," she said, and returned the nod. "Mr. Pike." She nodded again, appeared to blush, then looked down at her shoes.

Uncalled for, the image of that toy dog with it's head on a spring, bobbing in the rear window of my Dad's old '49 Buick, popped into my mind along with something else, but I was unsure just what. And what did she have to blush about, anyway? We'd just met.

"Shall we?" Eastlake turned and headed for the other end of the colonnade and the marble foyer, with Ms. Rivero anticipating his move.

Bernie and I nodded at each other and fell into step behind them.

I hadn't been up there in some years, but the gardens were pretty much as I remembered; the citrus trees, arbors and wading pool were all very formal. Although the building itself was undergoing a full-scale renovation, there were not many workmen around and the place was strangely quiet. Fog thinned and thickened, drifting eerily over the grounds. Bronze figures of long dead patricians stood about, materializing in and out of the mist as it shifted through the garden. It occurred to me that in another time, Eastlake could have lived in a villa very like this, on a hillside near Rome, under the reign of Augustus Caesar. I had no idea of his pedigree, but he certainly exuded a patrician air, almost as prevalent as the air of Calvin Klein's Obsession that he left streaming in his wake. As we walked silently along the colonnade, it came to mind that ancient Roman economy, and thus patrician life, was based on slavery. I wondered just what sort of economy existed between Eastlake and Rivero.

Associate Registrar Ronnie Rivero appeared to be in her late twenties or early thirties. Black hair curved about her face, down her neck to the shoulder. She had wonderfully sad dark eyes, full red lips and a figure more suited to motherhood than a marathon. Was that a slight but perceptible flicker of recognition in those sad eyes I noticed when Bernie introduced me? I would've remembered her, had we met before. My guess was that she knew something the rest of us didn't; she'd gone underbelly-white around the gills. I would have to give that some thought later. She wore a charcoal skirt, an appropriately artistic and colorful silk blouse, practical two-inch heels, and carried a bag over the shoulder just large enough to conceal a small caliber Beretta automatic. I calculated the odds, but came to no conclusion on that possibility. Presumably, they both left their rain togs in an office somewhere.

"So, Lieutenant, how can we help you?" Dr. Eastlake was the first to speak when we got to his office on the second floor. "Can we get you anything, coffee, water?"

"We're fine, thanks," Bernie said.

I could've used a cup of coffee, but at this point Bernie was doing all the talking.

The office was large, dim in the overcast light from the windows. The few furnishings left were heavy and dark, as were most of the antiques that I remembered throughout the place—in storage now, during the renovation. We could barely hear the sound of power tools running somewhere below. For the second time since I'd arrived, I had the disconcerting but not unpleasant sensation that I was adrift in time. There were few people to be seen, but there was the eerie sound of them moving around that echoed throughout the empty spaces of the Villa.

"Sit down gentlemen," Eastlake said, as he indicated two deep-red leather chairs across from his desk.

"To be honest, Dr. Eastlake, I'm not sure if you can help me," Bernie said as Eastlake sat behind his desk. "You were a close friend to Mr. Hollenbeck, I understand."

I stood next to the window, and looked out upon the grounds behind the Villa. Since there were no other chairs in the room, I'd assumed Ms. Rivero would sit on the black leather sofa along the wall. But she remained standing just inside the door, next to a large piece of furniture with a marble top that had survived at least three centuries, and resembled a very ornate credenza. She appeared nervous, rubbing her hands together.

"That's true," Eastlake said. "Possibly his closest friend. I've known Carter since I first came to the Getty, almost twenty years now."

"Excuse me, gentlemen," Ronnie said. "If you don't

40

need me at the moment, Lieutenant, I have some work in the renovation office."

"That's fine, Ms. Rivero," Bernie said. "We'll speak shortly."

He stood a moment as she departed.

Dr. Eastlake nodded and continued after Ms. Rivero closed the door. "Carter's death has been a terrible shock. I knew he was depressed, but I didn't know how depressed. He was a private man and didn't speak openly about his troubles, even with me, close as we were."

"Seems inconsistent then for him to fax such personal information to the Chief of Police, doesn't it?" Bernie said.

"Very. But he was under a great deal of pressure with the coming exhibition, not as much as I, as the Senior Curator, but nevertheless . . . And, if just half of the revelations in that note were true, his personal problems could've seemed insurmountably devastating. You have to realize that Carter was a perfectionist, often neurotically so. The least impropriety or disorder in his life could be terribly distressing to him. Not to speak ill of the dead, but he was sometimes over the edge when it came to his financial and personal affairs, as just about everyone here can tell you."

"Surely an established man in his position, on the board, a trustee, could not have been stretched to the point of suicide. Then to go to such lengths . . . "

"I can't really speak to that. All I can say is, I knew that he was suffering and after some thought, I would not be entirely surprised that he took his own life, if indeed he did so. Mind you, I do not dismiss the possibility that someone else may have done it. It's just that I can think of no one here who could have done such a

41

horrible thing. I've been here a long time. I know most of these people very well, and I can tell you that there's no one, absolutely no one here, with either the motive or the necessary access to have done this to Carter. Everyone at the Getty liked him, and his popularity throughout prominent circles of the city was legend. I'm therefore left with the inescapable conclusion that he must have done it himself, hard as that is for me to accept. And, strange as it is, there is the note as evidence to support it, circumstantial though it may be."

"Can you tell me what Hollenbeck might have been doing down here at that time of night?"

"I have no idea. This was no longer his purview. He had no business down here that I can think of. Though he was a big supporter of the new facilities, I knew he dreaded moving over there; he loved this place. His father had been a preeminent authority, and Carter had shared his enthusiasms for these early Greek works. These were the things he loved best."

"You mentioned the upcoming exhibition."

"Yes, some priceless artifacts from the Middle East at the time of Christ. In fact, they are consensually thought to be the actual utensils, among other things, used by Jesus and the disciples at the Last Supper."

"Are we talking Holy Grail, the actual Chalice here? Why haven't we heard about it? That would be priceless indeed."

"No, no. Nobody's calling it that. Just some simple, plain cups and bowls—not what you would imagine, but found very recently in an extremely promising archeological trove. Objects matching texts discovered among the Dead Sea Scrolls and elsewhere."

"Authenticated?"

"There are two schools there."

"Of course," Bernie said. "Were you and Mr. Hollenbeck students in the same school?"

"Same class even. I sense, Mr. Pike, that you have a question, something to do with this office, possibly."

I guessed my restless poking about the place somehow communicated itself to him. "Well, now that you mention it," I said, "I would expect you, as Senior Curator, to have your office up at the new place, what with this renovation."

"I do," he said, twiddling a pencil between his fingers. "This is not my office. This one is being maintained as a conference room until the renovation is almost complete. We need to meet down here on occasion for various reasons, and it just made sense to use the most comfortable room. It will be the last room done, along with the renovations office on the first floor—in fact, where Ms. Rivero is working now."

"Tell me," I said as I watched a couple workmen clearing debris outside, "with such important artifacts so recently discovered, how is it possible the Getty is able to convince the authorities there to part with them for an exhibition in the United States so soon—especially in light of all the recent tensions in the Middle East?"

"A number of reasons, really. First, the Getty was instrumental in the discovery. It was through research sponsored by the Getty that this site came to light. Secondly, along with permission to pursue a find, we always get permission in the contracts from the hosting government, in this case Jordan, to study and exhibit the discovery first. And Jordan, as you may know, has not been quite as hostile to the US as some of the other Arab states."

"Is this common practice?"

"Yes, it makes sense because our researchers are often the most qualified in the field. Many of them come from hosting countries and are the preeminent authorities. They apply here for money in the form of grants to pursue such research. Jordan's ministers did not expect this find to be of such monumental importance, and were reluctant to honor their contract when they found out. They did so, I'm not too modest to say, in part because I have close ties to the ministry of antiquities there. I made the trip personally, along with Ms. Rivero, to help convince the government that it was in their best interest to honor the contracts, and to oversee the transport of such valuable objects."

"I see. Tell me, how is it that the Getty has begun supporting archeological studies? Isn't that a little outside the mandate of an art museum?"

"Yes, true. The Getty research arm mostly supports arts related research. But when the possible scope of this find was brought to our attention, we felt that it was of such magnitude, it was important for us to pursue it. You must admit this forthcoming exhibition is going to draw some major attention. Indeed, it has already done so. It's a history-making event, any way you choose to look at it."

"I can see that. Thank you, Dr. Eastlake. By the way, who is the Senior Registrar?"

"That would be Dr. Penny Braithwate," He rolled a pencil on the desk under the palm of his hand.

"Is she available?"

"No, I'm sorry. She's on an extended leave of absence from the Getty. She fell while trying to replace a light bulb in her ceiling fixture at home. Apparently, she struck her head against the corner of a table. She's still in a coma. We've no idea when, or even if, she will return to us."

"Sorry to hear that, but that's why she didn't travel with you to Jordan?"

"That's right."

"Thanks again. Say Bernie, I think I'll get some air if you don't mind." I started for the door.

"I'll meet you outside later," Bernie said, then turned to Dr. Eastlake. "Say, just how do you think it's possible for Mr. Hollenbeck to bring down one of those stone boys on his own head? How much does one of those things weigh, anyway?"

I was out the door before I could hear the answer.

Six

WANDERED DOWN TO THE FIRST FLOOR IN SEARCH OF the coffee that Eastlake had offered me, and ended up in the gallery where Hollenbeck had been found reduced to a flattened, airless pulp under a big carved rock. The chamber was roped off with yellow crime-scene tape, and there was only one bank of work lights on. The malevolent stone had been righted. It wore the rust red evidence of Hollenbeck's fatal embrace. The place was empty but for the Kouri, three of them—one of which was still chained to the forks of the forklift. Standing there together, everything looked like one big piece of conceptual art, an enigmatic vision of delicacy and brute force. It made the room seem spooky, suspended out of time.

Under the circumstances, I wouldn't have been surprised to see Hollenbeck appear like Banquo's ghost, to point a finger and whisper the secrets of this case to me; he was murdered—he was not murdered. As I walked around absorbing the scene, looking at the stone-cold, silent witnesses, getting a whole new appreciation for the ancient Greek artists, it came to me how ironic that the

Kouri in question is itself questionable; some authorities consider it a fake. It's authenticity may never be resolved; the controversy rages on. It also came to me that this was all too stupid to be suicide, however it might appear—suicide fax notwithstanding. How improbable was that? And how could anyone have thought otherwise?

I was never sure how I knew these things; I just did. Aside from the obvious, the trouble he'd have engineering his own demise under one of these monsters, this was one of those times when I knew something as sure as I knew my own name. And, whether I liked it or not, there have been days when I woke up not quite knowing my own name, like this past Saturday for starters. Most of our lives were spent never knowing anything for sure—spinning around on a globe through the black void of space, going no one knows where. Does God exist? Will the Dodgers win the World Series? We spent our lives, awash in doubt, enduring the unfathomable. Well, I knew Hollenbeck had been murdered. It was more than a hunch. It was being in touch with that thing, that essence of existence where reality and I coalesced into some unassailable knowledge, some form of pure truth—if there was such a thing. That was no suicide in that room, and I knew it, instinctively—though, as of yet, I had no proof.

There's nothing mystical in it. When I think about it, I can see that in some ways I've spent my life trying to disprove things that I knew purely by instinct, and could've known in no other fashion. I'm good at knowing things unreasonably. It's why I can't give up the business. Being a private dick is the one thing that I'm really good at. Would you've asked Ali to give up his gloves, or Miles his trumpet? Not that I'm the greatest detective in the world, but I'm not bad. It took Shirl some years to come to an acceptance of that fact, that being a private eye is who I am, especially after Nathaniel was killed. Even now, she would rather see me doing something else. But I've come to face my own truth. It's only when I'm poised on the cusp of revelation that all seems right with the world. And not to make too grand an assertion, but revealing the essence that resides only at the center of things is my true calling.

"So, Mr. Pike, I see you've managed to get to the heart of the matter—the scene of the crime, I mean," Ronnie Rivero said, retrieving me from my reveries. "Gathering any clues?"

"To be honest, Ms. Rivero, you've caught me gathering wool I'm afraid."

"Please call me Ronnie."

"Well, Ronnie, I was looking for a cup of coffee when I wandered in here." I noticed that she had regained her color.

"It's in the office; come with me."

We went through an inconspicuous door at the far end of the room. It was faux painted to match the wall. Still, I should've noticed it before in my ramble around the gallery. I made a mental note to have Felia make me an appointment to get my eyes examined.

We were in the central office of a suite of small offices, which were occupied by several busy people.

"Architect's, contractor's staff. Bill Burnett, foreman. Hi Bill." She waved and stopped at his door.

"Hi Ronnie."

"This is Mr. Pike."

He waved from behind his mound of blueprints, and I returned the salute. We left Bill to his work and made our way to the coffeepot.

"Cream and sugar?"

"Just cream, thanks." She poured it into one of the Getty mugs that had been hanging on the pegboard over the pot and gave it to me.

"There are little cream containers there, help yourself," she said.

I over-creamed it with Half-&-Half from three of those little plastic tubs.

Outside, the rain had stopped and the fog had cleared considerably. We made our way over to one of the umbrella tables on the terrace of the outdoor café, brushed the rain off a couple of chairs as best we could, and sat out of the weather. The umbrellas were all gone, and the space was empty but for the tables and potted plants sitting in big concrete and ceramic pots. The gardeners were still employed, I surmised, because everything was immaculately kept.

"It's terrible what's happened to Mr. Hollenbeck," she said.

"Did you know him well?"

"Not at all. I knew who he was, of course; everybody did. About as well as I knew some of the other trustees, to see them around the grounds. We've rarely had occasion to speak."

"You never met him socially?"

"Openings, occasionally. But no. We lived and worked in entirely different realms. I'm just an aspiring Latina from East LA who went to college, and he, well . . . he was a socialite. But you already knew that."

"Can you think of anyone who might want to do such a thing to Mr. Hollenbeck?"

She paused, looked around as if she might be overheard, and said, "Sorry, no."

It occurred to me that she didn't see this as a probable suicide either. By the look on her face, she had more or less confirmed my suspicions about murder.

"Mr. Hollenbeck was a very nice man from what I could tell. He worked very hard for the Museum. He was always agitating to improve the quality of the exhibitions." She appeared hesitant to continue and looked around once again.

"Yes, go on."

"After the initial fanfare at the opening of the new facility, our attendance had fallen off. The Getty is the richest museum in the world, the only museum with a four billion dollar trust fund; and it ranks lower in mass appeal and draw than others around the country, some with far less in the way of resources to work with. That was a big problem for Mr. Hollenbeck, as it was to many others of us who took pride in working here. Fortunately, we now have new leadership that is dedicated to turning things around." She paused and looked out over the grounds, which were misting up again.

I was struck by something in her voice that seemed to float just below the surface of her words.

"Mr. Hollenbeck was particularly unsettled over an article he'd read a while back."

"What did it say that should bother him?"

"It was a slightly disparaging account of what happened out there, since the new Getty opened in 1997. It said that we were bookworms and disconnected, a theme-park for a bunch of Marians."

"Marians?"

"You know, librarians."

"Well, there are worse things to be called. But tell

51

me, how'd you know this about Mr. Hollenbeck, if you weren't that close?" I sipped my coffee.

"Well Mr. Hollenbeck was a pretty flamboyant personality and the object of much talk, gossip really, especially since he had been trying to get some changes made around here. He was pushing the Director, Dr. Eastlake, and the other trustees, whoever would listen, to open up the facilities, loosen up and do more for the city. He wanted to attract back some of the Hollywood people, take a more populist stance, and quit going over the heads of our audiences."

"What did he think about the upcoming show?"

"What was not to like? It could very well be the cup of Christ that we're about to put on display."

I noticed her expression soured somewhat when she said that. "When is that opening by the way?"

"It actually opens to the general public on Saturday, but there's a black-tie, invitation-only opening Friday night for all the supporters, trustees and dealers, the wealthy—you know—the well connected. It's unfortunate that Pen . . . Dr. Braithwate won't be able to attend. She was so looking forward to this. She's a devout Catholic."

"As you are?"

"I'm not so devout."

"I see."

She'd looked to the ground at the mention of Dr. Braithwate. Was that sadness tinged with fear? There was no doubt something else needed looking into here, but before I had the chance to ask, she stood abruptly and said, "Well, Mr. Pike, I see that you've finished your coffee. I suppose I should get back in there. Lieutenant Maldonado is probably looking for me by now. You think he'll put out one of those—what do you call them?" She smiled.

"An APB—an all points bulletin," I said, and stood, smiling back. I made a mental note to look into that Braithwate matter soon.

"That's it, an APB. It was nice meeting you, Mr. Pike."

"It was nice meeting you too, Ronnie. Could I ask you a favor?" She nodded. "Would you tell Detective Maldonado, when you see him, that I've headed back to town, and I'll call him later."

"Certainly. Maybe we'll meet again before this is over. Would you like to come to the opening?"

"I'm not that well connected." She looked a bit disappointed, so I said, "But hey, it might be fun."

"Consider yourself invited. I'll send you an invitation. Should I address it to Mr. and Mrs. Pike?"

"That'd be fine. Send it to the RD Detective Agency." I gave her my card. Was that another look of disappointment I spotted? She offered her hand, and I shook it. Her skin was papery dry and warm. After she turned to leave, I sat back down to make a few notes. I watched her dematerialize through the mist as she made her way back across the terrace, into the Villa. At that moment, I knew that that girl was in some kind of trouble—just as I knew that Hollenbeck had been murdered. Just what kind of trouble she was in was the mystery. I hoped it wasn't the murder kind.

Seven

FOG CLUNG TO THE HILLS IN WISPS AND TATTERS, AS the sun steamed the valley under a thinning veil of mist. It was a sauna. When I got back to the office around three, Felia was not at her desk. I assumed she'd either stepped down the hall to use the ladies' room, or had taken off for another audition. She was forever running out in a hurry to make a casting call and leaving the place unlocked. I also assumed that if she'd gone to an audition, she would have left a note on my desk telling me when she'd return. She usually did when she had to leave early. Of course, in my line of work, I knew it was dangerous to make assumptions or prefigure conclusions without getting a look at all the facts; things weren't always what they seemed at first glance. So her scream came as quite a surprise, when I opened the door and entered my office.

With the failing air conditioner running at full force, she hadn't heard me enter the outer office. She stood glaring at me while her hands were busy trying to cover her lacy black lingerie, which only served to accentuate her voluptuousness all the more. I could've testified to that voluptuousness in a court of law; there were no assumptions to be made about what I was looking at, whatsoever. I'd pretty much seen everything that needed seeing: five-foot-eight, stacked to the rafters, thick, curly blonde hair dancing on her shoulders. She was the sweet-alfalfa, milk-fed kind of girl that I would've bloodied any nose on the playground for, had she asked. If I was twenty years younger, and didn't know Shirl, I'd have been making a first-class fool of myself right then.

She had not recognized me with the black eyes, broken nose, contusions, and stitches. She must've thought that I was an ogre bent on doing her bodily harm. Although some of the swelling had gone down, I still looked like I had gone ten rounds with George Foreman or Smokin' Joe Frazier. What was worse was that I felt like it too, though I had taken a couple of Vicodin earlier. I backed out of the room, pulling the door closed behind me as quick as I could, and tried to memorize the vision of loveliness that I'd just seen. Someday, when I'm rocking on the porch of the old folks' home, and all I have left to keep me company are my memories, that memory of pretty Patty Porter from Muncie, Indiana— AKA Ophelia Tucker, her stage name, or Felia, as we called her—standing there in her delicious Victoria's Secrets is sure to warm the cockles of my black old heart.

"You nearly scared me to death, sneaking up on me like that," she yelled through the door.

"What are you doing half naked in there anyway?" I yelled back.

"I was getting ready to give you a big surprise—what do you think?"

"Obviously, you didn't expect me back."

"Boss, your powers of deduction never cease to amaze me."

I could hear her rustling around.

"Say, Boss, looks like you been in a car wreck over the weekend."

"No, just ran into a couple of disagreeable degenerates."

"That's what Donny said. I'd say damned disagreeable by the looks of it." She came out of my office zipping up her skirt and went to her desk. "I didn't want to go to the Ladies. You never know what's going to walk in down there. Come to think of it, it's almost as bad as what walks in here. So, what's up, Boss? I thought you weren't coming in." She put a carryall on the floor under her desk and her purse on top of it. She straightened the collar of her tailored cotton blouse, then came over and looked up at my face. "Wow. Are you gonna need cosmetic surgery when that heals? Donny said you got roughed up Friday, but he didn't say it was that bad."

"You think this is bad?" I said, pointing at my kisser. "You should see the other guys."

"You mean they're still alive?" She smiled.

I smiled. "Actually, I want you to be careful and keep the door locked when you're here alone. They may be back. Also, I need to get hold of Donny. He's not picking up his cell. I thought you might know why he hasn't called in."

"I don't know. I didn't see him over the weekend, but I spoke to him on the phone. He said he'd been busy with that Wilson matter down in El Segundo. He's okay, isn't he? He said he was. He wasn't lying to me, was he?"

"No, no. He was fine on Friday—just a little bruise on

his chin. You know Donny, can't keep a good man down."

She looked close to see if I was hiding something. "Okay, if you're sure; I'll call him later." She returned to her desk and put her purse in her lower desk drawer.

"By the way, what were you doing in there half-naked?" I said, turned, and went into my office. I crossed to the desk, put down my leather bag, and picked up the messages she'd left there earlier. "You do that often?"

"I just got back from an audition. I was changing clothes. You'll never guess who I read for today—go on, guess," she said, following me in.

"Ah—Steven Spielberg?" I ventured, scanning my messages.

"No silly, Quentin."

"Quentin?"

"Tarantino. You know, Pulp Fiction. That's why I had to wear my best lingerie. And you'll never guess who came in just as I was doing my lines. Well? Go on—guess."

"Harrison Ford?"

"It was John Travolta! Don't you ever go to the movies?"

"Not often. So tell me again why you were cavorting around in your best underduds."

"I was playing a stripper and had to strip in front of a mirror. The scene called for the girl to look at her naked body and speak this deep psychological mono-logue. It was about how her body was not who she was, and what she wants to do with her life, and how she was going to get along, when she got older and couldn't strip anymore—pretty powerful stuff."

"What happened to her in the end?"

"She realized that she'd never be who she wanted to be and went on a rampage with an Uzi, killing about a hundred people in a shopping mall before the SWAT team finally brought her down."

"Oh, based on a true story, I see. Well, how'd it go?" I tossed most of the messages into the wastebasket at the side of my desk.

"I don't think I got the part. He said that I reminded him of Mira and asked me if I'd go out with him sometime. I asked him if I did, would he give me the lead role? He said, 'Probably not.' We left it there."

"So, why was Travolta hanging out at your audition?"

"I don't know. He just watched the scene, whispered with Quentin, winked at me, gave a thumbs up, then shot me with his finger, and split."

I took off my trench and hung it on the pole behind the door, walked around and stood at my desk. The janitor had cleaned the office over the weekend. There were no bloodstains, no traces of Friday's fiasco except my license was pinned to the wall without a frame, and one of the client chairs had a broken leg, which I hadn't noticed in the fray.

"We need to get that chair fixed, or thrown away and replaced," I said.

"I'll get it out today."

"So what's this message from Susan Smith about?" I asked, waving the pink slip in my hand.

"You remember that appointment that stood you up last week? Well, she called back again, apologized profusely, and asked me for another appointment."

"Did she say what she wanted?"

"No, just that she had to see you, and . . . you ask me—well, Smith—not very creative, is she?"

"Did you book her?"

"Since she apologized so imploringly, yeah—9:00 am tomorrow. She wanted to come later today, but I couldn't be sure that I could confirm it with you."

"Okay, we'll see if she stands us up again. Get your pad and bring the checkbook. Was that fresh coffee I saw in the pot as I came in?"

"I made half a pot before I changed."

I went into the other room, got a cup, over-creamed it with Cremora, and returned to my desk. I kept thinking about my earlier interview with Ronnie Rivero and wondered why such a nice, young, educated woman had seemed so sad and vulnerable. I didn't know her from Eve, not that I wouldn't care to. But there was trouble there; I knew I'd have to find out about it, sooner or later. I pulled the holster with the Magnum from the waistband of my fatigues at my back and put it on the desk before I sat down.

Meanwhile, Felia went to her desk for a pad, pen, and checkbook, then sat in the chair across from me. Her eyes grew wide at the sight of the gun, so I put it away.

"First thing is, I'm serious about you being careful. The two guys who did this to me are threatening further mischief."

"Anything else I can do?"

"Just keep your eyes and ears open. In the meantime, Maldonado is checking them out. Next, take some petty cash and replace that license frame."

"Can't do, Boss. Petty cash already owes me thirty-five dollars."

"Here, take this, keep forty, get the frame and put the rest in the cash box," I said, as I peeled the only c-note from the wad of singles that I'd taken from my pocket. "What do our accounts receivable show?"

"Nobody came through last week, and there was nothing in the mail this morning."

"Carrington, Markley?"

"Nope."

"Washburn, Meyers, and Maloney?"

"Nada."

I was beginning to wonder what I was doing in this business, especially when I couldn't even collect the fees from my own customers. You knew it was getting bad, and you were getting soft, when your best clients didn't pay their bills. "Okay, I want you on the phone this afternoon. Tell Buck Carrington we need something on his account tomorrow, or the next time he wants some hard stuff done fast, he'll be calling the Pinkertons, and see how he likes that. Offer to pick it up. Talk to Madeleine Meyer's girl, Diane, over at Washburn, Meyers—she knows the witness we turned up made the Miller case for them. What've they got left on the books?"

"Can't be more than two-five. And without looking, I believe there's another three K overdue from Mankiewitz and Kline. It's been a couple months now."

"They're always late with payments," I said, as I reached for the Rolodex. I twirled up their number, punched it in, and handed the phone to Felia.

She was worth her weight in moon rocks when it came to collections. She could separate Shylock's last shekel from his cold grasping hands and convince him that it was his own idea, without even mussing her hair. When I couldn't pass Go or collect two hundred dollars, she rounded the board and landed on Free Parking. It was the same with information. Prying secrets out of clams was just a stroll down Boardwalk; she got pearls from oysters I couldn't even shuck. What I couldn't drag out of a source with a dredge, she landed on a fly rod. That's why she'd been doing case interviews on her own, for over a year now, although she was just a rookie.

"Hi Cat," she spoke into the mouthpiece. "How's it going? . . . Couldn't be better . . . He's pretty busy with school. How's Jack? . . . You guys pregnant yet? . . . hey, at least you're having some fun . . . Ask me if I care . . . Yeah, auditioned today for Quentin. Asked me out . . . no . . . no . . . definitely not . . ." Felia sat and listened a moment, then tossed her hair back and laughed out loud, "Are you kidding? Jack said that to Sammy?"

She held the phone away from her ear and rolled her eyes at me. I motioned for her to hurry up.

"Look Cat, my boss is giving me the evil eye. I'll call you later, and you can fill me in. Say, the reason I'm calling is that we haven't received anything on that Scranton case. Is there something I need to know . . . he what?" Her eyes narrowed to slits. "Can you put him on?"

Felia covered the mouthpiece and whispered to me, "Sammy Mankiewitz told her to hold back our payments until the settlement came in from the courts; the nerve of that guy. Get me the account book from the top drawer of my desk," she said, pointing to the outer office.

"That creep. A case like that could last a couple years." I went for the book.

"He's not going to get away with that . . . yes, Mr. Mankiewitz. This is Ophelia Tucker with RD DA. It appears your check has been lost in the mail, and I need to ask you to cut us another one . . . That was for work we did for you on the Scranton case . . . Yes. If you'll remember . . . yes, of course," she said brightly. Her gold flecked irises flashed fire as she looked up at me. "The bastard put me on hold." She held the phone with her shoulder while flipping pages in the account book as quick as she could. "Yes, I have that figure right here." She stabbed the number on the page with a well-mani-cured nail. "That was exactly $3,225. I'm sure you received . . ."

Eight

I LEFT FELIA HOLDING THE BAG WITH MONEYBAGS Mankiewitz and went down the hall to use the toilet. Coffee went right through me these days. Maybe it was my imagination, but ever since Davie's assault on my kidneys, my urination was a bit strained. For the first couple of days, I passed a little blood every time I pissed. Standing there, waiting for the stream, it occurred to me I was overdue on my prostate exam. Felia was going to have to make me a doctor's appointment as well. Meanwhile, I started thinking about my time at the Getty earlier that morning with Maldonado. Something bothered me about the interviews with Eastlake and Rivero, but I didn't know what. It would come to me later, no doubt.

Finished at the urinal, I walked over to the sink, leaned near, and examined my face in the mirror. The beard was coming in more salt than pepper. The stubble on my head was a dark cloud settling over me, as dark as memory, and reminded me of my Cherokee blood. Mongrel Red Men never went gray or bald. Tilting my face and looking close at the blood through the thin-skinned pouches beneath my eyes, there was the greenish glow of damaged tissue turning yellow and purple under the glare of fluorescence. It seemed to reflect off the morgue-white tile around the room, reminding me of war paint. The puffy flat line of a once prominent hawk-nose ran down the center of my face, like Mount Hollywood Drive zigzagging north to south through the seared dun summer color of Griffith Park. On my right cheek, the stitches left tracks of their own going nowhere. To the other side, the bruise from Mustafa's brass knuckles fanned across my reedy lower jaw like a delta, as gray as sunrise on a rainy day.

When it rained it poured, and here I was with nothing saved—not since Nathaniel died. That lowlife, Eddy the Eel, killed him, out to get me for putting his brother in jail. Only twenty, Nathaniel looked just like me, as I looked now in the reflection. His broken face and body, his naked remains on the cold stainless steel table for me to identify, claim as my own, and carry with me for the rest of my life. Like a memory, Nathaniel's bright red blood had decomposed to ruddy brown, the color of rot. Mindful of the stitches, I splashed water on my face to clear my head, washed my hands, took another Vicodin, and wandered back down the hall to the office.

"How'd it go?" I asked, crossing around to sit at my desk. "Mankiewitz turn you down?"

"Who knows? He said he would cut us a check first thing next week. But you know how that goes. We'll see."

"Losing your touch?"

"Don't think so. I told him if I didn't see a check by Wednesday, I'd send a couple of guys I know over to see him. He could write out a check then, before they broke his thumbs.

"You didn't."

"I did."

"You can't do that."

"I already did."

"Wha'd he say? No, don't tell me. I don't wanna know. He's gonna—"

"Don't worry, Boss. Hey. He wants to make a stink about it, we'll just send those two guys who did your face," she said, and laughed aloud.

"Yeah right—well—never mind. If anything comes in, make the deposit soon as possible. Now where were we? Oh yeah, I need you to find out the make and model number of that AC unit and get whoever services it over here. If they can't fix that noise, then scrap it and go buy us another one." The summer heat had not let up over the weekend and with this humidity, we were in for another week-long steam bath. I reached out a hand and pointed.

She pushed the checkbook across the desk toward me.

A quick gander inside told me we weren't buying new AC anytime soon, unless Mankiewitz's money came in, things picked up, and I started getting some better work. We could just about afford a small fan. Maybe that Susan Smith woman would come in tomorrow with a case and a big retainer. "On second thought, just get that one fixed as well as possible." I signed a blank check and a deposit slip and handed the book back to her. I took out my notebook and flipped through some notes I had taken at the Getty after my little chat with Ronnie. "Oh, by the way, have Donny call me about the Wilsons. I think we need to get that little matter cleared up as soon as possible. Call it a hunch."

"Are we on a new case I don't know about? Getting some new work?"

"Technically no, just helping Bernie with the Getty thing. But something's coming; things are heating up, and it's not just the weather."

"Well if we do get something, don't forget to get a contract in writing."

I paused and looked at Felia across the desk from me.

She glared right back for a moment. "If that's it then, I'll get to work on this in my office." She rose from the chair and started for the door.

"One more thing, I need you to make an appointment with my doctor."

"Oh no, it is worse than it looks." She paused, then started to come back around the desk.

"No, no, no, you've got it all wrong. I just need an overall exam. I haven't had one in years, and with these injuries, it seemed like a good idea." She stopped in her tracks when I raised my hands.

"Well, if you're sure. I'll make it right away. You're really all right though, aren't you—not as bad as you look?"

"I'm fine, I'm fine."

"Well, okay—as long as you're sure."

I nodded and took a sip of my coffee, which had gone cold. She hesitated, then turned, and went to her office. I pushed back from the desk, put my feet up and contemplated how to tell her that her sister's hubby, Bobby

Chandler, was a louse. I had taken time, on my way back from the Getty, to drive by the Big Star Motel in West Hollywood to see if her brother-in-law's Honda was parked next to his chippie's Chevelle, where I thought it would be. Yep, there they were, just like most days this past two weeks. I didn't know why I kept doing it. It had been obvious that he was stepping out on her sister, almost from the first day she'd asked me to look into it. I didn't want to see her hurt over it and knew she would be, for Mandy—not to mention what it was probably going to do to Mandy's marriage. I'd been putting off telling her in the hope that I could be wrong, even though I knew better. I'd even run Donny by it a couple days, secretly—something he wasn't comfortable doing—just to make sure I didn't miss something.

"Hey, Boss," Felia called from the outer office. "What's happening with that business with Bobby? You haven't said anything, and it's been almost a week and a half now." She stuck her head back in the door.

Was she psychic—reading my mind now? "Well, I've got a couple loose ends to look into, and then I'll give you the scoop."

"Okay, but Mandy's getting anxious, and I've got to tell her something. I don't think she's going to wait much longer before she wigs on me."

"Don't worry, I'll finish the report soon."

"Can't you just tell me now?"

"It'll be finished when it's finished. I've got to write it up. Just one more day."

I didn't know why I was so reluctant to tell her and just get it over with. After all, she and her sister pretty much already knew what was happening. She just need-ed me to confirm things so they could do whatever they were deciding to do about it. So yeah, I had done it—gotten the pictures, taken down the dates and times, made up a nice little package of evidence, good in any court in the land. But I know they're going to be disappointed, although I did what they'd asked me to do.

There are some things that people just don't want to hear, no matter how pleasant you try to make them. "Last call," or "you've got lung cancer," or "your soul mate's been boffing some busty brunette bimbo in a seedy little motel over in West Hollywood." Granted that last was better than hearing lung cancer news; but it still wasn't something anyone wanted to hear. Being the bearer of bad news was always the worst part of my job. No, I take that back. The worst part was when I wasn't disappointing people with bad news, they were disappointing me.

Nine

SHIRL SNORED SOFTLY INTO MY RIGHT EAR. I COULD feel her heart beating through the bed, out of sync with mine. Hers beat faster and somehow more urgently. We'd just finished the horizontal bop, using the only part of my body not hurting from my two-step with Mustafa and Davie. It was a long day, and it had been some time since we'd taken the opportunity for a little mattress mambo. She'd fallen to sleep in the afterglow and radiated an intense serenity that bordered on the nuclear, which made me envious of her freedom to just let it all go.

Earlier, I'd broken one of my own rules by drinking on the job. We'd been to dinner under the dim lights at Da Vinci's, on Melrose. We'd slurped down some icy cold Beefeaters martinis with the antipasto and a bottle of Merlot with the linguini. It would have been a culinary crime, after such a feast, to forego the brandy and coffee with the homemade spumoni. We'd come back to the house, and Shirl showed me her new paintings. We discussed how her work was finally making real progress

and how good she was feeling about it. After such gas-
tronomic, intellectual and sexual indulgence, I should've
been in the slumber mill sawing them off with her. But I
couldn't shut off my mind. I got up, went into the bathroom, washed my face, and used the toilet.

In the kitchen, I drank a glass of water. The clock on
the stove showed it was after one, later than I'd thought.

Something about the interviews at the Getty that
morning had been worming its way around in my sub-
conscious ever since. I sensed that it wouldn't drastically
alter the course of human events as we know them, but I
couldn't tell just what it was. It was probably the fact that
I was gallivanting all over the city working on a case I'd
been warned off of in the first place, or was this the case?
Not only that, but I didn't have a client to pay the bills,
even if it was. I thought it might've had to do with the
receptions I'd gotten from Eastlake and Rivero, which
were similar and yet different. But at this point things
weren't clear. And now there was Buddy Palmer, an actor
in this little drama, waiting in the wings. I had yet to discover what role he played. Then too, that fandango with
Mustafa and Davie still rankled; it was an itch that needed scratching. Although I'd been around long enough to
know what goes around comes around, I still had this
nagging feeling that I had left something undone. But
sooner or later, they were mine. Every dog gets his day.
Their names were inked on my dance card.

I went into the living room, pulled the drapes open
to let the moonlight through the sheers, and sat in the
overstuffed chair next to the window. It was quiet, as
quiet as LA ever got, except for the clock I bought her
for our fourteenth wedding anniversary. It ticked its
slow, deep metronomic tick on the mantle, in counter-

point to the hush of the room. The moon was full but hidden by clouds that scuttled past, sloughing shadows across the night. As I sat mulling over the events of the day, there was a car sitting down a ways across the street under the trees. Cars were rarely parked out there this time of night. I would've put it out of mind, but in the shifting moonlight, there appeared to be a figure sitting behind the wheel. With the shadows slinking across the landscape, I couldn't be sure.

I went into the bedroom, grabbed my fatigues, sneakers and Magnum, then went back to the living room to put them on. From where I stood next to the window, peeking around the edge of the curtains, there was definitely someone there. I went through the kitchen and out the back door as quick and quiet as I could. A car started, but by the time I was through the side gate and around to the front, it tore past me down the street. It was a late model Ford and impossible to make out the color or the tags. I stood staring down the block after it, letting the slow burn subside. I looked up at the moon, then down at my hands—to see if they were sprouting hair—and, after a moment, turned back to the house. This canine was going to have his day; that was a fact. I'd bet the farm on it.

Shirl met me at the door as I came back into the house.

"You gonna shoot me with that thing?" she said, standing there in her Baby Doll pajamas with her arms crossed.

"Sorry." I holstered the Magnum and took it into the bedroom.

"What's going on, Nes?" she said as she locked the back door.

"Nothing. Just thought I heard something out back."

"You gonna start lying to me now?" She was leaning against the counter with her derriere when I came back into the kitchen.

"No, no, you're right," I said and looked at her a moment. "It was probably nothing—just my imagination. I've been jumpy since Friday is all. Thought someone was watching the house; but more than likely, it was somebody from the neighbors."

"You want to tell me what's going on? You haven't said anything about what happened Friday," she said, pointing at my face. "I'd thought you would say something at dinner, but you didn't—and now this."

"What's to say? I haven't gotten to the bottom of things yet. Somehow, I'm involved in a case I know nothing about. A man's been murdered."

"What's that got to do with you?"

"I don't know."

"What's that got to do with your other cases?"

"Nothing, as far as I know."

"What's that got to do with those men who hurt you?"

"I don't know; maybe they're related somehow."

"What's Bernie got to say about it?"

"No more than I do. At this point, there's nothing to tie things together."

"Well, what about tonight?"

"I don't know what to say, Shirl."

She looked at me as though she were going to ask another question, but then turned to the counter by the sink and started to make coffee.

I crossed over and stood beside her. "I didn't want to say anything because I knew how much my work upset you. I didn't mean to bring it along with me tonight. I'm a detective, I know I'm supposed to have things figured out, but right now I haven't got a friggin' clue and that's what's bothering me." I could hear the clock ticking in the living room as I waited for her to say something.

"It's not your work that upsets me, you know. Well it does, but that's not the main thing."

"What then?" I knew where this conversation was headed. We'd been down this road so many times already, we were in the loop. Ever since Nathaniel had died, we never seemed to get beyond it. But that didn't stop us from plunging on full steam ahead.

"It's that you don't give me enough credit. You won't let me in."

"What are you talking about?" I knew better than to keep on speaking, but I just couldn't seem to stop myself. It was moments like this when I seriously considered going through with the divorce. We'd talked about it, and it too just sat there in limbo, in the loop.

"You never let me know what's going on—not really."

"I'm not purposefully hiding anything. There's nothing to tell you."

"Ever since Nathaniel was killed, you've gone out of your way to shut me out of your life. I feel like some kind of anchor around your neck, dragging you down." She started to tear up, then stopped herself.

I moved close to hug her, but she pulled away. "Shirl, you've got it all wrong. I'm just trying to protect you."

"You have a funny way of doing it, by keeping me in the dark." She filled the coffeepot with water, then poured it into the coffeemaker before turning it on.

"Look Shirl, some things you just don't need to know. Knowing too much can be a dangerous thing. Besides, this stuff just causes you to worry."

"I worry anyway. And who are you to say what I need to know and what I don't? Maybe if I'd known more, Nathaniel would still be alive—" She stopped, terror-stricken by what she'd said, and looked at me. "Oh Nes, I'm sorry." She turned and pulled me close to her. "I didn't mean it that way."

"I know." We were silent a moment, just holding each other.

"Do you?" she said. "It doesn't seem like it."

"Shirl, it's after two a.m. I can't think clearly about anything right now, except that I need to go back to my place so I won't be endangering you. You should go back to bed and get some rest; we can talk about this some other time, when we can think straight."

She just looked at me a moment, and I could see the tears she held in check, determined not to cry. I loved that about Shirl. She had grit and resolve I never had. She pulled away from me, straightened her shoulders, and clenched her jaw. She looked me square in the eye then turned to look out the window over the sink, which was dark under the cloud-ridden moon. She stood there some time before she turned back.

"Well okay, if that's the way you want it, if that's all we can manage, I'll play along for now." She switched off the coffee maker and turned back to look at me. "But you're not leaving here, not yet anyway. You're not getting off that easy."

"What do you mean?"

"If you're not gonna talk to me about what matters, then you're gonna help me put it out of my mind—at least for a little while. You're gonna fuck my brains out before you leave. You owe me that much; one more good turn around the floor, shall we say?"

"I thought we did that already."

"Uh-uh. You've just scratched the surface, Romeo. If that's all you've got to give me right now—okay, I'll take it. There's no such thing as a free lunch." She took my crotch in her hand. "If you can't give me what I need, you can at least give me something I want."

I just looked at her. "I love you, Shirl."

"I know. But no more talk, remember? They're your rules, and you've got some dues to pay, mister." She took me by the wrist and pulled me toward the bedroom, switching off the lights as we went. "Yes sir, Nes Honey." She pushed me back into bed. "This waltz—is mine."

Ten

Tuesday

SHIRL'S ALARM GOING OFF ON THE NIGHT TABLE NEXT to the bed woke me out of the deepest sleep I'd had in a long time. For a moment, I didn't realize where I was. It had been some time since I'd spent the night. Seven thirty and there was a distinct quiet about the place. She was already gone. Her scent lingered in the sheets and enticed me to lie there, luxuriating in it, but I was pressed for time. Shirl must've been tired, because she wasn't used to being up most of the night before going to work. She never called in and was always there at five.

I, on the other hand, was used to it. I did it all the time. With me it was a lifestyle. There was no sleeping longer than a three-hour stretch at any one time, if my life depended on it. Except this morning, which had me wondering if having her company in bed last night had made the difference. After Nathaniel was killed, my insomnia and round-the-clock restlessness were two of the major reasons for deciding to get my own place. With that, and the stress she suffered from my job—well, I just couldn't put her through it any longer.

I dressed while I drank the coffee she'd left for me in the pot. Out the door and in the Nova SS, the morning mist had already burned off, and the sun shone brighter than it had in some time. We were in for a scorcher. I drove to my place for a shower and fresh clothes before going to the office. Traffic on Santa Monica was bad, as usual, but there was no one tailing me for a change, and I got there with twenty minutes to spare. Felia was making coffee when I entered.

"Hey, Boss."

"Yo."

"How's Shirl this morning?" she asked, with a big fat grin on her face.

"She's fine." I said. "Why'd you ask?"

"Oh, I don't know. You looked sort of pleased with yourself when you came in, and I thought—well, never mind what I thought. Say, those bruises are looking better. Nothing like a little hot sex to help heal what's hurting, huh?"

"Really? Am I that transparent?"

"Not to the ordinary mortal, but I can sense these things."

"You can?"

"It's not hard, the way you look, with that grin and those moves . . ."

"What moves?" I asked, stopping at the door of my office and turning back to look at her.

"You know, sort of like Brad Pitt climbing out of the back of Thelma and Louise's Thunderbird."

"Ah, I see," I said, although I had no idea what she was talking about. "Say, have you heard anything from our nine o'clock?"

"Nope." She finished with the coffee maker and went back to her desk.

"Have you heard from Donny?"

"He said he needed to see you today. And Detective Maldonado called."

"What'd he say?"

"Just that he's got a make on your bad boys but he was gonna be out this morning, so he'd call you later. Oh, and maybe you should keep your cell turned on so he can reach you."

I had turned it off at Shirl's and forgotten to turn it back on. I didn't like using a cell, but when I had an emergency it was right there in my pocket. Otherwise, it often invaded my privacy. People were always reaching out to me at odd hours for one thing or another. I took it out of my fatigues and turned it on. It rang as if on cue, and I answered.

"Pike here."

"It's Maldonado.

"Oh hi, Bern, where are you?"

"Dexter's. I'm having a donut."

"Some guys have all the luck. Eat a bearclaw for me; I haven't had my breakfast yet."

"I've got to tell you, amigo, you've got a couple of nasty felons on your hands."

"Yeah? Tell me something I didn't know. Shirl there?"

"Si, and she's grinning like the Cheshire cat. What did you two do last night?"

"Do I ask you what you do under the full moon? So, what have you got for me?" I ducked into my office and sat at my desk.

"Ahmed Emil Mustafa, alias Ahmed Hussein, alias Emil Ben Haquowi, among others, is the bona fide, genuine, real bad boy. Alfred James Davie is his toady. Mustafa's sheet's as long as Prudhomme's Caddy and Davie's is almost as bad."

Maldonado was referring to LA's own Assistant District Attorney, Silvestre Prudhomme, a Cajun with a penchant for vintage Cadillacs, who sported white collars on blue-striped shirts, expensive leather "braces" to hold his pants up, and who hailed from a parish deep in a swamp of Louisiana. You get all kinds in LA.

"Mustafa's known throughout Europe and the Middle East." Bernie continued. "Arab father and French mother, very clever, the alleged perpetrator of over a half dozen murders in five separate countries. But he has always managed to elude the authorities, either on technicalities or on outright alibis. He was suspected of being cozy with one of the radical Arab groups who had contacts in Europe, prior to becoming known in France. 'It's rumored that he's done well out of murder for hire. More thug than terrorist, he's not politically motivated. He has continued to work his trade for the sheer pleasure of it, becoming affluent in recent years,' I'm quoting here, 'picking and choosing only those propositions or contracts that interest him.'"

"I guess he's a rich guy who likes to kill people, huh?"

"Certainly looks that way. You'll want to read this section on the way he works. It's a bit macabre. He prefers torture over murder, but it's murder that pays the bills. 'However, the compelling thing about him continues to be that he was never caught with the smoking gun.'"

Felia brought me coffee then went back to her office. I could hear Bernie shuffling papers over the phone. It occurred to me that Mustafa sounded like the kind of individual who might take a forklift and slowly lower a two-ton monster rock onto Hollenbeck, just to see how long he could continue to draw breath before expiring. This way Mustafa got his rocks off and a handsome paycheck too—two birds with one stone, so to speak. Of course, we were gonna need proof.

"What about Davie?" I asked.

"Davie's something else," Bernie continued. "In awe of his tall, homely friend, and not too swift, he has more or less applied himself to doing Mustafa's bidding, mostly the dirty work. With Mustafa to point him in the right direction, he's lethal."

And theoretically, it stands to reason that if Davie was driving the forklift, then Mustafa could've been down close to Hollenbeck's face watching for the precise moment his spirit left the body. It would've been orgasmic for someone with Mustafa's bent. However, at this point, it was pure speculation, so I kept it to myself. "I would've figured Mustafa for a loner. More than one chef in the kitchen can create a real mess. Davie could make him vulnerable, leaving too many loose ends."

"Si. But it looks like Señor Mustafa has taken our little Alfie under his wing. Prior to meeting Mustafa, Davie was unknown outside Sydney, where he bounced for several bars and collected for a small-time rackets mob. Mustafa does the thinking, and Davie does the heavy lifting. Interpol doesn't know how this odd couple got together, but they first noticed them in London at about the same time some valuable artwork went missing."

"You thinking what I'm thinking?"

"Probably coincidence. There's no evidence Mustafa has any interest in art. And Davie certainly doesn't.

There was nothing to tie them to the missing artwork, but it says here, MI6 suspected they had a hand in the disappearance of a sleaze-ball art dealer in London. Once again, they had alibis and no motives."

"Alibis or otherwise, stolen art can be real profitable, whether they have an interest in it or not. Any idea who they're working for now?"

"Could be on their own, though it doesn't fit their MO."

"I don't think so, either. Well, Bern, is that it?"

"For now. I'll fax this report over, when I get to the office. It's pretty interesting. I presume, amigo, if you were filing a formal complaint you would have already done so."

"Right."

"Then I suggest, ese, for the little good it'll do, stay out of their way. When I find them, I'll pick them up—if you want me to. We can put them through the system, and maybe they'll do some jail time on assault charges. Be hard to make a case for attempted murder though."

"No. Not yet. I need to find out what they're up to, and I can't very well do that if they're in lockup. Does that report show them with current LA addresses? I sure would like to know where they hang out."

"Unfortunately not. Look, I've got to go, departmental meeting at nine. By the time I get down there, I'll only be twenty-five minutes late."

"Hollenbeck was murdered. Too early to say definitively by whom."

"Yeah, I know. You work your hunch, and I'll work mine. I'll call you later for your take on Eastlake and Rivero."

"Okay—thanks Bern. I really appreciate it."

"Yeah. You owe me one."

"Tell Shirl I'll call her."

He called out, "Hey Shirl, Casanova said he'd call you. I don't know how he can call anyone with his cell always turned off, do you?

" . . . Hey compadré, she said something about 'more dues to pay.' What's that mean?" he said.

"Oh nothing. Hasta, muchacho."

"Mañana."

I turned off the phone, put it on my desk, and sipped my coffee. I needed some time to mull over what Maldonado had just told me. Who would've hired this killer to pay little ole me a social call? And more to the point, why? But that would have to wait. I looked at my watch. It was ten past nine, and I was beginning to think our Ms. Smith was standing us up again, when I heard someone, a woman by the sound of her voice, enter the outer office. I unclipped the Magnum from my belt and put it in my desk, leaving the drawer open. I stood up and walked around in time to meet Felia and whoa—.

I must've looked surprised, because Felia pointed at my lower jaw for me to close my mouth.

"Hey, Boss, guess what," she said, with a lilt to her speech. "This is our nine o'clock appointment, Susan Smith, only she isn't Susan Smith. She's—"

"I know. Thanks Felia. We met yesterday. Hello again, Ronnie."

"Hello, Mr. Pike," she said.

"Would you like coffee?" I said. "We could get you some water, or a soda if you prefer."

"Nothing for me, thanks." She turned and smiled at Felia who appeared relieved to not be making the trip downstairs to the drugstore fountain on the corner.

"If that's all, Boss, I'll be right outside if you need anything," she said as she gave Ronnie the slit-eyed once over. "By the way, I'm leaving at two for an audition and won't be back later."

"Fine. In the meantime, hold the calls until we're done here."

Felia nodded and closed the door on her way out.

Ronnie Rivero was dressed completely different than the first time I had seen her. The low-cut red number she wore clung to more curves than a Jag cruising Mulholland Drive. The dress accentuated her dark eyes and hair as well as her shape, but seemed out of place so early in the day. It looked like something she'd wear clubbing or pub-crawling. It may have added to my surprise at her unexpected appearance this morning. She seemed apprehensive and those expressive Latina eyes shone more fearful than sad. Although it was only a little past nine and we had yet to reach our high temp for the day, she was beading tiny droplets of moisture among the fine hairs on her upper lip.

"I guess you can't help noticing my dress."

"Yeah, it certainly invites attention. I'm sorry. Was I that blatant?"

"Oh no, I didn't mean it like that. I shouldn't have shown up here dressed like this. You see I spent the night at my brother Ramón's, one of his friend's girlfriend's bachelorette party. It's a long story, and I won't waste your time. I intended to go home and change before coming over here, but I had car trouble this morning and didn't want to stand you up again. Almost on time. Sorry."

"Not a problem. So, Ms. Smith," I said and smiled. "Tell me, what can I do for you today?" I pointed her to the unbroken client chair. She sat; I switched the AC on low then returned to my seat behind the desk.

"I'll explain that, but first let me apologize for missing our appointment last week. I've already apologized to Ms. Tucker." She put her purse on the corner of the desk then placed her hands in her lap. "I don't normally tell people one thing then do another." She picked at the broken polish on one of her fingernails.

"I'm sure you don't."

"It was rude of me, but I was unsure what to do, and since we had not met, I just blew it off. I guess that's why I used an alias, so nobody would know it was me. Sorry. I was afraid and thought the less said to anyone the better, until yesterday when you came out to the Villa. Then I realized that I really did need to talk to someone. And this morning, I was going to say that I'd had an emergency before and couldn't call." She looked up at me. "But I generally don't lie either, so I decided to come clean and ask you to forgive me. I'm in some kind of mess, and I don't know where else to turn for help."

"Why didn't you say something yesterday?"

"I wasn't sure I could trust you, and didn't know what I wanted to do."

"You trust me now?"

"I don't know."

"You know what you want to do?"

"Not really. But after you left, something inside me told me to come. I was hoping you could help, or at least point me in the direction of someone who can. I might be in danger."

"Have you thought about going to your attorney?"

"Yes, but I'm not sure he can help me."

"What about the police?"

"With all of the turmoil over Mr. Hollenbeck at the Getty right now, they might put me in jail first and ask questions later."

I was usually a sucker for a damsel in distress, but this morning I was not disposed—for a number of reasons—to go all gooey inside, don my shining armor, and go galloping off on my trusty stallion in search of some dragon that Little-Miss-Contrite here wanted me to slay. I wasn't even sure what kind of distress she was in, if any. Technically speaking, regardless of whatever else she may be involved with, she was a suspect in Maldonado's investigation, and I didn't like being played for a chump. Nevertheless, something in her manner told me she was in need of a little slack, and I decided to cut it for her, until she proved unworthy of it. "Go on," I said.

"I don't know what to say. I've never done anything like this before. I've never been in any trouble. I should ask you first how much you charge. I'm not rich, but I have a little savings."

"I get five hundred a day plus expenses; it depends on what kind of work it is and the resources I use. But we can talk about that later. There are no other principals involved; I would be working for you alone, correct?" She nodded. "First I need to know just what kind of trouble you think you're in, and why you think you need my help. You should know that as my client, whatever you tell me remains confidential." I took out my notebook and pen.

"It has to do with some irregularities I've uncovered in my job."

"Well, let's see, I know you're the Associate Registrar, but just what, exactly, does that entail?"

"A number of things, but the one that I'm worried

about has to do with the registration, cataloguing, and overseeing of the shipping and transport of valuable, make that priceless, artwork. I'm responsible for the direct control and whereabouts of any number of such materials, which can be anything you might imagine—ceramics, glass and paper, paintings and sculpture."

"You're pretty young to have that responsibility for a major museum, aren't you?

"Well, yes. But you see, Dr. Braithwaite was the one in charge. It was her department. I was her assistant. Since the accident, I've had to take over for her until they find a replacement. Dr. Eastlake is my stand-in supervisor. But it's my name on all the paperwork, you see. I'll be ruined if this gets out. I could lose my job, disgrace my family, get put in jail, or worse—maybe even be killed like poor Mr. Hollenbeck."

"Hold on there. Don't get ahead of yourself. You mentioned irregularities."

"Yes, sorry. I guess I'm nervous."

She looked nervous, but at the same time she seemed cool. The sharp, young professional just didn't jive with that sweet red dress. I knew she wasn't lying about having a problem. It's just that I wasn't sure what that problem was.

"It's okay. The irregularities?" I said.

"Yes. In this case, I believe the important artifacts for our upcoming show have all been stolen and some very clever forgeries put in their place."

"Holy mackerel! Let me get this straight. You're saying you think someone had the balls to steal Jesus Christ's Last Supper dinnerware?"

"Yes."

"Okay, then. Let's see, now . . . the way I figure it is

that the thief has to be either a heathen or an atheist—a true believer wouldn't risk the hell to pay."

Eleven

WHEN I LEFT THE OFFICE AROUND TEN-THIRTY TO
meet Donny for lunch at Adam's Rib Shack, my meeting
with Ronnie had changed everything. First, she had officially become my client by signing a written contract
and leaving a retainer. Felia was a stickler for doing
things by the book. Ronnie Rivero was now my boss,
which put Bernie and me into adversarial positions since
she was still, technically speaking, a suspect in the
Hollenbeck murder case. I had mixed feelings about
that, but I didn't really think there was much to worry
about. The way I saw it, I was going to find out who stole
those artifacts and clear my client's name with the museum. And I assumed that if I found the thief, then, more
than likely, I'd found the murderer as well, clearing my
client with the police to boot. It was win-win. In a sense,
Bernie and I were working for the same thing, even
though it wasn't my job to solve his murder case. But
there was another matter I had to attend to first.

Adam's Rib Shack was a good-sized dive off Sepulveda
Boulevard down in El Segundo. It wasn't dirty, but the

Naples yellow paint was peeling from the walls and vinyl upholstery tape almost obliterated the red naugahide booth-seats. It didn't seem to matter, since the steamy, aromatic atmosphere was lush with conversation and bustle. There were three waitresses and the joint was full; every race, nationality, and creed on the face of the Earth loved ribs, or so it seemed. I'd never been there before, but Donny had become a regular over the past couple of months. Dressed in his usual nondescript tan chinos and short-sleeved shirt, he was busy poring over some papers in a manila folder in a back booth when I slid in across from him.

"Hey Chief," he said, looking up at me.

"Donny, my man. How's it going?"

"Glad you made it. I almost lost this booth three times. People will kill you for a seat in this place."

"But it's only 11:15," I said, looking at the Coca Cola clock over the counter across the room. "I guess the ribs are good here, huh?"

"You got that right."

"So, where are we with the Wilson thing?"

"It's all set. Willy and Bruce will be along any time now, and here's the paperwork you wanted." He handed over a folder marked "The McFeety Bros."

"Are you sure they'll show?"

"Sylvia swears they eat lunch here every Tuesday and Friday, right over there by the door." Donny pointed to a booth where two other guys were poised over a couple of heaping platters, making pigs of themselves over the pork.

"Who's Sylvia?"

"She's that waitress over there."

"Well I hope she's right, or this is all for nothing."

"Don't worry, I've seen them here on those days often

enough to verify her statement. But if not, it's not a complete loss, Chief; there's always the ribs."

"Yeah, there's the ribs. Have you heard from Paco and Rueben?"

"Said they'd be here by noon, latest."

"Then I guess we're as ready as we can be."

I opened the folder and fingered my way through the documentation, stopping only now and then to ask Donny to clarify something in the paperwork. Willy and Bruce McFeety were a couple of scam artists. They owned a remodeling and construction company. Their specialty was latching onto an elderly couple in need of help with their house, and bleeding them dry for the repairs. They did this in any number of creative and devastating ways: shoddy work, cheap supplies, and undersizing materials when the people paid for something larger or better. But their favorite was to tear up the house, then press the couple for ever more money until the job was finished. They were masters and could string out the smallest job for months, doing only enough work to keep the authorities off their necks. If the couple threatened to call the police or the City Building Department, Willy and Bruce obliquely threatened physical retaliation, smiling all the while, but making sure the couple knew what was at stake. In fear for their lives from that point on, the couple usually did whatever the brothers wanted until the money ran out. Donny had spent the last couple of months compiling evidence against them.

"Everything looks good here, nice job," I said.

"Thanks. Things came together over the weekend. Most of the people I interviewed gave me a full account of their experiences and loss."

"Is that where you got that $150,000 figure?"

"Yep. If you noticed, I listed the Wilsons' figure separate. I got a total of eight cases. They've all agreed to testify in court when the case is prosecuted. The others were either too scared to talk, or I couldn't find them. With those figures, the McFeetys must've been busy little beavers over the past twelve years. Modus operandi was surprisingly similar across the board. You were right about the social security numbers. Once I got those, things opened up in all kinds of places. We've got enough there to see the McFeetys behind bars for at least five to eight years."

"That's good, but first things first. We've got to get the Wilsons' money back before we turn this over to the DA's office. There's no telling how long it would take afterwards, if they ever get it back." I closed the folder just as Sylvia came over to take our order.

"So, Donny, who's your big, handsome friend?" she said and put a glass of ice water on the table in front of me. Donny already had his.

"Sylvia, I'd like you to meet my boss, Nestor Pike."

"Well, Mr. Pike, I hope you don't mind my saying, but it looks like you made somebody real mad." She winked at Donny, then took a pad and pencil out of her uniform, and smiled at me with a smile that could've become an addiction.

"It doesn't take much these days."

"I suppose people've told you that you have a real unusual name. I never heard the name Nestor before." She was about thirty-five, shapely, a hundred twenty-five to thirty pounds, five-six, maybe seven, had big frosted hair, red lips and nails, and spoke with a southern drawl that almost made my mouth pucker trying to help her get the words out.

"Yeah, I get that a lot," I said. "My mother was a history buff."

"You mean there was some guy in history named Nestor?"

"That's what I was told. He was a wise old Greek who fought at the Siege of Troy and liked to tell people what to do and where to go." That was the stock answer I gave to everyone who asked about my name. I got asked all the time.

"So he was a fighter, like you?"

"Must've been."

"Then he couldn't have been too wise. Cause fighting's what happens when you try to tell people where to go and what to do. It looks like you went the full fifteen rounds. I hope you gave as good as you got."

"You better believe it, sweetheart, and then some."

"Serves 'em right," she said and smiled again. "Well, now that that's all straight, what are you gentlemen having for lunch?"

"What do you recommend?"

"Now you're funnin' me right? Listen, Hon, we don't serve nothing here but the best baby-back ribs and barb-que on the whole continent of North America." She held up a hand and looked at her nails as she said it.

"Ribs it is then," I said. "And how about some coleslaw on the side with a pickle and a cup of coffee?" I sipped the ice water.

"I'll have the same but bring me a Royal Crown Cola instead," Donny said.

"Comin' right up," she said, turned, and went back to the counter.

"Royal Crown Cola?"

"Well, they don't serve Coke."

"Hmm."

"So, Chief. Heard any more on Mustafa and Davie?"

"Yeah, but I want to put you on another case before the McFeetys get here, so I'll tell you later. I need you to do some surveillance for me. I want you to keep an eye on Ronnie Rivero, R-i-v-e-r-o."

Donny took out a small notebook and pen and started to write.

"Get with Felia after we leave here and help her with the file, you know, the usual background stuff. Ms. Rivero may be in danger, so pick up her track as soon as she gets off work at the Getty, up north on the San Diego Freeway. I want to know who she sees, who she talks to, and where she goes. Stick with her nights; you can sleep while she's at work. I'll be checking on her during the day. I'll let you know when you should back off. For the time being, don't let her know you're around. I don't want your presence to hinder her activities until we know more. I know that's tough, but since you're the best leg-man in the business, it shouldn't be a problem."

"I'll do the best I can."

"That's all I ask. Now, most important, remember what I told you about Mustafa and Davie; keep an eye open for them. They might be responsible for Hollenbeck, and she could be next. You'll need your piece. We're working both information and security here, so remember."

"Yeah, no client gets hurt on our watch. I know. I've got her covered. Is she the woman you saw this morning?" He put his notebook away.

"Yes."

Sylvia set our food on the table and smiled the while. The food looked great and smelled even better. Now I understood why there were so many people in the place, and so early. The food was the real addiction around here. Something this good should be illegal.

We finished our plates. I'd just settled back with my coffee when one of the McFeety brothers walked in and stood glaring at the two guys in what Donny had previously pointed out to be the McFeety's usual booth, up close to the front door.

"That's Willy." Donny said. "He's the soft one of the two, if you can call him soft."

Willy McFeety was what is known, in common parlance, as a bruiser. No wonder the older folks were so intimidated. Six-six, two-fifty to two-seventy-five, curly red hair, with hands like two slabs of the blue plate special, he wasn't someone you'd want to cross without some hefty major-medical. For a second, I had second thoughts about what I was about to do. Maybe I should get it over with before his big brother showed up. Just then a short, thin, dark-haired, ruddy-skinned, middle-aged man with sideburns, rosacea, and an Elvis pompadour came in the door, and stood next to Willy.

"Don't tell me," I said.

"Yep that's Bruce, the grim older half of the brothers McFeety. Believe it or not, they're twins."

"Huh!"

"Fraternal."

"Obviously. I thought you said he was the hard one."

"Hey, he may be short and skinny, but from everything I've heard, Chief, he's nothing but a cold, pitiless, cast-iron spike."

The two guys sitting in the McFeety's booth were beginning to wither noticeably under the glaring eyes of Willy McFeety. They finished their meal in a hurry, decided against dessert, and headed for the cash register. They didn't even wait for their check; the waitress had to take it to them at the counter. The McFeetys took the booth, even though there was a younger couple waiting ahead of them. The young man started to protest, but his girlfriend, apparently smarter than he was, said she preferred a booth in the back anyway and convinced him to wait by the counter for the next one.

"You boys want some of Maeve's homemade pie? We've got fresh lemon meringue, pecan, cherry a la mode, apple with cheddar, coconut crème, and chocolate meringue," Sylvia reeled off, as she freshened my coffee and began to clear away the plates.

"I guess we'll have to have some pie—since Rueben and Paco haven't shown up yet," I said. "Make mine cherry, but hold the cream."

"I'll have coconut," Donny said, just as the two Mexicans came in the front door.

Dark complexioned, their features displayed the indigenous characteristics of their Mestizo heritage, as well as the battle scars from a life in gangs. Paco wore a white ribbed muscle shirt. His gang-related tattoos cascaded from one side of his face, down his neck and over his shoulders onto his well-muscled arms. Rueben's tattoos were barely visible at his throat, disappearing beneath his bright floral short-sleeve shirt only to reemerge and cover his arms below the sleeves. Both of them wore their hair slicked back under nets. "Maldonado's boys just showed up," Donny said.

He referred to the fact that Maldonado had put me in touch with these two brave young men, ex-gang members who've broken away from their life in gangs. They were working with the city's task force to help at-risk youngsters stay free of gangs. I'd met Paco in Bern's company on a previous occasion. I hired him and Rueben to come down to Adam's Rib Shack and have lunch on me. I stood up, waved them over, and we shook hands all around. We made room in the booth so they could sit on the inside. Before I sat back down, I signaled Sylvia over. She brought our pie, took lunch orders, and left us to our business.

"So here, Paco, take this." I took the Glock 9mm from my waist and slipped it across the table to him.

He held it beneath the table to check the clip and chamber. "Hey, Dude, it's not loaded," he said.

"It's not supposed to be," I said around the pie in my mouth.

"It's a cool rod, mon, but what am I going to do with a gat that's not loaded?" He handed it back to me.

I pushed it back. "Keep it down, man. Put it in your waistband under the shirt. It's like this: Donny and me are going over there to talk to those two cholos." I nodded at the McFeetys. "At a certain moment, I'll point over to you. They'll look. I want you to nod back at me while they're looking. Then, when I give you a signal, I want you, Paco, to stand up and pull your shirt up, just enough to show them the butt of the gun stuck in your waistband. Try to do it so others can't see. But if they do, they do. Don't sweat it. Got it?"

"Si, mon. I show them the gun."

"Then you sit back down. Oh, and when Donny and I go over there, keep your eyes on them, give them a look, you know, like you would a rival gang-banger. That's all. I don't want you to do anything else, except have your lunch. This pie's great by the way. If anything happens, I want you to leave immediately, then meet me

at my office later. If nothing happens, the way it should-
n't, I want you to stay here in the booth till they're gone.
Is that clear?"

"As rain water, mon."

"When it's all over, you return my Glock, then I'll
pay you guys the hundred each we agreed on, and take
care of your lunch tab."

"Just for acting tough, mon?" Rueben said. "Chingada
madre."

"You won't be acting, will you?" I said.

"Hell no, mon," he said. "We are tough."

"Are we cool?" I said.

"Right on, vato," Rueben spoke again. Paco nodded.

"Okay Donny, it's showtime." I wiped my face and
hands with a napkin, took the folder, and stood up.

He threw down the last bite of his pie, wiped his face
and hands, and we left the table, just as Sylvia showed up
with Rueben and Paco's ribs.

Twelve

"**B**RUCE MCFEETY, NESTOR PIKE. I'M A PRIVATE detective," I said, leaning over the table and handing him one of my business cards—the one with the Thompson submachine gun blazing smoke and bullets across the middle, with the caption just below: "This Gun for Hire." I have different cards for different clients; the one I give out depends on the way I want to present myself. I wanted Bruce to see my tough side. "You don't know me, but I know you, and I've got a proposition I don't think you'll be able to turn down. Do you mind if we sit?"

He raised his eyebrows at his brother and looked noncommittal back at me. "Make it fast. I've got ribs comin', and I like to eat'em hot," he said through his adenoids.

I shoved in across from Bruce the Skinny, and Donny slid in across from Willy the Bruiser—who grimaced at being shoved over by me, since he was not used to being the shovee. It didn't get any cozier than that. But it made it impossible to reach the Magnum without getting up. I should have thought this out a little better. Oh well, no turning back now. Willy started to protest.

"Hang on, Willy," Bruce said. "So what's this deal you're so hot to promote that you've got to come in here and mess up my lunch?"

"You have no idea, Bruce. May I call you Bruce?"

Willy snorted, but I couldn't see his glare. I kept my eyes glued to Bruce, who reached up and scratched his scalp, careful not to muss his pomp. He stared a cold, dark stare.

"You have no idea, Bruce, just how messed up your lunch is going to be before it's all over."

"What's that supposed to mean? What do you want?"

"Let me ask you, Bruce. Do you know a guy named Manny Ortega?"

"Are you telling me you work for Manny Ortega? Not likely, man. You've got the wrong color and the wrong accent." He threw my business card on the table, like he'd just trumped my ace.

"See, Donny, I told you he was a smart guy." I picked up the card and put it back in my shirt pocket. "You're right, Bruce, I don't work for Manny. I work for Ed and Ruth Wilson, you know, the couple over on Fourth Street, whose kitchen you demolished and haven't fixed yet."

"Ah, so that's what this is all about. Okay, Willy, I think we've heard enough."

Just as he began to move, I threw my left forearm over into Willy's throat and pushed his head back, almost lifting him off his seat; I grabbed a fork from the table and stuck it to his belly. I had tried to grab the knife but would've settled for a spoon at that moment. "Another move, and I gut you like a flounder." He probably didn't know it was a fork; he went limp. "Okay, now you're going to listen to what I have to say. And there's no more rowdy stuff." I waited a moment, then put my arm down. The people in the booth behind us looked around in anger; then having seen the McFeetys, turned back to their ribs. Nobody else looked in our direction, though there was a general momentary lull in the sound level of the room.

"I'm not going to sit here and listen to this," Bruce said and started to push his way out of the booth. Donny held his place. Willy remained quiet.

"If that's the way you want it, I'll have to tell Manny you were uncooperative," I said and tossed the fork back on the table.

He stopped. "How do I know you're connected to Manny Ortega?"

"Look, you know and I know Manny runs everything around El Segundo, Inglewood and LA south. He doesn't tolerate other people making money on his ground without paying his commission. If you don't believe me, you can ask his man, Paco, sitting back there in my booth."

He looked over and saw Paco and Rueben glaring back at him. "Yeah, right. How do I know those are Manny's guys?"

"Good point. Let me put it to you this way. You don't sit here and talk to me, and do what I say, those men have orders from Manny to put you guys on ice when you leave here. See, I told Manny what I have in this folder. Well, not quite everything. I didn't tell him about the six hundred thousand bucks you've got stuck around in various banks. I'll get to that later. But he was a little upset, to say the least, when he found out how you two have been treating the old people in his Barrio. He was even more disappointed to find you making your pesos without his permission. He thought the McFeety Brothers Construction Company was legit. I gotta tell you, he was unhappy. He was going to have you killed right then; I convinced him to hold off, for now. But hey, that can be changed." I looked at him hard then turned and signaled Paco, who stood and flashed the Glock. He took his time and did it so well, even I got scared.

Bruce turned white. "You're bluffing," he said.

"Try me," I said.

He just stared at me until Willy broke in. "What about this six-hundred thousand in banks?" he said, glowering at Bruce.

"Listen," Bruce said. "I don't know nothin' about that."

"I'd be happy to show you," I said, opening the folder and sliding it over in his direction. Willy grabbed it first and slid it back over to our side of the table; he began flipping through the pages.

"So, this is a shakedown," Bruce said. "I should've known,"

"Not really. Call it restitution. All we want is for you to pay back my clients and their expenses. The total figure comes to $47,000."

"Hey, all we took from the Wilsons was $37,000."

"I know. The extra ten is our recovery fee. You also have to come up with another hundred fifty thousand for Manny, which is why those two are here," I pointed to Paco and Rueben. "They're much more demanding than we are. One hundred fifty thousand cash, today, is the only thing that will keep them from . . . well, you know."

"We haven't got that kind of money," he whined. He

was visibly deteriorating as we spoke, while Willy seemed to be getting more furious. It was all he could do to contain himself.

"Look Bruce, we're beyond this point already," I said. "Be grateful I told Manny that you only had $200,000 stashed away and not the full $600,000. That still leaves you $400,000, give or take . . ."

"Yeah? And how much more of that are you going to take?"

"I'll ignore that. Look at the bright side. I convinced him not to take the three grand left from the $200,000 I originally told him you had. I said you needed it to keep the company going. Why kill the golden goose, when he could become your partner? If you don't think that's fair, and do like I say, then I'll tell him I found another $400,000 that you've been holding out on him. And you know what happens then, or do I need to draw you a picture?"

"Well, why doesn't Manny take the Wilsons' money from you?"

"You know how it works, Bruce, or are you really that stupid? That's my fee for bringing this little matter and the $150,000 to him. I had to have him back me up, or you wouldn't give me what I want. Am I right?"

"Tell me again why you're such a good guy, and not taking all of it."

"Would you give it to me, knowing you'd have nothing left, even with Manny's guys sitting over there?" He was silent. "I didn't think so. This is not a negotiation. It's my deal or no deal. No deal, and you're dead meat. This way I've got what I need, Manny's satisfied for the time being, and it's the only way you get to keep any of it and stay alive. Everybody's happy. Right?" Just when I thought Willy was going to explode from the seething and snorting next to me, he slumped back in his seat and flung the folder toward Bruce. He spoke quietly, almost in a whisper.

"It's all in there, Bruce. You turd. You said we only had a hundred grand. You been keeping that money from me all this time. Was I ever gonna see any of it?" Bruce looked down at his hands.

"My own fuckin' brother and after all these years, after everything I've done for you, you shit. I'm gonna kick your ass when we get back. They've got everything. It's all right there: the banks, the money, the fuckin' people we took . . . it's all right there, in that fuckin' little folder. And now we got Manny Ortega fuckin' us up the ass. There'll be nothing left when he gets done. I ain't workin' for that asshole. From now on, you doing things my way. You hear? And we're gonna take the fuckin' deal with . . . what did you say your name was?"

"Nestor Pike."

"We're gonna take the fuckin' deal—with Nestor fuckin' Prick here—and save what we can. You hear me, you dick?"

"How are we gonna do that? Even if I wanted to, it's all tied up, and I ain't got that kind of money on me," Bruce said.

"No, but your friendly neighborhood Bank of America right around the corner does," I said, just as the waitress brought their food. "What say you and me walk around there, untie some of it, and make a little withdrawal."

If Bruce was a cold, pitiless iron spike, it was a cold, pitiless pig-iron spike. The fever in his brain, if he had a brain left, must've been tremendous, because his face, a true study in pain, appeared to melt. He looked at me, then his brother, where he found no solace, and then back to me. "You mind if I eat my ribs first?" he whined.

"I certainly do," I said to Bruce. I turned to Willy. "And who the hell are you calling a prick, motherfucker?"

Thirteen

On my way back to Hollywood, I stopped at a Wells Fargo branch and deposited the $197,000 that I'd taken from the McFeetys into my agency account. Then I swung by the Universal Paradigm building in Westwood to have a jaw with Buddy Palmer. It was the first time I'd been there. Yaeger Eastlake might've called it a twenty-five story juggernaut of minimalist aspirations in the International Style, but to me it was just a big gray box constructed of glass and steel, lacking all sense of grace. I parked the Nova SS beneath it and took the elevator up to the four-story marble lobby. The place was deserted except for one of Buddy's security guards in a business suit, who appeared to be dozing behind the big half-circle black granite desk across from me when I got off the elevator. On one end was a monster three-dimensional Frank Stella painting, from the Moby Dick series. At the other was a monumental metal sculpture twelve-foot tall by Raleigh Hanson titled Man Standing. It was as flat and uninspired as the Stella was brilliant and beautiful. Overhead, a gigantic Calder mobile flew like a raven, elegantly but uncharacteristically dark and triumphant.

From the directory next to the desk, I learned that the building headquartered Universal Paradigm and its subsidiaries, which held interests in commodities and financial markets all over the world. "Universal Paradigm for Solutions to the Universal Problems of Business." I suspected its cold, impersonal nature reflected the personality of its owner, G. Henry Carl. Also, I learned from the "information officer" behind the desk that Carl kept a residence on the top two floors. It made sense to me. Not only did he have some of the best views in town, but he and the rarest pieces from his private art collection were close to the helipad on the roof, in the event of fire. Buddy's office was on the twenty-third floor, just around the corner from the elevators. The suite was gray, the carpet was plush, and the air conditioner, formidably silent, was chillingly efficient. A stunning but icy young blonde dressed in business-black—with pale blue eyes, alabaster skin, and smelling of lavender—greeted me from behind her desk as I entered.

"May I help you?"

"Would you tell Buddy Palmer that I'd like a few minutes of his valuable time, please?"

"Of course, Mr.—?"

"Pike, Nestor Pike."

"You see, Mr. Pike . . ."

I felt the room temperature drop a degree.

"Mr. Palmer is in a meeting and won't be available until later. Would you care to make an appointment?"

"Could you tell me how long he'll be?"

"I really couldn't. He may be leaving. He isn't scheduled back for another appointment, until four this afternoon."

It felt like we were in for a heavy frost on the file cabinets, when the intercom sounded on her desk. She picked it up. "Yes sir?" She looked up, but appeared to stare right through me. "You may go right in, Mr. Pike. That door over there." She stood and pointed. Her left eye twitched with a tick that I hadn't noticed earlier.

"Thank you." I smiled for the camera concealed in the picture frame on the wall behind her. Just as I headed for the door to Buddy's office, it opened, and he burst into the room with his hand outstretched, and a smile gashed across his face. I'd forgotten; on Buddy, it was more grimace than smile.

"Nestor, the Pike, you old reprobate, how's it hanging?" he said and grabbed my hand. For a moment, I thought we were in a finger-crushing competition, until he gave up and let go.

"Buddy, the Palm," I said.

"Come in, come in. Take a load off; park it over there." He dragged me through the door of his spacious office and pushed me toward one of the two black leather chairs across from his football-field sized desk. I stopped to admire the view. There was the Santa Monica Pier to the west, and clear weather south beyond LAX. It was so clear that it felt like I could see all the way to San Diego. He stepped back to the door. "Inga, get Mr. Pike a cup of coffee—you haven't given up caffeine and sugar, have you?"

I shook my head. "With cream, please."

"So, how long has it been?" He crossed back to his desk and sat.

"A long time." I took a seat across from him.

Buddy Palmer was a five-foot, six-inch Jarhead, around one hundred and eighty-five pounds. His mousy-gray flat top was high and tight, unchanged since his Semper Fi days, except it was thinning in the crown. He wore a fitted white shirt with a button-down collar, dark-gray suit pants with suspenders that matched a coat hung in a closet somewhere out of sight, and a pair of black leather slippers that would've cost me a month's wages. My guess was they were all custom made to fit his overwrought physique. Oddly enough, his tasteful cranberry tie matched Inga's, the Ice Queen's, lipstick.

"Still working out, I see," I said.

Buddy had lifted weights as long as I had known him. He'd even won a number of state and regional bodybuilding competitions, the spoils of which lined the shelves and trophy cases around the room. "Not like I used to," he said. "This job keeps me pretty busy. I'm lucky to get to the gym a couple hours every other day. Not enough time to compete any more. But you look like you're still in fightin' shape." Not that he needed to go to a gym. He had one of those all-purpose Nautilus machines sitting across from the desk, next to the door of his executive washroom. Knowing Buddy, I'd have bet there was a sauna as well as a shower in there.

"I do what I can."

Inga, the Snow Princess, appeared with coffee, cream and sugar in silver service on a silver tray, and set it on the desk in front of me. I poured myself a cup in the corporate china, UP in gold on a gold crest to match the gold rim. It could have been Limoges. She took the pot of tea, a cup, and saucer from the tray, and set it beside Buddy. She poured nonfat, nondairy creamer and added a sugar substitute before giving it to him. It was Buddy all over.

"But it looks like the private eye game can be a little rough," he said, then nodded at my honor badges.

"Yeah, well, what can I say? It comes with the territory. On the other hand, this corporate thing of yours looks pretty cushy. Sure it won't make you too soft?"

"Nah. You know me." He reached down beside his chair, picked up a free weight, pumped a couple of biceps curls, then dropped it back to the carpet, which was so thick it hardly made a sound. "You ought to come work for UP and sell out that little three man operation of yours. What do you call it?" He blew on his tea and sipped.

"The RD DA," I took my card—the one with the Tommy gun on it—from my shirt pocket and tossed it to his desk.

"What does the RD stand for?" he said, picking it up.

"Run-Down."

"Ha!" he barked. "Damn good. You're not kidding?"

"Nope."

He reached over and propped my card against his Rolodex where he could see it. "Well, that's great; it fits you to a tee. But think it over. An operation like yours can't pay all that much, what with the overhead and having to take whatever comes your way. Besides, we could use a good operative like you. There're real benefits working in corporate security."

"You know, Buddy, I would; but I like working for myself. I really do. I do all right, and I don't have to take orders from morons who don't know the difference between a blackjack and a billyclub. But that's just me. It looks like you've done very well since leaving the LAPD. Tell me, just what is it you do around here?"

He didn't even flinch at the insult.

"I gotta tell you, Pike. It's sweet, it's profitable, and it's legit. I run Mr. Carl's personal bodyguard detail. I coordinate and direct the heads of all of UP's security services worldwide. I've even got time for a family life. I'm married to a wonderful woman. I have two beautiful daughters. I own a big house in Brentwood, close to O.J. Simpson's old place. There's no more departmental crap and red tape, no more IAB, no more thugs and assholes in my face. I come to work. I make decisions. I get things done, and I get paid very well. You gotta admire that."

I didn't have to admire anything and sipped the coffee, which was good. It tasted—expensive.

"But, listen to me going on like this . . ." He paused a moment before continuing. "I was sorry to hear about your son. What was his name?"

"Nathaniel."

"Yes, Nathaniel. Now that I have children of my own, I just can't imagine losing one of them."

I thought his remark ironic. Although I'd never had much respect for him early on, at the academy, I had none, nada, zilch for him now. In fact, making a show of treating me like a long lost friend was just that, a show. We'd been acquaintances at best. And I'd heard from a reliable source in the public defender's office that Buddy had fingered me for putting Eddy the Eel's brother away. Not that Eddy wouldn't have found out from someone else, but still, it was probable that Buddy's big mouth had set things in motion, resulting in Nathaniel's death. Not everyone who left the LAPD under suspicion was guilty; Buddy was. There were more allegations of police brutality on his record than he could count on his fingers and toes. He was careless and sadistic, and people got hurt as a result.

"So, Pike, let's cut to the chase. You didn't come all the way over here to ask me for a job."

I decided to toss it right out there and see how it would spin. "No, I didn't. I came to ask you why you pinned a tail on me yesterday."

"Ah, I see. Someone's dogging your tracks, and you don't know why? Well, well, that's not the Pikester I know. What kind of mess have you gotten yourself into this time, I wonder? Why, with talk like that, I'm beginning to think you couldn't cut it over here at UP."

"Your guy gave you up, Buddy. He said you wanted to know everything he could find out about my activities. So, what's the fucking deal, old pal?"

"Hey, lighten up there, Pikeman. Who was this mug?"

I hated like hell to tell him. Funny thing was, I don't know why I did. I didn't have to; I could've told him anything but that. "I didn't get his name."

"Well fancy that. Now I know you couldn't make it over here at UP; you didn't even get the dink's name. What kind of sloppy work is that? But hey, it doesn't matter; he wasn't my guy anyway. We've got history, you and me. If I want to know something about you, I'll call you up. Take my word for it. What you're up to is of no concern to Mr. Carl. And, if he has no concern, I've got even less, virtually none." He paused. "So, was there something else you wanted to talk with me about? If not, Piker old man, I'd love to shoot the shit some more, but . . . I'm a very busy guy."

I wasn't sure what to make of his response. Buddy the Palm was an accomplished liar and played a mean game of Poker. I wouldn't put it past him, but I couldn't remember now just what the tail had said. I couldn't be sure that the hump hadn't lied to me. He could've been a cooler customer than I'd given him credit for.

I gave it one more spin. "Have you come across a couple of foreigners lately, professionals by the names of Mustafa and Davie?"

"Not that I remember. They the guys . . .?" He smiled or grimaced. It was anybody's guess which.

I looked at him hard.

"I hear anything, I'll let you know. I've got your card right there." He pointed to his desk and did it again. This time, it was definitely a smile.

Fourteen

WHEN I LEFT BUDDY'S OFFICE, THE WINTER MAIDEN was nowhere to be seen. Her lavender scent still hung in the air, but now it reminded me of an ice cream freezer in a grocery store, cold, sickly sweet and turning sour. As I waited for the elevator in the hall, she came out of the ladies' restroom and went back to her office. She was blotting her eyes with a lacy white handkerchief. What I had earlier taken for a frosty demeanor now seemed nothing more than the defense posture of someone under a great deal of stress. Just goes to show how deceitful appearances can be. It appeared that someone had been hurting her feelings, and since it wasn't me, that left none other than my good ole buddy, Buddy Palmer. No surprise there; he was definitely the type to string an impressionable young woman along, promising her all sorts of things that he had no intention of delivering. But it was dangerous to indulge my intuition. For all I knew, she might've just gotten a phone call informing her that her mother had passed away.

When the elevator arrived, I got in and punched the

top button. Why not take a little tour of the upper two floors? It didn't hurt to reconnoiter the lay of the land; you could never tell when such information would come in handy. Just put it down to my nosy nature. Besides, maybe I'd run into G. Henry Carl himself, and he might give me some invaluable insider dope on the market. Then I could make a killing and retire to Cabo with Shirl. Failing that, I wouldn't mind a peek at his private art collection. But of course, the top three buttons were unlabeled and governed by a lock. When the elevator got to the roof, the door wouldn't open without the key. It was the same at the other two floors. I thought about picking the lock, but decided I didn't want to stir up a nest of Buddy's minions. Without looking up, I had no doubt that security had a camera hidden somewhere in the steel mesh above my head. Nothing ventured, nothing gained; it had been a long shot to begin with. I punched the button for the parking garage in the basement.

Ping. The elevator made a soft tone at every level until it eased to a stop back on the twenty-third, Buddy's floor. When the door opened, princess of the puffy eyes was standing there with her purse, a sweater, and a big woven, multi-colored, over-the-shoulder bag, stuffed to the gills.

"Oh, Mr. Pike, I—I thought you'd gone. I'll wait for the next one." She started to turn away.

"No, no. That's okay, you can ride down with me." I stepped forward to catch the door, which had just started to close. "Come on, Ms.—?"

"Braden, Inga Braden."

She was skittish but changed her mind, and joined me in the elevator. She stood against the wall, as far away from me as she could, and kept her eyes forward.

118

"So, Ms. Braden, how are you liking this LA heat wave?" I said as the door closed.

"You could never tell there was any kind of heat wave in this place. This whole damn building's just one big refrigerator. I hate it."

"Why don't they turn up the temperature?"

"I guess Mr. Carl has some kind of weird medical condition and can't tolerate heat. So the top three floors have to stay at 68 degrees or below."

"I'd noticed it was pretty cool up here. That must make it uncomfortable after a while."

"A lot he cares—" She looked wide-eyed at me, stopped talking, then looked back to the door. If security had cameras in the elevator, why not microphones? Buddy had broken a law or two in his time. It appeared that Inga, girl of the grim aspect, who'd thawed ever so slightly, had once again frosted over.

Ping.

As we descended, things began to tumble about in my brain. Inga reminded me a lot of Ronnie Rivero, even though they were complete opposites to look at— Inga, the chilly Ms. and Ms. Ronnie, the chili pepper. They were about the same age and both seemed to be overwhelmed with some sort of problem. Just what Inga's problem was, there was no way for me to say. No doubt, if Buddy Palmer was involved, it was a nasty one. But Ronnie was another matter. Our interview that morning had, in my mind, gone a long way toward clearing Ronnie in the Hollenbeck case. I had no proof that she wasn't a stone dead killer, but I'd seen too many of them, and she didn't fit the profile.

Ping.

I looked over at Inga. Her reserve was melting. She

119

looked as if she were going to cry again. She had asked me earlier if I'd wanted to make an appointment with Buddy just before he'd popped out of his office. He must've been watching from inside, although I'd seen no evidence of surveillance monitoring equipment there, which obviously, now that I thought about it, was hidden in that massive mahogany desk of his. Inga was under constant surveillance. As far as she knew, when Buddy was in house, he was watching her through that little peephole camera in the picture frame behind her. No wonder the poor girl had developed a twitch in her eye and gone off to the bathroom. It was the only place you could have any privacy, if indeed there were no concealed cameras there as well.

Ping.

At this point I wouldn't put anything past him. She had to have been following Buddy's instructions when he'd pulled the rug out from under her by coming out to greet me. Buddy had to have known that I was on my way up shortly after I'd first driven into the underground parking lot. He knew I was there before she did. There were security cameras everywhere. So why the big charade?

The door opened, and two men in full business uniform with briefcases got on. They were in the middle of a conversation about recent developments in the stock markets. Inga ignored them and kept her eyes front. But one of the men reminded me of Yaeger Eastlake—not so much his looks, but his imperial condescension toward the other man, obviously an underling. This man was a captain of commerce and used to such deference, an important man. Eastlake had exhibited a similar manner with Ronnie and had, more or less, dismissed me even as we'd spoken. Was it possible that he'd heard of me prior to our meeting? Anything was possible. He had ignored my bumps and bruises. Was it a matter too far beneath him to notice, or did he know about them before we met?

Ping.

Everyone I'd met since Friday had said something about my condition, except Eastlake and Rivero. But she had blushed and acted sheepishly. She had blushed, because—well, because—she had previously stood me up for an appointment that she had arranged the week before. Aha! There was one of those little worms that had been burrowing around in my brain since our meeting at the Getty. She had known who I was the week before. Someone—who didn't want me involved with her—had sent Mustafa and Davie to dissuade me from taking her case. Someone knew that she had made an appointment with me and decided that she had kept it. Until I could come up with something better, I had to assume that it was her case this someone didn't want me to take. And right now, this someone looked a lot like Yeager Eastlake. I downshifted into neutral and let it idle for a moment, and didn't think about anything. I just watched as the numbers on the digital readout above the door counted down the floors of our descent.

Ping. Ping. Ping.

I looked back over at Inga. She had regained her composure and was staring a hole through the back of the head of the man who had reminded me of Eastlake. Somewhere between the fourteenth and twelfth floors, it occurred to me that my Eastlake-Rivero hypothesis was a bit far-fetched and more improbable than I wanted to believe. But without it, I had nothing else to go on. Liar that he was, Buddy had been less than informative and, indeed, may not have been lying in this instance at all. I didn't see a connection.

Ping.

The elevator stopped at the eleventh floor. Two burly, swarthy Middle Eastern men in business suits, one blue, one gray, got on and stood with their backs to the door. They held their hands crossed in front of them and smiled at us from under those bushy black mustaches. They spoke quietly, in what I assumed to be Arabic. The one in the blue suit nodded to the other one toward me, and they both laughed. I didn't have to know the language to know that he had just made a joke about my face. I could see they were packing heat in slings under their arms, beneath their coats. They didn't speak again, but they were dangerous men, and their presence was an electrical charge in the tiny stainless steel box elevator that set the hair on the back of my neck erect. The captain of commerce was greatly put out to have been so unceremoniously moved from his central position in front of the door. But aside from a subtle single snort through his elevated proboscis, he continued with his conversation (albeit a lot more quietly) about stocks and bonds, unwilling to relinquish the hold he had over his protégé.

Ping.

The two Arabs didn't appear to know anyone. Inga showed no signs of recognition. I settled in for the rest of the ride. The two men turned to face each other so they could watch the door, and us, at the same time. They'd assured themselves that the rest of us posed no threat, although I noticed that the one in the gray suit kept bouncing an eye in my direction. But I ignored him, and he settled down. When the captain of commerce and his cohort got off in the lobby, I moved over and whispered to Inga, "So, Ms Braden, let me give you one of my cards. Perhaps we can talk some time?"

I handed her one of my cards with just "Nestor Pike, PI" and my phone number on it.

She was startled. "What?" Her gaze had been focused inward, and her mind was miles away.

"I said, perhaps we could talk."

"Oh, no—no. Sorry, I couldn't." She looked down at the card as if she didn't know how it had gotten into her hand.

"Taking the rest of the day off?" I asked.

"Oh no—I'm taking the rest of my life off. I just quit."

Ping.

Fifteen

IT SOUNDED GOOD TO ME. ALTHOUGH I COULDN'T take the rest of my life off, I could take the rest of the day. So I did. First, I met Maldonado at the gym. After we worked out, we went around the corner to Mick's Micropub on Melrose for some quick, quiet, and smooth homemade brew. I gave him the lowdown and paperwork on the McFeety brothers' scam. Later, I met Shirl for dinner at The Rusty Scupper in West Hollywood. It seemed like a date. She was already sitting there under the oars, fishnets, and marker buoys tippling a glass of a cheeky little Napa Valley Zinfandel when I arrived. I switched over to Corona with a lime. We were both having oysters, and I was making a concerted effort to cut some fresh bait and bring her more into the picture. It seemed strange and familiar at the same time. But I had real reservations about it.

"I still don't believe you did that to those men," Shirl said, as she toyed with an oyster—poking that little fork into it and swirling it around in the horseradish sauce.

"They had it coming." I said. "Bernie assured me

Fraud would be all over it like a cat on a rat, first thing in the morning. He didn't want that $400,000 to evaporate before they could get their hands on it. There would be others looking for restitution. In fact, he called a guy he knew in the division while we were still there." I slipped another oyster down the chute.

"And you got the money back for all those people?"

"Well, just the eight couples we could find at the time."

"Yes, but that's a lot. Most people scammed like that never see anything back."

"I am a trained sleuth, you know. What can I say? We got lucky they weren't any brighter than they were. They might not have given it over so easy."

"You may've been lucky, but you're also a good man, Nestor Pike. Not many men would have done what you did. If Nathaniel were here, he'd be so proud of you."

"Shirl, I was just doing my job. Okay? Besides, Donny did most of the work."

"Maybe, but you told him what to do, didn't you?"

"Well, sometimes. But still——"

"Look Nes, I'm just giving you some credit where credit is due."

"That's nice, Shirl, but—"

"Okay, okay. Don't look at me like that. So, tell me about the rest of your day. What's happening with that murder?"

"Shirl, I—"

"You don't have to tell me anymore, if you don't want to. I just thought . . . I'm sorry, I didn't mean to give you the third degree."

"It's okay. It's just kind of strange after so long. I mean . . . well . . . last night was—"

"Don't say any more. I know what it was, and I feel so different today. I know how painful it was for you, how tough it is to speak about it. It was just as bad for me. A day doesn't go by that I don't think about him. It's been five long years, and I still get so angry that I can't think straight. Still, it feels like you think I blame you."

"Well, I don't see how you can't, really—given how things turned out. That's not right either. I know you don't blame me, even if you should. Besides, I do enough of that for both of us. It's just that, if it weren't for the fact that . . . Shirl, I can't do this now; there's no sense crawling into something we can't get out of."

"Why won't you open up and talk to me about it?"

"There's no sense in it."

"Why not, if it will make our lives better?"

"What makes you think it would make our lives better?"

"Can they get any worse?"

"Things can always get worse. I felt like you, till Nathaniel . . . Look Shirl, I'm just hoping to find a way for us to be happy. I drink too much coffee, too much alcohol. I never drink enough water. I don't eat right, except when I'm with you. I forget things, if I don't write them down. I hesitate over every decision. I'm slower than I used to be, in more ways than one."

"At least you still work out."

"I have to. That's my job. I'm a detective. I hang out in seedy places with a lower class of people, some of whom would just as soon kill me as not. I break the law, never mind if I think it's for a greater good. I come and go at all hours, day or night, because my clients need me. I can't sleep half the time with the stuff twisting and twirling though my brain. But that's what they pay me for. It's what I do. I help them out of their petty squabbles, their problems with the law, their personal lives that have gotten turned upside down."

"What? I've been with you twenty-five years, and I don't know all that? What about your life? What about our life?"

"You don't think I think about that? I think about it all the time . . ." I stopped and looked at her. I took a long draught of my Corona. There we were, again.

She looked around the room, picked up her glass, and looked back at me through the rosy color of the wine. "I guess this isn't the time or place to talk about it. I don't know what I'm doing half the time."

We sat listening to the music.

"So, what is happening with that murder, that is, if you feel like telling me about it?" She swirled her wine around and looked hopeful.

"Well, let's see. The Mayor's hopping all over the Commissioner, the Commissioner's hopping all over Chief of Police and the Chief is hopping all over McCorkle. McCorkle is, of course, trying to hop all over Bernie, but nobody hops all over Bernie, least of all McCorkle."

"And?"

"And Bernie told me they still don't know a whole lot. They believe Hollenbeck was murdered somewhere else, and his body taken to the Villa. They don't know where. But I think he was killed on the spot, doesn't make sense otherwise."

"Do they know how?"

"They think he died as a result of blunt force trauma to the head, but they haven't found a murder weapon yet. They feel that the murderer apparently thought that crushing the body under the Kouri would hide the crime beneath a suicide. At least, that's their theory at this point. Nothing new, and I told Bernie it didn't sound very convincing. He confessed it was shallow and filling up fast. But that's all they have, and time's running out. I think some sicko lowered that rock on Hollenbeck just to see what it would look like to crush a man to death, slow and methodical. It was done with a forklift. Are you sure you want to hear this?" I champed another oyster down and followed with a draught of my Corona.

"Yes. I don't like the gory stuff while I'm eating, but go on." She popped a second oyster into her mouth, chewed once, swallowed, and sipped her rosy Zin.

I'd forgotten how much I liked to watch Shirl eat. She wasn't a finicky Pris, like some women I knew. She took another. "Well, okay," I said. "What I think aside, when I pointed out that Eastlake was still a good bet for further investigation, Bernie said, 'What am I, some kinda rookie cholo, like you gotta tell me how to do my job? And this from some gringo, whose woman has to dress him every morning.'" Shirl just looked at me. "Well, I guess you had to be there. Anyway, then he told me that Eastlake had a solid alibi for Thursday, none other than Raleigh Hanson, himself, in the flesh."

"Who's he again?"

"The sculptor. Hollenbeck's ex, you know, companion, partner, lover, whatever they're calling it these days."

"I remember. He's with Eastlake now?"

"Looks that way. He spent the night at Eastlake's mansion up in Coldwater Canyon. If true, they both have diamond-hard, crystal-clear alibis. And apparently it is, because Eastlake's housekeeper verified their statements, said she made dinner and was there until Eastlake and Hanson arrived late that afternoon."

"That's convenient."

"Nevertheless, they're still looking hard at Hanson. They think it might have been some kind of domestic squabble gotten outta hand. All hunches aside, I'm not sure that they're wrong. From what we can see, he had the motive and the means. Meanwhile, back at the scene of the crime, there're no prints, no DNA that matches anyone we know, yet, except Hollenbeck's, and still no motive. The good news is, they've stopped seriously contemplating Ronnie Rivero as a possible perpetrator of the crime, unless something else comes to light. But they're not closing any doors."

"Did he say why?"

"No, but he did say if I said that to anyone, including her, or if I withheld pertinent information concerning my client from the investigation, he'd throw my tail in jail."

"Would he do that again?"

"In a heart beat."

"Well, now that you've told me, it looks like I could get you arrested. So be warned, if you step out of line, Buster . . . Better yet, I think I'll blackmail you. Maybe now you'll take me to Cabo, like you promised."

"Oh yeah?"

"I don't know why I said that. If I want to take a vacation in Mexico, I don't need you to take me. I'm perfectly capable of going on my own. Eat the rest of those. I only wanted a taste." She tipped her little fork at the oysters and set it on the plate.

"Good point," I said. And I had no problem with the oysters. The only reason I didn't order a dozen more is because I didn't want to make a complete pig of myself in front of her, not that she would have cared. She had only eaten three out of the dozen. When I finished the others, I flagged down our waitress and ordered another Corona, but Shirl was still coddling her wine along. The waitress brought the Corona with the rest of our meal: grilled halibut, rice pilaf, steamed asparagus and fresh salad, which we ate like the French, after the main course. Over coffee and dessert, Shirl picked up our conversation again.

"You remember the first time we came here?" she said.

"Yes, of course."

"I was so excited. It was the first time we went out after Nathaniel was born. I felt like I'd been locked up for years."

"Yeah, I remember it took a long time for you to get back on your feet."

"I worried how we could afford such extravagance on a young cop's pay."

"We managed."

"Yep. We always did, somehow. So why is it so hard now?"

I didn't know what to say. I just looked at her. She looked vulnerable. I could see Nathaniel in her eyes. But I knew she wouldn't indulge herself the release of tears. She kept that for places that were more private. Tonight, she was beautiful in her simple but elegant black dress— her soft brown hair pulled up in casual wisps and curls on her head. She looked back at me, then away. In the silence that fell between us, I too looked around the room for some clue, something to tell me where we would go from there.

People were eating and drinking, talking, laughing, having fun. In the piano bar, someone played a jazzy rendition of "Stepping Out." People were singing along. The music mingling with the hubbub and murmur made the place vibrant, cheery, and the tinkle of the piano offered more hope than I could have imagined at the time. But still, I felt that we were two observers apart from our real lives, unable to find each other or connect. It was as if we were empty and transparent, wrapped with newsprint and packed away in a cardboard box, like a couple of glass tumblers from an old and incomplete set of crystal.

"What did you tell Bernie about the artifacts?" she said.

"What? Oh, yeah, that's a minor problem. Jail threat be damned, I didn't tell him anything about them. Stolen priceless artifacts look a lot like motives for murder. And at this point, it's just an unproved allegation yet to be substantiated on the part of my client. If they are missing, I don't want to expose that fact before I clear her of any wrongdoing in the matter."

"Won't he be mad if he finds out?"

"You can make book on it, Sweetie Puss. You wouldn't rat on me, would you?"

"Oh, I don't know. You're getting in pretty deep here, Nes Honey."

The piano player swung into another Tony Bennett favorite, a tune I couldn't remember the name of presently, but would feel really stupid about when I did. We sat and listened for a while.

"So what was the bad news?" she said.

"What? Oh, the bad news. Well, ahhhh, let's see. Now that I think about it, there really wasn't any bad news."

She looked at me funny, but I couldn't bring myself to tell her that Bernie hadn't come across any sign of Davie or Mustafa, or that I was beginning to wonder just a little bit about when and where they were going to materialize. If I wasn't careful, I'd end up fertilizing a small patch of grass out at Forest Lawn, or worse, as a cabbage-head in some sleazy nursing home, drooling down the front of my Elmer Fudd pajamas. They weren't the kind to make threats; they made promises. I already had the contusions to prove it, and I was painfully aware—my trusty little bottle of Vicodin notwithstanding—that just that morning, I had officially taken the very same case that they had so emphatically warned me to stay out of.

Sixteen

AS WE LEFT THE SCUPPER, I DECLINED SHIRL'S invitation to spend the night with her. Maybe it was silly, but I couldn't get past this anxiety that if I stayed with her again something bad was bound to happen. Nathaniel had been killed because of me, and I'd be damned before I'd let anything happen to Shirl. I was already pushing my luck, having stayed with her the night before. She was unfair game to anyone who wanted to get even with me, but game nonetheless. You can't meddle in people's lives, put a few of them in jail, and not make some of them downright vengeful. I had taken pains to cover my tracks the previous night, but still someone had been out there. And now, with this Mustafa-Davie threat, I was especially on edge about where I stayed, and with whom. So I tailed her back to her place and parked down the block, to make sure that she got in all right. She didn't know that I'd followed her home. She never did.

Although it was early yet, around eleven thirty, the street was quiet. It was a working class neighborhood, and the lights were out in most of the houses along the block. The night was warm and the sky was clear. I had taken only two Vicodin all day; but after a couple of brews with Bernie, I probably shouldn't have drunk that second Corona with Shirl. I was feeling a little drowsy and a bit euphoric. I never drank much when I was onto something even remotely dangerous. You never knew when you were going to need your wits about you. I'd been very irresponsible the night before. Contrary to the stereotype of the hard-boiled, hard-drinking PI, you didn't get many cases solved if you were a drunk. But since I had spread them out over a whole evening, and eaten well, I sat in my car under the trees looking at the moon with my windows rolled down—watching her house and feeling better than I had a right to.

Staking out her place, when she didn't know I was there, was something I did on occasion—a habit I'd gotten into after Nathaniel was killed. It was just a thing I needed to do now and again. I got this sense of peace that I could find nowhere else in my life. Sometimes when I sat outside her house like that I could somehow see beyond myself, into something larger, something that was usually hidden in my day to day routines. Sometimes I thought if I sat out there long enough, I would eventually find a way back in, to stay—without feeling this crippling guilt and crummy self-doubt. Maybe it was wishful thinking or an illusion; but sometimes sitting there alone in the dark gave me rare insight into realms of myself that I didn't even know existed. I always waited twenty-five or thirty minutes after her lights went out before I left. It made me feel good to know she was safe and sleeping peacefully. When I drove away, I realized that I'd been sitting in the same spot where I had seen the late model Ford the previous night.

On my way back to the crib, it occurred to me that Donny was sitting outside under the same moon, over at Ronnie Rivero's place in Santa Monica. Before I went to the apartment, I decided to swing by the office, make some coffee, and get a look at the Rivero file that Felia and Donny were supposed to have been working on that afternoon. Not that I expected to find a lot more than I already had, but I thought by toying around with some of the facts they'd gathered, maybe I could come up with a game plan for discovering where those holy relics had gotten to.

Besides, Ronnie Rivero was an enigma and starting to get a bit under my skin, in more ways than one—not the least of which was her sexuality. Maybe my time with Shirl was coming to a close, and I just didn't have the sense to see it. Everything changes. Change was inevitable. No one escapes it. Was it my time? Was I poised on this decisive cusp? Could I love another? My little world was ripe for change; who knows? Maybe a little nudge from Ronnie would tip the balance. Nothing was impossible; a kiss, and the world might twirl out of kilter and topple completely over . . . . What the hell was I thinking?

I noticed, as I pulled up to the curb, that the lights were on upstairs in my office windows. Donny and Felia rarely worked late, so there shouldn't have been anyone there at that time of night. Although Felia had a tendency to leave the place unlocked, it wasn't like her or Donny to leave the lights on. I, of course, had been known to do it pretty often, although I wasn't the last one to leave that day. I didn't see anyone moving across the windows, but that didn't mean anything. Things didn't feel right.

I got out of the car, unsheathed the Magnum, and checked the load. Then I slipped into the shadows under the bougainvillea at the entrance to the building. I thought about going up the fire escape, but decided it was too noisy. The surprise might've given me an ace-in-the-hole, but climbing in through the windows would've been too cumbersome to have taken advantage of it. Besides, they'd be locked. I probably couldn't reach the lower rung anyway. I turned the front-door knob and was not surprised to find the lock had been jimmied. I pushed it open and went into the hallway at the foot of the stairs. There were no lights burning on the first floor.

The building was old and the stairway dark. I made my way up the steps as silent as possible. Every other tread groaned like a five-dollar whore. So much for stealth; if somebody was up there, they'd hear me coming for sure. I stopped to listen at the head of the steps and heard nothing but the muffled city sounds outside and the creaking of the old building. All the lights were out, except for those shining through the frosted glass in my office door at the end of the hall. Felia's office was still dark. Just to be sure that no one was sneaking along behind me, I shouldered the bathroom doors open as I went; they were dark. Every doorknob along the hall tested secure. So, whoever was in my office wasn't there to rob the building indiscriminately. They'd come specifically to see me. I stooped below the glass outside my door and listened to the silence. My lock had been jimmied, too.

A moment later, a loud metallic clank came through

the inner office. Staying low, I pushed the door open and scooted inside Felia's office. The noise had stopped. Just as I was getting ready to move in and confront whoever was in my office, I realized they were gone. I could hear street noise and smell exhaust from out on the boulevard below through the open door. I heard someone outside yelling in a foreign language, maybe Arabic, but I couldn't be sure. I stood up and turned on the lights. The place had been tossed—but good.

The file cabinets were emptied and tipped over. There was paper everywhere. The coffeepot had been smashed against the wall, along with the computer. Felia's desk didn't have a drawer left in it. How they had missed the frosted glass with my name on it in the office door was beyond me. So much for Felia's office, and mine wasn't any better. The chairs were overturned and all the drawers pulled. Even the new frame that Felia bought for my PI license was in pieces on the floor. The only thing they didn't destroy was the AC unit, which didn't work very well anyway. The blinds were up, and one of the windows had been opened. I crossed the room, checked both ways first, and then stuck my head out. I was just in time to see two guys, in dark clothes, hot-footing it around the corner at the end of the block.

I looked around the room. Man, things were really beginning to knot my line; I'd just about had enough. It had already been four days since this began, and I still wasn't any closer to knowing what was going on than when it started. Well . . . maybe I was a little, but now this. Things were getting out of hand. I had nothing but questions, and I needed answers. It was going to be a long night. I holstered the Magnum and walked down to the drugstore to get some coffee, before I began to pick up the pieces and put them back together.

Who were these jokers? And what did they want anyway? By the looks of the place, probably the same thing I wanted—relevant information. This was, after all, the information age, was it not? Problem was, there wasn't much of that to go around these days. In fact, at this juncture of my existence, I didn't have much of anything worth a damn—least of all, relevant information. Except, maybe, my life. But hell, even at that, there were people out there who would argue that my life wasn't even worth that. And to be honest, with the way I felt right then, I was inclined to agree with them.

Seventeen

Wednesday

"**W**AKE UP, BOSS, WAKE UP," FELIA SAID, SHAKING me by the shoulder, which hurt like hell. "What happened? Are you all right?" At least I thought it was Felia; it sounded like her. Who was awake enough to know? There'd been dreams; and the images of the dreams were still dancing on the backside of my eyelids, although they were fading fast. When my eyes popped open, Felia was standing there, looking at me like she'd found her long-lost father.

"Yeah, I'm all right," I said. "But we had a couple of visitors last night." I sat up in my chair, wincing as my lower back screamed like a banshee. I'd been sleeping across my arm on my shoulder on the desk in front of me. How my body got twisted into that position was beyond me. No wonder that in one part of my dream, my arm was being slowly rotated, and pulled out of its socket by someone who looked a lot like Emil Mustafa. I tried to massage away the pain, but it had fallen to sleep and prickled with millions of pinpricks.

"They sure made a mess of things," she said.

"If you think this is bad, you should've seen it last night, before I got it all cleaned up."

"If this is your idea of cleaned up, it must've been indescribable."

"Well, I did leave the files for you; I wouldn't know where to start with those. You seem to have your own system. What time is it?" I'd forgotten that I was wearing my watch.

"A little after eight. How long have you been here?"

"Since around one this morning. I must've fallen to sleep about four thirty or five. I don't remember. Here, take this envelope; it contains the stuff you asked me for on Bobby Chandler. He's messing around with a young woman he works with over at CBS, but I guess you knew that already. It's all there."

I picked up the paperwork I'd done for her sister and handed it to her. She hesitated a moment before taking it from me. I could understand her reluctance to get the bad news, especially in black and white photos—the proof that her sister's marriage was about to come apart, for good. She didn't open it, just took it back into her office, where I could hear her putting it away.

"Hey, Boss," she said. "I could use another cup of coffee; and since they broke our pot, I guess I'll go down to the drugstore and get us a cup. You need anything else?"

"See if they'll give you some morphine," I said.

"Ha, ha!"

While Felia went for coffee, I straightened myself up and hobbled down to the restroom. I didn't feel rested, and my body hurt all over. The lack of horizontal sleep made the old bones ache, like it was going to rain again. Maybe it was, though it didn't look like it by the sunlight that was streaming through the office windows.

THE ART OF MURDER

In fact, my body felt worse than it had since I took that rousting from Mustafa and Davie. It was all catching up with me. Maybe Buddy Palmer was right; maybe it was time to sell out this little three-man circus of mine and do something else—get into something less painful. It wasn't like I was making any great strides in this case anyway. Not to mention, it was a damn thankless job at best. I didn't need this shit. Two weeks lying in the sand on a beach in Cabo, drinking tequila shooters, making love to Shirl day and night didn't sound too shabby right about now.

I splashed some water on my face and dried my hands.

What the hell was I thinking? I had a client who depended on me. I couldn't drop this and go hide out in Cabo San Lucas. There was time enough for that later. I had to do the best I could for now and think my way out of this. Besides, nobody ran me out of my own town.

I hadn't taken a pain pill since two o'clock yesterday afternoon, so I took a couple and drank some water. Coffee always dried me out. Then I went into a stall, wiped the seat down, dropped my trou', and sat on the porcelain throne to do a little kingly cogitating.

Granted, I'd only just taken the case officially yesterday. But hell, I was involved in this mess even before I knew I was. Ronnie Rivero had blown me off a week earlier. Usually, by this time in a case, I knew what I was dealing with, where the heat was coming from and from whom. But at this point I still didn't have a handle on it. This was Limbo. Something had to happen fast or I was gonna crash and burn before I could even get my own licks in. It was time to shit or get off the pot, as they say. Until now I'd taken the brunt of the pressure, because I was in the dark. Ipso facto, I had to shift the pressure to the other players, drop a little darkness into their lives for a change.

First things first, it was back to the scene of the crime. Only this time, it was a trip out to the new Getty, and not the Villa for me. If I wanted answers, that was where I'd find them. I finished up, washed my hands, and went back to the office. I was feeling better, now that I'd worked a few things out. Nothing worse than being stuck in Limbo.

"Hey Donny," I said when I got back to the office.

He was sitting across from Felia—who was sorting through the stacks of papers that I had put together in the wee hours of the morning and cussing under her breath. "Hey, Chief," he said, trying to look cheerful. Donny was a very empathic soul.

"I tried to keep things that looked as if they belonged together in the same stacks," I said to Felia. From the expression on her face, it appeared that I hadn't done a very good job.

"Everything's jumbled together," she said.

"I know; it's a bitch." I didn't know what else to say. I felt for her; I really did. It wasn't going to be easy straightening that mess out. "So, Donny," I said as I took a Styrofoam cup and the last two tubs of Half-&-Half from the desk and went to my office. "How'd it go last night?" I took off the plastic top, added the cream, and sipped the hot coffee. "Ahhh." Between that and the medication, maybe the old motor was gonna turn over after all.

"Piece of cake. Ms. Rivero went home straight from

work and stayed there all night." He came into my office and sat across the desk from me. "So far, she seems to be a pretty dull character. Hope the rest of this stakeout goes this peacefully. She went back to work this morning, and here I am. I was going to take Felia out for some breakfast before I went home to sleep, but I can see she needs to be here."

"If she wants to go, it's all right with me. She can finish up later. Say, Felia, how'd your audition go yesterday afternoon?" I yelled to her in the other room.

"Don't even go there, Boss," she yelled back. "I don't, I repeat, want to talk about it."

I knew when to keep my mouth shut. Donny just looked at me with his eyebrows raised. I raised mine back.

"So what's on the agenda for today?" Felia said joining us from the other office. Her brows were furled, not raised. "After we get the office straightened out, that is,"

"Well, let's see," I said. "We need a locksmith over here to fix the locks,"

"Already done. He's on his way."

"Make a list of everything missing or busted and call the insurance company."

"Right."

"Get me another license frame and look into replacing that computer. You may as well look into replacing that AC unit as well."

"But I've got a guy coming to repair that later this afternoon."

"Well okay, but if he wants an arm and a leg, go buy a new one."

"Hey, maybe we can get the insurance company to pay for that too. All we have to do is bust it up a little bit." I just stared at her. "Just kidding. God, what a look. I just thought, what with the premiums that they're charging us . . . ."

"As much as they deserve it, I'm real tempted. But never mind. After you get the files in order, you need to make out the restitution checks for those people who were scammed down in El Segundo. I'll sign them later. Retain ten percent from each and have the people involved sign contracts to reflect the fee. Call them; ask if they would prefer to have you mail their checks or come and pick them up."

"You bet."

"But before you do that, get me an appointment with Yeager Eastlake this morning, as soon as possible. Then call Ronnie Rivero—never mind that, I'll call her myself. I want to see that new file of hers that you and Donny were working on yesterday."

"Well, it may take a few minutes to hunt it up in all this mess."

"I know. I looked for it last night and couldn't find it. Maybe you'll know what you're looking for. Is there anything you can tell me about her, anything out of the ordinary?"

"Not really, basic stuff. I remember she's from East LA She's the same age as Mandy. She attended Cesar Chavez High School and graduated Magnum cum Laude. She was a Merit Scholar and went on full scholarship to UCLA for her BA, as well as for her MA in studio art—again with full honors; and she's almost finished with her Ph.D. in Museum Studies. She's real bright."

"Donny?"

"There's a woman I know over in juvenile records looking into something I came across by accident," said

Donny. "It may be nothing. I'll let you know what we come up with."

"Okay. Leave it in the file, and I'll look at it later. Get some sleep, then call me before you head out to pick up Ronnie's trail this evening. I may have something for you before you go. Felia, if you can get me that appointment now, you can go to breakfast."

"You got it."

"Okay, now get out of here. I want to finish my coffee in peace before I take off."

They cleared out, and I closed my eyes for a few moments. Then I drank the rest of my coffee and called Ronnie Rivero. I made an appointment to see her at the Getty in a couple of hours. Felia came back about ten minutes later.

"Eastlake wasn't in. The secretary said he's taking the day off and won't be back until tomorrow. Apparently, he's being recognized for some sort of curatorial coup, with a cocktail party in his honor at four this afternoon. The party's being given in G. Henry Carl's private art gallery, over at the Universal Paradigm building in Westwood—by invitation only."

"Can you get me one?"

"No can do. I already tried."

"Okay, never mind."

"Donny and I are going for breakfast after the locksmith leaves," she said.

"Fine," I said. "I'm outta here. I'll see you guys later." I stood and headed for the door.

"Thanks, Boss," she said as she took my elbow at the corner of the desk, then walked with me across the room.

"No sweat. Just get back—"

"No, I mean for helping Mandy with her divorce stuff." She stopped and turned to me before we went into the other office.

"Yeah, well, I'm sorry things—"

She hugged me tight, then leaned up and kissed me lightly on the cheek. "Mandy and I really appreciate it. I know how much you hate—"

I put my finger to her lip. "Okay, gotta go," I said and left her standing there. "See ya later," I said to Donny, as I passed through the office and went out the door—headed for Dexter's. I didn't know why, but all of a sudden I had the strongest urge to see Shirl. Besides, I needed to put some food on these pills; I was getting a bit light-headed.

Eighteen

RONNIE RIVERO WAS WAITING FOR ME AT THE TRAM stop in the Arrival Plaza at the top of the hill. She carried a putty-colored umbrella to ward off the sun. Wearing a tailored bone-colored blouse, some no-nonsense warm-gray slacks and comfortable shoes, she looked good enough to sit in on a Board of Directors' meeting, or she could, just as easily, have rolled up her sleeves and uncrated some art. I followed her up the steps, through the Museum's entrance, toward the Exhibitions Pavilion, where the Last Supper dinnerware exhibition was supposed to open on Saturday.

The new Getty Museum was a showplace, to quote the guidebook, "in which to experience and enjoy art in a unique setting that featured dramatic architecture, tranquil gardens, and breathtaking views." Seen in person, it is, indeed, a wonder in which to revel. You could take a guided tour, or you could follow your own nose to one phenomenal architectural, artistic, or educational experience after another. There was so much to see, it would take at least a couple of weeks to give this 750-acre rock garden a good going over. And I've got to say, any museum with Vincent's "Irises" on permanent display was aces in my book. It, alone, would be worth the price of admission, if they charged one. What a deal, and it only cost five bucks to park your ride. Now that I was there, I couldn't imagine how I'd missed the original opening. Had it already been six years?

"This is quite a place," I said as we walked. I was never much on small talk.

"Oh yes," she said. "Mr. Meier did a remarkable job. I love it. The travertine is so beautiful—the texture, subtlety, and interplay of the color." She pointed to the stone wall of one of the buildings. "Did you know the ancient Romans used the exact same stone from a quarry in Bagni di Tivoli for the Coliseum and the Trevi Fountain?"

"I haven't got that far in the guidebook yet. But I can see why; it certainly is beautiful."

"They also used it in the colonnade of St. Peter's Basilica. Believe it or not, it took a hundred ocean voyages to get all sixteen thousand tons of it over here. Though, to be honest, not everybody loves this place as much as I do. It's unfortunate, but Mr. Meier does have his critics."

"Don't we all?"

"Nobody I know, but let's not go there."

"Let's not."

There weren't many people on the grounds, and it was already after eleven. I noticed small groups of gawkers taking tours with the docents. Maybe the heat was keeping people away, and maybe there was truth to Hollenbeck's complaint about the lack of popularity that this elegant museum suffered from. There should've been a mob here, but the place was deserted. Of course, with the coming attractions, that was about to change. This place was about to become the new Temple on the Mount for all of modern Christendom. There were going to be more pilgrims crawling over this rock, at least for the next four months, than there were Carter's infamous little liver pills.

On the way to the Pavilion, Ronnie offered me coffee from the café cart on the plaza. But since I'd just come from breakfast at Dexter's, I declined. "Maybe later," I said. "Tell me, are things still set to open on Saturday?"

"Yes, and I'm dreading it," she said. "I don't know if the opening could be stopped now, even if word about the theft got out."

"What do you suppose they'd do if it did?"

"I've no idea, pull the items in question, I guess."

"Then we haven't got a whole lot of time. I'm assuming that hoards of experts, culture vultures, and the paparazzi, are gonna drop on this stone like a flock of buzzards on a carcass. They're gonna start asking some pretty nettlesome questions, and you're gonna need to give them some pretty straight answers, right?"

"Oh yes. I can't even begin to imagine."

"So don't take offense, but I have to ask this question. Are you absolutely, positively, without a doubt sure that there really was a theft?"

She stopped walking and turned to look at me. I stopped with her. "Well, it's funny you should ask," she said, "because I've been asking myself that very question for three weeks now. And the more I do, the less I'm sure."

"It's a fact of life, Missy. Take it from me, the more you learn, the less you know."

"Things would be so much easier if I was wrong about this."

"That's probably true."

"So, I go over to the gallery at least three times a day to look at the cups and bowls. If I wanted to turn them over and examine the identification and registration marks—which is where I could really tell if they had been replaced—I'd have to get special keys from Dr. Eastlake, or Security, to unlock the cases. It's a big job. The Plexiglas is heavy, bulletproof stuff; and I don't want people to know what I'm doing. I can't be seen handling the objects just for the fun of it. Then, I'm unsure if what I first saw in Jordan was different than what I see here. Lately, I've looked at these pieces so much, my memories of what I saw over there have almost faded completely. And now I'm afraid that I've drawn too much attention to myself."

"Didn't you uncrate the objects when they arrived? Couldn't you tell at that point?"

"Yes, along with Dr. Eastlake and the Jordanian courier who came with them. And that's when I got suspicious. But not everything was different, just certain pieces, and nobody said a word."

"You mean, even the courier didn't suspect anything?"

"No, and that makes me suspicious too."

"I see, so now you're saying it's possible that there wasn't a theft in the first place?"

She continued walking, and I followed. At this point I didn't know for sure where we were going, but decided that I'd find out when we got there.

"Well, it's possible," she said. "And to be honest, I really am beginning to doubt my own mind. No one around here, who might have, has raised any questions about the artifacts."

"I wonder what that has to say about the place?"

"Can I be the only one who feels this way? What if I said something, and it turned out I was wrong? Even Dr. Eastlake has shown no reservations about them; and he knows them better than anyone here does. He's eagerly promoting the show."

"Well, it's not hard to see why. As curator of the most controversial exhibit of the century, his stock is just about to split and go through the ceiling. Desire blinds even the rich and powerful. I understand he's being honored at some party this afternoon."

I grabbed the door for her, and she dropped the umbrella into a stand of a dozen or more identical umbrellas, just inside, on our way into the Pavilion. "Yes, he and the Minister from Jordan," she said. "And I'm not looking forward to it. The entire management staff has been invited. They strongly suggested that everyone attend."

I followed her across the hall and into an elevator, where she punched the button for the second floor. "I was wondering, with the private showing on Friday and the public opening on Saturday, why would Mr. Carl be hosting another affair today? That's an awful lot of parties."

"As I understand it, the Minister is a close acquaintance of Mr. Carl. Since he was the one primarily responsible for letting us have the artifacts in the first place, and because he has to leave tomorrow to be in Washington, DC on Friday, I think Mr. Carl chose this as a way to show our appreciation."

"Tight knit group, it seems—Eastlake, Carl, and this Minister from Jordan. What's his name?"

"Geshur Kedar. Officially, he's the Deputy Minister of Antiquities at the Jordanian Ministry of Culture."

On the second floor, we crossed through an exhibition hall where some walls were still being painted. I followed her into a small office and sat in the only chair in the room opposite the computer desk. Before she sat down, Ronnie opened a small file cabinet and rifled through some paperwork. She pulled a folder and dropped it next to the Indigo iMac.

"Some things from a previous show that I needed to return to my office," she said by way of explanation.

"I'd like to go to that party," I said. "Can you get me invited?"

"Of course. Come as my guest."

"Will you meet me in the lobby of the Universal Paradigm building at quarter after four? We'll be fashionably late."

"How fun, an assignation. Are you sure you won't mind being seen with me?" She smiled.

"Look Ronnie, if people think you and I have something in the works, the value of my stock is headed up. I wouldn't miss it for anything."

"Hey, I thought you said you were married."

"Yes I did. I didn't say I was dead."

She smiled again. "You'll need a suit," she said.

"That can be arranged."

"I bet you look very attractive all dressed up. Too bad about those bruises; although they do give you a certain rugged handsome—something, seen in a certain light."

"Beauty's in the eye of the beholder—but whatever, I just happened to think you might've had a point there. Who knows what tongues would start to wag if we showed up together. Given the circumstances, maybe it would flush a couple of bugs I've been looking for out of the woodwork. Could be dangerous, though. Maybe you should get me an invitation, and I could show up on my own."

She stopped smiling, sighed a big fake sigh, and looked disappointed. "Oh," she said and frowned. "I think we should go together. I'd feel safe with you there. I really would."

"Well, on second thought, same difference; chances are, no one would try anything with all those witnesses present. Besides, it might just break this case open. And I could use a break about now. If you're sure you feel all right about it, then we're on." I looked at her a moment. She tilted her head and looked up at me. For just an instant, she reminded me of Shirl—a young Shirl, the way she used to look up at me, quizzically, after we first got married. She'd been so young and so beautiful, like this woman. Though still beautiful, and young in many ways, Shirl was no longer the woman she used to be. But I was no longer the man I used to be, either. Who knows? Was it time to move on?

"Okay," I said. "I guess that's settled. Now tell me about your trip to Jordan. How long ago were you there?"

"Let's see. It's been almost a month now, three and a half weeks to be precise. I was only there two days, just long enough to see things identified and catalogued for the bills of lading. I worked on the transport documents and permits and conferred with my counterparts at the Ministry who were responsible for the actual shipping. I watched some of the objects being packed and crated. Then Dr. Eastlake sent me home early, directly after I signed all the appropriate paperwork. He stayed until everything was packed, crated, and shipped. He came back on the same plane with the Jordanian courier, four days later."

"Why'd it take so long? Why didn't you stay? Maybe he had something to do with the old switcheroo. He certainly had the time."

"You think Dr. Eastlake stole them?'

"Not impossible. He was there the whole time they were moving things around."

"Yes. That was supposed to be my job, but he said it wasn't safe for me to be there with the recent Israeli-Palestinian conflicts so explosive, especially an 'immodest young western woman in such a position of authority.' 'Immodest,' that was the word he used. Imagine. He said that he didn't want me to get hurt. I guess that I was attracting a lot of attention."

"I can understand that, especially in an Islamic country. Were the recent Middle Eastern clashes really a problem in Jordan?"

"Maybe, yes. There's this shadowy collusion between stolen artwork, terrorism, and the underground movement of contraband. It crosses every border in the region, especially in times of war. In many cases, the same people are involved. There's also a group of very rich, very conservative businessmen composed of powerful individuals from various Arab countries, which has been at sporadic odds with the Cultural Affairs Ministry this past decade—over letting Jordanian cultural treasures out of the country. They act as consultants to governments in the region, when they can, and work to get their lost cultural heritage returned. They're touchy about the willingness with which their governments have allowed their cultural objects and artifacts to go traveling around the world—especially in view of the outright rip-offs that have occurred over the years."

"Seems I've read something about that. And not just in the Middle East."

"It's worldwide. This group began to move against western collectors and museums, the main markets for which thieves have historically plundered the world's archeological sites. It was rumored that they funded proposals to steal back some of their treasures. They may even have funded murder contracts against some of the more brazen antiquities dealers in Europe and the US. At least, that's the word in some circles."

"I thought that sort of cultural grave-robbing had stopped."

"To some extent. There are new laws and most museums have reexamined their policies and developed new guidelines governing acquisitions, which makes that sort of thing unnecessary today. Many museums are really trying to return their questionable possessions. Even so, there are still many smugglers, unscrupulous dealers, and crooked collectors out there willing to create a booming black-market in stolen art. No doubt, museums are slow when it comes to parting with some of their best stuff. But to be fair, it takes a long time to unravel the threads of an object's history"

"Well, you'd think these business men would be working with their governments, not working against them."

"You would. And now they do sometimes, but they still don't trust the governments. For so many years the governments just let their cultural treasures get lost or stolen. And to complicate things, there's some speculation that this group has roots in Islamic fundamentalism. Some say they're connected to terrorist organizations across the Middle East as well. No one is really sure what their ultimate goals are or how deeply the roots go down."

"Not good. And not to change the subject, but how was this collection shipped to the US? Boat, plane?"

"Chartered plane, which the Getty paid for."

"I need to see all the relevant paperwork."

"Okay, if you keep it confidential. It's big trouble if they catch me giving it to you."

"No problem."

"The documentation's in my office, over in the East Building. All the staff offices are there. We can go later."

"I thought this was your office."

"Oh no, this is just a common-area staging office for the various exhibits that go through here."

"That's good. I thought it was a little dumpy for you. You people have more offices that are not your offices than anyone I know."

"Well, this one has the advantage of being private. I brought us here so we could talk without interruption. I've had the feeling for the past month now that someone has been tampering with things in my office. Nothing I could prove, just sometimes things seemed displaced; it's probably just my paranoia. Say, I could use a cup of tea." She stood, picked up the folder, and walked around the desk. "Why don't we take a walk down to the café cart and the Central Garden before I show you my other office. You really must see Robert Irwin's garden. I go down and sit there at just about this time every day."

"I'd like to see those objects as well," I said and followed her out of the office.

"Oh yes, those too. They're in another gallery on this floor. We'll come back. You'll want to spend some time with them."

There was a group of tourists waiting at the elevator.

"Let's take the steps," she said.

We went through the unfinished exhibition space, stepped over the gallery barrier across the hall, and headed down the stairway. With all the windows and the eggshell color of the enameled panels on the walls, it was as bright and clear as daylight throughout the space, which was a contrast to the dimly lit galleries.

"Not to change the subject again," I said. "But tell me about Dr. Braithwate."

"Well, let's see—what do you want to know?"

"It was her accident that put you up for this trip?"

"Yes. Poor Penny, I mean Dr. Braithwate, had been anticipating this exhibition for some months and was really looking forward to working on this collaboration. She wanted to make the trip to the Middle East."

"Did she and Dr. Eastlake get along?"

"As far as I know. I guess you've noticed that Dr. Eastlake has a manner about him that can tend to be a little—shall I say—arrogant? Dr. Braithwate always found funny little ways to deflate his pomposity, and I suppose he found her infuriating at times. But they had a working relationship and didn't let personal matters get in the way of their duties—not that I could see. On the other hand, he may've detested her, privately, for all I know. For her part, I never heard her disparage him professionally, although I must say we've had a number of good laughs over some foible or other of his personality."

"Would he have had any reason you can think of, any reason at all, to harm her?"

"Oh no. I never sat in on the upper level meetings, so I have no idea if they butted heads, or fought over policy, or whatever. I can only say that I don't think there was any real animosity between them. Penny didn't have an ugly bone in her body. No one would have wanted to hurt her. I just can't imagine such a thing. You don't think someone tried to kill her?"

"Not at all. I'm just following my nose around, to see where it leads me."

She looked at me strangely.

"Well, it's one way to solve this case. And besides, it led me to you—in a manner of speaking."

"Oh." She grabbed an umbrella from the stand at the door, and we left the Exhibition Pavilion, headed for that cup of tea she wanted.

I was ready for a cup of coffee myself. After we left the café cart, we made our way down to the garden. "You know what?" I asked.

"No, what?"

"Those artifacts had to have been stolen."

"What makes you say that?"

"Oh, I don't know. Occam's razor or Murphy's Law—who knows? Maybe it just makes a better story. They say everybody has one book to write. Maybe yours is a murder mystery."

"Oh God, I hope not. Couldn't it be something else?"

"A romance . . . maybe?"

Nineteen

The GETTY WAS AN HOUR'S DRIVE FROM MY PART OF town, and since I was already there, I decided to stick around a while and get a good look at the place. Ronnie had her tea, and I had a latté down in the Central Garden—on a bench under the sycamore yarwoods, where "we could visually meander through the azalea maze in the reflecting pool, or ponder the myriad splendors of Chalk lettuce, variegated Jacob's ladder, and Corkscrew rush," as it says in the brochure. I would've preferred just the regular coffee, but the young woman at the cart was sure that I would like the latté so much better, I just couldn't bring myself to disappoint her. Next time, I get the house blend. Anyway, Mr. Irwin's garden was over the top; I could've stayed there all day.

Afterwards, Ronnie led me up to her real office to show me the paperwork that I'd requested, then back to the Pavilion to see the artifacts. We shook hands and said our goodbyes there. She had work to finish before leaving to meet me later at Universal Paradigm. She told me to take my time and enjoy the artifacts, and that if anyone questioned my presence, just have them call her office. As soon as she left, I sat down in the gallery and made some notes so that I wouldn't forget our conversation. No one bothered me.

On first view, even barring the possibility that they may have been forgeries, the objects in question were less than awe-inspiring—until you considered it possible, however remotely, that these particular things may have been touched by none other than Jesus Christ himself. According to the accompanying legend, they were cups, bowls, and jugs common to the period. The fact that such fragile objects could survive human stewardship that long always mystified me in the first place. I was a skeptic, of course, and didn't see how anyone could be entirely sure that any particular person could've used these very objects two thousand years ago, let alone the Messiah.

Unless, of course, there were irrefutable documents to prove it. I guessed that was what this exhibition was all about, really—the dusty decaying documentation found in a jar, in a cliff, in a cave on the edge of a desert, in some godforsaken place in the Middle East. Scholars, experts, and theologians were going to be all over that one for the next two thousand years. If you really thought about it, a case could've been made for the proposition that with all of the praying and fighting, suffering and dying going on over there, God had long ago forsaken the Middle East—the Christ Almighty's musty cup notwithstanding. Inevitably, these things were just wedges to divide people, just more excuses to keep on fighting and killing. Apparently, the sheer joy of fighting and killing wasn't excuse enough. I left off looking at the artifacts and went out into the fresh air and sunshine wafting the Plaza. I'd had enough culture for the time being. I had to get my mind back on the business at hand.

I went back to the office to check in with Felia, make some calls, and review the notes of my meeting with Ronnie. As usual, traffic was backed up in every direction and moved slower than fishing for bullhead in a bathtub. While I crept along, I thought about our talk. Something bothered me, but I couldn't place what it was. Was it personal? Was it business? What was going on with this woman? I knew it would come to me; it always did. And there was Eastlake. I wanted to be ready when I met him at the party, later that afternoon. I had questions about his Middle East excursion, and the extent of his professional relationship with G. Henry Carl. Felia had returned from breakfast and was deep into piles of files when I entered. There were small stacks of paper and folders everywhere.

"How's it going?" I queried.

"Grrrr . . ." she said, flashing those gold irises of hers at me.

"That well, eh?" I was no fool; I left it there. She was going to be a real porcupine until she'd put every scrap of paper back where it belonged. There'd be no talking to her, no getting past those thorny barbs and needles, none of that chitchatting camaraderie she was usually so free about, unless it was an absolute emergency. I'd started over for a cup of coffee when I remembered we no longer had a coffee machine. I didn't say a word. I did an immediate about-face, went down to the drugstore on the corner, and bought us the least expensive Mr. Coffee I could find. For some reason that I've never been able to decipher, the cheap machines lasted longer and made tastier coffee, without all the bells and whistles. When I put the box on the cabinet in the corner where the old one used to sit, I knew better than to do it. Felia looked up, flashed those irises again, and cooed, "You're not really gonna leave it sittin' in the box like that, are you?"

"Of course not, Bright Eyes." I hopped to, unpacked it, made the coffee, and slipped into my office. She didn't have to tell me twice.

Once out of the line of fire—and being the highly trained professional investigator that I was—I could tell there was something different about the place. It took me a moment to realize, but, aha, there it was. The AC window unit purred like the big ole, re-bored, 396 cubic inch pussycat that idled under the hood of my trusty little 69 Nova SS, and it was cool as a Sno-cone in there. I had just decided that very morning that things had to change around there. And now here they were, beginning to change already.

I sat at my desk and pulled out my pen and notebook. I'd decided to make a list of the things that I knew for certain or could surmise deductively. Not that I didn't have something better to do with my time, but just then, I didn't know what that might be. Sometimes making a list helped me figure that out.

I recalled that Ronnie said she thought someone had been tampering with things in her office. She'd made an appointment to see me and, more than likely, had written it down on her calendar. If it were a desk calendar, someone could've seen it. If that someone were Eastlake (who else had more access to her office than he, especially with Dr. Braithwate out of the picture?), he would've been the bastard responsible for Mustafa and Davie's visit. Could his trip to the Middle East, and the possibility of hooking up with those two thugs over there, have been coincidental? I had other questions for Dr. Eastlake as well, but Felia came in, interrupting my meditations.

"Hey, Boss, I brought you a peace offering," she said and set a mug of coffee in front of me, along with the agency checkbook. "Sorry I was such a bitch earlier."

"Oh, think nothing of it. I guess you've finished with the files?"

"Nope. I just took a good look at myself and decided that I didn't need to let it get the best of me. I resolved to watch my mouth and be a better person."

"Well, that's good."

"I have no excuses for my previous behavior. You can give me a hundred and fifty lashes—right after you finish signing those checks."

"It won't be necessary. I intend to dock your wages."

"Ha, ha. You're a regular Jerry Seinfeld."

"Who?"

"Never mind. People will be coming in all day tomorrow looking for those." She indicated the checkbook. "Every one of those people opted to pick up their checks. It's my guess they'll go, lickety-split, right from here to the bank."

"How's the coffee?" I said, picking up the mug to sip.

"You make a great cup of coffee, Boss. I can only hope that if I study and work real hard, keep my nose to the grindstone, and dedicate my life to your astounding methodology, that maybe someday, like you, I, too, will be able to make a cup of the world's best coffee."

"Say, what was that resolution you just made?

"What resolution?"

"Hmmm, maybe I'll just give you those hundred and fifty lashes you so blatantly deserve. Unless you get back to work, now, while I sign these checks."

"Oh, Master, thank you Master, thank you. You're too good to me." She smiled and left the room.

"I know. Hey, by the way," I yelled after her. She stuck her head back in the door. "When Donny calls in, tell him to pick up his tail outside the underground parking tunnel at the Universal Paradigm building after four today. Ronnie Rivero's attending a party there, and I'm not sure when she'll be leaving. Make sure he understands that he's not to go out to the Getty."

"Universal Paradigm, after four today, you got it," she said and went back to her office.

I signed the checks, then called Bernie on my cell. "Hey Bern, it's me."

"Eh, como estas, Señor Pike?"

"I read the fax you sent me on Mustafa and Davie, and I was wondering if you had any more on their whereabouts."

"Sorry, Nes, nada, not even a fart in the breeze. But say, a little bird did tell me that you spent some time today with a certain young Latina lady. How'd you like the . . ."

All of a sudden, there was major static. He must've been on his cell phone in the car.

" . . . you hear me? I said, how'd you like the Getty?" he said.

"I was informed that it has its detractors. How'd you find out so soon? Where are you?"

" . . . to lunch . . . You forget, they didn't make me Lieutenant Detective for nothing. I assume you're working for her at this point. She's not your type, otherwise.

Besides, Shirl would . . . if she caught . . . —king around."

"Just a little security job. Don't get excited. She's nervous with the Hollenbeck murder so close to home. I keep an eye on her days, and Donny watches her nights, until you catch the bad guy, that is. You gonna do that anytime soon, I hope?"

"I'm working on it. You sound like McCorkle. Speaking of Ms. Rivero, you wouldn't be holding out on me, would you? What the hell am I saying? Of course you're holding out. Just what is it that you're not telling me?"

"You know me, Bern. I tell you everything. I've no secrets from you."

"Yeah, right."

"You know I won't compromise my client."

"You won't compromise this case either, if you know what's good for you."

"I can tell you this, from what I've been able to piece together, I know Eastlake's involved. I just don't know how."

"That's what my evidence points at."

"And what evidence is that?"

"Evidence that I can't share with you right now. McCorkle hit the roof when he found out that you were at the Villa with me while I interviewed Eastlake and Rivero. The Malibu people were miffed, too."

"Go ahead and be stingy, see if I care. You'll be sorry. Oh, by the way, how did you catch the Hollenbeck case? I meant to ask before. No wonder they're miffed. Last time I looked, that was Malibu jurisdiction."

"Believe it or not, they wanted help and asked for me personally."

"I'll be damned. That doesn't sound like Casey."

"It wasn't. Casey's gone, along with Mansfield and

Taliaferro. They were caught poking their chubbies into the various orifices of some sweet, young high school cheerleader in the back seat of a squad car after last Friday night's football game. Haven't you read the papers?"

"Not since last week. I've been too busy."

"Anyway, they're desperate for help over there. Hell, they'd probably even hire you at this point. This is your chance to get an honest job. Besides, this case crosses a number of jurisdictions. We think Hollenbeck was murdered at his place in Beverly Hills. Forensics is going over it for the second time, even as we speak. Oh, by the way, compadré, rumor has it Mankiewitz, that attorney you work for sometimes, went whining to ADA Prudhomme, said you threatened to break both his legs for not paying his bills."

"I'm pleading the fifth. Felia told him she'd send over a couple muscleheads to break his thumbs, not his legs, if he didn't cough up. It was a joke."

"Oh yeah? Well, Mankiewitz isn't laughing. He's threatening to file charges."

"That guy would do anything to get out of paying me what he owes me. Apparently, Felia doesn't like deadbeats anymore than I do."

"I'm surprised she didn't threaten to break his kneecaps herself."

"She threatened to break his thumbs, and she was probably saving the real threat, in case the bluff didn't work."

"Hola vato, going under an overpass, got to . . . " The static came back . . .

"Hey, Bern, Hollenbeck was killed right where you found him, at the Villa," I said. But he was already gone.

Twenty

WHEN I SHUT OFF THE PHONE I COULD HEAR A LOUD male voice in Felia's office. She was screaming back, just as loud. It sounded pretty nasty, but before I could get around my desk to see what was going on, Bobby Chandler burst through my door, into the room, with Felia trying to restrain him.

"Sorry, Boss. I couldn't stop him."

"It's okay, Felia. Let him go."

Bobby shook off Felia's grasp and stood facing me at the corner of my desk. I knew from my investigation that he was thirty-four, six-two, approximately one ninety; he had straight brown hair and freckles, which were splotchy, darker, and heavier across the bridge of his nose. If he'd been lying down, you could've fried an egg on his forehead.

"Mr. Chandler—what can I do for you?" I said, moving around to balance his press into the intimate space of the office.

He threw the large manila envelope he carried onto the desk and stood glaring at me from beside a client chair. The envelope looked to be the same one that I'd given Felia earlier that morning, containing all of the photos and information outlining his recent infidelity.

"You're the asshole that did this to me," he said.

"Watch your mouth, pal." I picked up the envelope and opened it. I took out some of the black and whites and tossed them on the desk one by one. "You caught me red-handed, Mr. Chandler. Yep. I followed you around a couple of weeks. You've been a naughty boy."

"What the hell do . . ."

"Of course, these prints don't compare to those of Ansel Adams, but I think I really captured the flesh and bone reality of the situation here, don't you agree?"

"I don't know who the fuck you think you are, but . . ."

"I told you to watch your language, pal; there's a lady present."

"Hell, she ain't no lady. She's my fucking sister-in-law, who thinks she's my goddamn mother."

"I won't tell you again," I said, as I put the last photo on the desk and stepped in close to get his attention.

"You don't scare me, old man." He pushed his chest out even further than it was, if that was possible.

"That's good. Because I wouldn't want you to wet yourself. You're about to get a beating if you don't cool your jets, rocket-man."

We stood posturing and threatening each other like a couple of schoolboys.

He looked as if he was about to back away, until he changed his mind and came across at me with a right hook. Moving to the side, I grabbed his arm and pulled him along the trajectory of his fist, dropping him across the client chair from which he fell unceremoniously to the floor, on his ass. Unfortunately, it had the opposite effect than I'd hoped for. Embarrassed but enraged, he got up, kicked the chair out of his way, and threw three more unsuccessful punches. My fancy footwork saved me. It appeared that my workout in the ring every week paid off. Meanwhile, Felia was yelling for him to stop and leave, or she would call the police. He ignored her and came at me again.

I dodged the punch and went around him as he struggled to regain his balance. I caught him from behind in a wrestling chokehold that should've put him to sleep. But he backpedaled me into the wall and broke loose. I ducked another wild punch, got in close, and delivered several straight shots to his solar plexus. It took the wind right out of him. He was a novice. It was like shooting fish in a barrel. Pushing him off, I followed up with a right jab, then a left, to his face. I meant to teach him a lesson and flatten his nose. But he moved, and I popped him directly between the eyes, on his forehead instead— damned near broke my left hand, which was still tender from Friday's bout with Mustafa and Davie. That's what I got for playing around with a blowhard. He dropped to the floor, like a hundred and ninety pound burlap bag of rutabagas.

I stood for a moment surprised, watching a large knot begin to grow where I had punched him. He didn't move, but his unseeing eyes were wide open. The knot began to look like a third eye, popping out of the middle of his forehead. Saliva ran from the side of his mouth and down his face. He looked dead. I got down to see if he was breathing. He was holding his breath, but finally gasped for air. Thank God. The last thing I needed was another accidental killing. Prudhomme would extradite me clear to Texas, just to have me executed by lethal injection at state expense. That, or I'd never see the light of day again.

"Would you look at that, Felia," I said, standing up. "He's out colder than a mackerel."

"Too bad you didn't break his damn neck while you were at it."

"I don't know. From the size of that goose egg, it looks like I might've broken his skull."

"Too good for him. He ought to be in the hospital, with every bone in his body broke into tiny, little, teeny-weeny pieces for what he did to my sister."

"Ah well, sometimes we don't always do what's right, or know what we're doing to those we care about."

"Oh yeah? Well, he knew what he was doing, all right. He's nothing but a cunt-hound."

"Felia!"

"Well—he is!"

"He may be, but . . ."

"He doesn't care for anybody but himself. If you only knew . . . but I don't want to go there. He makes me so angry I could just spit. Say, are you okay? Your knuckles look a little red and puffy there."

"I know, I'm fine. I just mean that we shouldn't be too quick to judge another person, since we haven't lived in that person's skin, is all I'm saying. I'm not trying to justify his actions. But he's not a criminal. It's just that sometimes we've got to make our mistakes."

"You'd think, though, by the age of thirty that he'd have some kind of handle on it."

"Yeah, you'd think so."

"But not him. Nah, he's just an asshole. He doesn't make mistakes; he creates disasters. He's put Mandy through some hard times, not to mention the kids. He deserves what he gets and then some, as far as I'm concerned."

"Well, maybe you're right. Just don't let it get to you."

"Not a chance. He's not giving me any grief, the bastard."

I spared her the blatant contradiction, but at the moment, unconscious or otherwise, I thought he appeared to be dishing a little grief all around. "Say, how about getting us some ice from downstairs? My hand's beginning to swell almost as much as that apple on his forehead."

"You've got it, Boss." She was already moving to the door.

My hand was throbbing. I tried to shake off the pain. I moved over to the desk and took out the pint of Early Times that I'd picked up at the drugstore when I went down for coffee, after those two thugs had ransacked the place last night. They'd stolen what was left of the other bottle stashed there. That was low, destroying a man's possessions, then stealing the last drop of his consolation. I knocked back a short snort. I remembered my meeting with Ronnie Rivero at the Getty later. And I wanted my wits about me when I talked to Eastlake. I put the bottle away, walked over to the window, pulled the blinds, and looked out on the city.

Well, here I was again, all roughed up from a bout of fisticuffs that I didn't ask for, or want, twice within a week. The place was a wreck. It was all just part of the business, one of the risks a PI ran every day. Mine was one of those confusing and dangerous professions, where I was constantly called out to take responsibility for my actions, and a mistake could cost me a life. On the other hand, months went by, a little footwork here, a little interviewing there, some consulting, easy stuff with nary a hint of violence. A day filled with peace is how I preferred it, not the way this happened. I was a peaceful man at heart. I liked peace. I liked long afternoons in the library, tracking down information I needed from the stacks, with an occasional cup of coffee outside in the sunlight. I liked using my gun for practice—shooting at the range, and not for killing. But I wouldn't change my life, even though sometimes it seemed to run in one of its downward cycles. If I had to take someone out and there was no other way, so be it; but I never went looking for it; and it never gave me pleasure.

The traffic out on the boulevard was not running at all. Cars and trucks sat like strings of beads, from one light to the next. When the lights changed, people were lucky if three vehicles moved through an intersection that was jammed from the other direction. When were they going to settle the MTA strike so things could get back to normal? I wondered the same about my life. When was it going to get back to normal? Since Friday, it had picked up speed, raced downhill toward some unknown disaster, and I wasn't in control. Even though La-La land appeared laid back and easygoing, there was an edge about life here in the city, in this time, and with the people who moved through it, clogging its arteries. Maybe this was normal. Sometimes when I sat down to clean the Magnum, I could see that edge as something to master. The smell of cleaning oil reassured me that there were things to be done, which put me in control. There was no situation that I couldn't think my way through, a case I couldn't solve. I just had to trust the process, follow the routine, and let the inspiration flow. But I must've liked it; I kept looking for that adrenaline rush.

Normal or otherwise, it appeared that I was nonviolent, until it came to the violence itself. Then I was all over it, like a sugar glaze on a cinnamon roll. I liked sugar glaze on cinnamon rolls, and I liked the violence when it was necessary to like the violence. Make no mistake. Sometimes there was no other choice; violence was necessary. Inside, it made me hard, shiny, untouchable, and cool as a low rider cruising the Sunset Strip. It was part of me. I was comfortable with that. And I was good at it. Humans were a complicated proposition every time, and it was not wise to underestimate them. You took things slow, not for granted. You didn't set your speed on cruise control within city limits. It left no options when things went awry. A person never knew what he could become on any given day, in any given circumstance. Maybe that's what got me out of bed in the mornings.

Bobby Chandler began to come around. I went back and picked up the chair. I helped him off the floor and sat him in it.

"Ow! Damn that hurts," he said, as he tentatively touched the tennis ball between his eyes. "What'd you hit me with?"

I showed him my fist, which looked like his knot.

"Serves you right. How long have I been out?"

"A couple of minutes," I said, as Felia came through the outer office.

She carried a small plastic bucket of ice, some of it already rolled up in a towel, which she handed to Bobby none too gently.

"Thanks," he mumbled and stared down at his feet, unwilling to look at her.

"You don't deserve it, you bastard."

"Hey, fuck you, Patty Porter. This whole damn thing's

your fault. If you'd stay the hell outta our lives, maybe we wouldn't be having these problems."

"Why you good for nothing . . ." Felia started to smack Bobby with the ice bucket. I got between them.

"Hold it right there, both of you," I said. "And Felia, pick up that ice before it melts all over. Now listen up, pal. I'm not telling you again. Next time, I'm putting you in the hospital."

He glared at me, slid down in his chair, then held the ice pack to his head, wincing as he did.

I sat on the edge of my desk, took the bucket from Felia, and put it in my lap. I eased my hand into the ice. I was glad it was my left, because I'm right handed with most things.

I looked from one to the other. "Well, what have you got to say for yourselves?"

Neither one spoke. They just glared at each other.

I set the bucket down, reached over with my good hand. I took the pint from the top drawer and handed it to Felia, who looked surprised. She rarely looked surprised.

"Take a shot at that," I said.

"I don't want any."

"Don't argue with me. I'm not in the mood for this." She took a small sip.

"Take another," I said. "Good. Now give it to him."

Bobby took it and belted down a respectable shot. He appeared grateful, as he handed it over to me.

"Now. I want to know. Are we all feeling better? Have we got this little fit out of our systems? Because if we don't, there's going to be hell to pay. I've got other things I need to be doing right now, and they don't include the both of you. Felia, haven't you got some work to do in the other room?"

She looked at me, and I could see the gold flecks of her irises narrow, then soften at the edges.

"Well—the files," she said. She looked again at Bobby, then me, nodded once, turned, and went back to her office.

"Now you. Is there anything else you want to discuss with me? You still think you can kick my ass, young man? You want to give it another shot? If so, let's settle it right now."

"You're a real tough bastard, aren't you?"

"You bet your ass I am. I've had lots of practice. So, what's it gonna be?"

He shook his head.

"Good. You want to go to the emergency and have that looked at?" I pointed to his head.

"I don't think so," he said. "But I would like to know, just what right you've got messing around in another man's personal life like that?" He pointed the icepack at the pictures on my desk.

"Someone asked me to. It's what I do."

"Yeah, and I bet I know who that was."

"It doesn't matter, does it? One way or another, your life's about to change big time, sonny boy, whether you like it or not. It's up to you if that's going to be a good thing or a bad thing. Think about it. You've got a couple of sweet young kids at home. You have a great job at the network, and a woman who loves you—at least that's what Felia tells me. Look, I'm not telling you how to live your life . . ."

"Yeah, right."

"Shut up, I'm not finished. You're a man at the crossroads. At your age, you need to look ahead and see where you want to be when you get to be my age—if you're lucky enough to live that long. At this rate, tough guy, you won't get there unless you start in that direction right now. It's your life, pal. You can make something of it, fuck it up, or lose it all, whichever you choose. Nobody gives a rat's ass. And I mean nobody, except maybe Mandy and the kids. Take it from me, dickhead. They're worth a lot more than you can afford to lose. I know what I'm talking about. Now get the fuck outta my office. You make me sick to my stomach, and I've got a party to go to."

Twenty-one

THE FIRST I SAW OF RONNIE RIVERO, AS I CROSSED THE lobby, was her three-inch spikes. Standing next to the big granite desk, her Betty Grables traveled first-class, all the way from the floor up into a black, shoulderless eye-magnet that only managed to conceal her pretty little keester by two or three inches. Clinging to that killer body, the dress was pure three-dimensional erotic art. The second thing I saw was Buddy Palmer standing next to her, with his back to me. Talk about the descent from Nirvana into the realm of the graceless . . .

They were talking. What was wrong with this picture? At the moment, I couldn't tell. But for some odd reason, it irritated the piss out of me. Buddy wore a light-gray silk suit, the price of which could've paid off my second mortgage. He knew how to pick threads, I'll give him that. Other finely dressed and festive partygoers were standing about in small groups, or moving between them. They grazed off hors d'oeuvre trays of shrimp and paté, and slurped up their colorful libations from the open bar spread beneath the mammoth Calder that soared above them, out in the center of the space. As I approached, Buddy broke away from his conversation with Ronnie and turned to greet me with his usual grimace.

"What is it, over five years? I go along minding my own business; I don't see hide or hair of you. All of a sudden, you show up two days in a row. What are the odds of that? And in a suit, too. I'm beginning to think that I'd slipped into a parallel universe and didn't know it."

"Not a chance, Buddy-cakes," I said. "It's a dream. When you wake up in the morning, we'll be gone; and all you'll have left is your teddy bear and a hangover."

He stuck it out there, so I shook it. He lost the finger-crushing contest yet again. Nestor Pike, two. Buddy the Palm, zero. I don't know why he bothered.

"So what happened to your other hand there? Looks like you been working the bag too hard."

"You always did have a sharp eye, Buddy-boy. Nothing gets past you."

"That's right. That's why I'm the boss around here. Speaking of jobs, all our vacancies have been filled. So what can I do for you this time, old pal?" It seemed to me that he laid an undue and less than flattering emphasis on the word old. "Don't tell me you're here for the party. You gotta have an invitation for this shindig. I don't remember seeing your name on the guest list."

"Oh, didn't she tell you? I'm Ronnie's date for this affair." I moved over and put my arm around her shoulder.

"Well, well, aren't you the lucky man? I had the good fortune to meet her myself, just now, before you arrived. Ms. Rivero." He nodded to her. "By the way, I thought you were married," he said to me, while looking at her, the bastard.

"Oh I am," I said. "Whatever you do, please don't tell my wife. She would never understand."

He looked up at me then back to her. She raised her eyebrows, snuggled a little closer to me, and smiled at him.

"If you'll excuse us, Ms. Rivero, I'd like to speak with my old friend, Mr. Pike, a moment." He overstressed the old again. It was beginning to wear thin. He took me by the elbow and walked me out of earshot. I went reluctantly. "So, Pike the staff, I gotta ask. Are you two—you know?" He made an obscene gesture that only I could see.

"C'mon, Buddy. You know me better than that. I don't kiss and tell . . . like some people might."

"Okay, so don't tell me; I don't want to know, anyway. But you've got the look of a man . . . Never mind. I gotta tell you, if you're packing a heater, I'll have to ask you to leave."

"Moi—packing? You stab me to the heart, Buddy, old chum, old buddy. Now why would I need reinforcements at a party like this? If I wanted to kill you, Buddy-boy, I'd do it with my own bare hands for the pure sensual pleasure of it." I held them up to show him. "They're lethal weapons. But hey," I said, dropping them. "I'm just here to network, look at the art, hobnob with my betters . . . say, nice threads." I reached over and fingered the silk of his lapel.

He took my wrist between his thumb and forefinger and lifted my hand off his suit. He held it away from him and let go, as if he were dropping a piece of trash into a can. "Then you won't mind if one of my associates pats you down?"

"Not in the least. Shall we do it right here, in front

of everybody, or would you like to take it somewhere a little more private? But I gotta ask first, and tell me the truth. I'll know if you're lying, you dog you. Did you pat Ms. Rivero down, before I got here?"

"Are you kidding? A blind man could see there's nothing hidden in that dress."

"Yeah, but tell me the thought didn't give you some cause for pause, Bud ole boy." I smiled, though I really wanted to smack him in the teeth.

"It went through my mind. So what? Do I look like I need Viagra to you?" He grinned back and glared over at her with what might've been lustful eyes; although with Buddy, it was always hard to tell what his expression concealed. Then he stared hard at me. "Would my man find anything?" he asked.

"Nope." I raised both arms straight out from my sides, like wings, giving him a full shot.

He just stared at me. "Never mind. For a moment there, I'd forgotten that you didn't like carrying ordinance."

"I don't dislike it—but are you sure?" I said and raised my arms a little higher.

He shook his head.

"Well, if you change your mind, you know where to find me."

He turned back to Ronnie and raised his voice. "Ms. Rivero, it was nice meeting you. I hope to see you again some time." He raised his hand but didn't wave.

"Mr. Palmer," she said and smiled.

He nodded, turned back to me, and whispered, "That little number's gonna give me wet dreams for a month." He grimaced and stomped off toward the elevators. He stopped and looked back. "You can put your arms down now, you dink." He wasn't smiling when he left this time either.

"So, Mr. Pike," Ronnie said, as I flapped my arms over to her. "What was that all about, if you don't mind my being so nosy?"

"Nothing really. Buddy and I go back a ways, and . . . well, it's a testosterone thing, I guess. I hope you didn't think me too forward a moment ago. Thanks for playing along."

"Oh, not a problem."

"Another testosterone thing?" She pointed at my injured hand. "Are you a disaster magnet? I hope you didn't get that because of me?"

"Oh no, another matter all together. But yeah, I guess it was testosterone, now that you mention it."

"Well, I'm glad it wasn't any worse than it is and that you made it here after all. I've got to say, you're looking very attractive this afternoon."

"And I'd have to say that you're about the best looking woman in the place."

"Thank you. You wear that color very well. It goes nicely with your bruises."

I was wearing my soft, sand-hued, single-breasted linen, and a pair of dark chocolate, calfskin loafers. Shirl had insisted that I have the suit made for my birthday, just before Nathaniel was killed. I wore it to his funeral, even though it wasn't black, because he had told me how much he liked it on me. Chullsu Kim had a friend in Koreatown who was an excellent tailor; I'd gotten a deal. I hardly ever wore it now, though it was the only suit I owned that wasn't a cop suit, out of date, or shiny in the knees. It fit great and looked new, and gave me a certain rakish quality, I thought.

"So, this doesn't look to be much of a party, although I've got to say that the harpist makes a nice touch," I said. "With all the stone surfaces and high space, it sounds like an echo chamber in here."

"It is nice, isn't it?—but this isn't the party," she said. "This is just the prelim, to soften you up for the real in-fighting upstairs."

"Oh, I see. Well, before we go up for the main event, would you like a drink?"

"A Harvey Wallbanger would be good."

"They still make those? You must be older than you look."

She shifted her beaded bag to her other hand, punch-ed me on the arm, and looked at me as if I had just dropped a barbecued cocktail weenie into the punch bowl.

"Be right back," I said.

A half-hour later, we stepped out of the elevator on the twenty-fourth floor into an elegantly appointed throng filling the gallery space. This elevator was an express and made no stops on the first twelve floors. Right after we got off, a rosy complexioned all-American linebacker in a white waiter's jacket, black bow-tie and slacks, the uniform of the evening, walked up to me.

"Mr. Pike?" he said.

"Yes."

"Would you come with me—please?"

"That depends."

"Mr. Palmer would like a word—sir."

"Oh, of course." I glanced at Ronnie.

"Will you excuse us, Miss?" he said. "This won't take long."

"Hold the fort, Ronnie," I whispered. "I'll meet you over by that Picasso as soon as I'm done with Applecheeks here." I left her standing by the elevators. "Lead on, McDuff."

He led me around the corner into a small, windowless office off the main space. Inside was a desk, a small file cabinet, a water cooler, and another door. Buddy was not present when we arrived, but another of Buddy's "waiters" was sitting on the corner of the desk waiting for us. He stood up as we came in. This one was the color and build of Evander Holyfield, but lacked the champ's good looks and winning personality. He kept tapping his thigh to some internal rhythm with one hand, like he had a ferret loose in his pants that was about to get the best of him, while trying to hide something in his other.

"With your permission, sir, Mr. Palmer said we should pat you down," Rosy the Beefcake said.

"You feel confident that you can manage that feat all by yourselves, do you?"

All of a sudden, he began to sweat. I had never before seen drops of perspiration literally pop out of the pores on someone's forehead. The twitch by the desk shifted his position and squared around to face me. "It looks that way to me, sir," he ventured, brave soul that he was. "Unless you'd like us to ex-cort you down to the loadin' dock in the freight elevator out back, and throw you in a dumpster."

They were polite; I'll give them that. I paused a moment, eyeing them both before I spoke. "Then by all means, let's have at it," I said, and raised my arms out to my sides.

Pink Cheeks didn't flinch. But first, he looked surprised and then relieved. He made one swipe across his face with the sleeve of his jacket and just stood there. The jitterbug had either gotten it together, or strangled his ferret—he appeared to relax.

"Well—you gonna do this or what? I haven't got all day," I said.

Although the Rose Man was a tad slow off the block, he was thorough. He started at my ankles and moved up my legs, while the black guy lit a smoke and sat back down on the desk to supervise.

"Touch me there again, sweetheart, and I'll blow in your ear," I said. "Then you'll have to marry me."

"Sorry sir; just following orders."

"Ahhh, you disappoint me, Grasshopper. That's what they said about ethnic cleansing in Bosnia."

He wouldn't look me in the eye, but his rosy complexion got rosier by the moment.

I couldn't see the camera that I knew had to be concealed somewhere in that room without going into a big search for it. But I could just imagine Buddy sitting in his office, gleefully slapping his knee at putting me through this little inconvenience, just trying to irritate me, get under my skin some. Buddy had always liked his immature little games. It was fortunate that Ronnie had agreed to hold the Magnum in her bag for me. When this hunch had first crawled up the back of my neck, down in the lobby, as much as I hated to, I had gone into the john, unclipped the piece from my belt, and then slipped it to her, just before we got on the elevator. At this point, I felt somewhat naked. I intended to retrieve it the very moment I found a spot that was not directly viewable by a security camera.

186

"Thank you, sir," he said. "Enjoy the party." He stepped away from me and opened the door.

"You bet," I said. "Are we cool?"

He nodded.

"Good. You can tell Buddy for me . . . never mind. I'll tell him myself."

The black guy yawned, belched, and then stabbed out his cigarette. From the smell of it, he must've been eating sardines with cocktail onions on his Limburger and toast points at some time during the festivities.

"Hey, nice bridgework there, Beaver Breath," I said, as I sauntered past him to the door.

"Hey, fuck you mothafucka," he said as the other guy caught his elbow and stood between us.

I let it slide. At the moment, I was trying to decide just what I wanted to tell Buddy, or if I wanted to say anything at all. To be honest, I was a bit surprised at my own reaction to this little charade. I hated to admit it, but he had gotten under my skin—a smidgen. His cavalier attitude toward my client irritated me. And he knew that I was carrying to begin with. If he didn't want me there, why didn't he just throw me out? The two ham hocks he'd sent over to frisk me might have pulled it off, although I didn't give them very good odds on it.

Maybe it was G. Henry Carl who didn't want me there. Did he even know who I was? Maybe Buddy sensed that I could be unpredictable, if he'd proceeded against me too blatantly. Maybe he knew someone could get hurt in the process, and that it might bring down some unwanted publicity on Universal Paradigm. That was all Buddy needed, another unexplained accidental death over here. By the looks of things, some important people were there, and it wouldn't do for Buddy to call too much attention to the proceedings. It was my guess that Mr. Carl would not be pleased.

So now, I felt better. Buddy was squirming. Good. I was a thorn under his leathery tanned hide. Even better. Unless he got downright hostile and threw me out, he was forced to endure it for the time being, while I got to enjoy some really fine art. And God knows what else I might get to enjoy while I was up there. So without further delay, I was going to start with Ronnie Rivero, standing right over there next to Mr. Carl's second rate Picasso. I guess when it comes right down to it, in some ways, Buddy and I were not all that different. We both had an accidental death on our hands, we were both married men, and I was also having impure thoughts of a sexual nature . . .

Twenty-two

THE PLACE WAS BUZZING. SOMEWHERE OUT OF SIGHT, A string quartet was whipsawing Mozart and somehow blending into the predominant undertones of gossip, hearsay, and bold-faced yarn-ripping. People of every conceivable description were swimming about in small pods, ravaging the tables already sparse with food and beverage. Servers and bussers were cruising the feeding frenzy like remora scavenging for scraps. The entire twenty-fourth floor had been divided into a number of free-flowing, interconnected galleries, just like the MOCA downtown. Unlike the MOCA, however, there were large potted guavas, fichus, and figs randomly placed throughout. They lent an earthy appeal to an otherwise sterile, though undeniably artistic, environment. Serious twentieth-century fine art—that's art with a capital "A," especially the conceptual stuff—rarely tolerated such intrusion, organic or otherwise, to the sanctified domain—except as a matter for irony, much like some of the people who collected it.

When I rejoined Ronnie, she was standing next to

189

Yeager Eastlake and a small group of people, none of whom I knew. She seemed to draw a crowd wherever she went. Of course, in that dress, it was a no-brainer why. On the other hand, about half of her little group looked to be gay. They all stood about in sophisticated poses under the dissolute gaze of one of Picasso's least successful pipe-smoking Musketeers, who was also, I fancied, dismayed at their indifference to his expressive, if not entirely cubist, presence.

"Dr. Eastlake, just the man I want to see," I said, as I dove right into the middle of this little pool of fine art aficionados—sending ripples of disdain and condescension throughout the tableau. Nothing like the trusty old cannonball to make a few waves in a stagnant pond.

"Mr. Pike, isn't it?" he said, but refrained from offering his hand as he turned to me.

Was that a sneer or just a little dyspepsia? I hadn't known Eastlake long enough to tell. "You remembered," I said.

"Well, it's an unusual name. Is it not?"

"Yes, I suppose. It's not your regular Smith, Jones— or Yeager Eastlake."

"Touché. Very good, Mr. Pike. Allow me to introduce you. Everyone, this is Mr. Pike, a member of our worthy LAPD."

Was that a tinge of sarcasm I heard, especially in view of the past Ramparts investigations and revelations concerning the LAPD? As an ex-cop, even after five years, I was still a bit touchy when someone disparaged our men in blue—although some of those men, too many really, didn't deserve to wear the uniform. "No, I'm sorry Dr. Eastlake," I said. "I'm no longer a cop. I'm just a private citizen, a private detective, actually."

"Well, gentlemen, ladies, it seems that I'm in error. Excuse us, please," he said, taking me by the elbow and guiding me a little ways apart from the group. What was with this elbow thing? First Buddy and now Eastlake. "Did you not tell me you were with the Police Department the other day?"

"Oh no. I apologize, if we gave you the wrong impression. I believe Detective Maldonado introduced me as his colleague. And that's true enough. I was acting as a friend and consultant."

"I see. Then, are you here in that capacity today?"

"No. Actually, I'm here as a guest, to browse the collection and congratulate you on your accomplishment with the upcoming exhibition."

"Oh, I see, and yes, thank you. It was so good of you to come."

The sincerity of his last statement was, of course, suspect, since he had basted it rather liberally with the oil of sarcasm. On the other hand, maybe he'd sensed my own small slick of insincerity, which I'll admit, bordered on being an outright falsehood.

"But I didn't realize that you had an interest in the fine arts, Mr. Pike." He appeared distracted and glanced around the room as he spoke. Was he looking for someone special?

"Oh yes, a keen interest, for some years now. In fact, my wife's a painter of some promise, and I was hoping that you could spare me a few moments so we could talk about such things. There are several questions I'd like to ask you."

"Of course, there's nothing I like better than speaking with someone who has 'a keen interest,' as you say. But you really need to talk with my administrative assis-

191

tant out on the hill. Call the office. She's in complete control of my calendar." It didn't take a professional to know he was pulling the old dodge.

"I was thinking, you might give me a few minutes today, before you left. Shouldn't take long."

"Normally, I'd be more than happy to oblige you, Mr. Pike. But as you see, I've got my hands full. We have visitors from out of the country. Mr. Carl is due any moment. The evening agenda is full. No, I'm afraid you'll have to speak to Greta. She's a real stickler about keeping track of my time."

"Oh, I sympathize, believe me. I know exactly what you mean. My girl's just the same. Hell, I can't even step down to the toilet to take a crap without passing it by her first." He looked up, sharply. I guess that I'd finally gotten his full attention.

"You're not really interested in discussing the collection, are you, Mr. Pike?"

"Well, no, not really. Although, I would like to get your take on that Musketeer over there. It's from Picasso's last period, the early seventies—his dotage, I believe." I flashed him my pearly-whites.

He looked at me a moment. "What is it that you really wish to discuss, if I might ask?"

"To be honest, I was interested in your trip to the Middle East. Ms. Rivero tells me you sent her home early and had to manage everything on your own. Must've been difficult for you, without a qualified registrar to help out?"

"Well, of course. But the Ministry was very accommodating. Furthermore, pedant that I am, I'm not completely without skills or experience in these areas. I've been around a long time, Mr. Pike."

"Oh, far be it from me to suggest that you are, Dr. Eastlake. I'm just wondering what you would say if someone were to tell you that some of the more important items that you brought back from Jordan were outright forgeries. Could the Ministry have made a switch on you?"

He looked like he was about to have a heart attack.

"Absolutely impossible," he piped out, loud enough to draw heads in our direction. He lowered his voice. "Why, that's perfectly outrageous. Where did you get such a scandalous idea?"

"Oh, a little birdie I know was singing outside my window." For a moment, I thought he was going to croak on the spot. His jaw dropped open. "Hey, lighten up Doc," I said. "That was just a little joke." His tan seemed to fade slightly. He was going white around the gills. I didn't think he'd take me literally.

"Having me on, were you? You have a depraved sense of humor, Mr. Pike."

"What can I say? Nobody's perfect. But seriously, I've been thinking about what you said the other day, about why the Jordanian government would allow some of its most precious possessions to leave their country. And I thought, what if they didn't allow it?"

"Well, it's not uncommon for governments to send reproductions. That's what the Egyptians did with Tutankamen, once they realized the enormous risks they were running with the original artifacts. We could have made such an agreement with the Jordanians, but we didn't. We had prior contracts that gave us the right to study and display the originals. We held them to their word which, as you may know, isn't quite the same thing culturally to some people in the Middle East that it is to us."

193

"If true, then consider the influence such primary and holy Christian relics give to an Islamic State. Maybe they decided to circumvent the contracts, send forgeries . . ."

"Please, stop using that word. We prefer the term, reproductions. It's less inflammatory."

"Okay, reproductions. They could blame you when the real artifacts were discovered missing, as they were sure to be someday. And they could legitimately seek restitution through your insurance company, which is who, by the way?"

"That's really none of your business, Mr. Pike. Although I'm sure, it's a matter of public record at this point. The Getty uses several firms, though it's not my place to discuss such business with you."

"I believe your primary underwriter on this matter is Universal Paradigm—correct?" When he just stared at me, I smiled at him. "I can get that from another source," I said.

"As I told you, Mr. Pike, I shan't discuss it with you. And don't ask the sum they were insured for. I wouldn't tell you anyway. Look here, Mr. Pike, your snooping around can get people in trouble. If Ms. Rivero has been speaking out of turn and spreading rumors, I won't be the only one to see that she's firmly reprimanded. She could be drummed out of her profession for good."

"Ms. Rivero had nothing to do with this," I lied through another smile.

"This is no laughing matter. Have you any idea what these accusations could mean? No, of course you don't. It's no skin off your nose. Reputations could be shattered. But then, maybe you do realize what's at stake. I'm beginning to think it would be unwise to underestimate you." Just then, there was some cheering and applause. The string quartet quit playing. Eastlake stopped dead in his tracks and looked across the room, then back at me, hard, as if to memorize the face of his most hated adversary. "Now, Mr. Pike, if you'll excuse me. Mr. Carl has arrived, and I think you've wasted quite enough of my valuable time with these unwarranted and potentially slanderous speculations. I suggest you keep them to yourself from now on and let the matter drop, before someone gets hurt."

He turned abruptly and walked back to the group. He whispered something to one of the men; they excused themselves and left together. Ronnie Rivero, who had been half-heartedly talking with another of the men standing there while covertly watching all this, quickly made her way over to me.

"What was that all about? I think you've upset Dr. Eastlake. I've never seen him so . . . well, so out of himself. He gave me such an evil look."

"It was all very interesting. That was Carl, right?"

She nodded.

"Say, who was that Eastlake left with?"

"That was our esteemed visitor, Geshur Kedar, the Cultural Affairs Minister from Jordan. And the woman who followed them was his wife, Yasmine."

Geshur Kedar was dark complexioned, of medium height, and had no distinct facial characteristics. Though a trained sleuth, I would've found it hard to give the cops a good description of him, even if he had just murdered his wife right there in front of me. He was just that nondescript. She, on the other hand, was unforgettable. She was just that homely. And her dress was either an ultra-chic, retro-fashion statement, or horribly out of touch with the times. Such distinctions were sometimes hard to make in our post post-modern era. I could've been wrong, but I opted for the latter.

"How about the black gentleman?" I said.

"Oh that's Bel, Belvedere Whiting, of the Whiting/Harper Galleries, which I'm sure you must be familiar with. And the man next to him, dressed in charcoal, is his primo bean counter and partner, Bruno Harper."

"Dealers."

I'd been in every art gallery in LA at one time or another over the years. These two had been around longer than most, and dealt the less trendy, more classical stuff, including Greco-Roman antiquities. If memory served, I'd seen some miraculous Etruscan bronzes at their space, down in Venice Beach, some years earlier. Bel Whiting was a tall, elegant African-American with a café-au-lait complexion. Highly polished, deftly manicured, and wearing a dark-blue Armani, he spoke with an upper crust British accent whose authenticity fell suspect when it occasionally landed on my ear, above the din of the room. It was my guess that there was more Louisiana than London in his pedigree. His sidekick, Bruno, was an authentic, silver-haired fireplug of a man, if I ever saw one.

"The big guy, who was hitting on me earlier, is Raleigh Hanson."

"Ah, so that's Raleigh Hanson. You say he was hitting on you? How's that possible? I thought he was gay."

"He's bisexual, actually. He always hits on me. He hits on everybody."

"Why do you put up with it?"

"It's no big deal. It's our little ritual. He hits on me.

I laugh and call him a pig. Then he laughs and tries to wrestle me into submission, but I always win. C'mon, I'll show you."

We walked over to where Hanson was standing, holding an empty glass and looking bored to tears with Whiting and Harper. He was tall, tanned, squared-jawed, and blonde. He appeared to have just come from a photo shoot for a modeling spread in GQ, although he wore a blue blazer and an ascot, an outfit I hadn't seen on anyone since the sixties. He had one of those faces you couldn't help but like immediately, with a smile so charming it could've gotten him laid in a monastery. It was my guess that he was not used to hearing the word no, unless it came from Ronnie. It was also my guess that it wouldn't be too long in the future when that would begin to change. He appeared to have had a few too many. Whiting and Harper thought so, too. They turned and fled, as if someone had just cut the cheese, when Hanson said something that I couldn't hear, right before we got there. They disappeared into the sea of humanity that washed back and forth across the room.

"Hey, Raleigh, I'd like you to meet a friend of mine," Ronnie said, as we walked up to him.

He handed her his empty glass. She put it on the tray of a passing waiter.

"Nestor Pike," I said, as I reached out and shook hands with him. The grip of his monster hand, I hated to say, was a real bone-crusher. It looked as if I was going to lose the Grand Lizardship Finger Crushing Title to this drunken upstart, until he took pity on this poor flipper of mine and turned it loose.

"So, Mr. Pike, tell me," he said. "Where'd you meet our saucy little hot tamale here?" He finished mangling my good hand with his right, massaged my right shoulder with his left, and moved over to put an arm around her shoulder. But she was fast and deflected him before he could get a real grip, even though he was a veritable octopus.

"You pig," she said.

His laugh was a bark. He thoroughly enjoyed it. "You think we can get another drink around this place?" he said, pulling away and scanning the room with some sort of internal alcohol detector.

"No doubt," I said. "I could use one myself." I looked around for one of those waiters with a tray of bubbly that I'd seen earlier.

"Now you're talkin,'" he said, really looking at me for the first time with those red-rimmed eyes of his, as if he'd found his long-lost drinking buddy. "Wha' kinda work you do, Mr.—ah . . ."

"Pike, Nestor Pike."

"Where the hell d'you get a name like that?"

"You wouldn't believe me if I told you."

"Tha's kinda fishy, you ask me . . . Pike, fishy, get it?" He almost doubled over in mirth.

We just looked at him.

"What a coupla sore heads. Where's your sense of humor, man?" he said, after he caught his breath. "Never mind. Hey, either one of you guys know where my dear fren' Cap'n Eastlake went? He just jumped ship . . . 'thout saying a word . . . We were supposed to . . . Never mind. Say, I thought we were gonna get us another drink. You guys, stay right here. Don't move, okay? I'll get 'em. What'll you have Chiquita—a banana daiquiri?" he said and laughed aloud, again. "No, seriously, tell me what you want—besides me that is." He couldn't contain himself over that one. His laugh was infectious. I almost lost it myself; the joke was so stupid. "Okay, enough. I'm done. What'll it be?"

She just looked at him a moment.

"Well?" he said.

"Surprise me," she said finally.

He surprised us both. He left. Without warning, he walked over, got into an elevator just before the door closed, punched the button, and never looked back.

"You'd better come with me," I said, a moment later.

"What?"

"I said, come with me, young lady." I grabbed her by the elbow and started to drag her to a corner. She couldn't move real fast on those heels of hers.

"Ow!"

"Sorry."

"Where're we going?"

"Over there behind that fichus. You've got my piece, and I need to have it—right now.

"Why, Mr. Pike, I'm flattered. But this is hardly the time or place . . ."

"The Magnum, sweetheart, the Magnum."

"Oh."

"I think I just saw Ahmed Emil Mustafa standing in the back of that elevator talking to Alfred James Davie."

"Ahmed Emil who?"

"Never mind, Missy. Just give me the gun."

Twenty-three

"WHERE ARE WE GOING?" RONNIE SAID AGAIN JUST moments later, as I dragged her around the corner toward the little office where the two "waiters" had frisked me earlier.

"Ah, Señorita, you keep asking the same weighty, philosophical, and ultimately unanswerable question," I said. "It ranks right up there with 'Who are we?' and 'Where'd we come from?' At this point, all I can tell you is that the game's afoot, my dear Rivero." We ducked into the office, out of sight.

"The what . . ."

I grabbed her and covered her mouth. I crossed my lips with a finger and shushed her. "The bug," I whispered. "I don't want them to know we're in here, if we can help it." She nodded, and I let her go. I began to check out the room for the surveillance equipment that I knew just had to be there. After a minute of silent searching, there was no camera and no bug. Either Buddy wasn't as paranoid as I thought he was, I was more paranoid than I thought I was, I was losing my

201

touch, or all of the above. Well, either way, surprise me. I took the holster with the Magnum out of my coat pocket where it was making a big, unsightly bulge. I clipped it on my belt, at my back where it belonged. I was dressed again.

"Okay listen, Ronnie," I whispered as I sat on the edge of the desk and pointed her to the chair next to me. She sat. "I just saw the two guys who gave me these lumps, in the elevator; at least I think I did."

"They beat you up in an elevator?"

"No, they came to my office last Friday afternoon and beat me up. I think they were in the back of the same elevator that Raleigh Hanson got on just now."

"Oh."

"I didn't see if it was it headed up or down. Did you happen to notice?"

"No, sorry. Hey, why are we still whispering?"

"I don't know," I spoke out loud. "I also think that it was your case they didn't want me to take. When you made the appointment with me, did you tell anyone?"

"Of course not, I didn't want anyone to know what I was thinking about doing."

"Did you write it down where people could find it?"

"I put it in my appointment book, which I keep in my desk while I'm at work. My office is always open. It didn't occur to me that anyone would be looking through my stuff."

"I thought so. Did you write down both appointments, or just the one you canceled?"

"Just the first one."

"Then, theoretically, they don't know you hired me. They must've assumed that you kept the first appointment. That's why they came to see me. Have you told anyone?"

"No. Before I made my first appointment with you, I asked my brother, Ramón, if he knew of a private detective I could hire. I didn't know who to go to. He said I should just look in the phone book, but then gave me your name a couple of days later."

"Did he say how he got it?"

"He didn't say, and I didn't ask. He just said that somebody told him you were good."

"All right. Unsolicited testimonials are the best sort of advertising. I love it."

"Hello. Can we stick to the subject here? What are we going to do about these men? Are they looking for me or you?"

"I have no way of knowing. I don't think they saw me, so I'm guessing they don't know I'm here—unless someone told them I was. I doubt they would do anything with all these people about, but you can never tell. They might try to use the crowd as a cover, but I don't think so. Either way, we don't want to take any chances that we don't have to. Are you parked in the garage downstairs?"

"Yes."

"Too bad. Which level?"

"Two."

"They'll probably be down there lurking about, waiting for you to leave—unless they're looking for me. In which case, they'll have a harder time of it. I parked down the block. I didn't want to be trapped downstairs if I needed to leave in a hurry."

I went over to the door and cracked it open. I wanted to see if anyone noticed us leave the party. Ronnie stood up to follow me. There was no out-of-the-ordinary activity, no one looking in our direction. I closed the door.

203

"Guess who I just saw," I said.

"I have no idea—Bruce Willis?"

"No, Raleigh Hanson."

"Raleigh Hanson?"

"The one and only. He's holding three drinks and standing there looking totally mystified." I opened the door and looked out again.

Ronnie came over and peeked. She smelled terrific up close.

"He must've gone all the way to the lobby for those drinks," I said.

"Why would he do that?"

"I have no idea. But do you think you could get him to escort you down to your car?" I closed the door again.

"No problem. He'd follow me anywhere."

"I guess you could say that about a number of guys . . . Hell, I'd follow you myself, if I wasn't already spoken for."

"That's so sweet of you," she said, looking up at me. She looked sad.

I wondered what that meant. Some days a man could be sorely tempted. For a moment, I thought she was going to kiss me. In fact, I wished that she had—until I thought better of it. I was flattered to think that maybe she had feelings for me, casual as they might be. They would, however, have to go unrequited forever or, at least, until Shirl gave me the old heave-ho permanently. As it stood, all Ronnie and I could ever hope to have between us would be pure, hot, unbridled, passionate, tender, raunchy, meaningless sex—but who knows? Some days a man could be sorely tempted, sorely tempted indeed. "Okay," I said. "As much as I hate to suggest it, it would probably be the wise thing for you to get

Raleigh Hanson to take you down to the garage."

"Aren't we going together?"

"Together, you and I attract too much attention. And that's just what we don't need right now. Grab Raleigh, wait until an elevator's almost full, and then go with the crowd. I'll keep an eye on you to make sure that you don't get on with the wrong people. It wouldn't do for you to take the ride with Mustafa or Davie on board. Make Raleigh see you to your car. If you have to, promise to meet him somewhere. When you get down to the garage, make some kind of excuse and leave him. Then go home and stay there. Lock your doors."

"What if he or somebody else follows me?"

"Don't worry. Nobody will follow you that I don't want to follow you. You won't see me, but I'll keep my eyes on you." I didn't tell her that those eyes were actually Donny Mack's eyes. She didn't need to know that yet. I was hoping that he'd gotten the message I left him with Felia, to pick Ronnie up here as she left the party. I had good people. I would've already heard something if Donny weren't going to be there.

"Are you sure that I can't go with you?"

"At the moment, I don't want to risk getting you mixed up in something between me, Mustafa, and Davie. We have to get out separately. But have no fear; I'll be close. And like I said, I'll keep my eyes on you. Now get going before Raleigh decides to pull his disappearing act and leave us again." I looked out the door to check on him once more. Raleigh was talking to a young woman who had taken one of the drinks off his hands. He was in his element. He had a doting audience of one, and a drink in each mitt. "Oh no, Raleigh's found another woman. Well, I'll be damned. That's Inga Braden."

"Inga who?"

"Braden, Buddy's secretary. She told me she quit her job just yesterday. I wonder what she's doing back here. There goes our plan, if you can't get Raleigh's full attention."

Ronnie just looked at me as if I was having a senior moment.

I slapped myself on the forehead. "Of course, silly me. What was I saying? He'd have to be a dead man." On the other hand, and I didn't say this in front of Ronnie, Inga was not without considerable charms and assets of her own. This was going to be interesting. The smell of cat was in the air. I watched Ronnie cross over to them. I made a mental note to get out more often for a little girl watching. I'd forgotten what sheer pleasure it could be to witness a well-structured, purposeful woman putting her moves into motion. It only took forty-seven seconds for Ronnie to displace Inga—who made an airy gesture with her hand and just sort of sauntered away, looking as if Ronnie had just tossed her from an airplane without a parachute. I know, because I timed it. I watched them for another minute, until she had maneuvered Raleigh around the corner into a small group of people waiting near the elevators. He was clay in the hands of a master. As they moved out of sight, I followed them around the corner to make sure the elevator was clear. When they disappeared inside, I went back to the office, making sure no one paid any attention to me. Inside, I took out my cell and punched up Donny's number.

"Donny Mack here."

"Where are you?"

"Hey, Chief. Believe it or not, I'm parked just two

cars from your Nova, watching the tunnel to the parking garage. How's the party going?"

"Great. The champagne's bubbly. The caviar's black. Everybody showed up; we've even got Mustafa and Davie prowling the premises."

"You need me to come in? I can be up there in five minutes. Besides, I've got a score to settle with Davie."

I knew just how he felt. "Actually, Donny, Ms. Rivero's already on her way down. I wanted to alert you, so you could run interference if someone tails her. Stay close, and don't let anyone get between you."

"Aren't you leaving with her?"

"I thought I would snoop around up here a bit, if you think you can keep her out of trouble. I'll see that she's safe until she's mobile, then you've got her. Right?"

"Right."

"If it looks like you've got a problem, or nosy strangers in tow, call me back immediately. I'll join you. Got it?"

"Got it."

"And let me know when you get her home safe and sound, right?"

"It's as good as done."

That was a load off my mind. Donny was a good man. Some day he was going to own RD DA. I loved that boy like a son.

Twenty-four

I POCKETED THE CELL, TOOK OUT THE MAGNUM, AND checked the load. This baby was ready for anything. Back into the holster it went. From the crack in the door, everything appeared clear; nobody took any undue interest. This room was already checked out, except for the second door, which was on the opposite wall from the gallery. No time like the present. Ronnie was already on the move. So was I—through the mystery door and into the small warehouse area full of crating, shipping, and storing materials. This crazy desire to stop and search through the empty crates, boxes, and everything else tugged at me. But time was of the essence, and who knew what to look for, if anything. That half-used roll of strapping tape and the razor knife on the workbench, in the middle of the area, looked as if they might come in handy. Into my pocket they went.

Huge racks held large paintings along one wall. They begged me to rummage through them. But hell, I hadn't even had a chance to rummage through the collection of paintings and sculpture hanging in the galleries. Better luck next time. On the other wall, an extremely large set of double doors that opened, I presumed, directly into the gallery was locked. The party was popping full blast on the other side. The sound vibrated through the crack between the doors. At least they wouldn't be coming at me from that direction. At the far end of the room, the industrial-sized freight elevator—the very one old Beaver Breath had threatened earlier to give me a ride in—stood open, beckoning me. I knew it had to be close.

The elevator took me down to the loading dock area—at the lobby level, in the back of the building—without a hitch. Before opening the door and getting off, I looked out one of the glass slots to try and find the surveillance cameras. Unless there was another hidden in a blind spot, that one was the only one in sight. It was placed with a full view of the loading dock and doors. Several large crates and boxes cluttered the area, and a small forklift sitting on the dock blocked access to the loading doors. Only a couple of work lights were burning; the main overheads were off. From where I crouched in the elevator, the area was silent and appeared deserted. Everybody should've been gone for the day. I checked my watch. Yep, five-thirty. I was on a roll. But just then, two armed-security men in uniform came in through the doorway to the stairwell. Apparently they were on rounds because they took a leisurely inspection tour over the area with their flashlights and stopped to call in an all clear to their control. They proceeded back through the stairwell doors, the way they came. My time was running out, and Ronnie was probably already down in the parking garage.

I lowered the grate and slid the big doors open as quietly as possible. Keeping to the walls in case of motion-sensing devices—not that that would really be of any help if there were any activated—made me feel like the professional snoop that I was. Potential alarms were either silent or had not been tripped. Over at the stairwell door, and peeping through the safety glass window, I spotted the camera on the ceiling above the railing, in the center of the stairwell, focused at the door. The red light glowed.

The camera was watching, so it was a gamble. The odds were better than fifty-fifty in my favor, with security clearance just now called in, that the surveillance man upstairs was not bothering to follow up and check his visuals. I cracked the door wide enough to listen for the guards. All clear. It was against the law to lock a fire exit during business hours, but it was after hours. Better safe than sorry. A couple strips of tape over the lock slot in the doorframe prevented the door from locking behind me. No sense closing any avenues of escape, if it came to that. After cutting more tape, I slipped into the stairwell, climbed the railing, and taped off the lens of the camera as quickly as possible. If the camera jockey looked now, all he would see would be the opaque light through the strings of the strapping tape. It would appear to be a malfunctioning unit, a maintenance problem, nothing more. If he had seen me, then the jig was up, and Buddy's goons would be all over me like a nest of ants on a monkey carcass. There was no time to worry about it. I went down the stairs to the second level, where Ronnie had parked her car. At the door to the garage area I didn't stop to look through the safety glass window before pushing on through. A disgruntled Raleigh Hanson caught me in both arms as I ran into him at full throttle. He let go of me, stood back, and brushed at his blazer.

"Oh, Raleigh Hanson! I'm sorry," I said. "I didn't

expect you there. I was in a hurry to find Ronnie Rivero. Have you seen her?"

"It's Pike, isn't it?"

I nodded.

"Yeah, Pike, I just left the dizzy bitch—oh, sorry. I forgot she was a fren' of yours. She's over there." He pointed down to the end of the row of parked cars. It was really too late, although I'd gotten there just in time to see Ronnie back the little red Mazda Miata out, and drive up the ramp at the far end to the first level. No harm done. She was alone, which suited me just fine. I dodged several cars and ran down to the end of the row to watch. Her car switched back one level up and zipped out the exit tunnel at the opposite end, only pausing long enough to flash her taillights as she went. She was in Donny's hands now. And there was no sign of Mustafa or Davie. I was lucky. They were involved in some ugly business elsewhere at present, no doubt. Had they really been upstairs in the elevator? Must've been them. No time to start second-guessing myself now. What the hell would they be doing here? I'd have to get to those questions later. Right now there were more pressing matters at hand; I had to find them first. There was nothing left for me down here. I did a quick surveillance of the area and headed back to the stairwell adjacent to the elevator. Raleigh was still there, waiting for me.

"Ah, Mr. Hanson, on your way home? Did you enjoy the party?" I walked past him, toward the stairwell to the loading dock and the freight elevator that would take me back upstairs unseen.

"For a while there, it looked to be better than it turned out. Are you goin' back up?" He fell awkwardly into step beside me.

"Well, to be honest, I don't think I've decided just yet," I said, as I stopped and faced him.

He stopped and looked back at me. He had a strange sort of sparkle in his eye.

Until now, he hadn't been included in my immediate plans, which were still formulating in my devious little brain even as we spoke. The gallery, storage areas, and G. Henry Carl's quarters up on the twenty-fifth floor were just screaming out for me to give them a good tossing. But I certainly wouldn't be able to do that with him tagging along, unless he had some personal influence in the situation, and could take me into Carl's quarters with him. I didn't know if Raleigh was connected that well or not, but Carl did own that big sculpture of his up in the lobby. And Raleigh, Mr. Personality Plus, just might have a way into the inner sanctum that I hadn't considered. But even if he could open the door, it probably wasn't a good idea to have him there. He was sure to cramp my style. I wouldn't get much in the way of in-depth snooping done. I decided to play it by ear. At least it didn't hurt to move in that direction, until things proved to be otherwise. "What about you?" I asked.

"Oh yes, yes, of course. It's still pretty early, and I'm completely free . . . well, that is until about ten. I have a late dinner engagement with Yeager, I think. But until then, Nestor—it's Nestor, right?"

"Yeah, that's right. But call me Nes."

"Okay. Until then, Nes, I'm all yours."

"Why, Raleigh, if I didn't know better, I'd swear you were hitting on me."

"Well, Nes, what makes you think—" He hiccuped. "—you know better?"

Twenty-five

"**A**FTER YOU," I SAID AS THE ELEVATOR DOORS SLID open. As we rode the elevator back up to the lobby, I wasn't sure that I wanted Raleigh Hanson standing behind me in his condition. People I didn't know, standing too close at my back, made me nervous. I think it had something to do with being a shamus, but I hadn't really given it all that much thought. It was that old saw about always sitting with your face to the door and your back to a wall. Raleigh seemed like a nice enough guy, but you never knew about people these days. And I hadn't forgotten that Maldonado was looking at him as one of the prime suspects in the Hollenbeck murder. I reached over and hit the button for the lobby, which was already lit up. Whoever used this elevator last had hit every button up to the twelfth floor, as far as it went. It was a local. We both faced the doors.

"I was sorry to hear about Carter Hollenbeck's death," I said.

"Oh? I wasn't aware that you knew Carter," he said as the doors of the elevator bumped shut. "And I knew

215

everyone Carter knew." All of a sudden, he didn't appear to be quite as drunk as he had earlier.

"Well, I didn't really. But I knew what a fine crusader he was for the programs out at the Getty; I think he'll be missed out there."

"Damn right he'll be missed," he said and looked sharply at me. "That bunch of pompous, sycophantic, backstabbing assholes deserves what it gets without him. Hell, he was the heart and soul of that place."

I was a bit surprised at his vehemence, so I turned to face him. "It sounds like you really miss him?"

"I do miss him—more than you'll ever know, Pike." I wondered what had happened to his calling me Nes. "Yes, Carter and I had our differences at the end . . ."

"What do you mean?"

"Well, we lived together a number of good years. I don't want to sound corny, but we were devoted to each other, despite what you may have heard to the contrary. I have no idea what you think of homosexual relationships—and frankly, I don't give a shit—but Carter and I were soul mates and life partners, and we would still be together today if he hadn't gone off the deep end, there at the last."

He stopped a moment as if recalling something unpleasant. I didn't want to interrupt.

"The only reason I left is because we couldn't stop fighting. I was afraid that he was going to get hurt. He was pushing my buttons, day in and day out. He became impossible. If things had gone on that way, we might've come to blows. At our age, that's not only unseemly, it's dangerous. As big as I am, and as frail as Carter was, I might've hurt him—by accident. That's when I left, shortly before he found out about his mother's estate."

Ping.

The elevator door opened on the first level of the parking garage. Raleigh appeared oblivious to everything around him. He just stood silent and turned to stare forward. When I could see there was no one waiting, I punched the lobby button again and continued. "There was some talk that that is why you left him in the first place, because his money ran out."

"Yeah, I know. But I don't care what they say. I know it's not true—and more importantly, Carter knew it. That's all that matters to me. Hell, I have money, lots of money. Carter wouldn't take it. We fought over that as well. He was trying to change the ground rules on me after all those years."

The door slid shut.

"Well if that's true, what's all this business with Ronnie Rivero and Yeager Eastlake?"

"It's really none of your business, Mr. Pike—but since you're a friend of Ronnie's, and you seem like a nice guy, I'll tell you anyway. It's just a game with Ronnie and me. Sure, I'd sleep with her, if I got the chance. And she really had me going today. I thought for sure . . . but never mind, it doesn't mean anything. She knows that. I know that. And now, you know it. I guess that's why we never have and probably never will. Maybe that's why I can say I will, if I get the chance, because there's really no chance of that ever happening. But Yeager and me is another thing. We were together for a while years ago, and now he's my friend. He knew about Carter and me, and respected our relationship."

"What about the others?"

"What others?"

"Well, you know—you have quite the reputation for getting around town."

"You mean sleeping around town, don't you? So fucking what? What are you, the cock patrol? Who I sleep with is my business. Carter and I had things worked out to our own personal satisfaction, and I don't see that anybody else matters. But, just so you know, since you've been decent about things so far, there were no others. Well, not many, anyway, over the years. It's mostly hot air and innuendo, which I can't say that I mind entirely. It certainly doesn't hurt the sale of my sculptures, if I'm known to be a little . . . well, outrageous in my behavior. If anything, it seems to drive sales up, especially when the gossip columns get hold of it."

"You're right. It's none of my business. I only bring it up because the LAPD is looking into those matters in connection with Carter's death, and I can tell you, without speaking out of turn, you're topping the list of suspects."

"Tell me something that I don't know, Mr. Pike. It's all pretty easy for you, isn't it?—standing on the outside, looking in through the frosted glass. You think you know what you're seeing, but there're no details. You can't see what's really there because you're not on the inside, where it counts. Carter and I loved each other. I was hoping that he would come to his senses, so we could get back together. I don't know why I'm telling you all this."

"I guess you've got to tell someone. It may as well be me. Besides, I'm a good listener. I know what it's like to lose somebody close."

Speaking of close, I wondered just how close Buddy Palmer was to all of this. I didn't want to think about what he was going to make out of it, if he was listening in. At this point, I wasn't sure of just what Buddy could see or hear. He had thrown me earlier, with that clean

218

office upstairs. The elevator may have been clean, but I doubted it. I tried to take a quick look around without disturbing Raleigh, or letting him know what I was doing. I didn't see anything. If Buddy was listening in, he was certainly getting an earful.

"Now I find out that Carter was dying of cancer," Raleigh continued. "He was trying to push me away. He had a tumor in his brain the size of a golf ball. It made him erratic, gave him all these crazy ideas. He never told me. He didn't want me worrying over him. But I knew something was wrong. I thought it was Alzheimer's . . ." Raleigh's speech halted. He stopped abruptly and took a handkerchief from his pocket, sucked it all in, and wiped the traces of emotion, the budding tears, the anxiety, everything from his face. His expression grew hard, chiseled into sharp relief on his already sharp features. He leaned in close and whispered, "Listen Pike, I'll give you ten thousand dollars if you'll find the bastard who murdered Carter. And when you do, and prove it, I'll give you another forty thousand dollars—to kill the motherfucker."

Ping.

God, I hoped Buddy didn't hear that. If he did, he was a witness to Raleigh proposing a contract for me to off someone. Worse still, it was probably on tape. That kind of leverage could get ugly. Buddy's got some nasty clutches. And I didn't want to get tangled up in them.

The elevator door opened on the lobby, where a group of departing revelers waited to get on, apparently headed for the garage. This elevator didn't go to the top; it was headed down. We got off and walked over to wait for an express up to the gallery. Just as it arrived, Raleigh turned to me.

"Look Pike, I think I've had enough for the evening. So, if you don't mind, I'm going to leave you here. It was nice to meet you. Maybe we'll see each other again sometime. Sorry about unloading on you like that. I don't normally do that to perfect strangers . . . . You are perfect aren't you?" He winked at me and laughed out his big barking laugh, and once again seemed more inebriated than he had previously been in the elevator.

"Not by a long shot, and don't worry about it. If you want to talk, call me at this number." I offered him one of my cards with just the name and number on it. I didn't want to tell him that he'd probably done enough talking for the rest of his life, considering everything he'd said in the elevator. Contracting murder was a felony, the last time I looked.

He took the card and stuck his other hand out. I shook it. He won the Title without even trying. I didn't give him much of a contest. My heart wasn't in it. He crossed the lobby, paused a moment at his sculpture, Man Walking, and lit a cigarette. Then he left the building through the Santa Monica Boulevard exit. I don't know why because I had no evidence, but it occurred to me that Raleigh's big sculpture, however large and abstract, might've been a portrait of Carter Hollenbeck. For some reason it looked better to me now than it had earlier.

Ping.

Turning back to the elevator just in time to see the doors close, I decided to skip the direct approach and sneak up to the gallery the same way I came down. Besides, all signs of my previous excursions through the nether reaches of the building needed to be eradicated before someone caught on to me. When it appeared that no one was looking in my direction, I moved nonchalantly over to the stairwell doors and, after checking through the glass, ducked inside. The red light on the camera was still burning. I climbed the railing and pulled the tape from the lens, jumped down, and slipped inside the loading dock area. The odds on being seen were definitely not as good for me now as they were, although everything was where it should be, as it was left earlier. I took the tape off the doorframe. So far, so good—still no alarms. Across the loading dock to the freight elevator, I hit the button to return to the gallery warehouse upstairs.

Five minutes later, I returned the packing tape and razor to the table from which I'd borrowed them, straightened my jacket, and pushed through the door into the little office.

Surprise! Rosy the Beefcake and his sidekick, The Twitch—the same two guys who had frisked me earlier—were standing there waiting for me. I knew they were looking for me because Beaver Breath was holding what looked to be a Colt Special Combat pointed in my general direction. Pink Cheeks spoke into a walky-talky.

"He's here . . . just came in. Standing at the door . . . yes sir." He turned it off and clipped it to his belt. "Have a seat, Mr. Pike."

I held my position at the door. I wanted to keep as many options open as possible.

"The boss wants to see you, before we escort you out of the building," he said, smiling a nasty little smile. "He'll be right in. I've got to say, Mr. Pike, it looks like you been a bad boy, squirreling around all over the place," Somehow, I got the feeling that he anticipated giving me a few more lumps, as if I didn't have enough already.

"Well, you see, boys," I said and closed the door, "I've got this mad thing for elevators. What can I say? I'm absolutely crazy about 'em. I can't get enough of 'em. I get the chance, I ride 'em till I drop. I'd ride an elevator sooner than any carnival ride you can name—God's honest truth. Hell, I'd even rather ride one than a roller coaster. Now that big heavy-duty freight elevator sitting in there was just more than I could pass up."

They looked at me as if I had just deleted my operating system. "Yeah, right. Don't worry, Mr. Pike. Me and Marvin here are gonna give you that ride we promised you earlier."

"Oh goody. I can hardly wait," I said. I could hear the string quartet's muffled playing through the door. The party was still in full swing, but it didn't look like I was going to be attending, much less do any snooping around upstairs. Damn, I did want to see some of that good art before I left. But the jig was up. Time to cut my losses, if not the cheese, and get my ass out of there. I had to start thinking fast; Marvin's ferret was on the loose again and looked to be headed in my direction.

"My frien' Tommy said for you to sid-down," Marvin said as he came toward me. He was about to prod me into the chair by the desk with the Colt. Big mistake. I admit—I'm very touchy when someone attempts to push me around with a gun. I probably overreacted. Just as he raised the gun, I turned and grabbed his wrist, angling the weapon at the floor, nearly breaking his arm in the scuffle. It went off—without warning. The slug hit him in the top of the arch of his foot. He started screaming and fell to the floor, tearing at his shoe. I probably broke his finger in the trigger guard when I twisted the piece from his grasp as he fell. He grabbed his shoe, then started rocking his foot back and forth. It seemed that he couldn't make up his mind whether to rock, tear off the shoe, or try to straighten out his finger. Blood was beginning to puddle over the floor.

"Uh, uh, uh," I said, leveling the piece at Rosy who'd been a teeny bit slow on the uptake. Caught dead in his tracks, he stood and glared malevolently while his ears and neck flushed scarlet.

"Damn, that's got to hurt," I said. "Tsk, tsk, tsk, it looks like Beaver Breath's gonna need a little foot surgery."

Buddy burst in through the door. "I just heard a gun," he said. "What the hell's going on in here? Oh shit!" He spotted Marvin writhing around on the floor.

"Marvin here had a little accident while helping me to my seat," I said. "Can you believe it? This damn thing just went off as he was showing it to me." I pointed it at Buddy.

He flinched. Got him. I let him sweat a second or two before I crossed over to him, took the clip out of the weapon, and emptied the chamber. Rosy, the Grease-Ball, looked like he wanted to kill me. I suppose he did.

"Here, take this. I've got plenty of guns of my own," I said, and handed the empty Colt to Buddy. I tossed the clip across the desk and onto the floor behind it. "You'd better call 911—and by the way, I'd get a tourniquet on that leg of his; Marvin's loosing some serious blood there." I went to the door, looking back at Buddy, who just stood there with his mouth wide open.

"Oh, and don't bother about me," I said. "I'll see myself out."

As I closed the door behind me, Buddy yelled. "Hey,

Pike, call me tomorrow. Mr. Carl would like to meet you."

I didn't stop to answer. I just managed to catch an express to the lobby and left the building, just like Elvis: "Thank you, thank you, very much."

Twenty-six

WHEN I LOOKED AT MY WATCH, I COULDN'T BELIEVE that it was only quarter after seven. It had been a long day, especially since I hadn't slept well—folded like a pretzel across my desk the night before. Every day this week had been a long day. Hell, it had been a long week, and it was only Wednesday. By the time I left the Universal Paradigm building, the adrenaline had worn off; sleep or no sleep, it felt as if reality was about to cave in on me like shoddy construction. I was tired of the art world. I was tired of people, their petty problems, their noise, their posing, and their neediness.

Even though I hadn't had much to drink, the champagne had given me cottonmouth. I'd forgotten to drink water and felt dehydrated. My head ached. My feet hurt. All the puffing, chin music, and knuckle dusting of the past few days had caught up with me and were giving me fits. I hadn't taken a painkiller all day because of the fuzzy side effects; they made me too groggy. And although it was after seven, the day hadn't cooled much. Sweat soaked my shirt down the middle of my back—not to mention that the dirt and stink of the street took its toll. I'd had enough for one day. What I needed was a shower, a stiff bourbon, and time alone in my cool, dark grotto to put things in perspective. An all-out, no-holds-barred, dead-to-the-world, thirty-minute nap wouldn't hurt either. And that's where I was going.

Unfortunately, there was no going anywhere. When I got to the car, it was sitting at the curb with tires as flat as a couple of single cheese pizzas with no pepperoni. Someone had knifed the rear wheels. What were the odds that the perp was someone connected to Buddy Palmer, the Arabs, or Mustafa and Davie? For all I knew it could just as easily have been one of the McFeety Brothers seeking vengeance. It was anybody's guess. For that matter, there were even pretty good odds that it was simply an unrelated random act of violence, and I would never know who did it. Hell, even in the best of times—these were by no means the best of times—LA was meaner than shit. None of the surrounding vehicles had flat tires, however, so I jumped to the depressing assumption that it must've been some asshole that I'd crossed earlier. More than likely, though, it was someone connected to this case.

After the truck picked up the Nova in Westwood and towed it back to a tire shop close to my place over in Hollywood, it was already quarter to ten. They were closed, of course. I'd have to call them when they opened in the morning and order some new tires put on. In the meantime, I was on foot. As I checked my watch, it occurred to me that Raleigh Hanson was probably on his way to his late dinner engagement with Yeager Eastlake. In this case, it reminded me that I hadn't eaten anything since the party. And even then I hadn't eaten much. I took out my cell, used the pre-programmed speed dial and ordered Mu Shu Pork, egg rolls, and Won Ton Soup to be delivered to my place. I gave the tow truck driver one of those colorful, new-style Andrew Jacksons to drop me off on his way back, hoping to get home before the food got there. It was that or call a cab and wait for it.

My place was a large, high-ceilinged, one-bedroom with wrought-iron filigree on the lift and balcony, situated on a side street across from Paramount Studios, just off Melrose. It was on the top floor of an old, three-story, eighteen-unit Mediterranean-Mexican Rococo style apartment building called the Villa Pancho. When we arrived, I could see lights upstairs in my living room window. I had the truck driver go past and drop me down the block. As usual, Melrose was busy. The traffic was a low howl that could still be heard in the middle of the block, buzzing like cicadas under the foliage, though this was a pretty modest and quiet middle-class neighborhood. As I walked back along the dark street, I kept to the grass at the edge of the sidewalk in the shadow of the trees, preferring silence to the sound of footsteps on pavement. The adrenaline was beginning to flow again. Was it déjà vu, or reruns of my previous night? The punks, whoever they were, had decided that rousting my office wasn't enough. Now they had to do my place over as well.

I wasn't in the mood for this—on second thought, maybe I was. It was a black mood, getting blacker by the moment. Now that I thought about it, it was the perfect mood for what I contemplated. As I approached the front of the building I could smell the sweet fresh-cut grass on either side of the walk, Nelson, the maintenance guy, had finally gotten around to cutting and watering the lawn. I didn't stop to admire his handiwork. There wasn't much to see in the dark anyway. I drew my piece and checked the cylinder again. They weren't getting away with it this time—not if I had anything to do with it.

They might've expected me to come in from the rear of the building where I parked my car. On the other hand, they might not have expected me at all, especially if they were the ones who had slashed my tires. But there was no way for me to know that.

I took my time. I stopped and crossed the street where I had a better angle from which to see up into the windows. So much for that, the shades were drawn and I couldn't remember if I had left them that way. I watched a couple of minutes anyway, just because—and sure enough, a shadow crossed the window once, then back again. My mood got blacker. Until then, I had cherished the slim hope that maybe I'd left the lights on, or that they, whoever they were, were already gone.

Well, there was no time like the present. Besides, my food was due any moment and it was better when eaten hot. I crossed the street back to the fence, pushed through the wrought-iron gate, and moved up the walk—took the portico steps two at a time, keyed the entrance lock, avoided the noisy elevator, and took the carpeted stairs to the third floor. A light bulb was out at the end of the hall, just down from my apartment. How long had it been like that? Mr. Rostopovich in 6B, two doors from mine, an elderly, kind-hearted widower, had made cabbage soup for dinner. He always made it on Wednesday; I had a standing invitation to try it out. He swore by it; said with his glandular problem, it was the only thing that helped him keep his weight below three hundred and fifty pounds. One learns to tolerate the smell, if not to love it. I tiptoed down the creaky old hall to my door as quiet as possible and tried to look through the peephole. Ah, there was the little scrap of duct tape I'd forgotten that I kept over it on the inside, so peepers like me couldn't see in.

Across the hall and one door over Mrs. Spencer—who always reminded me of Colombo, with that glass eye staring off in all directions—had her TV blaring full blast. She was a widow, hard of hearing, and kept it on for company twenty-four hours a day. She was watching Murder, She Wrote. I could just make out Angela Lansbury's sing-songy speech patterns through the door. The sound would give me away when entering my apartment. There was nothing for it. Who had time to stand around all night, hoping for a lull in the action?

I slipped the key into the lock and turned it ever so quietly. Just as it clicked over, someone on the other side pulled the door open, jerking it out of my hand.

"C'mon in, Nes Honey. Quit playing detective out there, and put that thing away before I take it away and shoot you with it."

"Damn it, Shirl! You almost gave me a heart attack—not to mention that I could've shot you."

"You wouldn't shoot me. You love me too much."

There was no arguing with that. "But Jesus H. Christ, why didn't you tell me you were gonna be here?"

"I wanted to surprise you . . ."

I threw my hands up in the air. "Okay, okay, okay—so what're you doing here, Shirl?" I said as I holstered the Magnum, closed the door, and flipped the lock behind me.

"What does it look like, Handsome? I was waiting for you. Forgive me?"

What it looked like was a black satin teddy draped over some serious curves, but in my fatigue I might've been dreaming. "Okay, I'm easy," I said. "I forgive you."

"Good, I'm glad. And I'm glad that I came. Cause you always turn me on in that suit." She plastered herself against me, then kissed me as if she hadn't seen me since The Beatles hit the charts with Sgt. Pepper's Lonely Hearts Club Band. She pulled away, looked up at me, and smiled the smile of the innocent, though she was anything but. Then she left me adrift in a cloud of Shalimar and sashayed back into the living room. My fingers tingled in the memory of her flesh, and the static in the fabric that just barely hid her matching panties, which flashed seductively above her long, graceful legs.

"So how'd you know it was me?" I said as I followed her in, took off my jacket, and went to the bedroom to change my clothes.

"I heard you coming down the hall. I'd know your pussyfooting around anywhere."

"Oh yeah? Well I guess that old carpet out there has seen better days."

"Maybe so, but you've just got a distinctive way is all."

"I see. Okay—so what's with the getup, Shirl?"

"What getup?"

"You know what I mean."

"Don't you like it?"

"What's not to like, but—kinda looks like you're planning on sleeping here tonight."

"I wasn't planning that far ahead, but since you've invited me—I accept."

I didn't have to be in the room with her to see those

big wide eyes and that mischievous little grin of hers. I could hear them in her voice. "Now listen to me, Shirl . . ." Just then the buzzer to the intercom went off in the entryway.

She spoke into the blower on the wall, paused for an answer, and yelled back to me, "Did you order something from Panda Palace? It's here." She buzzed the delivery person into the building.

When I rejoined her in the living room, I was wearing a pair of shorts and T-shirt. I wanted to eat before I took my shower. I noticed the large painting hanging over the sofa and the other one on the wall next to the kitchen, neither of which I remembered seeing when I came in.

"Were those hanging there when I arrived?" I asked.

"Of course."

"What're they doing here?"

"I thought you might like to have them. They certainly do brighten up the place."

"You've been a busy woman, haven't you?" Why the paintings hadn't filtered into my consciousness before now was beyond me. I must've been more beat than I thought, or I'd been so busy ogling Shirl that I couldn't see anything else. Those two paintings were the only two things hanging on the walls. Obviously, they were Shirl's. They weren't bad either, but I liked my space sparse.

"Well, what do you think?" she asked.

"I think—"

Mu Shu pork arrived with a resounding knock at the door. Famished, I went out to the entryway, lifted the duct tape off the peephole, and checked for some shiny black hair and almond-shaped eyes. I paid the young man and brought dinner back into the kitchen.

Shirl joined me there. She had put on her knee-length gown. "Say, that looks good," she said, watching me open the cartons.

"Would you like some?"

"Are you sure? I know you weren't expecting company. What are we drinking?"

"You'll have to settle for some tap water on the rocks." I found a half bottle of brandy that I'd forgotten Shirl left here some time ago, to go with our fortune cookie for desert. We split the food onto plates and sat down to eat in silence at the kitchen table. When we finished, she got up, took the dishes and silverware, and put them in the sink. She ran water over them.

"Why don't you leave those," I said. "Bring the bottle, a couple of glasses and come sit down."

"I'll make some decaf first," she said.

"Since when do I keep decaf in there?"

"I brought it with me."

"Oh." I left off with the sparkling after-dinner conversation and went into the living room. Before I sat down, I looked around the room. With those paintings hanging there, it seemed smaller than it ever did. It seemed like a different room, not my place anymore. There was the same old comfortable sofa, the same old overstuffed chair, which was not so comfortable anymore, and the same old ring-worn coffee table. There was a prehistoric, black and white, thirteen-inch TV that I never used, sitting on a set of stacked metal TV trays, looking forlorn against an empty wall. The room that had looked so cavernous with so little stuff in it, now seemed jammed to the rafters.

There was a time when I would've preferred it another way. But now, putting paintings on the walls seemed like an outlandish extravagance of the soul. No one deserved such beauty, light, and happiness. The idea of hanging artwork, even something by Shirl, felt somehow like a betrayal to my memory of Nathaniel. Weird as it was, it made me angry. Or maybe, I was just worn out and everything looked darker, meaner, and smaller than it actually was—including me.

I plopped down in the overstuffed chair to wait for her and fell asleep. The next thing I knew, she was sitting on the arm of the chair next to me, sipping her coffee, and gently running her hand over my head. She whispered something about putting me to bed so that I could get some real sleep. Just then, my cell rang. I sat up in the chair, rubbed my eyes, took the cell out of my pocket, and cracked it open. Shirl got up and went in the other room.

"Yeah?"

"Chief, that you?"

"Yeah!"

"You sound different."

"What is it, Donny?"

"You sound so loud. Are you all right?"

"Yeah! I just woke up. What do you need?"

"Ronnie Rivero gave me the slip."

"She what?"

"When she got home, she parked the Miata in the carport and went inside, just like before. I thought she was in for the night. Remember, I called to tell you she was home safe and sound, like you said, about seven thirty?"

"Yeah! Yeah, I remember."

"Well, I just went to get a coffee to go. I was ten minutes at the most. I'd waited till she put her lights out, thinking she was in bed, as usual. She must've left while

I was gone. Her car isn't there anymore, and all her lights are out. I've been looking around the place ever since. I thought I'd better call."

"Right. Any idea which way she might've gone?"

"Nope. Sorry, Chief."

"Don't sweat it, Donny. Everybody loses somebody sometime. Hang out there for the next couple of hours; see if she comes back. Let me know if she does. After that, go home and get some sleep. I'll see you tomorrow if I don't talk to you before then."

"You got it. I'm really sorry, Chief."

"It's okay, Donny." I terminated his call and hit the button to speed-dial Ronnie's cell phone. She didn't answer, and I got her service. I didn't leave a message. I tried it again with the same results.

Par for the course or not, things were starting to come apart at the seams. It had been a long day all right. What else could go wrong? I had a premonition that it was going to get uglier before it was all over.

Just then, Shirl came in from the bedroom. She was dressed in jeans and blouse and had her overnighter slung over her shoulder. I got up from the chair and followed her into the entryway. She turned toward me when she got to the door.

"Where are you going?" I asked.

"Home. You don't need me here, right now."

"But I do. I want you to stay. Are you angry at me for some reason?"

"No. Not really. You just need to get some sleep now, and I need to go home. I don't know why I came over here in the first place. Things are not going to change, are they? You're so busy with work, when there are other matters, more important matters, that need your attention."

I crossed to her. "Look, we can talk about it—get to the bottom of things." I took hold of her elbows, but I didn't try to move her. Shirl had a will of her own and was not to be coerced by anyone—not even me.

She measured her hands' span, thumb to thumb across my chest.

"C'mon. We'll straighten things out," I coaxed, looking deep into her eyes at all the thoughts that darted through her mind, and that, sadly, I couldn't decipher.

"I've heard that before," she said.

"I know."

"You won't talk about Nathaniel. You'll never put his death behind you until it's too late and you ruin everything between us."

"That's not true, Shirl. I'll do whatever it takes to make things work. Come back in and sit down with me." Just then, my cell rang, again. Like a moron, I hadn't turned it off the last time. She blinked, and what had looked like a change of heart before, had gone hard and cold somewhere deep in the center of her being. It rang again. I just looked at her.

"Aren't you going to answer that?" she said as she pulled away from me.

"I don't need to."

"Oh, yes you do."

"Will you wait?" I said. It rang again.

"Answer it," she said.

"I'll shut it off. They'll call back."

"Oh no, take it now. I insist."

I looked at her a moment, then took the cell out of my pocket. "This'd better be damn good," I barked. ". . . oh, Ronnie . . . Are you all right? Where are you?"

Shirl turned around and quietly let herself out.

"Hang on a sec," I said to Ronnie. I walked out behind Shirl and watched her all the way down the hall. She didn't look back. For the life of me, I couldn't call out to her not to go. I don't know why. I just stood and watched, with this catch in my throat, as she turned down the stairs out of my sight. I don't know how long I stood there, just looking at the empty place where she used to be. I guess it was until I heard Ronnie screaming in the cell—something about there being "blood everywhere . . ."

Twenty-seven

BY THE TIME I CHANGED CLOTHES, WOKE MR. Rostopovich, convinced him to loan me—well, rent me—"the apple of his eye," his two-tone white/lime green, 1959 Oldsmobile convertible, and got out to Eastlake's domicile in Beverly Hills, I thought I was gonna die. If not in a fiery, head-on collision from the wayward steering over hill and valley, then from the noxious cloud of carbon monoxide that permeated this deathtrap. The big boat chugged, backfired, and smoked until I almost puked. Even with the top down, it was still tough breathing, not to mention reading the street signs in the dark through the smoky haze wafting into the car. About all I could say for it was that it got me out there in one piece, although the jury was still out on whether or not I had any lungs left. How the hell did this thing pass emissions testing? Maybe I was driving it illegally. Just my luck. And I didn't set any land speed records in the process, either. Silly me, I thought a cab would be too slow. Fortunately, Ronnie had given me good directions, otherwise it could've been a real nightmare. If I ever, ever get my hands on the mug who knifed my tires . . . .

Eastlake's lair was located north of Sunset Boulevard and Beverly Drive, out past Greystone Park in Coldwater Canyon. He lived in what was euphemistically called a cottage, on one of the large estates that are common in that area, if you could call any of them common. They were all different. The Tudor style gatehouse—with four bedrooms of its own, a smaller thatched version of the slate-roofed mansion—was set back on the property and secluded among the moss-backed old evergreens, oaks, and larch much favored as landscaping that reflected the cottage's historical origins. It was a perfect picture, right out of some nineteenth-century English novel. By the looks of it, it had been a long time since it had had any connection to the mansion, which was hidden farther back in the trees almost completely out of sight. Funny thing was, I would never have guessed Eastlake for such a romanticist. I saw his tastes running toward the ultra-chic white, angular, sort of opulent minimalist post-modern modern, "Architectural Digest," avant-garde kind of stuff. Now that I was here, I could see how this made sense, but I couldn't see how I had missed it in the first place.

When Ronnie let me in through the big oak door—with its iron strap hinge, and its top shaped to fit the stone arched-doorway—I could see that she had calmed down some. In fact, she was downright cool. Devoid of expression, her face reflected the gray lead crystal of the bubble glass in the door window through which I peered—just as I was about to ring the chimes. She turned the porch light on and let me in before I could press the button, and stood hugging the door edge. I noticed there was blood on the front of her shirt. It was a long-sleeved silver satin blouse with button-down pockets covering her breasts—useless on a chest like hers. She wore it out, over her jeans.

She raised her eyebrows and nodded her head, indicating that the real show was on the inside. "He's in there," she said. Her voice sounded hollow, uninflected, as if life had become too much to bear.

"Eastlake?" I said. "Is he dead?"

She nodded.

"You sure?"

She nodded again.

"Anyone else?"

She shook her head.

I started for the living room, across the slate floor through the vestibule, but paused at the staircase. "Have you been upstairs?" I said as she closed the door and followed me in.

She shook her head again.

"Good. Now stay right there and don't touch anything else until I get back." I pulled the Magnum and made a quick foray up through the second floor where I found two small bedrooms, a master bedroom with changing area, a study, and a large central bath with two sinks, whirlpool, and shower. The crapper and bidet each had their own little cubby. I touched nothing but the light switches, and I used the barrel of my gun for that. The rooms were smaller than the outside of the house had led me to believe. Maybe it was the overcrowding. The furniture was antique, and the wall art leaned toward Russian iconography. Though I was no expert on either one, from what I could see, everything appeared to be less than top quality. I would have expected better from an aesthete like Eastlake. Nothing seemed amiss, with everything in its place. Beds were made. There were new toothbrushes on the hanger. The towels were unused on racks, as if arranged for expected company, without a speck of dust anywhere. I knew from a previous conversation with Maldonado that Eastlake had a housekeeper who also did his cooking. I could see that she was excellent. I was glad I didn't have to be the one to tell her that she was out of a job, especially since I couldn't afford her.

As I switched off the lights, I holstered the Magnum and went back downstairs. My little reconnoiter through the second floor had eased my mind about unwanted company. I found Ronnie sitting on the chair next to the sideboard, across from the staircase in the vestibule. "You want to tell me what happened?" I said as I went into the living room.

"The door was open. The lights were on. He was like that when I found him," she said in that monotone voice. She got up and followed me in.

Eastlake was still in his suit from the party earlier at the Universal Paradigm building. He'd been shot several times, in the head, upward through the eye, one in the mouth, and the third in the groin. I wondered what that could mean, if anything. It appeared as if he'd struggled with someone before he was killed. He was sprawled halfway across the coffee table and the sofa—an ornate piece of furniture from some period other than the present. It looked expensive, and his scalp had spattered the print all fleshy, hairy, and pink. I got down close for a good look. I was tempted to turn his head over to get a gander at the exit wounds, but I was afraid parts of his brain would plop out on the floor. I didn't want to disturb things too much. I was going to have to call Maldonado and clue him in, and I didn't want him, or worse, McCorkle, climbing up my ass for fucking around with the evidence.

"Have you touched anything in here? I said. "Think. Anything at all?"

She shook her head.

"Have you seen a weapon?"

I guessed the cat had got her tongue for good, because she shook her head again.

"Sure you didn't touch anything? Well?"

"You already asked me that for Christ's sake! Yes, yes I'm sure." She glared at me.

"Don't get excited, Ronnie; just making sure is all. Now then, do me a favor and go stand outside. And try not to shed anything while you do it. The forensics guys will be all over this place in an hour, and I don't want them finding hide, hair, nails, moles, warts, or anything else that would give them a sample of your DNA. Got it?" I had already told her most of this on the phone when she'd called me earlier.

After she left, I made another foray through the ground floor with the same results as I'd gotten on the second floor. Kitchen, bedroom with full bath, cellar, gym, all shipshape, except the living room. I found out pretty much what I usually found out from a crime scene, nothing—except that somebody had sent Eastlake on his final journey into the next world, and made a big mess in the process. I also picked up a shell casing, one of three, which were still on the Persian rug where they'd fallen, and stuck it in my pocket. I didn't find the weapon, and the casings were strange to me; they looked to be an odd caliber, but I was no expert. Apparently, our murderer was either a novice or had left them there for purposes of his own. Maybe he was thumbing his nose at the cops. Who knows why these assholes do what they do?

Outside on the porch, the air was finally cooling down. It was about time. I'd forgotten to wind my watch, but I knew it had to be after midnight, probably closer to one. The stars were twinkling; there wasn't a cloud in the sky. The trees gave out with low moans and rustled in the breeze that raked lightly over the grounds. The moon was past full. Back down in the valley, LA looked pretty good from up this way; but then many things look good in the dark. From some other perspective, LA looked like any other vermin-infested rat hole. It was true. Beauty was skin deep and resided only in the eye of the beholder. Speaking of beauty, I went over to Rostopovich's bomb, took the T-shirt I'd brought for Ronnie from the front seat, walked over by her car, and gave it to her. "Here," I said. "Gimme that blouse and put this on."

"What for?"

"Because I know what to do with it. So strip."

"Now?"

"No, tomorrow at the Laker's game. Yes, now, what do you think?"

"But I love that blouse."

"You can have it back, if you still want it after the police and the crime lab get done with it." I guess I was a little snappish with her. Being called out at this hour, after what I'd been through that day, was getting under my skin. I sure could've used a cup of coffee. Shirl's brandy was working itself into a cotton-mouthed headache like the one I'd had earlier. And for once I really felt like I could sleep the sleep of Eastlake in there.

"God, this shirt stinks," she said. "What'd you do,

burn a tire in it?" She waved it around in front of her.

"Look, just put the friggin' thing on. It's all I've got." I watched her remove the blouse. "Is that a blood spot on your bra?—there, between your breasts."

"No it's just a little embroidered heart. Too bad, huh? You want a closer look?" She arched her back and gave me a wicked grin.

It's a good thing I was a professional. It was too bad. "No thanks. I see it just fine from here."

That wicked grin of hers had been one of pure sarcasm. Sex was the last thing on her mind after what she'd been through that night—which, come to think of it, she seemed to have handled better than I would've imagined. I was guessing she'd never seen much in the way of dead bodies, brains, blood, and such. I wondered how she'd managed to maintain her cool. There was more to her than met the eye, by a long shot. I was gonna have to be careful.

I watched her pull the T-shirt over her head. It swallowed her whole. "There now, aren't you pretty?" I said.

She ignored that.

"How'd you get the blood on this blouse?" I said, as she handed it to me.

"I must've touched him when I leaned over to hear if he was still breathing."

"Why didn't you call 911?"

"I was calling you. Besides, he was already dead when I found him."

"How did you know that?"

"He wasn't breathing. His head was spattered all over. Call it woman's intuition."

"Why didn't you just leave when you saw what was up?"

"I don't know. I just didn't. I couldn't take my eyes

off him, all that blood, everywhere. I didn't know what else to do. So I called you. What else was I supposed to do? Why have you got to be so rude and so damned bossy?"

"Look, sweetheart. I don't know if it's occurred to you, but it looks to me like you could be in a lot of trouble here. With Hollenbeck's murder still unsolved, the police are going to be very interested in speaking to you again. Especially when they find out that you were here tonight. And believe me, they will find out. I'll probably have to tell them eventually. And they will undoubtedly try to place you on the scene at the time of death. You have a connection with both victims, and this one is going to renew their interest in you, big time. I don't know if they've discovered that certain priceless artifacts are missing yet. But when they do, they're going to have what looks a lot like motive. And when that happens, they'll put this juggernaut into high gear."

"What does that mean?"

"Well, there's almost no stopping it. They may come looking for you in the morning. You'll need a good attorney. Now I'm gonna try to straighten this out, but frankly, I'm just not sure what else I'll be able to do to keep you out of jail. They'll want you for questioning, if nothing else. At least if you play this my way, you won't have to go tonight, maybe. You want to tell me what you were doing up here?"

"Dr. Eastlake called me to come up."

"When was that?"

"Oh, I'm not sure. Ten, ten-thirty."

"What did he say?"

"He said he'd heard some disturbing rumors and needed to discuss them with me face to face, tonight, before Minister Kedar left for Washington, DC tomorrow. When I complained that I was just going to bed, he said my job was in jeopardy, and if I knew what was good for me, I'd 'get my fanny up here, post haste.' Those were his exact words. Now tell me, what's with that?"

"Could you tell if there had been anyone else here?" She shook her head.

"You didn't see Raleigh Hanson after you arrived, by any chance?"

"No, should I have?"

"Not necessarily. Look, I want you to go home. And don't get stopped for speeding on your way."

"I don't speed."

"Whatever. And when you get there this time, stay there, no matter who calls you, unless it's me. You got that?"

"Yes sir, anything else, sir?"

"Call me when the police get there."

"You're not going to let them take me to jail, are you?"

"I'll do what I can."

"I didn't do this. You believe me, don't you?" She stepped closer, reached out, and touched me on the hand.

I didn't know if I believed her or not. God knows I wanted to, although things had changed again. It certainly didn't look good. But until I knew otherwise, she was still my client; and deserved or not, she was getting my loyalty, the benefit of the doubt, and whatever else I could do to keep her out of trouble. After all, how could anyone not believe such innocent, big brown eyes, such flawlessly beautiful skin, or such full, red cupid's-bow lips?

Twenty-eight

I WATCHED THE TAILLIGHTS FLASH, AS THE MIATA zipped down through the trees along the cobblestone drive. I waited until she'd cleared the gate at the road before calling the police. No sense letting the tape they make when 911 calls come in record the sound of her vehicle leaving the scene of the crime—giving them proof that somebody else had been here. Then I called Maldonado, woke him up, and told him that I was just sitting and thinking about him, and watching Eastlake's dead body decompose out here in the hinterlands of Beverly Hills. I asked if he would like to join me. I also asked if he'd mind bringing me a cup of coffee, since my body was about to die of caffeine deprivation. He didn't say one way or another; I think he was still asleep. So I gave him the address and told him how much I had missed him, and that I just couldn't wait to see him. It was true, too, if he was bringing me some Mocha Java. I could tell he wasn't happy about my intrusion into his dream life, but there was nothing I could do about that. Why did I have the feeling that our friendship was going to be sorely tested over the next couple of days?

He wasn't going to like the fact that I'd been keeping things from him—things I fully intended to keep from him a little longer, if possible. And now there were some new things I needed to keep from him as well, unless I was forced by circumstances beyond my control to spill my guts. It really wasn't that big a deal; but then again, it was. Powerful and destructive forces were shaping up here that could steamroll my client right into a death sentence, guilty or otherwise. She'd hired me to see that that didn't happen. Given the past problems with certain LA cops planting evidence and lying in court to make their cases, it was nothing to joke about. Not that Bernie would ever be involved in something crooked; I knew better than that. But he wasn't working this thing alone, and some of the others—like Deputy Chief McCorkle and Asst. District Attorney Prudhomme for starters—weren't too meticulous about procedures, as long as they got the numbers they needed. That was the kind of game they played with us intermediaries. I would give them everything I could, but I had my job to do, just like they did.

I called Donny and told him that Ronnie was headed home, to keep an eye on her after she got there. I thought about calling Shirl and begging her to forgive me, to let me come over and spend the night—but my night wasn't likely to be over until sometime tomorrow. What was I thinking? This was tomorrow. Besides, Shirl had to be at Dexter's by five. Time was running out, and I had to get it in gear. People were on a mad dash to get to the scene of the crime, and there were things to do before they got here.

First thing was to take the shell casing from my pocket and stick it in my shoe, out of sight and touch.

Ronnie's bloody blouse went into a never-to-be-found cozy little spot under the spare tire in the trunk of the Rostopovich lime-green monster. Kindly but mercenary old man that he was, Rostopovich was also a pack rat; they'd never find anything under all that garbage. Back in the house, I made another sweep of the ground floor, just to be sure there was nothing remotely connected to my client—nada. I took off my T-shirt, wiped down the front door, light switch, chair, sideboard in the vestibule, and put it back on. In the living room, one final, on-my-knees inspection of the body and the surrounding area; it wouldn't do for them to find one of Ronnie's long, black hairs draped across his nose. There would be a hell of a lot of explaining to do, before I was ready to do it. I knew I was breaking the law, but I intended to give the evidence to Bernie in a day or two, if for some reason I didn't bust this case wide open before then. When I did that, my tampering became a moot point—maybe. Meanwhile this would buy us a little time—I hoped.

But it was probably all for naught. They were going to figure out that she'd been out here when they got hold of Eastlake's phone records and realized that he had spoken to her just an hour before he was killed. At the least it would bring her back into the full glare of their deliberations. Bernie already knew that I was on her payroll. I couldn't worry about that now. After five days, things were coming to a head soon. With two murders, two old friends who'd worked together, both dead, it wouldn't be long before something had to give. And when it did, I was going to be all over it like the paparazzi on Angelina.

I heard a siren and went outside to await my fate. It was a Beverly Hills black and white followed by an

EMT wagon. I wasn't sure they wouldn't arrest me first and ask questions later. Coming onto a murder scene, cops had to be careful. Many of them didn't like private dicks and threw us in jail on occasion, just to discourage us from hanging around where they thought we had no business. Nevertheless, when their headlights came to rest on me, sitting on the top step at the front door, I had my wallet—with my PI license visible—held out in front of me with my other hand over my head. It wasn't fear; it was prudence. I didn't want to get shot for a perp by a nervous cop hyped on sugar, caffeine, and adrenaline. Turning a spotlight on me, they got out of the cruiser, drew their weapons; the driver, a large fellow at six-foot-five and about two-hundred and twenty pounds approached.

"Evening officer," I said. "It's a beautiful night,"

"Yes it is," he said. "Would you stand over here, sir? Slowly. What's the problem?"

"There's a stiff inside," I said as I stood and stepped down to meet him.

"Anyone else?" he said, motioning his partner inside.

"No," I said.

"Who are you?"

"Name's Nestor Pike. I'm a private investigator. I used to be on the job. Lt. Detective Maldonado is a friend of mine. I called the homicide in."

"You don't mean, Burning House Maldonado?"

"Yes sir. That's the man."

"Well, damn. When he saved that family from the fire three years ago, he made us all proud to be cops." He was referring to the incident that gave Maldonado his nickname, Bernie, short for Burning House. Bern's given name was Oscar. "And he's hell of a nice guy too," he

continued. "Too bad I can't say the same for that nee-
dled-nosed prick he works for . . ."

"You mean, McCorkle?"

"Yeah, that's the one . . . But hey, either way, it don't
cut no ice around here. Got me?"

"Gotcha." I didn't take it personally. He was just piss-
ing on a weed to mark his territory.

"You carrying?" he asked and signaled the paramedics
to go around us inside.

"Yes sir."

The other officer came back out and joined us.
"There's a dead guy like he said," he said.

Couldn't have been much of a search, I thought; but
I kept it to myself.

"Okay, Mr. Pike, you know the drill," the first officer said. "My partner, Officer Hartley here, is going to
pat you down."

I turned around and laced my fingers across the back
of my head.

Officer Hartley, six-two, about one eighty, one eighty-
five, put his gun away, came around, and frisked me. He
took the Magnum, checked the load, and asked to see my
identification. I turned, took my ID, license and permit
for the piece from my wallet, and handed them to him.
He went back to the cruiser and called in. After a few
moments, he came over and gave them back, except for
the Magnum, which he handed to his partner.

"Everything checks out," he said. "Go ahead and
interview him, I'll finish in the house." He headed back
inside.

"So, Mr. Pike, I'm Officer Blake. And I'll hold on to
this, until I clear it with the detectives," He put my gun
in his belt.

"Sure thing. It hasn't been fired recently."

"If you don't mind, Mr. Pike, step over here with me," he said, and walked over to stand in front of the cruiser. He holstered his weapon and took out a small leather-bound notebook with a pen. "What can you tell me about what went on out here tonight?"

"Absolutely nothing," I said, following him. "I just got here and found the place all lit up like this, with Dr. Eastlake lying in there dead. I called 911."

"How'd you know he was dead?"

"Doesn't take a genius to figure it out; his brains are all over the couch."

"I guess you'd be right about that. What were you doing here in the first place?"

"I'd come out to see Eastlake. It was a private matter."

Officer Blake questioned me like that for another five minutes, then told me to wait by my car until the detectives got here.

"Nice ride," he said. "Did you do that shiny metallic, lime-green and white paint job yourself, or did Earl Schibe do it?"

"God punishes those who scoff at others in their times of need," I said. "But I don't know. This fine vehicle belongs to Mr. Vladimir Rostopovich, my neighbor."

He laughed. "Mind if I search it?"

"Knock yourself out." I tossed him the keys.

He checked the glove box and glanced around at all the crap in the backseat and foot wells. He took one look in the trunk, closed it right up, and gave the keys back to me. He laughed again, shook his head, and went over to his cruiser to call in. By this time, three more cruisers, the forensics personnel, and the ME had shown up. They were bustling around, busy as one-legged men at an ass-kicking contest. They turned this place inside out, a for real and true crime scene, with flashing lights, yellow tape, and the works. I'd seen too many of them. Across the road, in earshot along the canyon, lights were coming on in homes among the trees.

Just about then, Maldonado's big unmarked Chevy pulled up and parked off the drive in the grass, over behind one of the cruisers. Another detective, I presumed, someone I didn't know, got out of the passenger's side. They met Officer Blake, who gave Bernie my gun. They stood at the front of the cruiser and spoke together for a few moments before Bernie spotted me standing by the convertible and ambled over. The other man went into the house with Officer Blake.

"Okay, Señor Pike," he said, handing me the Magnum and a couple bags from Dunkin' Donuts. "What have we got here, and what, by the grace of Our Dear Lady of Guadalupe, have you got to do with it?"

"Hey, Bern, nice to see you, too," I said. "Thanks for the coffee." That Señor Pike didn't bode well. "Donuts too! Man, you're a real life saver." I holstered the piece and opened a bag.

"Yeah, well get your manos off, vato, that jelly baby's mine," he said, taking it from my hand. "You got something else for me? This better be good, amigo." He munched his way around the red filling that oozed out on his fingers, saving the best part for last. He held it out away from him and leaned over to eat it so it wouldn't drop on his coat.

I opened the other bag and set both cups on the hood of the great green machine, along with a couple of those small tubs of Half-&-Half which I stirred into my coffee. "Ahhh, man." That first sip always touched me, right down deep inside where I live. The crullers weren't as good as Dex's, but I couldn't afford to be fussy.

"There's some real heat coming off the commissioner's office," he continued as he licked the jelly from his fingers.

"Well, it's like this, Bern," I said, as I wiped my hands and tossed him some napkins from the bag.

He wiped his hands and chin, pulled the lid off his cup, and washed the donut down, then looked me square in the eyes and waited.

"Where to begin?" I said. "Ah, let me see . . . well . . . there are a number of foreign operatives from Jordan here in LA right now."

"And what would these cholos have to do with anything?"

"They may be responsible for both of these murders."

"Are you talking about those two skels who gave you that shellacking last Friday, Mustafa and Davie?"

"Not entirely. There are others. By the way, have you got anything else on Mustafa and Davie?"

He shook his head. "And what the hell do these others want?"

"I'm not sure, but they're connected to the Jordanian Minister of Culture, a man by the name of Geshur Kedar. Recently, there was a theft of several very valuable items which the Jordanians are either responsible for or trying to track. I haven't been able to determine which. I saw them in an elevator at the Universal Paradigm building yesterday. Middle Eastern intelligence professionals from one service or another, if you ask me. I didn't talk to them. Kedar is leaving town tomorrow for Washington DC."

"That explains the call I got from the FBI yesterday. They wanted to know if we'd come across any unusual activity in the past month involving either Arab aliens or Arabs with diplomatic immunity."

"Don't they ever talk to Interpol?"

"You know how it is. The left hand doesn't know that the right hand is jerking off. They wanted the poop on some names we'd never heard of before."

"Are you telling me the Feds are involved in this now?"

"Oh no, not yet. But they have asked that we notify them, if the people they mentioned come to our attention—even though they showed no real interest in either Mustafa or Davie. Go figure."

"Run that by me again."

"What part of 'showed no real interest' didn't you understand?"

"That part about 'showed no real interest.'"

"Well, it's just that they were not familiar with Mustafa and Davie and didn't care. Said they'd look into it is all."

"No shit? . . . Then you already knew about these other guys?" I couldn't tell if Bern was buying the smoke screen that I was laying down. He kept his poker face on. Hell, he was probably blowing some smoke of his own.

"Not exactly."

Like what did Bern mean by that?

"I wondered why the Feds were being so cryptic, especially in view of all the tensions in the Middle East" he said. "Where'd this theft take place?"

"I don't know."

"What does this have to do with . . . Ah. Si . . . El sol, he rises . . . the upcoming exhibition at the Getty!"

"Yeah. First Hollenbeck and now Eastlake . . ."

He turned to look back at the house without speaking for a few moments. Finally, he turned back to me and said, "Is there anything else, anything at all you'd like to tell me, Nes?"

I knew he knew that I knew that he knew that I was keeping something from him. "Well let me see . . . ahhh . . . nope, not that I can think of right off the top of my head."

"Sure?"

"Yep."

"Oookay, if you say so," he said. "You driving this?" He looked down at my rented wheels.

I just looked at him.

"Where's your car?"

"Don't ask."

"Okay. . . . But give me the name of the Low Rider you had to kill to steal this macho machine, por favor," he said, patting the green monster affectionately on one of its crumpled fenders.

"Et tu, Brute?"

"By the way, McCorkle wants to see your smiley face in Prudhomme's office in the morning, eleven o'clock sharp. Said he'd send a cruiser, if you wanted him to, make that, if he needs to."

"Ha, ha." No wonder the poker face. "What do they want with me?"

"Well, if it was me, vato, I'd be asking you just what you and the gorgeous young Ms. Rivero have been up to for the last forty-eight hours. I don't know what they want; they've been pretty secretive with me lately. But if I were you, amigo, I'd be wearing my cast-iron briefs and bring along a good bail bondsman."

"What if I don't show?"

"You'll show."

"You gonna be there?"

"Oh yeah, I'm invited to the party. But if I wasn't, I still wouldn't miss it for all the chimichangas in Chihuahua."

And even in the dark of night—with the trees moaning and the moon past full—Burning House Maldonado has got the whitest teeth, in the biggest mouth, of anybody I know.

Twenty-nine

Thursday

THE LARGE COFFEE AND DONUTS THAT BERNIE HAD brought me revved me right up. The sugar and caffeine raised my spirits and boosted my energy. Unfortunately, as is often the case with sugar and caffeine—on no sleep and an empty belly—it also triggered an attack of paranoia, self-doubt, and dire foreboding. Helloooo jitters! By the time I finished with Bernie, cleared the gate at Eastlake's in the Rostopovich-mobile, and was back on the road for home, I was playing the sugar blues.

What the hell was I doing?—wiping out evidence, stealing it from the scene of a crime, and lying to Officer Blake like a streetwalker off the Sunset Strip. It couldn't get any worse than that, unless I had capped Eastlake myself and tried to cover it up. The licensing board would take my license, no questions asked. Hell, the way I felt, I would've gone down there, turned it in, and given myself a big fine to boot, if the licensing board had been open at two in the morning. Worst of all, I wasn't treating Bernie right. This was not my normal MO. On top of that, there was something rotten in the state of

Denmark other than herring. Besides acting like a three-bit, ass-dragging felon late for a date with his mattress, something bothered me deeply about this, and it wasn't my conscience.

Back at the Villa Pancho, I took the nasty telltale evidence from the green monster, stuck it—along with the shell casing from my shoe—in a plastic bag, and stashed it in the freezer of my refrigerator for safe keeping. In the bedroom, I kicked off my shoes and pulled off my socks. I unclipped the Magnum, put it under my pillow, and threw myself onto my trusty old, queen-sized bed. "And though I'd plunged into the deep, dark silence and embraced this rare, fleeting sleep, I could find no rest or solace in the arms of oblivion . . ."

I was at the Getty looking for Shirl; but for some reason I had to take this tour first. That was the rule; there was no escaping it. Everyone rode the tram and took the tour. The sun reflected off the Travertine, giving the whole hillside a white glare, reminiscent of one of Hollywood's many renditions of heaven. I had to shield my eyes with a pair of Rayban Aviators. What had happened to my regular pair of Vuarnet's? No one would recognize me. I caught a glimpse of Shirl hurrying into one of the buildings across the plaza.

By the time I got there, presto chango. I was transported to the old Getty Villa office a world away, where I had first interviewed Eastlake. And there he was, sprawled across his desk, his head blown apart like a watermelon. Great! With Eastlake dead, how was I ever going to find Shirl now? What a stupid question. I looked down at my watch and realized it was past time to meet Bernie at the new Getty, out on the 405. The lime-green Nova was waiting at the foot of the hill with a couple of flat tires, and I had to call a cab to get me back there. I didn't have time to be pissed.

When I arrived and took the tram to the Arrival Plaza, Penn Gillette and his sidekick, the ever silent Teller, were waiting for me. I wasn't all that surprised to find them there. There was a crowd watching as they performed one of their magic tricks. Shirl, dressed in a magician assistant's costume—an elaborate headdress, one of those sequined bathing suits with a ruff around the fanny, and black fishnet stockings with four-inch heels—was standing on the platform between them. They assisted her into one of those tall magic boxes and twirled it around, so you could see there was no way to escape. Teller ran a number of gleaming scimitars through it, as Penn made his usual round of pithy and biting observations and directions to the audience. Teller, as usual, was silent.

At the end, Penn pulled one of the swords from the box, twirled it around over his head, and, in one blinding swoop, lopped off the head of my son, Nathaniel, who was standing next to him, wearing Teller's suit. The crowd gasped and then broke into a rousing round of applause. It was a pretty astonishing effect. A wave of deep sorrow passed through me and almost knocked me out. Teller jumped up with Eddy the Eel's smiling head attached to his body, and all the blood was gone. Everything was back to normal—except for the indescribable anger that had replaced my sorrow. I was hyperventilating. I had practiced the art of murder and wanted to kill someone at that moment, more than anything I could describe. They pulled out the rest of the swords, opened the box, and Shirl was gone. In her place, Eastlake came out dressed in Shirl's costume, and the crowd went wild.

Either I passed out, or someone knocked me out from behind. As I began to come to, with the crowd noise ringing in my ears, Penn Gillette was kneeling over me. Holding me up with my collar in one hand, he was slapping me across the face with his other. What in hell was he doing that for? Teller was standing on the other side of me smirking, pointing his finger at me. The sun had gone under a cloud, and the white glare of the Travertine had turned dingy beige.

As the sound of the crowd began to fade away, Penn let go of my collar and stood over me, then walked out of the room. I went back under, briefly. Teller kneeled down and poked me with his finger. I looked over to see him but Penn and Teller, as usual, had pulled off one final, awe-inspiring magic trick. Presto chango for the third time, right in front of my eyes, Teller went out of focus then refocused as the tank, Alfred James Davie, standing right next to my bed. He was pointing a Glock at me. Penn went fuzzy then unfazed into Ahmed Emil Mustafa, who just at that moment had lumbered back into the room and threw a glass of water into my face. My first thought was—as I choked, sputtered, and wiped at the water—this nightmare has just begun. I was back in the land of the living, and reality sucked the big one.

"Ah, Mr. Pike, I see you are, what do you say . . . quite the Sleeping Beauty," Mustafa said in that doomsday voice of his. I almost couldn't make it out with his Middle Eastern accent coming through those hoary yellow teeth and that shit-eating, metallic grin.

I reached under the pillow, but the Magnum was

gone. This particular moment of reality really sucked.

"Looking for this, mate?" Davie said, pulling back his sport coat and patting it where it stuck out of his belt-line. "Nice piece, but I prefer a Glock, as you can see." He almost doubled over laughing.

That was my own Glock he held on me—definitely the notch I'd put across the face of the trigger guard. He had taken it from my dresser by the door, where I kept it when it wasn't in use.

"Morning boys," I said in the best bravado that I could manage; my eyes were still partially stuck together. "What time is it, anybody know? I seem to have forgotten to wind my watch." I surmised that it was still early, just after dawn, by the light coming through the blind on the window.

"Nancyboy forgot to crank his timepiece," Davie said.

I loved how Australians always said toime for time and might for mate.

"Too busy cranking his dingo," he continued over his shoulder at Mustafa, as the latter went into the bathroom across the hallway.

I could hear him over there, checking out the medicine cabinet, removing the lid from the toilet tank. He pulled back the shower curtain. I could've told him that I didn't have any other weapons in the place, but he didn't ask. When he came back in, I was sitting on the edge of the bed, and Davie had moved over to keep me in clear view.

"So, Mr. Pike, I see you have gotten yourself involved in our affairs, in spite of our kindly efforts to steer you away from them," Mustafa said. "Apparently, you do not know what is good for you, or you do not listen, or you think we are liars and won't follow up as we have said."

"Well, it's like this, see. I didn't have a case. And I still don't know which case you're referring to, exactly." My mind was racing around, looking for something to hang its hat on. "Say, how'd you guys get in here anyway, without my hearing you?"

"Against all probability to the contrary, you are as dumb as you look after all, aren't you?" he said. "Would you have believed it, Mr. Davie?"

"Not bloody likely."

"Well, you gonna tell me or what?" I said.

"We strolled in." Davie said. "You left it open—forgot to lock your own bloody door, mate. Nessyboy must've been too tired, eh?"

I really couldn't stand that smug, sneering attitude of theirs. I vowed then, as I had vowed that first time, that I was going to even the score with these two if it killed me. At this point, I wasn't sure that it wouldn't, or that all this earnest vowing of mine was going to get me anywhere. Unfortunately, it was about all I could do at the moment. How the hell had I allowed them to get the drop on me, again, twice in a week? They'd materialized out of thin air both times. I was losing it. This was getting to be monotonous, and it pissed me off—mightily. Maybe it really was time for me to get out of this racket. Maybe I was finally past it for good.

"You're a lucky man, Mr. Pike," Mustafa said.

I liked the sound of that—especially since I didn't feel all that lucky just at the moment.

"We're not going to kill you—yet."

I liked the sound of that even better, except for the yet part.

" . . . unless you force us to, in which case we will be happy . . ."

"Yeah, I got it."

"Our associate has deemed it a prudent course of action to take a meeting with you, personally."

"Oh, yes?" Things were getting brighter by the moment. Of course, I wasn't forgetting the provisional nature of the situation as it stood, but things were definitely looking up. Now all I needed was a good cup of joe.

"Yes, as I said, you're a lucky man, Mr. Pike."

"Well, if you don't mind my asking, when is this lucky event supposed to take place?"

"No time like the present, I believe your saying goes," Mustafa continued.

"Kinda early, don't you think? Can't be later than five thirty, five forty-five."

"Five twenty-one to be precise," Davie said, looking at his watch. "It's getting late, mate. We're expected before six." He wasn't speaking to me.

"Wait a minute! I didn't sleep through the day, did I? We're talking six a.m. Thursday, right?"

"My employer wants you wide awake when he meets you," Mustafa said as he put his gun away and took out a cell phone. "So get some clothes, and Mr. Davie here will accompany you while you shower."

"I've got a good idea. Why don't you gentlemen come back this afternoon and I'll go along with you, over to see your boss then. In the meantime, I can finish my beauty sleep, get a shower, a bite to eat, and have a cup of coffee. I'll be fresher than the Virgin Mary. Wha'd'ya say?"

"Move it, Mr. Pike, and don't dawdle, or Mr. Davie will find it necessary to hurry you along. I can guarantee you will not like it . . ." He turned abruptly and went back into the living room. I could hear him speaking on his cell. I got some clean clothes from the dresser under the ever-watchful but beady little eyes of Alfie the dozer. "So, who is your associate?" I said, padding barefoot across the hall into the bathroom, with Davie on my heels.

"You'll find that out soon enough, Bucko. In the meantime, keep your yap shut unless you're spoken to first. Got that mate?"

"I'm not your might."

"You've got that right, mate," he said, swiping me across the back of the head with the barrel of the Glock. "Like I said, keep your mouth shut, Bucko."

"Whatever you say, Baldy." It wasn't much, but it was all I could come up with through the purple haze left over from the muzzle of that Glock. Maybe a cold shower would help keep the swelling down.

Thirty

BY THE TIME WE'D PULLED INTO THE UNIVERSAL Paradigm garage beneath the building, it was a quarter after six. I'd already figured out we were headed to see G. Henry Carl almost before we'd left my place. Chalk it up to one of those things that just made sense, that wouldn't have made any kind of sense otherwise. We'd entered through Carl's private entrance on the parking level, took his plush personal elevator, which only had three buttons, directly to an office on the twenty-fourth floor. It was set apart from the gallery areas that I had already seen and looked more like a living room than an office. I noticed the chill as I stepped off the elevator. It felt cooler than the sixty-eight degrees that Carl had ordered maintained on the top three floors, but then I hadn't had my full ration of sleep or any breakfast, and unstoked, the furnace was running on low. I wasn't sure why we were here.

The room was white, expansive, and surprising. Most surprising was the simple, form-follows-function spiral stairway standing in the corner. Minimalist in feeling, the room contained an eclectic assemblage of furniture, a rust-red leather sofa across from two deep-green wingback chairs, all sitting on an intricate pattern of Moroccan design, not so minimalist, inlaid into the light hardwood floor. A large, ultra-modern mahogany table with a matching deep-mahogany colored leather deskchair on the backside, simple but elegant, stood opposite the sofa across the room. A substantial group of fine color-field abstractions—including pieces by the likes of Albers and Marden, among others I didn't recognize-hung uniformly across an iron-paneled wall which had oxidized to a rich rust surface. These paintings were nothing like the works I'd seen in the main gallery during the party. They belonged in a museum so that the rest of us peons could enjoy them. Here, they were reserved for the privileged few. Carl was not there as we arrived. Mustafa pointed me to the wingbacks and indicated I should sit.

And then, surprise of surprises, the men put away their weapons. Mustafa had kept his piece on me the whole trip over as Davie drove the big Lincoln Navigator SUV. It had been a silent ride. I never once caught him with his guard down.

Before I sat, I walked over to the floor-to-ceiling windows that looked out on the Pacific side in the morning shade. They were shielded on the inside by a set of open louvers that were retractable into the wall at either end. From there I could see the Santa Monica Pier materializing and dematerializing in the fog. A blanket of evershifting mist covered the city. Couldn't see south central LA at all. But LA looked good like this, too. The morning rush was already on; the MTA strike was still not settled. From the twenty-fourth floor, things below continued to look small and insignificant. Appearances were, as always, deceiving. Davie remained standing by the elevator. He needn't have bothered; I wasn't going anywhere. By the time we'd settled in for the ride over here, Mustafa and Davie's presence to the contrary, I'd decided it was a good time to meet the big dawg who had sicced these hounds on me in the first place.

"So, Mr. Pike, I see you are enjoying the view."

A man that I assumed to be G. Henry Carl had come partway down the spiral stairway and stood looking at me from across the room. I'd not actually seen him the day before, at the party. Pictures that I'd seen of him in the paper, over the years, led me to believe that he was a younger man. He was dressed in a pair of ox-blood wingtips, a blue pinstripe, white shirt, and a conservative dark tie that looked as if they might've come from the racks at any good department store in the city. I guessed that he was a frugal man. His skin and complexion appeared to have been pulled tight to the bone and polished with pumice, to the texture and color of vellum. The monk's ring of once dark but now gray close-cropped hair gave him a sincere, if somewhat pale, grandfatherly air, though everything about his manner suggested he was anything but grandfatherly. He had a small, dark, asymmetrical blotch over his left eye, just above a hairline that no longer existed. It reminded me of Mikhail Gorbachev's birthmark, only it was on the opposite side. His only concession to fashion was the ultra-thin gold watch on his wrist. At this distance, I assumed it to be a Cartiér; Rolex just didn't appear to be his style. He had a slight lisp to his speech, but his voice was pleasant enough.

"Yes, the view's good from here," I said, as he came the rest of the way down the staircase.

Having descended so god-like from the heavens above, he made no effort to shake my hand when he came across the room. We were not going to be friends, and he already knew that I had no weapon. He was short and thin and appeared frail, though his demeanor was not. His pale gray eyes were piercing and close together. Was that some sort of worry I saw lurking behind that veiled look? I had the vague sensation that he was wrestling with a problem of some importance, and that maybe I held the only key to the solution. Was there a slight shift in the balance of power in the room? Though outnumbered three to one, for the first time that morning I felt as if I was on level ground. My only problem was, I was twenty-four stories in the air and didn't know what bargaining chip I held. But whatever it was, I hoped that I was holding it, and that it was a good one.

"Well, Mr. Pike, it would appear that someone owes you an apology. Was your ride over a pleasant one?"

"As pleasant as could be expected, under the circumstances. But as a matter of fact, in the first place, I would like to know just where the hell you get off, sending Lucy and Ethel here to my office last week, and then to my apartment this morning."

"I'm afraid you have me at a disadvantage. I've no excuses for their behavior, Mr. Pike. These gentlemen, 'Lucy and Ethel' as you so colorfully call them, do not take their orders from me, though we do work together on occasion. Actually, they work for someone else, someone with whom I share several interests. But that is neither here nor there. Seems you are a hard man to dissuade from something, once you set you mind to it."

"Actually, Mr. Carl . . . it is G. Henry Carl, CEO of

Universal Paradigm that I'm speaking to, isn't it?—just for the record."

He nodded ever so slightly, unwilling to give even that little bit away.

"It's like this—Hank. Once someone orders me not to do something is just about the time I decide that I really need to do that very thing. Know what I mean? It's obviously a flaw in my character, but what are you going to do? You see, when Ahmed and Alfred here came to my place and roughed me up, well, they more or less sealed our fate. I had no choice but to take the case. You follow me there?" I knew that I was scooting across thin ice here. But Mustafa and Davie made no move, showed no inclination to object to my flippant use of their first names. Something was up; these boys were being entirely too congenial and reserved for my taste. It wasn't like them. It gave me the creeps. I almost preferred a good clean round of knock down, drag out; at least I knew where I stood in that case. I was beginning to think I couldn't get a rise out of these humps if I'd stripped naked, waltzed up, and smacked them both in the kisser. Even Carl didn't flinch when I called him Hank.

"You realize that I could have you removed for speaking that way to me."

Ah, finally. "Highly unlikely, but nothing's impossible, I suppose. However, that's not why you went to all this trouble to bring me over here."

"You're right, of course, Mr. Pike. I admire your— brass—shall I say. You've shown me that I have a lot to learn about human nature. You must allow me to make things up to you. I'm afraid my friends here have been somewhat zealous in their attention to their duties, in their treatment of you. I will, of course, write you a check for any and all expenses that you have incurred as a result of their actions; and further, will include any reasonable sum you should name for any pain and suffering you have experienced at their hands. Would say . . . ten-thousand dollars be sufficient?"

Hmmm. Now I knew something was wrong. Here he was offering me restitution for all the pain and suffering these yahoos had put me through. It must be a big payoff indeed, to have reversed the tactics of my new-found friend, Mr. G. Henry Carl, of none other than Universal Paradigm. I didn't know quite what to say . . . "Say twenty large and promise to keep these jokers on a tighter leash," was all I could manage. My brain had hitherto not contemplated such an unexpected and fruitful turn of events.

"Consider it done."

"And while we're at it, your friend, Mr. Davie, over there, has some things of mine that I would like returned."

"Of course," he said. "Give them to him, Mr. Davie,"

It looked for a moment as if it were going to pain Davie beyond endurance to do so. But after first disarming them, he promptly returned my weapons and cell. To be honest, I didn't deserve them back after having lost them so ignominiously in the first place. But fine by me, as long as I had them. Suddenly, I didn't feel quite so vulnerable. For just an instant, it crossed my mind to ram the Glock's clip into place and pump a couple of these full metal jackets through both Mustafa and Davie; little holes in, big holes out, short and sweet. But I could see that Mustafa was not asleep, though his lids hooded his eyes. Leaning nonchalantly against the stairway railing, he was the perfect picture of ease and relaxation. His right hand rested comfortably on the second button, just inside his jacket, below the sling under his arm.

Besides, I was in some new territory with Messieurs Mustafa and Davie. There'd been a subtle shift in our dynamic, and the vows I'd made earlier notwithstanding, my revenge was destined to take a new tack, a temporary detour. Just what that might be or where it might lead, I didn't know yet—but it would come to me. Just like what they had coming was coming to them, sooner or later. I owed it to them. It was one of the missions of my life. Payback was as sure as death or taxes. So for now, I clipped the empty Magnum to my belt, stuck the Glock in my waistband, and set our differences aside.

"You see our earlier appraisal of certain situations was skewed, as it seems, and now we must make amends where we can. I hope this suits you. Anything else, Mr. Pike?" Carl said.

"That check you were going to write . . ."

"Yes, well—remind me of that once again when our business here is finished, and you are ready to depart," he said, as he walked over behind the mahogany table that sat across from the windows in front of the rusting wall.

I almost said that he and I had no further business, at least for the present. But something held my tongue. I was ready to depart then and there, but was still intrigued. Why had Carl gotten me over here in the first place and then pulled the old switcheroo on me? It was another character flaw of mine; I was too damned nosy for my own good. Still, all things being equal, it didn't seem right. It felt kind of like I was shaking hands with old man Potter, selling out the ole Bailey Building and Loan with Christmas just around the corner.

"Can I get you a cup of coffee, Mr. Pike?"

The man was smooth; I'd give him that. I had seen the carafe sitting there on the silver service all along, but hadn't dared to hope. Things were not going as I might've expected them to, and I didn't need that disappointment to spoil what looked, so far, like a perfect run. Besides, I hadn't wanted to consort with the enemy by taking something he offered me, putting me under minor obligations. But twenty thou' was something else again. Things were in flux. I had to go with the flow and adapt to the situation. It was part of what made me good at my job. If I had to stoop to drinking coffee with the opposition, just to get the poop on the real deal, then so be it. He poured me a cup in the company china with the gold rims and all, and it made me wonder where Buddy Palmer was this morning, and why he wasn't here. Could it be that he was out of the loop on this one, not part and parcel of this little scenario being played out by Carl and his chorus girls? The number of possibilities was growing.

"There's cream and sugar," he said. "Help yourself to the pastry." He was going for the jugular.

I had to draw the line somewhere. Coffee was a necessity, like air or water, but pastry?—well that was something else altogether. "Never touch the stuff," I said. "It's how I keep my young Greek-god-like figure."

He ignored my levity and moved over to one of the chairs across from the sofa, indicating that I should join him with my coffee. "I think we're all squared away here, gentlemen, if you would like to wait for me in my office upstairs," he said to Mustafa and Davie. "Cook will make you breakfast, if you ask." They nodded, eyed me ferociously, and made a quick retreat up the spiral stairway. Mustafa found it difficult to watch me cream my coffee, as he went round and round. He, like Davie, had remained strangely quiet the whole time.

"I've already had my breakfast, but would you care for something, Mr. Pike?" It began to sound like he was trying to bribe me.

Every man had his price, and I was no exception. But I doubted he could afford mine. "No thanks, coffee's fine." I was still unsure what to make of this. It appeared I was about to find out. The coffee was deep and rich and tasted like hickory nuts. I almost had the cup polished off by the time I joined him at the other wingback. I drink my coffee anyway I can get it, but I liked it best hot, with one of Dex's bearclaws. "So tell me, Hank. Just what is it you want from me?"

"To put it bluntly, Mr. Pike, I need you to locate some priceless missing artifacts."

"You don't say?"

"I do say. Dr. Eastlake tells me that there is a distinct possibility that the Getty will not be able to open its forthcoming show on Saturday. Certain of the show's artifacts have been called into question, and I believe your client, Ms. Rivero, might know something about them."

News traveled fast. I guess word was out about Ronnie and me. "I'm really not at liberty to discuss what my client may or may not know about some artifacts, missing or otherwise."

"I could make it worth your while to help me discover the facts of the matter. I'm sure that, on her salary, it will take some time for Ms. Rivero to come up with the resources to pay your fees, if indeed she ever managed to do so without a job or the possibility of ever working in her field again. All we would need would be for her to produce the missing pieces, or proof that she doesn't have them. I would be happy to double the twenty-thousand for your assistance in this matter."

Anyway I chose to look at it, it was tainted money—not to mention that I harbored a major conflict of interest. Nevertheless, it was mighty tempting to score that forty Gs and donate it to a charity for children. There was no doubt in my mind that he'd refuse if I didn't contractually promise to deliver the goods or information he wanted, and I couldn't do that at any price. "What business is this of yours?" I asked. "You're not directly associated with the Getty."

"True enough. But Dr. Eastlake is a long and dear friend of mine, and he stands to be embarrassed if these irregularities come to light. I would like to prevent that if I could."

I debated for a moment; should I tell him now about Eastlake's demise or let him find it out on the news? It was surprising that he hadn't already heard. "Two things, Mr. Carl—first, I can't help you with your problem. I'm under contract, and there's this little matter of ethics. Second, you should know that Yeager Eastlake was murdered at his place in Beverly Hills last night."

Carl didn't move a muscle. He showed no emotion, except that his already pale complexion went a shade lighter. "Enjoy your coffee, Mr. Pike," he said a moment later, as he stood and headed for the spiral stairway. "Meanwhile, I trust you will excuse my abrupt departure. You may leave the way you came in." He stopped and turned to me at the foot of the steps. "My personal elevator is at your disposal; use it, soon," he said. Then, quicker than I thought possible for a man of his size and age, he scooted up the stairs two at a time and was gone. Hmm, I guess all bets were off.

Thirty-one

THE FIRST THING I DID AFTER CARL DISAPPEARED through the ceiling was reload the Glock. Then I punched the down button in his personal elevator, without getting in, and let myself out through a door in the south wall that would lead me into the art gallery and the public elevators. Bingo. The lights were on, and the place was empty, but I didn't stop to view the paintings that I'd missed the day before. The clean up crew from the party had already finished and gone. Carl could make things happen; I'd give him that. The express opened up on the ground floor and surprised one of Buddy's security-lackeys who manned the desk. He had to let me out personally, since the lobby was closed to public traffic until eight. I wondered if Buddy knew what was going on here, so early, right under his nose—or if he was even in yet. No time to stop and worry about it.

Outside, I called the Yellow Cab Company and told them to have a driver pick me up on Santa Monica Boulevard, three blocks east of the UP building. No sense hanging out in the immediate vicinity any longer than necessary. It wouldn't have surprised me to know that Mustafa and Davie were already looking for me, although they would probably come at me in a more opportune time and place, not so close to home. Or, for that matter, if they were even coming for me at all. No way of knowing for sure, but I wasn't taking any chances. How was that for paranoia? And it wasn't even eight yet.

While I shanked it over for my rendezvous with the cab, I made a call to the tire shop and begged them to match up a couple of tires on the Nova ASAP. I let it be known that there was an extra fifty in it, if the job was done by the time I got there. I took the cab back to my apartment and made the driver cruise around the block, twice, before I got out and went in. I retrieved the bag of evidence that I'd filched from Eastlake's out of the Fridge, put the shell casing in my pocket, and slipped Rostopovich's car keys under his door on the way out. The cab dropped me at the tire shop. The Nova was ready, and within an hour and a half from the time I'd left Universal Paradigm, even in that traffic, I was standing outside Dexter's Diner and Donut Shoppe, looking at the big, black and white "Help Wanted" sign in the window.

It was total chaos on the inside. The place was more jammed than usual, and Shirl was not in evidence. There was another waitress working, a girl who occasionally helped out, but she didn't know the ropes, and orders were backing up. People were coming in, turning around, and walking right back out. The bell was ringing. There were nothing but plain donuts left, and no place to sit. Fortunately, Bernie was holding his usual seat at the counter. He was wearing the same clothes I'd seen on him at Eastlake's. He looked like hell, for him, although nobody else would notice. He pulled his police badge, showed it to the guy next to him, and told him he was commandeering that stool as a matter of police business. The guy, who apparently hadn't ordered yet, became pretty vocal about the abuses of power in our society, but then gave it up and stomped out of the place. Bernie called me over.

As I plopped down next to Bern, Dex was running from one end of the counter to the other, waiting on the customers, his chef's hat tilted at a precarious angle. On his second pass, I reached over and grabbed his elbow. "So Dex, where's Shirl this morning?" I said.

"You tell me, Nes," he said. "You're the one's married to her."

"You mean she didn't show up?"

"Called me last night and said she was sorry, but she had to have some time off. Didn't know how long. Said she'd let me know in a day or so. In the meantime, I'm just sort of hanging here."

"That's not like Shirl."

"Tell me about it."

"Is she ill?"

"She didn't say."

"Say, since you're out here, you have your son doing the cooking, I suppose?"

"Yeah."

"Swell."

"Hey, Nes, I gotta get back to work," he said, pulling his elbow gently from my grasp. He didn't want to drop three plates of bacon, eggs, hash browns, and three orders of toast.

I sat back down. From previous experience, we knew that Chops wasn't that good a cook anyway, primarily because he hated it and thought it beneath his dignity to cook for white folks. He had visions of becoming the next gangster-rap star, although he had no contacts in, or knowledge of, the entertainment business. Go figure. We skipped breakfast and got coffee with a couple of plain donuts.

"That was mean of you, running that poor sap off like that," I said to Bern.

"He'll get over it," Bernie said. "So, how's it hangin'?"

"Precariously, by a thread," I said, referring to my state of mind.

"What do you suppose has happened to Shirl?"

"Well, Bern, it's a personal matter. But I think Shirl's pretty unhappy with me right now."

"You think?" He laughed out loud. "I don't want to bum you out, but in case you didn't know, amigo, she's not alone. I hope your insurance policy covers assholes, because the last I heard McCorkle and Prudhomme are set to ream you a new one. I haven't seen McCorkle this happy since the last time he thought he had you jigged over that rogue cop-turned-drug dealer."

"You know what it's about?"

"Uh-uh. Muy mysteriosos. They're keeping me in the dark on this one. They know we're compadrés. But I can tell you this, they seem pretty confident, whatever it is."

We fell into an embarrassing silence for a moment and just sipped our coffee. This wasn't going to get things done. May as well get it over with. I decided to just grab the bear by the tail and hang on for dear life. So I said, "Hey Bern, I need you to do me a favor."

He just sat there with this look of surprise turning to awe, and finally to anger, on his face. "This Gringo says that right out loud," he said, and turned to look around the room, as if to get confirmation from everyone there. He turned back to me when it wasn't forthcoming. "Well, pinche! Like I'm not already giving him the biggest set of favors a cop could give a friend by not asking him questions that I know he hasn't got the answers to. I'm bent over backwards here, Nes, or hadn't you noticed? You've got some mucho grande fucking brass balls, compadré."

"Give me a break here, Bern . . . just a little longer."

"Look, Nes, I'm stretched to the limit; this can't go on. I had to check my own asshole insurance this morning because of you and the raw deal going down out at Eastlake's last night. I've been able to contain the situation so far, but me and my pension are on the carpet this time if McCorkle gets wind of it."

"Like hell, you're a fucking hero for saving that family three years ago, for Christ's sake. They can't touch you, and you know it."

"Since when do you care? Hell, I ought to be slapping the cuffs on you right now. Evidence missing, evidence wiped out. And prints, not yours by the way, with blood spatters all over the little powder room behind the staircase in the vestibule—when you claimed you'd been there all alone. I've got a hunch that they belong to Ms Ronnie Rivero, and we'll find that out, believe me, when I get probable cause to pick her up and have her prints made."

It was good to know they hadn't picked her up yet. But hell, how'd I miss that one? I'd seen the door back there but assumed it was a closet or something. Who puts a powder room under a staircase? Besides, Ronnie had said she hadn't touched things anywhere else in the house. You just can't trust the clients. I knew better. What was I thinking? What else had she lied to me about? I was beginning to get this sick feeling deep down in the pit of my stomach.

"Did you think I wouldn't find out?" Bernie continued. "Though I can't prove it yet, there had also been at least two other cars out there last night, besides that giant green chili you were driving . . . by the way, did you get your car back?"

"Yeah, it needed a couple of new tires was all. Look Bern, everything will clear up soon. I promise. Give me until the end of the day. That's all I ask. Just meet me outside Prudhomme's office, and you can have all the evidence back before the meeting with McCorkle this morning, if you'll just do me this one favor. I'll have some other things for you by then as well, I swear. What do you say?"

"Toda madre. You're a real piece of work, amigo. Never satisfied. Always looking for more. I don't know why I put up with you. I've been defending you to the brass at the department ever since you left. I am sorry about Nathaniel. Not like you, of course; he was not mine. But ah, mi corazon! It breaks anyway, whether you think so or not. I feel it, here inside, deep in my bones." He struck himself across his chest. "You're not the first man in the world to lose a son."

"What do you know about it?"

"More than you'd give me credit for."

I wasn't sure what Bernie meant by that. He'd never spoken to me about the reasons he was still single. He'd never spoken of family—though somehow over the years, I'd discovered that he had come from a large one, somewhere in Mexico. It was also common knowledge that he had suffered some sort of tragedy in his past, but no one I'd ever talked to knew what it was. It dawned on me. I was ashamed to realize that when it came right down to it, I knew so little about my friend and his life, when he knew so much about me and mine. Some people are just more self-centered than others. Yeah, right. Some friend I was. He was right; I'd pretty much been a prick ever since Nathaniel was killed.

But for now, that didn't change the situation I was in right then, with the meeting between me and McCorkle and Prudhomme looming, or the fact that this case was still a long way from giving me the answers I needed. I couldn't let up now; too much depended on it.

"So, are you gonna give me that favor, or are you gonna sit here and rip me a new one before Laurel and Hardy get their chance?" I said.

He just sat and looked at me a moment, as if he couldn't believe that the sun had risen that morning. "Did you hear a word I said?" he asked.

"Yeah."

"Is there anything you want to tell me?"

"Ah, no—not yet."

"Sure?"

"Yep. Say, haven't we been through this before?"

He looked at the ceiling as if he expected to see scads of big, white, fluffy clouds overhead. "Okay. Against my better judgment, okay. Mary, Mother of God, protect us from such fools, madmen, and evil doers . . . Don't you ever say I never did anything for you . . . Well, what is it?"

"Thanks, Bern. Tell me, do your guys know who made the shooter's ammo?"

"A small munitions manufacturer in Brazil called L'Argente. Why?"

"Do you know where he got it?"

"No, but we're looking hard. You can't find that kind of lead just anywhere. You got anything you can give me now?"

"Not yet."

"Is that your favor then?"

"No. I need you to run a California vanity plate through the DMV. The plate reads Hafiz 3, H-A-F-I-Z-3. It's riding a black late-model Lincoln Navigator. I need to know who it belongs to and the requisite address."

"That's it? Okay. Happy now, or is there something else I can do for you while I'm at it? I live only to serve you." Sarcasm wasn't usually Bern's style.

"Well, now that you mention it," I said, "you could pick up this check. I haven't been able to rob a bank yet this morning, and I spent my last buck on those new tires of mine."

He sighed a long sigh. "Anything else?"

"Not unless something comes to mind later."

"Well, if it does, amigo, don't call me. Your credit just ran out, until I see the first of many installments on the debts you already owe."

Thirty-two

WHEN I GOT TO THE OFFICE, DONNY WAS UP TO HIS elbows in dry coffee grounds. He had just spilled them all over Felia's desk—trying to remove the plastic lid from an almost full can of coffee when it slipped from his grip.

"Boy, Felia's gonna be pissed if she sees that," I said. "Where is she, by the way? She ought to be here by now."

"I don't know. Been trying to call her. Been trying to call you, too, ever since Ronnie didn't arrive at her place last night like you said she would."

"What? Ronnie didn't show?"

"Sorry, Chief. I've been trying to reach you since about two-thirty this morning. When I couldn't get you, I tried Felia, but she wasn't answering her cell either. And there was no answer on her home line." He pushed several mounds of grounds off the desk into the can. He stopped to look at me.

"Well, hell, isn't anybody where they're supposed to be this morning?"

"Boy, Chief, you look rough. What happened to the back of your head?"

285

"Guess."

"Not Mustafa and Davie?"

"You always were a smart lad, Donny, my boy. Now if I were you, I'd clean up that mess before Felia gets here. She's not gonna like coffee grounds all over her desk or that stack of files. By the way, how long have you been here?"

He resumed gathering the coffee grounds into little piles and pushing them off the desk into the can. "Just got here. Thought I'd make some coffee. Ha! When I couldn't reach anyone last night, I went home and got some sleep. Knew I'd see somebody here this morning; but I thought it would be Felia who showed up first."

"So, Ronnie Rivero didn't go home last night. How long were you there?"

"I dunno. Three, four hours, then I went home."

"Hmmm. Wonder what little game she's playing. There's something funny happening here. Wish I knew what it was. Look, Donny, I know there hasn't been much time, but I need you to dig deeper. The stakeout's over. Now I need everything you can find, a complete bio, financial records, phone records for the past month, anything you can uncover that will help me figure out her part in this. And I need it last month. Get Felia on it, too. Did that source of yours over in Juvie come through with anything yet?"

"No, but I expect to hear something soon."

"I need everything you two can put together by eleven this morning, before my meeting with McCorkle and Prudhomme."

"What's with that?"

"No idea. They're jerking my chain, putting me through a few hoops for their sick, sadistic pleasure.

Nothing better to do than harass a handsome, clean-living, hard-working PI. Who knows? But I'll be in a better position if I have something I can give them. In fact, I may need you downtown to go bail for me. But I'll call if it comes to that."

"Well, I guess that's what happens for blowing the whistle on your boss's incompetence." He was referring to the murder case of a young man connected to a prominent, socially connected, wealthy family that McCorkle had botched by arresting the wrong person. He and Prudhomme, out to make names for themselves, under pressure from the commissioner's office, had stuck it out to the bitter end. I, however, found substantial evidence to the contrary that ultimately blew their trumped-up, circumstantial evidence clean out of the water. While trying to back peddle and save his cajones, McCorkle then botched the arrest of the actual murderers, who got off with a wrist spanking on technicalities. It came back to bite them on the ass, and I've been on their to do list ever since. I'm afraid that I've never been much of a team player, especially when the team was such a bunch of nincompoops. "You'd never catch me making that mistake."

"I better not. You gonna finish cleaning that mess up and make some coffee, or what?"

Just then, Felia walked through the door. "What mess?" she asked, moving around the desk, pushing Donny to the side. "Oh damn . . . Okay, ladies, which one of you did this?"

We looked at each other and then to her. She seemed a little irritated this morning. Donny raised his hand like a third grader called on by his teacher.

"I thought so," she said, and then shifted gears. "Oh well. Be a sweetheart, Donny—go down to the bathroom and bring back a bunch of wet paper towels." She leaned over and kissed him on the cheek.

Donny blushed and left without saying a word as she put her stuff away.

"You'd think an office of this caliber would have a Dust Buster, wouldn't you?" she said.

To be fair, Donny had most of the coffee already back in the can by the time Felia had arrived.

"So, Missy," I said, ignoring the barb and looking at my watch, which I realized I still hadn't wound yet. "What's the deal coming in here at this hour? Don't you know we've got a lot to do to put this Rivero matter in the finished column? Get with Donny on it ASAP. Let the files go for now."

"Don't start with me, Boss. I've had a rotten night. That prick brother-in-law of mine beat the crap outta Mandy, and I've been over in the emergency room, sitting with the kids most of the night. I swear I'm gonna shoot that bastard when I get my hands on him."

"So much for good fatherly advice."

"What?"

"Nothing. Is she all right?"

"A broken jaw, some contusions, but she'll make it."

"Did she press charges?"

"Yeah. I pressed them for her."

"Good."

"They've already picked him up. They're holding him over for arraignment tomorrow. Then I guess he makes bail."

"See if you can find out when that will be."

"What for?"

"I want to see that someone's there to meet him with condolences and flowers when he gets out."

"Look, Boss, I don't want you to . . ."

"Never mind, Felia. It's all too bad . . . for Mandy, the kids . . . him, too, really."

"It is too bad. Mandy's crushed. So don't be wasting any sympathy on that jerk. And I was having such a good day yesterday, too."

"Oh yeah?"

Just then Donny came back with the paper towel and proceeded to help her wipe down the desk and floor.

"Thanks, baby," she said. "Yeah, it was a great day; I got a call back from Tarantino. He wants to see me read something else for that role in his film."

"All right!" Donny said and hugged her.

"Fantastic!" I said.

"Yeah, maybe. And maybe he just wants another peek at my boobs," she said.

"I can't say that I blame him," Donny said and stood there beaming.

She pulled away and slapped him on the arm. "What are you smiling about?"

"Oh nothing," he said.

"Well, don't just stand there grinning like a dork. Take that pot and get me some water for the coffee maker," she said to Donny. "And you," she said, pointing at me. "I put a couple messages on your desk last night before I left. Did you get them?"

"Not yet," I said and turned to my office.

"By the way, FYI we got that check marked 'paid in full' from Mankiewitz yesterday, right on time," she said, smiling as if there was no tomorrow.

"Great. I guess you did have a good day. Well, just make sure you get that sucker cashed sometime this morning. That way you can come down to the tank and go my bail when they throw me in jail, for you threatening to break his thumbs in the first place."

"What does that mean?"

I stopped and turned back to her. "Just that I've got a meeting with McCorkle and Prudhomme at eleven, and I understand Mankiewitz made a formal complaint to the ADA; they want me over there to talk about it."

"Are you kidding me?"

"I'm not sure what they want, but I guess that's on the agenda."

"I'm sorry, Boss. I didn't mean for it to cause you . . ."

"Never mind. They got squat . . . Gotcha." I smiled and went into my office.

"Oh you . . ." she said.

I tried to call Shirl, but she wasn't answering. Felia had left two messages on my desk. Inga Braden had called, left her number but no message. That was intriguing. I took out my cell and punched her number. I left my name and cell number on her machine and asked her to call. The second was from Prudhomme's office, a secretary officially requesting my person for a meeting, eleven this morning. Donny came back into the office, and the two of them talked quietly. I walked over to the door, asked Felia for a cup of coffee when it was ready, and closed it. I went back and sat behind my desk, put my feet up, and shut my eyes.

I needed some time to think. It was heating up. Things were beginning to take shape in my mind. Answers to my questions danced seductively just out of reach. With a few more crucial parts of the puzzle in hand, the solution to this case would start to reveal itself, piece by piece, just like a stripper in a club. Ronnie Rivero had some things to explain. I was going to pay her a visit when I could find her. That business with Carl, Mustafa, and Davie was eye opening, but brought up more questions to answer. Inga Braden had something to add, otherwise why would she have bothered to call? Yeah, though I had to see her, too, I had to see Chullsu first. But there was somebody missing, someone I'd overlooked somehow, someone who could help me unravel this case and put it to rest. My cell rang. "Pike here," I said.

"It's Maldonado."

"What'cha got, Bern?"

"Hafiz Al Hassan, the owner of a house out in Topanga Canyon, 46069 Blue Sail Drive. He's the owner of that Lincoln SUV you asked me to track."

"That's right over there by the Getty Villa . . ." I jotted it down in my trusty little notebook.

"Yeah."

" . . . where they found Hollenbeck."

"You're right."

"Thanks, Bern. Gotta go. A million things to do before I get to that meeting. If I'm late, you guys start without me."

"Yeah, right. Look, Nes, you'd better not miss. . ."
I didn't hear the rest cuz I hung up on him. He'd get over it—sooner or later.

Thirty-three

CHULLSU WAS BUSY WITH A CLIENT WHEN I ENTERED his shop, so I strolled around looking at the guns and ammo in the display cases. While I waited, Jason Kim, his nineteen year-old son, lugging a beach bag and one of those short needle-nosed surfboards, came in through Chullsu's shooting alley in back. Jason, who always reminded me of Keanu Reeves, was wearing long baggy shorts, a T-shirt, and reddish-blonde tips in his short, spiky hair. He was headed for the front door, until he saw me and veered over.

"Wassup, dude?" he yelled, walking up. He dropped his bag and vigorously shook my hand, first knocking his knuckles into mine.

"Long time no see. How's it going?"

"No complaints, man. You?"

"It's all good; what can I say?"

"It doesn't look too good. Somebody been wailing on your ass, dude. You let 'em get away with that?" he asked, pointing at my face.

"Not a chance."

"Yeah. Payback done righteous is sweet sweet. Did you shoot the motherfucker? Like pow?" he said, making a gun with his fist and fingers, as if he knew all about such things.

"Not yet, but who knows?"

"Hey, gnarly . . . but I gotta run, dude. Gotta meet the boys, pick up the girls . . ." He winked, then smiled. "Had a storm out there last night. I hear we got some stiff waves on the roll man."

"I hear you got a job."

"Yeah, but I got the day off. Called in sick." He leaned over, whispered, "Don't tell my dad," and laughed. "He thinks they gave me the day off for inventory." He smiled again and picked up his bag. Jason was always in a good mood.

"Your secret's safe with me," I said.

"Thanks, dude. I'm outta here."

Jason yelled bye to his dad as he flew out the front door. Chullsu handed his customer the change from his purchase and tried to catch Jason before he got out the door, but was too late. He joined me where I was looking across the counter at a locked-down rack of high-powered assault weapons.

"That kid gimme heartburn. He think I don't know he play hooky, go to beach."

"Yeah, he thinks he's pretty clever all right."

"He good kid, but too much like Missy Kim . . . So Mista Nesta, how you do? Look like you got in new fight since I seen you. Got big goose egg now. How many little pill you take for tha' one?"

"Well, you know how it goes, Chullsu. Some days are better than others."

"Yeh, yeh, I know wha' you mean. Some day I can't

see fores' for tree. Wha' can I do for you today? You need more bullet already? How many cowboy you kill?"

"I haven't killed anybody—yet, but I know a couple guys who would look better aired out with a few holes in them."

"Yeh, yeh. Beauty is fleeting with years. They not think they look so good with hole."

"Probably not. Say Chullsu, The reason I came by . . . I want to know if you can tell me about this ammo." I took out the shell casing that I'd stolen last night at Eastlake's and handed it to him.

He turned it over a couple times. "Yeh, yeh. I know tha'. Tha' L'Argente, small maker in Brazil. See brown lacquer casing." He held it up for me to look at. "Copycat Russian Wolf TCJ bullet with green lacquer casing. Where you get this?"

I knew about Wolf Ammo. I used it for practice. The factory in Tula Russia had made high quality ammunitions for over a hundred years. Their line of Total Copper Jacket bullets with green lacquer casings was a less expensive TCJ, expressly made for the gigantic American shooter's market. "I got it at a murder scene over in Beverly Hills. What else can you tell me about it?"

"Can't buy quantity yet. I don't have big stock. I had six box. I sold two box. Brand new. Have to order through catalogue, or go online to website. For trial period, I exclusive distributor for LA, three month. In six month, everyone carry L'Argente."

"Why haven't you shown it to me so I could try it out?

"I don't know how good. I not shoot yet; no time to try. Tha' why they only send me six box."

"If you're the exclusive distributor, then you sold this bullet to the shooter. And if you had it on trial, why'd you sell it to him and not order it from the catalogue?"

"He ask for by name. I only need two box to try, so I sold to him two box. I give you other two box," he said, turned, and went down the counter.

"Did you get his name?" I said, as I followed him.

"No."

"Did he pay in cash or with a check?"

"He pay cash."

"Can you tell me what he looked like?"

"He big for Spanic guy. Tall. Long black hair, combed back. Skinny mustache." He went behind the counter, stooped down, and popped back up with the two boxes of L'Argente's. He shoved them over to me. "You take," he said.

"Ever seen him before?" I said. I took out my wallet and realized I didn't have any money on me.

"Couple time. Not very friendly. Smar' ass." He returned the casing to me.

"I'll have to get these next time," I said, as I put my wallet away and pushed the ammo back to him.

"No, no. You take now. It free to me, so it free to you," he said, pushing them back even closer. He looked like it would crush him if I refused.

"Okay, okay," I said. "Just till I can pay you."

"I lock door. We go in back and shoot now. Wha' you say?"

"Can't now. I'll come back another time."

"Yeh, yeh. Come back, we shoot hell out of this ammo. See how good." He smiled from ear to ear, took a paper bag from beneath the counter, and wrapped them up. Chullsu's description of the guy had sounded vaguely familiar, like a description of someone I knew or had seen before. It would come to me later, I supposed.

"Thanks, Chullsu. Say, since you mentioned Ms. Kim, how is she by the way?"

"Ah, woman, she gimme no res'. Now she do Kundalini all time. She say, make her sex better. She wan' me to take yoga. I tell her 'frosty day in hell when I take yoga.'"

"What did she say to that?"

"I can' repeat in English, no translation. She say, I don' take up yoga, she bring mother to live with us. Pull back out trying exercise called Dying Swan. Motherfucker hurt like hell; though' I was dying."

"I thought you were walking a little funny today, but I didn't want to say anything."

"You got any little pill lef'?"

"Sure. Here, take these; I won't use them," I dug the bottle of Vicodin out of my pocket and handed it to him. "Sounds like you're going to need them."

"That not all I gonna need. Viagra not enough for her. Now she wan' bigger dick. She say I need penile implant. She know good doctor, she see on Oprah. I tell her, 'Go to Hell! Live with fucking ancestor!'"

"I don't blame you." My cell started ringing, and I had to try to stop laughing before I could answer. "Excuse me, Chullsu." I moved away from him and took out the phone. "Pike here."

"Mr. Pike?"

It was the Ice Queen. I recognized her voice; it reminded me of the lavender scent she wore. "Yes?"

"This is Inga Braden. Could you meet me for a drink later? I have some information that I think you will find interesting."

297

"And this information is concerning what?"

"A mutual friend and his little black-haired Ho."

"Oh, I see. Where would you like to meet?"

"Is The Carousel okay?"

"On Melrose, over in Westwood?"

"Yes, say . . . around one?"

"You bet." I assumed that I'd be done with McCorkle and Prudhomme by then. If not, then taking a meeting with her probably didn't matter anyway, regardless of what she had to tell me, cuz I'd be in jail.

She hung up without saying anything further.

"Hey, Chullsu, gotta go," I said, putting the cell away and heading for the door.

"Wai', wai', Mista Nesta, you forgot bullet," he said and brought them over to me.

"No, you keep them. I'll come back next week; we can shoot them together."

"Yeh, yeh. Tha' good idea."

"Thanks. Now be sure and stick to your guns. Whatever you do, don't let them give you that implant."

"Hell no. With my luck, they cut boner off. I tell her, 'no one touch dragon of love. Have to kill me firs'.' I say, 'I know good doctor—sew pussy, make tight.' See how she like tha'."

Out on the sidewalk, I stopped laughing long enough to compose myself and try to remember where I was going and what I was doing. Ah yes, I had to rob a bank for the cash to meet Snow Princess for a drink . . . I was sad, really, because I just knew that after talking with Chullsu, my day was going downhill from there on out. Especially since I was due in Prudhomme's office in one stinking measly little hour.

Thirty-four

TWENTY MINUTES BEFORE THE SCHEDULED MEETING with McCorkle, I met Bernie outside ADA Prudhomme's office. "Here's the evidence you were missing from Eastlake's last night," I said, handing him the plastic bag with Ronnie's bloody blouse and the brown shell casing in it.

"Why did you take it in the first place, vato?"

By the sound of his voice, I could tell he was miffed about the evidence, and my hanging up on him earlier. He had a lot to be miffed at me about. I was going to have to make it up to him somehow. So I told him about Ronnie calling me the night before from Eastlake's, and what she had said about that night. I asked him to hold off on picking her up, until I could see her later that afternoon.

"I don't know why I let you talk me into this, ese. No good's going to come of it."

"Look, Bern, I'll come with her to see that she surrenders herself in your office at the Parker Center Station for questioning, no later than nine a.m. tomorrow morning. Okay? I just need to know the extent of her involvement. Believe me, she'll lawyer up, then clam up, if you pick her up now. And who knows how long it will take to crack this case without her help? You said I could have until the end of the day." Fact of the matter was, he didn't know exactly where to find her, or he would have already picked her up. But then, I didn't know where she was either; she hadn't gone home last night.

"No doubt, I'll live to regret it," he said.

"In the meantime, amigo, I hate to do this to you, but . . ."

"But si, si—you will anyway, I know."

"You're gonna have to make some excuses for me. I can't make their little party this morning. Show them that new evidence." I pointed to the plastic bag that I'd given him, with Ronnie's bloody shirt in it. "Tell them I just turned it up. Say that I'm out looking for my client so I can bring her in, in the morning, which is true enough." That was pushing Bern beyond his limits, I figured; but to my surprise, he said okay. Without giving him time to reconsider his folly, I removed myself from his presence post haste.

Since it was only eleven and I had to be back in the city by one, there was just enough time to drive out to Topanga Canyon, given favorable traffic. I wanted to get the lay of the land and see what connection, if any, existed between Mr. Hafiz Al Hassan, Mustafa, and Davie. Traffic was light and I arrived at the gates of the address on Blue Sail Drive in under thirty-five minutes, slowing to a crawl as I passed by.

It was a large estate, with a sentry house manned by a mug in a crewcut, tie, and blazer. The gates were ten feet high, hung on stone columns, fanning inward, like a two-fisted hand of pinochle cards. From the center of the coral-colored scallop shell entryway, the exposed-aggregate drive wound it's way steeply up through three lawns and stonewalled terraced gardens and dropped you in a circular courtyard, with a triple-decker fountain in the center at the front door. From there, it diddled its way seaward around the back. Across from the house, a four-bay ramada sheltered a small Mercedes limo, a Mercedes Kompressor and, voilá, the big, black Lincoln Navigator SUV. I assumed it to be the same one Mustafa and Davie kidnapped me in just that very morning, though the plates were beneath my view.

The house, a humongous and rambling cream-colored Mission-style confection—replete with bell towers, ten inch vigas sticking from the stucco walls, and red roof-tiles that topped the massive but ornately carved rafters—was draped in the perennial California gold, red, and lavender bougainvillea. It was too precious for words, crowning the top of the hillside. With its many wrought-iron balconies overlooking the gardens below and out to the Pacific beyond, it looked like it belonged on one of the back lots at Warner Brother's Studios. Zorro, in a purple cape and mask studded with sequins and zirconia, was going to charge up on his black stallion at any moment. Damn, there I was without my sword. The place was a complete surprise. With an owner whose name was Hafiz Al Hassan, I'd been expecting some sort of desert palace, like something out of Casablanca.

I wasn't wearing the right costume for this picture, or well-heeled enough to get through such majestic gates in broad daylight, so I made plans to come back when fewer eyes would be watching, later that night.

Driving up the road a ways, around to the side and back, and looking for a way into the grounds revealed a small service road, which, by the looks of it, was in disuse, overgrown at the property line. The old gate, not as grand as the front, was heavily chained and covered in bougainvillea, which climbed all along the wrought-iron around the property and reminded me to bring leather gloves.

There were no sidewalks or curbs beside the asphalt street, though there was room for them between the road and the fence that terminated abruptly at the neighbor's two-tiered rock and concrete-stucco wall. On the other side, and a bit further up the road, was a secluded turn-around under some trees. The Nova would be well hidden, not too conspicuous sitting there after dark, if I got in and out fast. I pulled over, parked, took my binoculars from the trunk, and looked back across the ravine toward the house and grounds. Two small outbuildings sat screened by trees to the side and back from the patio, courtyard, and pool areas directly connected to the house and guesthouse. Fortunately, there were no kennels in evidence, but security cameras were liberally placed around the house. I plotted a route along the unused service drive to the outbuildings, while trying to avoid as many cameras as possible through the courtyard to the main house. I could enter from the back where there was likely to be less vigilance.

From this position, there was no way of telling what the house screened on the other side of the hill. If there were time, I'd drive around there before I left. Just then, a couple of suits came out of the house. One of the men went over to the limo and drove it around to the front door. Geshur Kedar—or his evil twin, Hafiz Al

Hassan—came out of the front door, accompanied by two more blazers carrying luggage, and two women dressed in mufti. They were completely hidden from view in black veils and skirts that covered their feet and wiped out any slipper tracks left in their wakes. Kedar leaned over, kissed each of the women, and helped them into the limo. The suits put six bags of luggage into the trunk of the car. With everything secure, and a wave from Kedar, the limo moved around the fountain, quickly down the drive, and through the previously opened gate that closed immediately as the limo cleared. It turned south and sped away.

Kedar walked over and spoke to the two men who turned and went back inside as Mustafa and Davie came out. Davie walked straight to the Navigator; Mustafa walked over and stood listening to Kedar. He nodded his head once, before Kedar turned abruptly and went into the house. Mustafa turned back to the car, which Davie had just driven around. Before getting in, Mustafa paused to look around; something had caught his attention. He scanned the hillside, as if he felt my eyes watching him. With my binocs I could see him and his cold, expressionless, deep-set black eyes clearly. They were persistent in their search, but unconcerned—little black points, like pencil dots on fresh white paper.

After a moment they fell on me. He'd found the source of that prickle on the back of his neck. I doubted he could see my car—or knew for sure who was using the glasses in the shade under the trees—from this distance. But now he knew that he was being watched. And though he showed no reaction to this knowledge, he and Davie would soon be up here to see about it.

He got into the car. That was my cue to split. I'd seen

everything that I'd needed to see. There was no longer any reason for me to hang around here, or come back later, for that matter. My elaborate plan to return in the dark of night, to toss the place, was moot; it was time to turn things over to Bern and his men. Things had speeded up; people were leaving town. Call it a hunch, but I knew that somewhere over there, in Disneyland-on-the-hill, he'd find distinct evidence linking Mustafa, Davie, and Kedar to the Hollenbeck murder. I just wondered where Chip and Dale were off to now in that big SUV. I drove up the canyon. Whatever truce we'd had that morning at Carl's had been terminated, and this was not the time or place to discuss it.

On the way back to town, I called Bern and blew the whistle on Hafiz Al Hassan. I told him everything I'd seen and suspected and suggested that if he wanted to interview Mrs. Kedar, who was at that very moment on her way to LAX, he might need to send a car to the airport, post haste. He said he'd also get a search warrant while he was at it and send a demolition crew out to Topanga Canyon, with an APB on Mustafa and Davie next on the list. They shouldn't be too hard to spot in that rig, looking the way they did. What was it Jason Kim had said earlier? Oh yeah, "Payback done righteous is sweet sweet." Well, this wasn't as sweet as it might've been; but then maybe nobody got hurt, and that would be sweet enough, if not entirely righteous. And not to put too fine a point on it, if Prudhomme did his job, maybe they'd be doing some hard time—for a long time.

Thirty-five

T HE CAROUSEL WAS A YOUNG EXECUTIVE'S EATERY AND watering hole in Westwood, not far from the Universal Paradigm building. Done in etched glass, exposed halogen lighting, and the calculated risk of perforated, galvanized steel, with not one prancing pony or gamboling goose in sight, it was the next rung up the evolutionary ladder from the cozy fern, oak, and brass yuppie dives of the eighties. When I arrived, Inga Braden, wearing a bright yellow sundress with spaghetti straps—which was an extraordinary change from her monochrome-black work outfit—was already sitting at a dark corner table in the bar, drinking a martini up, and holding three stuffed olives impaled on a little pink sword.

With her shoulder-length hair, coral-colored lipstick, and a pair of bangle earrings that I thought had gone the way of the seventies, she appeared to be flying in the face of all fashion decorum—not that I was an expert. But what a turnabout from the Ice Queen that I'd first met at Buddy's office. It looked as if she had quit her job once again, and this wasn't her first drink. On the contrary, the napkin in front of her had two little pink swords on it, just like the one she held in her long tapered fingers; and this drink had hardly been touched. She wore an expression of genial irritation when I first walked in. But then, she'd been waiting for me twenty-five minutes. Lunch traffic had turned fierce on the way back from Topanga Canyon.

"Sorry I'm late," I said, slipping into the chair across from her. "It was good of you to wait." I snagged a buxom young waitress—in a tight tee with black and white horizontal stripes and a dark green mini-skirt over matching tights and platform shoes—as she bounced by. I ordered a gin and tonic with a twist, and asked her to hold the gin.

"Oh, how clever of you," the waitress said. "There's one in every crowd." She batted her big baby blues, shook her shock of curly red hair at me, and continued: "We have open mike stand-up comedy here every Friday and Saturday nights. You should come back then, for an audience who could really appreciate such side-splitting humor."

"Touché."

"Touché? What's that, the name of your designer aftershave?"

"Ouch. Are you performing this weekend?"

"I'm always performing."

"I can see that."

"Why don't you join me?"

"I couldn't hope to compete with the likes of you."

"Who said anything about competing?" She smiled wickedly.

"I'll bet you're a real crowd-pleaser."

"Standing ovation every time."

I was beginning to think she and I were talking about two different things. Inga didn't appear to find our little exchange amusing and did some major damage to her drink as she waited for me to quit farting around. She was skittish and almost polished it off in one long gulp.

"So how about that tonic?" I said. "And another martini for the lady."

"One triple-decker martini and one Geritol comin' right up, Dad," she said, winked, then rolled off toward the bar. I hadn't seen this much perkiness since I'd joined the Mickey Mouse Club. Speaking of winks, the Ice Queen's eyes appeared to have been leaking recently; they were red and puffy. When she caught me looking at them, she took her purse and excused herself to the ladies room. While she was gone, I got hold of the waitress—whose nametag read Roxanne—and ordered two grilled-chicken breasts, blue-plate specials with lettuce, tomato, onion, and Mayo with fries on the side to go with the drinks. I figured if Inga didn't want hers, I could eat it later; I was ravenous, having had nothing but coffee all day. Roxanne brought our drinks.

When Inga got back to the table, I didn't speak. I just waited for her to tell me what she wanted to tell me in her own good time, without my clumsy prying. She'd made some adjustments to her eye makeup and looked as if she could face the rest of the day.

"So, Mr. Pike, aren't you just the tiniest bit curious why I asked you over here?"

"I assumed that you'd found me so attractive that you just had to get to know me better."

She didn't know quite how to take that at first. She seemed flustered, distraught.

"Lighten up, sweetheart. I'm teasing."

"Oh yes, yes of course . . ." She sighed a big sigh. "Sometimes I just get so overwhelmed by things . . . I don't know. I'm so embarrassed."

"Not at all. Look, I just figured you'd say something when you wanted me to know. Okay?"

"I see. I guess you're pretty confident about things. I suppose you should be. You are an attractive man, even under all those wounds. But what if I had changed my mind?"

"Well, that's a woman's prerogative, or so the women I know keep saying. Believe me, you wouldn't be the first woman to disappoint me."

"Who would dare disappoint you, Mr. Pike? Besides, what do men know of disappointment? You're not the ones sitting home nights, waiting for the phone to ring." The frosty condensation on her martini glass reminded me of hot breath on a cold morning. She had this air about her; she wore this cool anger like a cloak. But it gave me the feeling she was softer than she wanted to appear. She tippled back on her martini and ate one of the olives.

"Well I don't know about that," I said. "But I suppose it could get to feeling that way, if the man you're sitting around waiting for is Buddy Palmer."

Ow, that touched a raw nerve. A look of pure disgust flashed across her face when I'd mentioned Buddy's name—like she'd just discovered a roach in her drink. I wasn't surprised. I always had a similar feeling when I thought of Buddy Palmer, too.

"You're a cruel man, Mr. Pike. I can see that in those big green eyes of yours. I know about such things. At least I thought I did. Buddy's eyes are like that at times, cold, indifferent, and hard. Are you cold, indifferent, and hard, Mr. Pike?"

I took that to be a rhetorical question.

"You've probably even killed a man or two in your time . . . Am I right?"

I didn't answer that one either. She seemed to be doing fine without prompting from me. Besides, she really didn't want to know that I had killed more men than I cared to remember. Viet Nam was a war, of course, and those Viet Cong soldiers probably didn't deserve to die any more than I did; the others were self-defense. And there were some I should've killed, but didn't. Either way, it never mattered; they still haunted me some nights, when I got too tired even for sleep.

"Of course I am. Men like you and Buddy take what you want, and then just throw it away when you're done with it. You never think about the consequences, how much pain you cause others, as long as you have what you want. That's what counts, isn't it?—no matter who you hurt in the process." Her martini kicked in somewhere in the middle of that speech and slurred the last couple of words she spoke. She brushed at the skirt of her dress that didn't appear to need brushing; but what did I know?

"I'm afraid you don't have a very high opinion of me, Ms. Braden."

"Do you really care, Mr. Pike? Don't take it personally. Right now, I don't have a high opinion of any man. I don't even have a high opinion of myself." But she appeared to remember something that made her features soften momentarily, and I wondered about the relationship she'd had with her father.

"Call me Nes," I said.

"What?" She seemed taken aback by this suggestion.

"I said, call me Nes. That's my name."

"I heard you the first time. I just wondered why this sudden invitation to familiarity. You think we're gonna be friends?"

"Not impossible."

"Trust me, Mr. Pike; we're not gonna be friends."

"Okay. So we're not going to be friends . . . where does that leave us?"

"Right where we started." She sipped her martini and ate another olive.

"It's your call, sweetheart," I said and waited, since she appeared to be in the lead here.

"Are you married, Mr. Pike?"

"Yes. And please . . . call me Nes. It doesn't mean we have to be friends. It's just that 'Mr. Pike' makes me feel so old, especially when a young person, such as yourself, calls me that."

She gave me the once-over with an appraising eye. "All right, Mr. Pike, . . . Nesh it is. Married a long time?"

"Twenty years."

"That qualifies. Happily?"

"That depends on your definition of happiness. But for the most part, yes, though we don't live together."

"What's this? Do I detect a serpent in the garden? Hmmm."

"It's my work, she . . ."

"Let me guess. You stay out all hours, day and night. She sits and worries herself to distraction over you. She never knows when you'll show up. You never call, except when you need her to do something for you. You meet other women, and you're constantly—well, for lack of a better term—pumping them for information; and all in the line of duty to your clients. Something like that, Nesh?"

310

"Well I can't speak for Buddy, and I really have no need to justify my life to you, Ms. Braden, but yes, Shirl and I have our problems, though not the infidelities that you imagine. We've been hashing out some differences over the past few years, ever since our son was killed."

She stopped drinking her Martini in mid-sip and looked at me through the edge of her glass, as if looking through a prism.

Why did I feel like a bug under a microscope? How had I gotten myself into this personal conversation, shooting my mouth off in all directions? Here I was, sitting and talking to a complete stranger, the Ice Queen herself, about my personal life—when I couldn't bring myself to discuss it with Shirl. The irony was galling. "Look, sweetheart, I didn't come over here to waste your time with my sad tale. You brought me down here to tell me something. So was that it?"

She paused for a long moment, looking at her drink as she swirled it about in the glass. "Call me Inga," she said.

"Call you Inga?" I guessed it was my turn to look surprised.

"That's what I said; it's my name."

"I know that," I said and narrowed my eyelids at her. "But if I do, you should know it doesn't mean that we're gonna be friends."

"That's all right. I deserved that. It's just that 'Ms. Braden' was my mother, and I'm nothing like my mother."

I didn't want to burst her bubble, but in my experience, women who said that tended to be like their mothers in one way or another, no matter how much they thought, hoped, or professed otherwise. "All right, Inga, now that that's settled, why did you call me over here?

I'm assuming you know something about Buddy and his 'black-haired ho'—by which slur I guess you refer to my client, Ronnie Rivero—that you think I should know about."

"What would you say if I told you they were sleeping together?"

"It wouldn't surprise me. At this point in my life, not much does. But I take it you just found this out, and it's a bit of a shock. Right?"

"Yes, it's true; you don't care?" she said. Her already fragile demeanor seemed on the verge of crumbling altogether.

"It's none of my business, except insofar as it has some bearing on the case she hired me to pursue."

"That bitch," she spat. "Buddy was going to leave his wife, he said. For the past six months, he's been promising that he would leave her, so we could be together. He said we could get married when his kids got a little older." She took another tissue from her purse and dabbed at her eyes. "I'm sorry," she said. "I just didn't see this coming. I know I should have, but I didn't. That's what makes it so bad."

I wondered if Buddy's wife had seen Inga coming. Hell, if I knew Buddy, she'd probably seen a lot more than Inga.

"Don't worry about it," I said. "It's okay,"

"You'd think as old as I am that I would've known right away."

"Sometimes there are things we just don't want to know." For some reason, the memory of Ronnie Rivero standing in my office, in that hot red dress, popped into my mind. I shoved it aside. "When did you find out?"

"Last night."

312

"At Buddy's office?"

"Yes. Coitus interruptus. I walked right in on them, caught them on the very same couch where Buddy and I first made love. I've been so dense, such a fool. You cannot imagine. He was fucking that bitch all along. I knew they occasionally met each other, but I thought it was something to do with Carl's art collection. It always looked that way. Then, one day, everything that's happened over the past six months just fell into place, everything they've been doing since Buddy first heard about the Getty show. Did you know that they were planning to steal some valuable artifacts and blackmail Dr. Eastlake and Mr. Carl?"

Right then, I knew more about some things than I wanted to know about anything. Everything fell into place all right. I knew just how she felt. Young fool that she was, she didn't understand that there was no fool quite as dense as an old fool . . . but I couldn't go there now.

Just then, Roxanne delivered our sandwiches.

Inga's watery eyes flashed up at me through her pain. "Food? You ordered food?"

"Just thought you'd like something to buff the edge off those martinis. What—you don't like chicken?" I cracked wise.

I thought she was choking, until she burst out with a long hysterical laugh that continued until all the previous tension seemed to drain away from her. The residue of her smile, even under a deluge of tears, was radiant. I didn't know she could smile like that.

She stood up. "Excuse me, I know that wasn't funny, but I just couldn't help myself," she blubbered and wiped at her eyes with a tissue from her purse. "I'll be right back; I have to fix my eyes." She left the table.

"Would you pack this stuff to go and bring me the check, please?" I said to Roxanne as I stood to watch Inga leave.

"Is she gonna be okay?" she asked, handing me the check—looking troubled at first, then angry.

"Oh yeah, she's tough, she'll be fine; I think the worst is over."

"It's obvious you're no comedian; that punch line was crap. What kinda clown are you, anyway? You think you're a real heartbreaker, don't you? Jesus, you men are all alike; you make me sick. Well, just in case you've got the wrong idea, Slick, you can forget about these babies." She reached up and boosted her boobs from underneath with a shimmy. "And comedy nights, too." Then she made a face, stuck her tongue out, turned her back, and stomped off toward the bar, her tight little tush all aquiver with indignation.

"Well I guess they told me, chauvinist pig that I am," I said to myself, since I was the only one left standing there.

Thirty-six

THE HEAT WAVES SHIMMERING AND RISING OFF THE
Carousel parking lot were lolling the tongue and curling
the lips of a mangy-looking German Shepherd as it hot-
pawed its way over the asphalt. It must've been hungry to
have been driven out from under the dusty but cooler
shade of an oleander or hydrangea bush, somewhere in
this heat. The sun had burnt off all cloud cover. The
smog had risen, and the city sparkled through the mid-
afternoon salt-spray rainbows drifting in from the ocean.
I'd left Inga—the not-so-icy Ice Queen—inside, where
she'd decided to eat her chicken sandwich and drink a
cup of black coffee after all. I would've joined her for coffee, if I'd had the time. She promised to get a cab home.

To be honest, I wasn't sure that I wanted to sit com-
miserating and licking our wounds together like a couple of old dogs. Right now, the last thing I wanted was a
good look at myself through my own eyes, especially
when it came down to Ronnie Rivero. I knew I wouldn't
like what I would see; it was looking evermore likely that
this dark angel had played me like a harp.

As I carried my doggie box over to the Nova, a white

Ford panel van parked across the lot caught my eye when a tall, swarthy man with a bushy mustache got out of the passenger-side door. He was dressed in a gray business suit. I flashed back to a similar van from earlier, just after I'd left the Kedar estate out on Blue Sail Drive, up the hill in Topanga Canyon. The ACME PLUMBING sign on its side had led me to assume that it was a service van on call in the area, an unwarranted assumption I now realized. A second man, shorter and lighter, also with a bushy mustache but wearing a blue suit, came around the front of the van and joined the first man, who was eyeing me directly. He adjusted the sling beneath his jacket under his arm as they came in my direction.

I turned to face them.

"You are Mr. Pike, yes?" the tall man said, after they'd walked up and stood at right angles to me. I had to turn my head from one to the other to keep them in view. Traffic was heavy on the street. But, for now, we were alone in the parking lot.

The man's Middle Eastern accent and good looks reminded me that I had seen these two on the elevator at Universal Paradigm, the day of my meeting with Buddy Palmer. They'd laughed about my face.

"Mr. who?" I said.

"Ha ha. You Americans, all with these senses of humor. You are liking lots of jokes. You are Nestor Pike. I am Debir; this is my partner, Jarmouthe. We would like to speak with you." They had the look of the Israeli Secret Service all over them but, for all I knew, they could just as easily have been Jordanian Intelligence, or Egyptian, though that was unlikely. They didn't offer to shake hands.

"And believe you me, I'd like nothing better than to

mince a few choice words with you, too," I said. "But right now, I'm late for a date with Tyra Banks over at the House of Blues. I'm in the phone book; stop by the office sometime. Nice to meet you boys." I started to put the key in the door of the Nova.

"Ah, that is too bad," he said as he reached up, pulled what looked like one of those Israeli special forces weapons from beneath his jacket, and aimed it at me. "I'm afraid we must insist that you join us—now." I was afraid he was about to do something like that. He'd done this sort of thing before. With his lids at half-mast, he appeared bored with the predictability of our little scenario.

"Well, since you put it so persuasively, how can I resist?" I put the keys back in my pocket. "Where to? It's your party. Shall we go back inside?" I nodded toward The Carousel. What was this city coming to? A man couldn't stop for lunch with a pretty young woman without getting hijacked in broad daylight. I looked up and down the street. Where was a cop when you needed one?

"Sorry, but our van is right over there and will do very well." He took me by the elbow and walked in close, to shield his weapon from view. We crossed the parking lot and the one called Jarmouthe quickly frisked me. He took everything I had before we got in the side of the van that was still running and cool inside. This hadn't been my day; people kept taking my guns away. This guy even got my lunch. One of these days, I might not get them back. I might get myself shot instead.

"So, gentlemen, what can I do for you now that you have my undivided attention?" I said after we settled in. The one calling himself Debir sat across from me where he could keep his weapon clear. Jarmouthe sat in front, where he could keep one eye on the parking lot outside.

To my chagrin, he removed my sandwich from the Styrofoam container and took a big bite, smacking his lips before he put it back in the box. He wiped his hands with a napkin from the bag.

"We understand that you work for Veronica Rivero, yes?" Debir said.

"I'm not at liberty to speak about Ms. Rivero," I said, glaring at Jarmouthe. Not only was I not at liberty to speak about my client, the thought of doing so gave me a sick feeling. No sense getting into it with Debir. Besides, after what Jarmouthe did to my sandwich, I knew that he was the one I ultimately had to watch out for. And Inga thought I was a cruel man. Ha!

"Don't play games with us, Mr. Pike. We know she has hired you."

"Then why ask me?"

Debir looked at me a moment then said, "Yes, I see your point. Shall we start over?"

"Whatever it takes."

"Then you will tell us what you were doing at the Topanga Canyon estate this morning."

"I don't tell anybody anything without good cause. Aside from that Roscoe you're pointing at me, so far you haven't shown me any convincing reason to be cooperative. Who do you think you are anyway?" When in doubt, push a few buttons and see what lights up. Was that a twitch at the corner of his eye? That remark also caught Jarmouthe's attention. He laid his bright sharp eyes squarely on my face.

"An intelligent person would consider this convincing enough," Debir said, indicating the gun. "But I can see you are going to make this much harder than it has to be." Jarmouthe remained silent, though he hadn't missed a move. It seemed that I had an Arab Penn and Teller on my hands. Here was hoping that they weren't going to try and make me disappear.

"Where do you get off, coming into my city and sticking that gun into my face? And what the hell were you doing out there in Topanga Canyon, spying on me?"

"We were not spying on you. You just happened to come along at the wrong time."

"Who are you?"

"I told you our names."

"Your first names, your last names, your real names? Who do you work for, and what's this operation you're running?"

"Enough of this. You are in no position to ask questions." He nodded at Jarmouthe.

"Would you like to start over again?" I said. "They say the third time's the charm."

The sarcasm wasn't wasted on him, although Jarmouthe appeared totally unmoved, as if he didn't understand English to begin with, though I knew better. What he understood were knives. He pulled out a foot-long switchblade, popped the clutch on it, and cut a few curlicues through the air in front of him. There was no bleeding heart hanging on his sleeve, unless it had belonged to someone else first. He got out of the front, came around, and slid into the seat next to me. The party was about to get ugly.

It occurred to me that maybe discretion was the better part of valor after all. And that for the time being, Debir was right. I was in no position to make demands of any sort. "Look," I said. "You need some information, and I need some information. We're not necessarily adversaries here, are we? Maybe we can find some common ground before we start down the road to ruin."

"Ah, I see we are finally making impressions upon you. No, maybe not adversaries. That is what we must find out. So first, you will tell us of your interest in Minister Kedar?"

"If you will do the same, quid pro quo."

"What is this quid pro . . .?"

"Quo. It just means that we trade a piece for a piece."

"Then you will start."

"Well, I had no interest in Minister Kedar, per se. I was following the black SUV to see where and to who it would lead me."

"So you must have knowledge of Mustafa and Davie?"

"Oh yes, only too well, but not as well as I'm going to. I have a little unfinished business with them before this is all over. And you?"

"Ah yes, I see," he said and smiled. "You mean your face. I wish you luck with your vengeance. They will not be easy. But if I were you, I would sit back and wait to see what happens with them first."

"Thanks, but all I'm gonna need are my weapons back."

"You will have them when we are finished here. In the meantime, quid pro? . . ."

"Quid pro quo."

"Yes, Quid pro quo. Jarmouthe and I work for a consortium of Middle Eastern businessmen who are concerned about the loss of their cultural heritage."

Why didn't that sound true to my ear? Could my newfound friends be lying to me, and so soon after we'd just met? What had Ronnie told me about a group of businessmen dedicated to protecting their cultural heritage? These two were anything but businessmen, although I could say, clearly, that they were all business. But I wasn't buying that story for a minute. Meanwhile, I said, "Isn't that also a concern of the Minister?"

Debir smiled wryly. "The Minister has many concerns, some that do not always coincide with ours. We have been sent here to track the disappearance of some artifacts that belong to one of our member countries."

"You, too? Fancy that. It seems everyone's looking for something. I presume they're all the same ones. Do you know when and where they were stolen?"

"Oh, no, Mr. Pike. Quid pro quo, remember? You were following the SUV in the hopes of also finding what does not belong to you or your client?"

"Yes, if we can find them or the people who've stolen them, then we can clear my client. She's worried they will fire her from the Museum and ruin her reputation. She just wants to see that they're returned to the proper owners." Amazing, he appeared to be buying this hogwash. After what Inga had just told me, I didn't know what Ronnie Rivero was really up to. But finding out had become my first priority. More than anything, I hated being played for a sucker.

"How thoughtful of her," Debir said.

His sarcasm wasn't wasted on me. Maybe he knew more about her game than I did. "So, just what is your interest in my client?" I said.

"She was working at the Ministry in Amman with Dr. Eastlake. He sent her home, but she did not leave. She stayed in the country two days after he thought she was gone . . . We had never seen her before."

"Yes, and . . .?"

"And she was seen consorting with artisans who are

known to create forgeries for export to the black market in antiquities."

It seemed that Ronnie Rivero was not the sweet, pretty little rose she appeared to be, but rather an onion, and a hot one at that. She certainly had more layers than I'd anticipated if what Debir and Inga had just told me was true. I had reason to doubt them on other things, but not this. Why hadn't I seen it before? No sense going there, I'd seen it now; it was time to go see her. And that was precisely what I was going to do, if I ever escaped these Bedouins.

"But still, she is not what you call the big fish. There are others. But because of her, you are now jeopardizing a long investigation, which Jarmouthe and I cannot permit you to do."

"I see. So, let me guess . . . you're looking hard at Kedar and G. Henry Carl because they're major players, the ones with money, power, and worldwide influence, the whole Universal Paradigm conglomerate. Yeah, I see that, one big smuggling ring of ancient antiquities. So what, did Hollenbeck get too close? Did he catch Eastlake stealing the goods right off the Getty shelves?"

"Speculation can be dangerous, Mr. Pike."

"You should know that Mr. Carl tried to hire me, just this morning, to help him find some missing artifacts."

"Are you saying he has discovered that the pieces he had stolen were forgeries?"

"No," I said, and then had a flash of insight that almost knocked me down. "But you might, if you worked for somebody's government, and you'd started that way from the beginning, as a sting operation set to net the big fish, as you call them."

"You have a fanciful imagination, Mr. Pike. I wouldn't lean on it too hard, if I were you. You never know when it will let you down."

"You won't confirm what I just told you?"

He just looked at me, giving no indication one way or another. Finally he said, "I cannot say. But you have been warned to stay clear of this operation. We cannot tell you again. Next time we will remove you from the situation all together."

"Then tell me this, Mustafa and Davie are the clean up crew; they do the wet work, right? Hollenbeck was theirs?"

Again, he gave me the look and more silence.

"But they didn't do Eastlake, did they?" I said.

"Goodbye, Mr. Pike." Debir said, nodding again to Jarmouthe, who folded his spike and put it away. He got out, went back around to the side door, and opened it. The heat, smell, and sound of the street flooded the van.

"Really, so soon? But I was just starting to like you guys."

"You've been warned, Mr. Pike," he said and put his weapon away. "We cannot be responsible if harm should come to you." He got out of the van and I slid out after him. "Give him back his things," he said to Jarmouthe, who gave everything back—including my sandwich.

"Keep it," I said. "I'm not hungry."

"Take some advice and stay away from Mustafa and Davie," Debir said. "They will not be around long, and we wouldn't want to see our new friend get hurt."

Was that a veiled threat about hitting Mustafa and Davie? No, sir, not on my turf. Mustafa and Davie owed me, and I had plans to collect. But if these two, whoever they were, had plans of their own, well, they were gonna have to get in line, cuz I was here first.

Thirty-seven

JARMOUTHE HAD INSISTED ON RETURNING MY LUNCH to me. I watched him and Debir drive off in the van before crossing the lot to throw it in the Dumpster. Just as I was about to chuck it, the lop-tailed Shepherd I'd seen earlier came trotting around the corner. He appeared to be following his nose as he came warily in my direction. The way my day had gone so far, I was about to get dog bit. He stopped ten feet away and looked mournfully up at me, as though he didn't know whether to run or fight. I opened the boxed lunch and set it on the ground in front of me.

"Here ya go, Rin Tin Tin. Looks like you could use a bite to eat."

He edged a little closer, but was too skittish to approach while I stood over it. I backed up a step and stooped down, careful not to look him directly in the eye. He came in with his head stretched out, sniffing from side to side; his nose got the better of him. I guess he figured that if I was going to kill him, he'd die a happy dog. He didn't have a collar. He was starving and filthy.

His coat was dull, shedding heavily, and he stank. The poor animal needed attention. He dropped the whole sandwich in two bites, and immediately followed up on the fries. I reached over and scratched him behind the ear. He didn't even growl. To look at him, you would've thought I'd done it a million times.

When he started to shovel the box around with his tongue, licking out the scraps, I picked it up and dropped it in the Dumpster. He just stood looking at me through those big golden-browns of his, as if I might have dessert hidden on me somewhere. His tongue hung, drooling on the asphalt. "God, you're a sorry sight," I said. "Not much I can do about it. But you've eaten something, at least. It'll get you by for a while. So, adios, Rin Tin Tinman, and good luck." I turned, walked back to the Nova, and keyed the lock. Just as I opened the door he slipped up behind me and sat back on his haunches. He looked at me with his ears cocked. Just then I could have sworn that he said, "Take me with you." I looked at him for a moment and couldn't believe what I was about to do. I would never have so much as contemplated such a thing before. I didn't know what came over me. I must be getting soft, was all I could think. Oh, what the hell. In for a penny, in for a pound. "All right, get in you mangy cur, but just until we can find a shelter." I pulled the back of my seat forward, so he could get in the rear. He wasn't in the least bashful about accepting a ride from a stranger and jumped right up into the seat as if he belonged there.

"Don't get too comfortable back there, pal. Like I said, it's just until we can get you to a shelter. And quit drooling all over my seats." He licked his chops, tried to turn in a circle but gave up, and lay down with his head on his paws. I knew that he knew exactly what I'd said. Great. Now I had this critter on my hands who, apparently, thought that he'd found himself a sucker that was going to adopt him and take him home.

When I got back to the office a half-hour later, Donny was manning the fort and working on that Rivero file at Felia's desk.

"Where's Felia?" I asked.

"She went to her interview with Tarantino. I told her to go ahead, there wasn't much more she could do here. We were almost finished and we got everything you asked for. Say, who's your doggie friend there?" Donny said.

"Donny, Tinman, Tinman, Donny."

"How'd you know his name was Tinman?"

"He told me on the way over."

"Whatever you say; you're the boss."

I sat on the corner of the desk and watched as Tinman snooped around the office, poking his nose into everything. That dog had the makings of a good PI.

"Hey, you don't have to take my word for it. Ask him yourself."

"Now you're jerking me around. Dogs can't talk."

"Yeah, I know . . . if you say so . . . but go ahead, ask him. He's got a voice like James Earl Jones. Sounds just like Darth Vader, for Christ's sake."

"Hey, dogs don't talk in this universe, and I'm not falling for that one."

"Okay, fine. I didn't believe it either."

"Do I look like a fool to you?"

"Not a bit, but what have you got to lose? I'm telling you. It's amazing. Go ahead, ask him his name."

Donny looked at me like I was crazy, but finally gave up his skepticism just long enough to say, "Here boy. C'mon. Is that your name? Tinman?"

Having recognized his new name, Tinman stopped his in-depth nasal investigation long enough to stare a blank at Donny.

"Gotcha," I said.

"What?"

"I mean—asking a dog if he can talk. Really now."

"Damn, I don't believe I let you get by me with that."

"Yeah, I'm too good."

"But hey, don't worry, Chief. I don't get mad, I just get even."

"Yeah, we'll see." I fake-punched his nose and went over to the coffee machine. "Say, how old is this coffee?"

"Felia just made it before she left. She said you'd be in looking for a cup sometime soon."

"I guess she knows me pretty well. So, what have you got on Ronnie?" I poured myself a cup and joined him at Felia's desk where he pulled out some phone records.

"Well, these records tell me she's been in close contact with a guy named Ramón Diaz, among others. I ran a check on him with a guy I know over in the hall of records, and Diaz turns out to be—"

"Her brother, right?"

"How'd you know?"

"Ronnie mentioned him the day she hired me."

"He's a half-brother. They share the mother in common, different fathers. Diaz is an ex-con from Florida. He's got a sheet as long as my arm, mostly petty theft,

B&E, and some deadly weapons assault charges. He did five years on a manslaughter charge and just got out of jail there about a year ago. I'm guessing he came out here to reconnect to family and start over. His number first showed up on Ronnie's phone records about eight months ago." He shuffled the pages to show me what he had.

"Interesting. You've got his address?"

"Yeah, and his phone records, his credit rating, and his dishonorable discharge from the Marines. He lives over there in Westlake, just north of MacArthur Park, on South Park View. You think she's over there?"

"Yep. Rough neighborhood. Write it down on that." I tossed him my notebook. "Good work, Donny. By the way, are you going to be around for a while?"

"I was going to be here until Felia got back, then we were going to dinner. She didn't know how long she'd be on the audition." He finished writing the number and handed the notebook back to me.

"Then never mind. I was going to ask you to call one of those mobile dog-grooming outfits and have them come over here to give that animal a bath."

"He could certainly use one."

"But I'll do something else. I've got to talk to Ronnie, and I don't know what I'm going to do with Tinman in the meantime.

"You're not going to keep him?"

"Just until I can think of what else to do with him. I was going to put him in a shelter, but he'd probably never find a home. He'd be in a cage the rest of his life. I couldn't do that to him, and I couldn't leave him on the street. So here I am, a stray mutt on my hands and no time for it."

"Hey, sounds to me like you're going soft there, Chief."

"Yeah, right, about as soft as concrete. Say, Donny, you going to be around tomorrow?"

"I can be, if you want me to."

"Well, I need to talk something over with you, but I don't have time now."

"Can you tell me what it's about?"

"I was wondering what you would think about taking over here for a while."

"Well, I always hoped that—"

"Let's talk about it tomorrow. I just wanted you to think about it until then. I've got to go now. I'm guessing that Maldonado's about one second away from picking Ronnie up, if he hasn't already, and I'm thinking he probably should. But I've got to find out where I stand in the middle of this, before he does. I may have to do some time of my own, if Prudhomme and McCorkle can prove I've been aiding and abetting her in illegal activities, which, as it turns out, might not be too hard to do. And unfortunately, it's beginning to look as if she's up to her neck in it, and I'm up to my ass. I think I've been had, big time.

"Speaking of being had, did Felia tell you that Ronnie's retainer check bounced?"

"Now I'm not going to get paid? Great—what else can go wrong with this fiasco?"

"You got me. I don't know what to say. Is there anything I can do?"

"How about going to the bank and getting some bail money for me. Ten large ought to do it, just in case. If I have to call, then you can bring it downtown and get me out."

"Sure thing."

I wrote the check out, and Donny took off. I went into my office to see if Felia had left any other messages on my desk. McCorkle had called, expressing his disappointment at not seeing me earlier and informing me that he was putting a cruiser on the street, just for me, if I didn't call him by five today. Tinman followed me in and stood waiting. "What am I going to do with you?" I said.

"You could take me over to Shirl's. She's got a nice big backyard."

I swear that dog had to be a ventriloquist, because his mouth didn't move a muscle.

I took out my cell and tried to call Shirl again, but she wasn't home or answering her phone. I left her a message to call me. I'd been thinking about her all day, ever since I found out that she hadn't gone to work that morning. It was really beginning to worry me, and I wasn't the worrying sort. I'd called a couple times over the day with no luck. I'd just have to keep trying until I reached her. In the meantime, Tinman had had a great idea, although I knew that Shirl wasn't going to like it one bit. But, in fact, driving over there would give me the chance to see if she was there and check the place out. Anyway, right then, I didn't have a choice. Tinman had to go somewhere. Of course, I knew it really wasn't Tinman's idea, but from the look on his face, as he stood there gazing so soulfully up at me, it sure had seemed that way. I had to be out of my mind. I needed a dog like I needed another dick. I wish I knew what I was doing. Life was sure getting complicated.

Thirty-eight

I WASN'T GETTING ANY YOUNGER, SITTING AROUND the office and bemoaning my fate. So I dropped Tinman in the backyard at Shirl's place. I left water and opened a couple of cans of tuna in a bowl. It was all I could find, and he seemed to like it. He was so hungry he would have eaten my shorts if I'd given them to him. But at least now he wouldn't die of starvation. It would have to do until I could make other arrangements.

Tinman made himself right at home. He dug out a good-sized bed under one of the hydrangea bushes along the fence and settled in for the duration. Shirl was going to have my keester as a trophy on the mantle. Nothing to do about it for the time being, except leave a note telling her his name and that I'd be back to pick him up as soon as possible. I looked the place over and there seemed to have been no foul play. Nothing was amiss, except that she was gone. And there was nothing extraordinary with that, as far as I knew. So it was off to South Park View for me.

When I arrived, I parked down the block and walked

the rest of the way. Ronnie's little red Miata sat behind a late model tan Ford, in the driveway, on a steep incline. I'd seen that car or one just like it the other day, though I couldn't remember the plate from the first one I'd seen. There was probably a thousand more right there in LA, but it raised the hackles on the back of my neck anyway. If I wasn't mistaken, it belonged to the guy who had followed me over to Chullsu's. He'd received a broken nose from our meeting on that occasion. He was not gonna be happy to see me. So Ramón Diaz, Ronnie's brother, had been working for Buddy Palmer all this time. The plot turned to gravy.

The house was one of those small California cottages gone to seed. It sat up on the patchy half-dead Bermuda grass, which was behind a retaining wall, three feet above the sidewalk. They had the high ground, that was sure. There was nothing to do but make a full frontal assault, storm the gate, and knock on the front door. I checked the Magnum, which I had clipped to my right side, and then the Glock, which I had clipped at the small of my back. Before I went in I called Bern on my cell and told him where I was, and what I was about to do. He said that he'd be right over, and for me to wait outside until he got there. I thought he knew me better than that. I had answers to get first.

"Well, well, well, look who's here, Ronnie. Speak of the Devil, Nestor Pike, of all the fucking people in the world, come right in, dickhead," Ramón said as he pulled a .38 Smith and Wesson out of his waistband. He pointed it at me through the screen, as he pushed it open and backed away. "I won't say it's nice to see you, but I'm glad you're here. Ronnie and I have just been talking about you."

I went in. "Oh yeah?" I said. There was a suitcase sitting by the door. It looked like I got there just in time.

Ronnie Rivero, wearing jeans and a light blue T-shirt, was leaning against the archway into the dining room, holding an ashtray as she smoked a cigarette. She had a mouse on her right eye, and her lip appeared to have been busted on the left. There was an ugly bruise on the left side of her neck. With all the contusions, bangs and bruises, we looked like the front line of the L.A. Rams after a long losing season. Through the archway into the other room I noticed a fresh white shirt wrapped in cellophane, a pack of Marlboros, a book of matches, two glasses, a half bottle of Scotch, a little vial of white powder, and one of Chullsu's boxes of L'Argente brown lacquered TCJs lying on the dining room table. It was circumstantial to be sure, but it was all I needed to know who had put three holes into Yeager Eastlake.

"It was all good, I hope," I said.

Ramón was dressed in a pair of dark polyester slacks and a dazzling-white muscle shirt. His hair, slicked back, gleamed with Vitalis. He wore a heavy aftershave that mingled with the smell of body sweat and liquor. Perspiration beaded his forehead as the small AC unit labored in the window. I had overestimated how soft he was, sitting behind the wheel of his car. With his shirt off, he didn't look soft at all. He obviously worked out and was as tall as me. But he seemed agitated, nervous. He wore a narrow, woven, black leather belt with a gold buckle, and his stylish black shoes were highly polished. I hadn't noticed the other day how white his teeth were. It was somewhat amazing that they could be noticed at all, what with that big white nose bandage across his face, beneath the blood shot eyes and purple shiners.

His flicked his gun at my open shirt, and I pulled it back on both sides so he could frisk me. He took the Magnum, the one that broke his nose, and then made a big, big amateur mistake; he forgot to check my back. He'd just failed PI 101—the pat down. Maybe he'd had one too many Scotches; maybe the coke had fuzzed his brain to mush; maybe he was just plain stupid. I opted for D: all of the above. He pointed me to a threadbare overstuffed chair across the room, and told me to sit.

"So you gonna drink all that Dewar's by yourself?" I said. I nodded toward the dining room and sat.

"Get him a drink," Ramón said to Ronnie as he walked around close and sat on the arm of the couch above me, with the gun sort of aimed in my general direction. "Yeah, as a matter of fact, be my guest. I don't hold no grudges. I'd like you to have a drink before we get down to business. Wanna snort some coke? You can have that, too, just so you know there're no hard feelings. It's all about business, right? You'd do the same, right? Nobody gets over on you, right? Tell me I'm wrong about that."

"You've got a point there, I must admit. I knew you weren't all bad."

"Oh no, I'm not bad at all, but I do get even. I was just telling Ronnie, before you came, how I was gonna settle the score with you when the time was right. An eye for an eye, so it's a nose for a nose. That seems only fair to me. I just didn't think it'd be this easy—you walking right in here like that. I was gonna stop by your office and see you before I left town. But the tables are turned. Now you're sitting there without a weapon, and I got the upper hand. Man, I shoulda bought me a lottery ticket today. I can't lose."

I noticed that Ronnie had been crying when she came back from the kitchen with a fresh glass. She poured two fingers and brought it into me.

Though Dewar's was all right for sipping, I tossed it down in one pass and set the glass on the end table next to me. "I'm assuming that it was you, Ramón, who put those copper slugs into Dr. Eastlake," I said. "LAPD's already got you figured, you know. Those shells you like so much are sure enough dead giveaways. How'd you find them?"

"My cellmate in Florida knew about them from his time in Brazil. He swore by them, but I like them cause they're cheap."

"Yeah, me too." I was lying to gain his confidence, so I could get some information before Bernie got there. "You want to tell me why you killed Dr. Eastlake?"

"It was an accident, man, I swear. We were arguing over those damned artifacts—and the money. That faggot tried to take my gun away from me."

"Hold on there, Ramón. One bullet's an accident, maybe, but three . . . three looks like premeditation in any court in the land."

"Yeah, well maybe, but it's not true. The bastard tried to get my gun, and it went off, and then, I don't know what happened exactly. It was like he got even angrier and angrier. He was punching me in the face, the throat, everywhere. I was just trying to defend myself. That asshole was a lot stronger than he looked. He damn near kicked my ass. If I hadn't had the gun, who knows what he would've done. Hell, I'd probably be dead instead of him."

"You're not gonna sell that to a jury. You're young, big, and strong. He was middle-aged. And he was shot, at least once, where he was lying across the table."

"Well, by that time, I was just so fucking mad, I couldn't see anything but stars—lights were flashing in my eyes . . . I mean, I just blew my fucking top. It was his own damn fault. If he had just backed off and gave us what we wanted, none of this would've happened."

"Yes, and if you had listened to me and left the guns out of this, none of it would've happened," Ronnie said, raising her voice to him.

"Shut up, or I'll give you some more lumps to go with those I already gave you," he said to her. He looked at me. "Have you got any idea what a pain in the ass she can be?"

"No, but I imagine she can be one if she wants to," I said. I turned to Ronnie. "So, how'd you get mixed up in this mess in the first place?"

"They forced me into it. After Ramón showed up and found out about the work I was doing on this show, he got this plan and wouldn't let it go. I didn't want any part of it, but he kept at me, about all the money we could make. He wouldn't stop . . ."

"Yeah? Go on."

"Well, he went to Buddy, and they both started pressuring me to help them. When they injured Penny Braithwaite so that I could replace her . . ."

"Wait a minute," I said to Ramón. "She's telling me that you put Registrar Braithwaite in a coma. She didn't fall?"

"Hey, that was an accident, too. I was just trying to scare her a little bit, so she'd back off and keep her mouth shut. How'd I know she was gonna put up a fight? What's wrong with these people? Doesn't anyone take me seriously? You'd think they could see just by looking at me that I wasn't the kind of guy to mess around with."

"I got it," I said.

"They said I was an accomplice to attempted murder, whether I liked it or not," said Ronnie. "And if I didn't help them and they went down, then I was going down with them. Originally, all this was supposed to be just a little game of switch and hide, and return the stuff when they gave us the money, two hundred and fifty thousand dollars." She stubbed her cigarette out. She set the ashtray on the coffee table and sat at the other end of the sofa.

"Just two hundred fifty thousand for the Holy Grail?"

"Oh, no. Everybody got greedy—now it's two million. That's what my brother thinks two hundred and fifty thousand means."

"Hell, they were ripe for the picking. They got more money than God and had a bunch of things to hide. They're fucking thieves for Christ's sake. Eastlake and Carl would have been ruined. Believe me, they didn't want it getting out . . ." he said.

"So what happened?" I asked.

"We couldn't find the right things," she said. "Everything that came in was a forgery, everything I'd shipped from Jordan, and the articles we switched at Universal Paradigm. There were no genuine artifacts to be found anywhere."

"What did Eastlake have to do with this?"

"Eastlake knew about the forgeries at the Getty, because he had helped Carl to steal the real ones, which also turned out to be fakes," she said. "There never were any authentic artifacts."

"My, my. What about Hollenbeck?"

"Buddy said it was Carl who had Hollenbeck killed, because he found out about them. Buddy said the same thing was going to happen to me if I didn't do like they said, because Carl had brought in professional killers from Europe."

"Yeah, Mustafa and Davie," I said. "So, I'm thinking it must've gotten pretty nerve-wracking, trying to blackmail these guys."

"Yeah, that's when everything went crazy, when we threatened to blow the whistle on them if they didn't give us the money," Ramón said.

"What was Buddy's part in this?" I said.

"It was his idea to switch and ransom," she said. "Ramón just wanted to steal the stuff. Buddy knew about Carl's involvement with Minister Kedar and the smuggling they'd been doing. He said it was going on ever since he started working there. There was some really big money changing hands. 'Why not take a little for ourselves,' he said. He could give us the access we needed at Universal Paradigm. It was supposed to be a piece of cake."

"Then why'd you hire me, knowing I might expose the whole thing?"

"That was another one of Buddy's great ideas. Are you sure you want to hear it?"

"Go on."

"As long as you're sure. You know that I don't personally feel this way."

"Don't worry about me, Dolly. I can handle anything you or Buddy dish out."

"Okay, but remember you asked for it. He said you'd lost your edge and your nerve as well. That you'd been wallowing in self-pity for the last five years, and lost most of your business right along with it. The RD Detective Agency was going bust cuz you were a loser.

He said you were on the outs with the police, and the DA's office; they were looking to hurt you, if they could. That if anything went wrong with our plans, it wouldn't take much to plant a little evidence and make you the fall guy, as long as you were already involved somehow."

"Good ole Buddy," I said.

"Enough of this crap!" Ramón said. "Me and you got some unfinished business here before I leave, and I gotta leave now. It's eye for eye and nose for nose, remember? So what do you say, vato? It's either I pop you across that nose of yours, or I put a slug in you somewhere it won't kill you, which I ought to do anyway."

"Well, as long as I got the choice, I guess it's the nose for a nose, although mine's already busted."

"Good, it'll hurt more that way. What the hell, you got it coming, right? But just to show you I'm not a vindictive guy, I'll give it a nice little rap, right there across the bridge," he said, pointing the barrel of the gun at it. "Just enough to break it nice and clean, okay?—like you did for me."

"Okay, it's a deal. But only if you give me another shot of that Scotch first, and have one with me."

"Hell, yeah. Ronnie, bring that bottle in here and hurry up."

She went into the dining room and returned with the glasses and Scotch. She poured everyone a round.

"Here's to a clean break, in more ways than one," Ramón said, and we all tossed them down, even Ronnie. "Now, let's get on with it, so I can get outta here." He set the glass down and wiped his mouth.

I slid up onto the edge of my chair, set the glass on the coffee table, and leaned my face out. "Okay," I said.

"Just be sure you step around in front here, close enough so you don't miss my nose and hit me in the eye by mistake."

"You got it bro . . ." he said.

Just as he got into place in front of me and raised the gun, I came up into his crotch with a shoulder-driven fist that must've put his balls right up into the back of his mouth. That'll teach him to call me a dickhead.

Ronnie screamed, jumped up, and stumbled back into the dining room.

I moved out of the way, as Ramón clutched what was left of his testicles and doubled over headfirst into the chair where I'd been sitting. That had to hurt big time. He turned blue, vomited, and couldn't breathe. The doorbell rang.

"That'll be Lt. Detective Maldonado, let him in," I said to Ronnie, as I retrieved the weapons that Ramón had dropped.

She just stood there with her hands over her mouth.

"Ronnie," I said, "Let Detective Maldonado in. Oh, and by the way, I'd advise you, for what it's worth, to keep your mouth shut until you can get yourself an attorney. You're gonna need one."

Thirty-nine

WHEN BERNIE CAME IN, WE ALL WATCHED RAMÓN writhing around on the floor where he'd fallen out of the chair. Ronnie went over and sat on the sofa, looking stunned.

"So, ese, just couldn't wait for me, eh?"

"You know me better than that, right Bern?"

"Si."

"Ramón there just confessed to shooting Eastlake."

"Did he now? Looks kind of like a forced confession to me."

"Nah. I was a witness. She was an accomplice. Here, you're going to want this. It's his. I think it's the one that killed Eastlake." I handed him the .38 S&W by the end of the barrel.

Outside, a couple of black and whites showed up, and the officers came in to take statements, read their rights, cuff them, and get Ramón to a hospital. Bernie and I stepped out to the porch and watched as they took Ronnie to a squad car.

"Buddy Palmer was the third triplet in this little tri-

343

angle. More than likely, you could pick him up over at Universal Paradigm, if you hurry," I said.

"Buddy Palmer's dead," he said.

"What?"

"Yeah. Cholo was shot in the temple with one of his own guns, at powder burn range, while sitting at his desk. Looks kind of like suicide, but isn't. His secretary found him, so she says. She called it in from the scene, had blood all over her. On the other hand, Mustafa and Davie have disappeared. That big black Navigator they were driving was found abandoned out back at the UP loading dock."

"You got to be kidding."

"No, no, amigo. You know I don't kid about murder. So, what do you know about any of this?"

"Just that Inga was pretty distraught over his messing around on her. I don't think Inga's got the ovaries it takes to pull the trigger execution style, but you never know about a woman scorned."

"Yeah, and in this case, it's hard to imagine anyone else getting close enough to do the job. Besides, all those growth hormones in the food chain is changing testosterone levels in young women, makes them bigger and more aggressive."

"It's not impossible, I suppose, but Inga's not really the Ice Queen she sometimes appeared to be."

"You're probably right, amigo. We'll give her every benefit of the doubt. Looks more like Mustafa's MO anyway."

"You know that he and Davie killed Hollenbeck, right?"

"Yeah, but what I don't get is how."

"Easy, they crushed the breath out of him by slowly

lowering that Kouri on him with a forklift. It suffocated him before it crushed his bones."

"But why?"

"Who knows? But just imagine young Ahmed Emil, sexually, ritually, incessantly abused throughout his childhood. Seeking his revenge on flies, insects, and little furry mammals until he graduated to a rabbit, a cat, and maybe a dog. I read that in the file you sent me. The connection between torture, death and orgasm was established as a teenager . . ."

"I know, the classic recipe for a psychopathic serial killer, but why crush him with a rock?"

"The irony, of course. The things we love most hurt most. He killed Hollenbeck with one of the very things that Hollenbeck loved most. Oh yeah, Mustafa got off big time, savoring the irony as he watched the life slowly flicker and ebb from Carter Hollenbeck's eye. My guess is that to someone like Mustafa, it would be more gratifying than sex. There's a cautionary tale in there somewhere. So, you don't know what happened to the gruesome twosome?"

"Nope, but we got guys out searching all over for them. They must've been very well paid, because it looks like they're sticking around town at their peril to tie up all the loose ends that could convict Carl and Kedar. You appear to be the last name on their list."

"Hmmm . . . What are you guys doing about Carl and Kedar? They're really the top of the food chain here."

"Nothing. The Feds have it and are moving against people, but very hush, hush. They're working with the Jordanians to crack the smuggling operation."

"Yeah, a couple of their agents paid me a visit earlier, nice guys, real gentlemen."

"They're prowling for Mustafa and Davie too."

"Carl and Kedar?"

"Minister Kedar had joined Ms. Kedar, and both were detained at LAX, but not for long. They're now on their way, at government expense, to Washington DC; they will, no doubt, have many, many questions to answer when they arrive. G. Henry Carl, on the other hand, is nowhere to be found. But you watch, he'll show up someplace soon with his crack legal team that will keep him insulated and free. It'll go on for years. He'll never do any time. He's just got too damned much money."

"That's depressing. But speaking of time, what time have you got, Bern?"

"Six o'clock, straight up and down."

"Same here. So, I have to ask, . . . you going to arrest me too? McCorkle said he was sending a cruiser out if I didn't get back to him by five today. If not, I've got to go, I'm worried about Shirl."

"I should and throw away the key, too, after all the crap you've pulled on me lately."

"I wouldn't blame you if you did . . . I got taken Bern, big time, like a goddamn rookie."

"Hey, it happens to the best of us."

"Yeah, I know. Doesn't help though."

"Nah, never does, ese, never does . . . What's this about Shirl?"

"She's not picking up her phone. I haven't been able to reach her since she left my place last night."

"Then you need to get out of here now. Anyway, I'm not arresting you today; McCorkle's got to do his own dirty work. But if I were you, vato, I'd get me a good attorney."

"Don't worry, I will . . . and thanks . . . say, Bern, are we okay here?"

"Sure thing, ese. And let me know if you have a problem finding Shirl."

On the way to Shirl's place I stopped off at a Von's grocery and picked up a couple rotisserie chickens, some mashed potatoes with gravy, coleslaw, rolls, and a box of those Milkbone dog biscuits for large dogs. Her Mustang was there in the drive, but she wasn't in the house when I entered. I stopped in the kitchen and looked out the window. She was out back, barefoot in a pair of shorts, a tie up blouse with no bra, giving Tinman a bath in a washtub—lucky dog. She was soaking wet and covered in suds. She'd never looked so good. I didn't deserve to be married to a woman like her, especially after the fiasco I'd just been through. To think that Ronnie Rivero could've cut into me . . . no sense going there, only chagrin and depression lay down that road. But Shirl looked happy outside, as happy as I'd seen her in some time, playing with the dog. Tinman, on the other hand, wore an expression on his face that could only have been called severe depression.

"Oh it's you," she said, as I came out the back door. "I thought I heard your car drive up."

Just then, Tinman tried to make a break for it.

"Oh no you don't, Buster. Not until I get that god-awful smell out of that mangy fur coat of yours," she said, grabbing him by the scruff of the neck just in time, sitting him back down on his haunches in the water. He gave me a heartrending look, and my heart did rend and went out to him, but there was nothing to be done. When Shirl had her mind set on something, there was no denying her. "Would you hand me that hose?"

"So, stranger, where you been all day?" I said as I gave her the running water.

"Oh, here and there."

"Why didn't you pick up your phone? You had me worried to death."

"Cause I had it shut off, and I was busy. Besides, I can take care of myself. I had things to do."

"Well, you sure left old Dex in the lurch."

"Hey, old Dex can manage just fine without me for a day or so. The world's not ending if Shirl decides to take a day off, now and again. And, I'm warning you now, you all need to get used to it."

"Hey, I think you need more time off. I always said so, but that was pretty short notice. So where were you?"

"As if it was any of your business . . . I've been on the UCLA campus all day."

"What were you doing over there?"

"I was seeing people, talking to counselors, and signing up for some classes, next term. I've decided to finish my degree. I've been offered a gallery, and I'm going to paint seriously."

"Well that's great, and I'm glad, but that came up pretty quick, didn't it?"

"No. I've been thinking about it for quite some time now. Are you really getting in my face about this?" She stopped rinsing Tinman to look up at me. "Hand me that towel."

"Ah, no. No, I'm not," I said. I tossed her the towel, then went over, and turned off the hose. "I ah . . . just brought some dinner and hoped you and I could have a nice meal, maybe a little conversation."

"Look, Nes, I've got to get on with my life. And that's what I'm doing. I kept waiting for you to . . . I don't know, change, I guess. But I finally realized that you've got some real deep problems getting by Nathaniel's death. I mean, I always knew you did, but I thought you'd have learned to deal with them by now. But you haven't, and it doesn't look like you're going to."

"What if something were to happen to you, and it was my fault, just like Nathaniel? It's not that simple, Shirl."

"It's not? Looks that way from where I stand. If something happens to me, it happens. We can't live our lives fearful of what the day's going to bring. It was no different for me, you know. I miss Nathaniel just as much as you do. And you can't say otherwise. Not only that, but I live with the possibility that you're going to be killed every day of my life. I manage. I realize that's who you are. I wouldn't mind if you quit, but I don't want you to if you don't want to. We've got to go on as we are."

"Yeah, I know. You're right, and maybe things are different now."

"Since when?"

"This morning."

"How so?"

"I don't know."

"Well, what happened?"

"Nothing in particular. It wasn't any one thing, so much as I just realized that my life had come to some kind of dead end."

"Hmmm, what does that mean?"

"I know I'm the detective, but I haven't got a clue . . .

I just thought . . . maybe I should come back here with you. We could mend some fences, work some things out. You could take over my apartment and use it as a painting studio. I'd take some real time off, a couple of months, six months; let Felia and Donny run the RD DA on their own for a while. You and I could take that Cabo trip you always wanted."

"If you really wanted to go to Cabo, we'd have been there by now. I'll have to think about that. Besides, I like having my own space. I love you, Nes, but I don't really think you'd want that either. We'll have to talk about it . . . but not right now. I've got to finish this and get out of these wet clothes. So, where'd you find the mutt?"

"Yeah, well, before you blow your stack about that, don't worry. I'm going to take him home with me. He needed a place to stay and—"

"I love him. He's great."

Tinman looked sheepish; I swear to God he did.

"You do? He is?" I said.

"Yeah, really. He sits; he stays; he rolls over; he's got the full repertoire. And just look at those eyes. What's not to love?"

"Then you're saying . . . you love him, he's great . . . and we can keep him?"

"I wouldn't have it any other way."

"All right! That's a surprise! Hear that, Tinman, you mangy mutt? You got yourself a home."

His ears went up at the mention of his name, and he smiled. Well, it'd be a smile on my face.

"This calls for a toast," I said. "I'll get us a beer," I started back inside for the fridge.

"I'm out of beer," she said, and ruffled Tinman with the towel one last time, then turned him loose.

He shook himself, thoroughly wringing out his coat all over us, then ran around the yard, barking for the sheer ecstasy of finally being free of her clutches.

"Actually, I'm out of everything alcoholic," she said. "You'll have to go down to the corner if you want beer." She tilted the tub over, pouring Tinman's bath water onto the grass.

"Okay, I'll be right back. Anything else?" I headed around the side yard for the Nova.

"Get some champagne," she said. "Two bottles; I feel like celebrating, and I'm thirsty."

Forty

AS I GOT INTO THE NOVA, IT DAWNED ON ME THAT the sun was setting and it was beautiful. My watch showed it was quarter past seven, though I don't remember setting it; the night was coming on. Somehow, the world seemed a better place than it had all week. That feeling always surprised me when it happened. The promise of relief in the air, from the heat, hinted at a change in the weather. And the case I'd been on since last Friday was, for all intents and purposes, over. Although my client turned out to be one of the bad guys, and was probably not going to pay me for my troubles, time, or expenses, I felt good. I'd helped clear two murder cases, some of the perps were hauled off to jail, and who knows, maybe Bernie and the Feds would get lucky and put the big fish away after all. Stranger things had happened in my life—like me picking up a stray dog for one, and Shirl falling in love with him for two.

Bernie was still worried that Mustafa and Davie were on the prowl for me, but I didn't see any reason for that. I really knew nothing about them, Kedar, or Carl's oper-

353

ations, and I assumed they were too professional to waste their time and energy on senseless acts of revenge. They didn't have a lot of time to waste anyway; there were lots of people looking to put them in jail. They knew it was past time to get out of town. Besides, what had I done to them? I'd taken the worst beating. I deserved revenge, if anyone did. And, at this point in my life, for whatever reason—not one I could think of right at the moment—I was strangely willing to let it go, to give it up and let sleeping dogs lie. What had come over me? If I was willing to forego what was owed me in this situation, then I saw no further threat from them. Professionals didn't go searching out trouble they didn't need.

So I was looking forward to some chicken, mashed potatoes, gravy, and being with Shirl for a change. Who knows, maybe she wanted me to spend the night. That was certainly okay by me. Maybe it was time to get things out on the table for good, clear the decks, put our lives into some kind of order. On the other hand, maybe she didn't want me to spend the night. She'd had a long day, and I was feeling washed out. Maybe I should eat and go back to my crib. We both could use the rest. Whatever, I was easy, in a rare mood, and I'd cross that bridge if I ever got that far.

After I'd bought the beer and champagne and was on my way back to Shirl's, I noticed a mauve, late model Grand Marquis Merc with tinted windows, sitting two houses down and across the street from her place. I couldn't tell if there were people in it. It had not been there fifteen minutes earlier, when I'd left for the beer. The plates were not familiar, though I had no reason to suspect they should be. But it was weird; I had a real bad feeling about that car sitting there. When my feelings were this strong, it was not wise to deny them. They'd saved my ass on more than one occasion. And I was never wrong about them. This was not good, not good at all.

I drove past the house, down to the end of the street, around the corner, one street over, back up to the middle of the block, and parked the car. There was a pathway between the houses. The gate was unlocked, and it was a simple matter to slip across the neighbor's property to the grapestake fence at the back of Shirl's yard. Just as I started to go over it, there was a soft but deep growl on the other side. I'd forgotten about Tinman. "Tinman, it's me," I called softly. The neighbors had turned on the porch lights. It was either get over the fence or maybe get shot as a trespasser.

Shirl must've gone back inside because Tinman stood alone in the last of the fading light. He was showing some big, ugly teeth and he had the full set aimed right in my direction. "It's me, Tinman," I said a little louder. He stopped growling and smiled that silly grin of his, if you could call that a grin. The neighbors turned their porch light off, without coming to investigate. I got over the fence but scraped my elbow in the process. At least I didn't fall on my ass. I stooped to one knee, among the hydrangea bushes, where I could see what was happening at the house and not draw unwanted attention to myself.

Tinman trotted over, smelled me, and started licking at my face. I grabbed him and pulled him into the bushes with me. Nothing feels or smells quite like a big, wet stray dog, fresh off the streets. I hoped that rank odor would wear off in time, before it became a permanent addition to our lives. I had noticed on my way to the store that it still lingered in the Nova after just that one ride. But I had to worry about that later. Right now, I wasn't sure what was going on at the house. Shirl had gone in and couldn't be seen at any of the windows. I unsheathed the Glock and reseated the magazine. Fifteen rounds ought to do whatever needed doing. If not, I had five more in the Magnum. If that didn't do it, I was shit out of luck, as well as shells, and deserved what I got for such lousy shooting.

I told Tinman to be quiet and stay. His ears perked up; he sat back on his haunches, tilted his head, and looked eagerly up at me. I guess he thought we were playing some kind of game. I made my way over to the flagstone patio just off the back door. The lights were on in the kitchen, but no one was there. Tinman stayed in the bushes as long as he could and joined me. He started barking, as if he were trying to get me to chase him around the yard.

"Shhhh, Tinman, stop it, shhhh," I whispered urgently and went to grab him, but he sprinted out into the yard. I heard movement in the house and ducked around the corner, just in time to keep from being seen by Davie, as he came out to investigate the noise. Tinman started barking at him and running around. Davie did a quick reconnaissance out into the yard, ignoring the dog. He had his jacket off and carried what looked like a blue steel Colt .38, but I couldn't be sure in that light. I was ready to drop him if he looked to shoot Tinman.

It had finally happened, the thing I'd dreaded more than anything I could imagine. This was the living nightmare that came back, night after night. This was the scenario that brought the cold sweats and soaked the sheets, the terror that always got me out of bed after just three hours. It wasn't only Eddy the Eel, or Bobby Chandler, or Mustafa and Davie. It was anybody with an urge for payback, anybody that thought I had done them some injustice and wanted their revenge, to extract their pound of flesh. It was always there, never ending, the malformed, bitter fruit of my labors. As long as I loved Shirl, or anyone for that matter, I would never be free of it. It would hound me to my grave.

What was it Buddy had said? Oh yeah, I'd lost my edge and my nerve as well. Maybe so, but had I lived this long and come this far to see everything I cared about taken from me? They had Shirl in there and were going to kill her, or me, or both of us, if I didn't do something about it pretty damned quick. Well, we'll see. Edge or no edge, this wasn't happening. I couldn't let it—not tonight. It was simply not acceptable, nerves or no nerves. Nobody tramples my life like this—nobody.

"It's just the bloody dog," Davie said, as he went back into the house and shut the door. He turned the back door lights off, and the brilliance of the stars popped out in the clear night sky. Tinman ran up to me and barked again. I told him to sit, and he sat back on his haunches. "Lay down," I said and pointed. "Good boy. Now roll over. Good boy." I stooped, scratched his belly, and told him to stay, before going over and peeking through the window. "Good boy." The kitchen lights were out. I tried the door; it was locked. I still had my keys to the place and let myself in. I closed the creaky, old screen behind me, very carefully, but left the back door ajar as I entered. No use in letting the sound of the latch give me away.

I crossed the kitchen to the dining room doorway and listened before looking around the corner. There was the deep rumble of Mustafa's voice, but I couldn't make out what he was saying. Then someone smacked someone hard across the face. It must've been Shirl, but she didn't cry out.

"When's he coming back then?" Davie said, raising his voice.

There was another pause and another smack. God, she was tough.

Sticking to the perimeter, I crossed the dining room, silently, passed the table, until I was close enough to see around the archway into the living room.

"You boys looking for me?" I said, as I walked into the room, racked a shell into the chamber, and dropped the Glock on them. Mustafa stood surprised, over by the window, where he'd been looking out from the edge of the curtains onto the street. I caught him off balance. Davie stood right next to Shirl in the overstuffed chair. Blood was dripping from her nose; her cheeks were blazing red and swollen, but she was defiant. There were no tears running down her face.

Things had already gone too far. There was no stopping what was about to happen. I knew it, maybe before I had even gone into the room. Even though I had the drop on them, this was not going to end peacefully. There was only this one moment . . . Davie was rubbing the knuckles of his right hand. He grabbed Shirley up in front of him with his other hand over her mouth, choking off her scream. She fought back, but he clamped down on her like a vice, leaving nothing of himself but a chancy headshot over her shoulder. There was no time to think about it, only this one moment . . .

"Put the gun down mate, before I break your Sheila's neck," he barked.

I knew he was quick but hadn't realized he could move that fast, especially since everything seemed to be happening in slow motion.

Meanwhile Mustafa had gone for the piece under his lapel. My first round took out Davie's right eye and most of the right side of his head. It knocked him sideways and backward into the chair; he pulled Shirl down on top of him. She screamed as I turned and put two rounds into Mustafa's chest as fast as I could—but not before he put a bullet through my left arm, almost taking me off my feet. He whirled with the impact and grabbed the curtains to catch his fall. He let off another round in my direction as I put two more into his face and blew out the back of his head. He fell to the floor taking the curtains, rods, and all with him. I blacked out on my feet. It was some kind of daze or trance; I was so caught up in this one moment, in the killing . . .

"Stop it, Nes! Stop it! They're already dead."

I could finally hear Shirl speaking and came to my senses. My jaw hurt from clenching and grinding my teeth.

She pulled me away from the bodies. Her face was bruised, swollen, and bloody, but right then, it was the most beautiful face I had ever seen. The bastards had gotten to her, and I had not been able to stop them. I had failed her—again. The anger I felt was pure and hard and sharp as a razor. It cut deeper than I could've imagined. I was pumping shells into them, first one, then the other. The Glock's clip was empty before she'd managed to drag me away. I guess fifteen rounds were not enough—after all.

"It's okay . . . I'm okay," I said.

"Oh, Nes, I thought they were going to kill you . . ."

Shirl moved in close and hugged me around the chest, pulling me with her.

"I know. I know . . . it's okay now. Everything's all right." I put my good arm around her shoulder and dropped the gun on the dining room table as we stumbled through the house and out to the kitchen.

"You're hurt, Nes . . ."

"It's not bad."

"I need your cell. I've got to call 911."

"It's in my pocket. Call Bernie, too. But it's nothing, just an arm wound."

"No, Nes, it's your head . . . you're bleeding; you've been shot in the head," she said, as we went outside through the back door.

For a moment, I smelled the ripe, rich odor of wet canine and saw the stars as they blazed brilliantly into focus overhead. I knew Polaris, the North Star over there. I knew Mars and Venus were not stars. I knew that I would catch that unnamed star falling in my direction. But then all of a sudden, I knew nothing at all. The universe went dark.

Forty-one

HERE IT WAS, LATE FRIDAY AFTERNOON, AGAIN. AND as usual at the end of a week, busy or otherwise, I sat with my feet propped on the desk, entertaining my customary three fingers of Early Times bourbon in a coffee cup. I was feeling a bit uncomfortable, what with the sling on my left arm and the bandage covering the graze over my temple, not to mention the rest of my stitches, knots, bangs, bruises, and contusions in their various stages of healing. But the warm amber liquid slipped down my gullet slicker than oysters and was pleasantly, if not miraculously, beginning to mitigate all of these aches and pains, including some of the mental ones.

Outside, the sun hung low and golden over the Pacific. And I was perusing the pages of my previous night's exploits in the LA Times through the slats of shadow that fell across my lap. To read how they wrote it, you'd think I was some kind of hero or something. But the investigation was proceeding, and they'd turned me loose on my own recognizance, bolstered by evidentiary suspicions that it was self-defense—even though I

361

had flipped out and pumped those boys full of lead. What are you going to do? Sometimes you lose it.

"Hello! Anybody here?" someone yelled from the outer office. Damn, I'd forgotten to lock the door after Felia and Donny left. I have to quit doing that. It was unprofessional. It was just that I hadn't intended to be here any length of time. I was going to finish my bourbon and read this paper before I went back to the crib to be with Shirl. She'd moved into my place until the LAPD was through at the house. Bernie had assured me they'd be getting everything they needed as fast as they could and then releasing the crime scene. It didn't matter. It was an interesting proposition living with Shirl again, for a change. There was no telling what this was going to do to our relationship. I looked forward to finding out, but I wasn't nurturing any expectations, one way or another.

"I'm in here," I called to the guy out front and stood up to meet him as he came in.

"Hi," the young man in a messenger's uniform said, as he stuck his head through the door.

"Come in. What can I do for ya?"

"Got this envelope for Nestor Pike."

"Who?"

"Pike, Nestor Pike, is what it says here," he said, offering up the evidence on his clipboard.

"Oh, Pike. Thought you said 'Spike.' We got no Spike here."

"No, I said, Pike, Nestor Pike,"

I was starting to rattle his cage a smidgen. The boy had no sense of humor. "Yeah, well Pike. Nah, he's not here. But you want me to give it to him for you, tell him who it's from?"

"I can't. He's gotta sign for it."

"I could sign for him."

"Nope, he's got to do it."

"Is it from a process server or an attorney?"

He stopped and looked down at the clipboard and read, "Have no idea. It just says Raleigh Hanson."

"Oh yeah, then I'm your man. You can give it to me. I'm Pike."

He looked skeptical.

I flipped out my wallet and showed him my license.

Doubting Thomas reached out and pulled it up for a closer look through his specks. "What's with that Billy Idol thing?" he said and pushed it back, then handed me the clipboard for my signature. After I signed, he gave me the envelope.

I ignored the question, but he continued.

"Hey, you been in a terrorist attack or what?" he said and laughed.

"Nope, just a little disagreement with a couple of smart asses who asked me too many questions. They're both dead now." I gave him a couple bucks before he left. My left hand wasn't completely useless, and I managed to get the envelope open with the least amount of pain. "Well, well, well. Would you look at that," I said, talking to myself since there was no one else around. I went over, sat behind my desk, and took another slug of that Early Times.

It was a short note, and a check for fifty thousand dollars. Hmmm. All the note said was, 'Thanks, RH,' written in a florid hand.

Imagine that. Here was fifty thousand semoleans, fifty large, right here in my greedy little mitts, with my very own name on it, for me, alone, to cash or not to cash, to do with entirely as I pleased. Could take that trip to Cabo, no sweat; erase that second mortgage off the house for Shirl; get her some flowers, new clothes, and pay for her classes. I could get a new AC unit and a dust buster for the office, that new Colt I've been eyeballing over at Chullsu's Emporium . . . Yeah, well, too bad I couldn't keep it; it was blood money. Raleigh was paying me off for killing Mustafa and Davie. He was a man of his word; I'd give him that. The money looked awful good and I could use it, that's sure. Besides, if anyone needed killing, they did. But I didn't like it; I didn't set out to kill them. I was not a hit man. At least I didn't think so.

On the other hand, who knows, maybe I did. I'd been over that scene in my head, time and again, ever since it happened. I still can't see what I could have done differently. Should I have waited and called for backup? Shirl could've been dead by the time help arrived. Did I have a choice? And what about all that vowing to get even? Was it talk, or was I serious? It appeared that I was serious, deadly serious. After all, I was not one to make idle threats. I didn't know how to answer these questions. Maybe I'd never know. Maybe in the long run, it wasn't important. Maybe it wasn't so much what I'd done, but how I'd gone about doing it that mattered. To be honest, I was too tired to think about it.

But was I really going to return this money after what I had been through? It wasn't like I'd intentionally set out to kill them or told Hanson that I would. I'd not taken the contract. Could I keep it even if he didn't owe me anything? I decided to talk it over with Shirl. For the time being, I could at least carry the check around in my wallet for a few days. It made me feel flush. I pulled out

my cell and was just about to call her when I heard someone else moving around in Felia's office. I'd forgotten to
lock that damn door again. This time I went out there.

"Good afternoon, officers. What can I do for you?"

It was a couple of LAPD's finest, who appeared to be
near retirement and looking forward to their pensions.

"Yeah, you Nestor Pike?" the short one with hairy
fingers said.

"Yes sir. Got me right on the first try."

"May we see your ID?" he said.

"You bet." I whipped it out and showed them.

"Okay, Mr. Pike, you'll have to come with us. Since
you're in a sling there. I'll just cuff your hands in front
of you, if you don't mind, sir." He reached back for his
cuffs.

"Can you boys tell me what this is all about?"

"You bet. Deputy Chief McCorkle sent us over here
to pick you up. He said something about a meeting you
missed with him and Assistant District Attorney
Prudhomme." He just looked at me a moment, as if he
had something he would rather be doing than messing
around in my and McCorkle's business.

"Oh yeah, I forgot. I must be getting senile in my old
age. Say, either one of you boys know Lt. Detective
Bernie Maldonado?"

"I do, sir," hairy fingers said. "Burning House
Maldonado, everybody knows him." He had his cuffs
out, waiting for me to offer up my wrists.

"Well, I should tell you guys, before you make this
big mistake that you're about to make, that Bern's not
going to be very happy if you take me over to
Prudhomme's office without checking it through him
first. In fact, he's going to be downright furious . . ."

"But McCorkle gave us specific . . . Hey, wait a minute. I know you. You're the guy in the paper that killed those two thugs last night?"

"That'd be me."

"Well I'll be damned. Look here, Bob; we got us a real-life hero. And it looks like he's had a bad time of it, too. Now, this is a problem. I don't think we should piss off the Lt. Detective . . . Maybe we should call him. What do you think?" He turned to his partner, the tall slim one.

"Well, Otto, since you asked, I don't really see any reason to bother Detective Maldonado with this crap or, for that matter, get all mixed up in this departmental bickering, do you?" Bob said.

"Maybe you're right . . . We could just tell McCorkle that we couldn't find him. That'd be okay with you, Pike? You wouldn't rat us out, would ya?"

I just smiled at him and said, "You boys want a shot of some Early Times I've got stashed back there in my office?"

"What do you think, Bob?" Otto asked.

"You know, Otto, technically speaking, we were going off duty when they gave us this shit job in the first place. And in the second place, a little bourbon never hurt anyone, as far as I know."

"I see your point there, Bob . . . so what d'ya say?"

"I say you never look a gift horse in the mouth, Otto."

"You're a man after my own heart." Otto put his cuffs away.

"Mine, too," I said, as I turned and headed for my office. "If you boys will follow me—"

On the way in, I folded Hanson's check and stuck it in my pocket. Who knows, maybe I'd keep it after all. Who the hell was I to look a gift horse in the mouth?

Don West was born in Murray, Kentucky but grew up in Detroit, Michigan. He graduated from Michigan State University in 1969, and went on to complete an MFA in theater direction at The Ohio University in 1973.

He's currently at work on his third novel. His collection of short stories titled PERFECT RELATION-SHIPS, will be published in the coming year. He, his wife, Barbara, and their cats, live in Tucson, Arizona.

He's been writing, drawing, and painting since childhood and has shown his work in galleries across the country.

Visit his websites: www.BoomerFiction.com and www.artdonwest.com.

Acclaim for DREAM OF THE GREAT BLUE

Don West's first novel DREAM OF THE GREAT BLUE was a nominated finalist in ForeWord Magazine's BOOK OF THE YEAR AWARDS for 2005.

". . . . beautifully written and quietly poignant . . . . West paints a contemplative and almost Socratic picture about the nature of human existence . . . . Using finely detailed strokes, dipped in day-to-day life in lieu of broad plotlines . . . ."

"West is a master of metaphor—neither waxing too sentimental nor blatantly cramming his lessons into his text. Rather like a Shakespearean character, he uses both art and nature as the mirrors with which to reflect his philosophical message."

"He artistically conveys how meaning, and a touch of regret, is to be found within life's daily details—in thoughts, in meals, in art and in one another. But examining one's life is not easy. For Jack and Maggie, there is a hovering mortality, though each handles growing old a little differently. . . . West illustrates this with grace."

—Leigh Rich, Tucson Weekly

"Literary in tone, with strong sexual passages, the book explores the ennui, infidelity, and dwindling health and financial resources that can make middle age challenging."

—Betty Webb, Scottsdale Tribune

"West sets his first novel at Pacific Beach, where Jack and Maggie have come for their annual seven days of rest and relaxation at the ocean. After being married for thirty years, the couple (especially Jack) is challenged by the changes brought about by growing older."

—Paula Chaffee Scardamalia, ForeWord Magazine 2006

Order your copy online at www.BoomerFiction.com or buy it at any fine bookstore.